The Men Who Mastered Time

The Men Who Mastered Time

DAVID BUTLER

HEINEMANN

William Heinemann Ltd
10 Upper Grosvenor Street, London W1X 9PA

LONDON   MELBOURNE
JOHANNESBURG   AUCKLAND

First published 1986
Copyright © David Butler 1986
ISBN 0 434 09906 6

Printed in Great Britain by
St Edmundsbury Press,
Bury St Edmunds, Suffolk

For Frances and Rebecca

Acknowledgements

For Inayat Khan's background in India I am indebted to *Freedom at Midnight* by Dominique Lapierre and Larry Collins. For information about the Yuan rulers in China I am indebted to *The Mongols* by E. D. Phillips and to *China under Mongol Rule* edited by John D. Langlois Jr. For the Mongol invasion of Europe in 1241–2 I owe a debt to *The Tartar Khan's Englishman* by Gabriel Ronay. For Steerforth's explanation of the Michelson–Morley experiments, I am indebted to C. V. Durell's *Readable Relativity*. Three books on Samuel Taylor Coleridge were of great value: Norman Fruman's *Coleridge: the Damaged Archangel*, Molly Lefebure's *Samuel Taylor Coleridge: A Bondage of Opium* and, of course, *The Road to Xanadu* by John Livingstone Lowes. My final and most telling debts are to Messer Marco Polo and to Samuel Taylor Coleridge, himself and alone.

Contents

❧ PROLOGUE ❧

The Poet's Eye

On a cold and damp November afternoon my former pupil and long-time friend Lord Augustus Steerforth came unexpectedly to see me in my rooms in college. When the young man who works in the porter's lodge knocked at my door to see if Steerforth was to be admitted, I must confess that I had fallen asleep at my desk. Whether the torpor to which I had succumbed was a testimony to the soporific qualities of the undergraduate's essay I was reading, or rather to the fire-building skills of the college servant who looks after me (the room being filled with almost tangible heat from the open hearth), I cannot with certainty say. But I recall the thin pale face of the lodge porter's assistant peering round the edge of the door and muttering some initially inaudible message. For some reason the college servants have in recent years taken to muttering, even those who used to speak quite audibly. This young fellow is no exception, and I had to ask him to repeat himself.

'Lord Steerforth is unexpectedly here, sir. The porter sent me to ask whether you would receive him, although he has no appointment.' As soon as the youth had been sent off in haste to fetch Steerforth, I picked up the telephone to give the porter a piece of my mind. He should have known better than to keep Steerforth waiting in the lodge. But in the end I changed my mind. Steerforth, like many of the truest of true English aristocrats, has a way of relishing the company of all sorts and conditions of men, and had probably enjoyed a few minutes of conversation with the porter. I replaced the telephone and at length heard Steerforth's solid tread on the staircase, saw his squarish frame in the doorway and grasped his hand. It had begun to snow heavily now and even in the short walk from the lodge he had acquired a heavy white dusting. I took his hat and coat and hung them near the fire. While Steerforth busied himself with the seemingly endless task of igniting his pipe, I set the kettle to boil and began searching in various cupboards for biscuits. I could not find any. Like many academic bachelors of a certain age, I always seem to be planning to introduce a greater measure of order into my affairs, but never quite get well enough organised to do so. At the age of seventy-six it may well be doubted whether I am likely to effect any major or permanent change in my life. Yet more improbable things do happen to old men, as you will find if you do me the honour to read on.

Like some animal arrived in a new habitation, Steerforth prowled around for a while before settling, looking at the invitation cards on my mantelpiece and commenting briefly on the relative attractiveness of the various dinners and sherry parties to which I was bidden, then transferring his attention to the different prints hung on my study walls, examining them as if he had never seen them before, despite the fact that he knew them all well and had himself presented some of them to me. All in all, Augustus Steerforth seemed uncharacteristically ill at ease, even jumpy.

At last he settled himself into an armchair and gazed for some time into the fire without speaking. I had only one or two small table-lamps lighted, so that the glow from the fire lit up his features and gleamed in his eyes. His face was not exactly handsome, but open and friendly and pugnacious. The firelight leapt on his golden hair and turned the curls to flame.

During the thirty years I had known Steerforth, first as a schoolboy under my tutelage as his housemaster, then as a pupil at the college where I had been his moral tutor, and finally as a personal friend as well as a benefactor to the college, his career had been one of outstanding success. He had certainly had the innate ability to be a first-rate mathematician, having taken an excellent First and then worked for some years on a number of research projects. On at least one of these projects he had collaborated closely with his old school friend and rival, Inayat Khan, the great Pakistani physicist, though the nature of that joint work had been kept a close secret even from those of us who knew both Khan and Steerforth well. There had been trips abroad for unstated purposes.

Steerforth had too many diverse interests ever to immerse

himself wholly in his academic and scientific career for very long at one time. He had played both cricket and rugby for the university. He had become a county cricketer while still a schoolboy and had gone on to captain Middlesex at cricket for three or four seasons. He had come very close to the England team on more than one occasion and had even been spoken of in some quarters as a possible England captain of the future. But he seemed to lose his form at critical moments and, by his late twenties, seemed at last to have missed the call. A team was chosen and announced for a tour of Australia: Steerforth did not expect to be chosen and was not. I was with him on the evening the team set off and I remember seeing them on television as they left London Airport, looking joyous and invincible in their new England blazers. He had never said anything that smacked of envy or dissatisfaction, but I sensed that this was the only serious regret in his otherwise outstanding career. He would, privately but quite sincerely, have given every penny of his considerable fortune to step out and bat in a Test Match against Australia. Later an unsuccessful marriage was to cast a shadow over Steerforth's life; but at that stage he had little acquaintance with failure and showed little sign of wishing to acquire it.

Several weeks after the departure of the England cricket team, Steerforth had come to see me on another cold and blustery winter's evening, though somewhat later in the year, just a week or so before Christmas. He was sitting then just as he was this evening, pipe in hand before a blazing fire. I was prattling on about an essay written by one of my more brilliant pupils, pouring out glasses of pale dry sherry and looking forward to the hour or so before dinner which he and I would spend in bachelor talk, cosseted against the icy wind and the dark gusting rain squalls. And then the telephone rang. It was the porter's lodge.

'I'm sorry to disturb you, Professor Hawkesworth, but is Mr Steerforth still with you?'

'Yes, Mr Steerforth is still here. Who wants him?'

'The President of the Marylebone Cricket Club and the Chairman of the England selectors,' answered the porter, reserving his most matter-of-fact tone for this part of his announcement. I handed the telephone to Steerforth without a word. In the electric silence as he listened, I too could hear the words coming from the headquarters of world cricket. One of the England batsmen now in Australia had broken a finger in a fielding accident and was to be sent straight home. Steerforth muttered the conventional words of sympathy for the injured player that were obligatory in these circumstances. Two or three of the players who might have been chosen as replacements were unavailable.

'I am calling to ask you, Mr Steerforth, if you would like to join the team in Australia as a replacement? We are inviting you to do so.' At this even Steerforth was momentarily nonplussed and had to hold the back of a chair to steady himself.

'Yes sir. I should be delighted and honoured to join the team.'

'Excellent. In that case perhaps you could come to Lord's tomorrow to discuss the arrangements. It might save time if you were to bring your gear with you.'

Steerforth sat in silence for some moments when this conversation had ended, too deeply moved to say a word. Then I shook his hand – or rather nearly wrung it to a pulp – and gave him his sherry. At length he managed to pull himself together.

'By Jove . . . Australia!' was all he could manage even then. That evening I rang Khan and the three of us dined at the Randolph to celebrate. By now Steerforth was beginning to relish his good fortune. I bought a bottle of rather fine champagne and we drank to Steerforth's success Down Under. When he went off to pack, Khan smiled at me and I swear that there was a tear in his eye as he watched Steerforth step between the tables. By now the news was out. One of the diners in the restaurant recognised Steerforth, set down his knife and fork and seized his hand as he passed by. Steerforth grinned and a round of applause broke out, enthusiastically led by Inayat Khan.

Within a couple of days he was gone. Within a week he was playing in a state match against Victoria at the Melbourne Cricket Ground, the largest cricket stadium in the world. In the first innings, perhaps even Steerforth's classic imperturbability ruffled by nerves on this occasion, he made a duck. In the second innings he was lucky: he should have been caught before he had scored. He grabbed his reprieve with both hands and went on to make a century off the tiring Victorian bowlers under the torrid Melbourne sky. On such chances and mischances does life depend.

Only cricket lovers in England know how strange it is in the midst of the ice and snow of an English winter to hear early morning cricket broadcasts from the blazing heat of the Australian summer. As we struggle to warm our frozen limbs by the fire, our cricketers battle against heat exhaustion on the baked turf of Brisbane, Perth, Melbourne, Sydney or Adelaide. One morning as I shaved I heard that, a number of the established players having lost their form just at the same moment when their unfortunate team-mate was invalided back to England, Augustus Steerforth had been chosen to play for England in a Test Match. Thus he fulfilled his ambition, at a point in his career when it seemed that it had eluded him. At once I sent him a telegram of congratulations on behalf of Khan and myself. Then of course I was obliged to rise even earlier in the spiky cold of an Oxford January and February to hear the scores in that and the subsequent Test Matches. Steerforth kept his place for the remainder of the series and played in three Test Matches. His performances were solid and consistent, though at this most elevated level of the game not quite as brilliant as in its lower forms. I have kept the press cuttings from that series. Steerforth averaged about twenty-five runs an innings and had the great and – for him – uniquely satisfying experience of scoring a fifty for England at Sydney Cricket Ground. All the journalists, British and Australian alike, were struck by the qualities of doggedness and pugnacity he brought to the English batting, creating resolve in more talented players than himself. 'Whatever the circumstances,' wrote one, 'his is one wicket that will never be given or thrown away. Watching him stand there with that expression of utter resolution on his face, you sometimes have the impression that John Bull himself has padded up, grabbed a bat and gone out to do battle with the Old Enemy.'

In later years his career followed perhaps predictable paths for one with his family connection. He was in his middle thirties when his father died, bequeathing to his son both the family title with the estate of Bain Brook and the highly successful publishing house of Steerforth & Sons. He took all his new responsibilities seriously, including an occasional and thoughtful intervention from the cross benches in the House of Lords and the running of the publishing company. He combined these activities as best he could with intermittent work of a scientific nature, including the joint project with Khan. He was married briefly and, I believe, disastrously, though he rarely spoke about such matters. His wife now lived in California with the two children and seemed likely to remain there at least until the boy succeeded to the title and the house. This then was the man I saw before me in the light of the fire, a mathematician and a sportsman, aristocrat and successful publisher. Was there an occasional glimmer of dissatisfaction with his lot, even of ennui, a hint that the prizes of life had come a little too easily into his determined hands? If so, he had schooled himself by the age of forty-five to suppress such hints, to banish any trace of self-indulgence to the attic of his life.

So much for the past. I had made up the fire with fresh coals when Steerforth arrived for this his latest visit and I now saw that his overcoat and hat were beginning to steam in the heat. I poured more tea for both of us. Steerforth's eyes seemed to glitter in the firelight with an almost alarming intensity, but still he seemed oblivious of my presence.

Watching Steerforth's eyes gleaming in the firelight and the smoke curling from his pipe, I was suddenly reminded of Coleridge's lines:

> The poet's eye in his tipsy hour
> Hath a magnifying power
> Or rather emancipates his eyes
> Of the accidents of size.
> In unctuous cone of kindling coal,
> Or smoke from his pipe's bole,
>   His eye can see
>   Phantoms of sublimity.

At length Steerforth roused himself from his reverie and, with a particularly vehement pull on his pipe, he turned his face to me.

'Hawkesworth,' he began, 'we have known each other for a long time, have we not? Ever since I was a child in fact. I suppose you would not call me a fanciful person, would you? Not given to wild flights of the imagination, could we agree? Well, I want to tell you a story that will puzzle you. But I swear to you, Hawkesworth, that every word I propose to tell you about Khan and myself and our work together is the plain truth. He and I, working here in Oxford and abroad, have unravelled one of the greatest secrets of the universe. It is one that man has dreamed of solving for many years. But it's a nightmare too, one that awakens me in terror when it's upon me. And if I am right in what I have worked out, if I have correctly guessed Inayat Khan's plans, why then the fate of all mankind may be in the balance. Yes, all mankind. Not just those alive today, but those who ever lived and those who may live in the future. So may I tell you my story?'

Although it was a little early for drinks, I had a presentiment that Steerforth's narrative might well demand something stronger than tea. I poured each of us a measure of malt whisky, gleaming like gold in the firelight. The wind arose in the college gardens, swept around the quadrangle and hurled itself like a beast of prey against the shutters. An undergraduate called hoarsely to another in the cold courtyard below. I raised my glass to Steerforth and we drank.

'Tell me, Hawkesworth,' said Steerforth quietly, 'when did you first set eyes on Inayat Khan?'

ᨠ CHAPTER 1 ᨡ

The Flames of Two Candles

When did I first set eyes on Inayat Khan? When Steerforth asked me that question on that cold November evening in 1980 I thought I knew the answer straightaway. I first saw Inayat Khan playing cricket in the summer of 1948 when I was a newly appointed housemaster at a certain public school on the north–western fringes of London. Inayat Khan was then a boy of twelve, in his first year at the school. Today I find it much harder to say just when I first saw Khan. He was a boy when I saw him on that far-off summer day in 1948. As a man I was to see him as a mediaeval potentate. Which is first?

Even at the age of twelve, Inayat Khan was physically well-developed. He was not above medium height for his age but his shoulders were broad and set well back on his frame. As his team took the field, a casual observer might have taken Khan for just another cheerful and outgoing schoolboy, distinguished from his fellows only by his darker skin and blue-black hair. There was, however, a sombre side to his nature which was not surprising in view of his childhood experiences. For the day of which I now write was in the summer of 1948, and only one year earlier Khan had faced the horrors and dangers of escaping from his native India during the violent upheavals that surrounded Independence. In August 1947, as one of the Moslem leaders had said, the people of India went mad. For a time the violence was everywhere. New Delhi, Old Delhi, Amritsar, Lahore and the bazaar at Rawalpindi – all were the scenes of sudden and hideous outbreaks of in-humanity all the more shocking because of the basic gentleness of the Indian people.

Khan very rarely spoke of his own experiences. Just once when we were alone in a compartment of a train from London to Oxford, when the train stopped inexplicably for an hour at Didcot, he told me most of that horrendous story, perhaps as much as he could bear to remember or to put into words. On August 17th, just under a year before I first saw him in the cricket match, Inayat Khan was with his family at their home in Amritsar. His father was a prosperous and aristocratic Moslem trader with a thriving sugar business and a distinguished record in the life of the local community. It was a sultry and oppressive day and the young Inayat sought whatever fresh air was to be obtained by playing marbles in front of the house. His parents and sisters were within. Late in the afternoon a party of armed Sikhs began to make their way up the street, driving the Moslem families out of their houses. Some instinct for self-preservation must have guided Inayat. He quietly gathered up his toys and slowly crossed the road, managing to hide himself in the sugar cane without attracting the attention of the Sikhs. By the time he reached this point in his story, the Oxford train had begun to move again. It was now dark. Khan stared out across the meadows and the ploughed fields of the Oxfordshire landscape, his face reflected in the windows of the train. I could see every flicker of emotion that passed across his features. But he could look through the glass at the dark fields and the occasional lighted window that we passed. His anguish was not nakedly visible, which mattered to him.

When all the Moslem families were in the street, the Sikhs began to torture the women. From other houses nearby Inayat had heard, even above the screams of his mother and sisters, the sound of gunshots. At first he thought that the Moslems were fighting back. Later he found that some of the Moslems had killed their own daughters to save them from a more frightful fate.

Later a patrol of the Punjab Boundary Force arrived and rescued those few Moslems who had survived the attack. Of his family only Inayat Khan was left alive. He was taken away to safety and later sent to Paris, where he had an aunt living in the Avenue de Suffren. It was she who later made arrangements for him to be educated in England. He never told me (or anyone else as far as I knew) exactly how his family died, though I believe that he certainly witnessed their deaths from his hiding-place in the sugar cane. I feel certain that they must have died slowly and hideously, and that Inayat must have had to suppress for his own safety the cries of terror that welled in his throat.

But there is another thing about Khan, another psychological oddity about him, which prompts a suspicion almost too fearful to contemplate. In all the years I have known him, I have never known Khan to respond with anything but the most extreme distaste to the presence of a dog. Lapdog or wolfhound, they are all alike to him. Psychologists are, of course, familiar with the phenomenon of cynophobia. Most cynophobes experience a sensation of mild distaste if a dog is near them, or of unreasoning nervousness if a dog barks or growls at them. Khan's symptoms are much more acute. He literally cannot bear to be in the same room as a dog and even looks venomously if one passes him in the street. I have seen him get off a train and wait an hour for the next one rather than sit for two or three stations in the same compartment as a dog. Most English people of course are rather keen on dogs, and those who have been exposed to Khan's phobia are rather puzzled by it, perhaps ascribing it to the general oddness that English people regard as being part and parcel of foreign nationality. But it is a thought almost too hideous to contemplate that a young boy might have been obliged to watch in horrified silence while his parents and sisters were literally butchered and fed to the dogs.

Perhaps Inayat Khan confided more of the details of his escape to his aunt in Paris than to any of us. She may have concluded that only an English public school education could afford horrors to make those of his earlier years seem with hindsight tolerable. At any rate she sent him off to England with all the mandatory impedimenta, including sea-trunk and tuck-box, at the beginning of the next academic year.

In English public schools in the 1940s, sports fixtures between the different houses were taken pretty seriously. As Khan paced out his run-up there were competing calls of encouragement for the two sides from the crowded area below the old elm tree. Khan bowled as fast as any boy of his age I had ever seen, including one or two who went on to bowl for England. Although he was not particularly big, his bowling action was supple and whippy and he knew how to get all his weight and energy into the delivery.

He was much too fast for the schoolboy batsman at the far end. After playing and missing once or twice, and after being hit a thudding blow on the pads as he tried to play a forward defensive stroke, he saw the last ball of Khan's first over smash the wicket and send one of the stumps cartwheeling off towards the wicket-keeper, stationed a pitch's length or more towards the boundary.

The young batsman surveyed his wrecked wicket, tucked his bat under his arm, murmured a word of congratulations to the bowler and made for the pavilion steps. As for Khan's supporters in the crowd, they went quite wild with ecstasy, while the opposing supporters plunged their hands in their pockets and scuffed the grass with their feet. For a time Khan's tail was high as the opposition crumbled. Three or four batsmen went out, not so much dismissed as destroyed.

At the other end from Khan was a schoolboy bowler of perfectly respectable speed and accuracy. Compared with Khan, his bowling seemed positively benign. Soon the batsmen became so reluctant to face Khan that they refused easy singles to stay at the other end. The only (and relatively minor) compensation to the batting team was that schoolboy fielders could hardly be expected to take catches at this speed, so that several snicks went for four. Nevertheless the score was still under thirty when the fifth wicket fell. Coming down the pavilion steps to bat next I saw a boy with close-cropped blond hair, stocky shoulders and rather large, square hands. He looked in his own way as much a natural athlete as Khan, and had the habit, as many athletes do, of carrying his arms a little apart from his sides, as though to be ready for any emergency. The first ball he faced was a beauty, very fast and curving inwards in its flight. He dropped his bat quickly on to the ball and sent it rolling back up the wicket. It was the first ball from Khan to be played off the middle of the bat. The next ball pitched on the line of the off-stump and cut away towards the slips. The batsman had no time to remove his bat. But he slackened his grip on the bat handle so that the ball fell inertly from the bat's edge to the ground. The next ball after that was short-pitched, almost a bouncer; it was played downwards with a steeply angled bat. After another over or two the new batsman found himself facing the less menacing bowler. He hit a four through the covers with a fine swing of the bat, and two past mid-on with a well-timed push. Off the last ball of the over, which was short, he struck a sweep shot down to long leg. There were two easy runs but the batsman walked through for a single. Clearly he felt confident of his ability to handle Khan.

Khan's dark eyes glinted. It was obvious that he relished a challenge. Turning at the end of his long run, he flung himself at the bowling crease. This delivery seemed positively to fly from Khan's hand. The ball bounced short and reared high, a genuine bumper. Fast as it was, the batsman was faster. He turned square

on to the bowler, facing him down the track, his eyes fastened on
the ball with almost fixed intensity. The blade flashed like a sabre,
there was a deep and mellow note as the ball hit the meat of the
bat and the next second the crowd by the pavilion steps scattered
as the ball descended among them. Khan stood at the end of his
follow through, not ten yards from the batsman. He gazed with
disbelief. He had bowled his fastest ball of the day and it had been
hooked for six. I could readily understand his astonishment. While
the ball was being retrieved, I turned to one of the spectators.

'What is that boy's name?' I asked.

'Steerforth,' he replied. 'Augustus Steerforth.' These then are
the two protagonists of my story, one a fugitive from his native
land and the other the heir to one of England's premier titles.

After this the match gradually became a much more even
struggle. At the age of twelve even the strongest of boys cannot
bowl flat out for more than an hour. Khan was now wilting and
would soon have to be rested. When Steerforth failed for once to
take a single off the last ball of an over, so that Khan got a
chance to bowl at the weaker player, the ball caught the inside
edge and streaked away between the batsman's legs for four.

'Good shot,' said Steerforth with a grin. Khan scowled and
took his sweater. Steerforth played that day like the future England batsman he was. The team score was now over one hundred
for five wickets. As a last resort a leg-spin bowler of rather dubious
quality had been produced, with a peculiar action and little control
over length or direction. Some merriment was manifest in the
crowd, as well as some excitement at the onslaught Steerforth
might at any moment unleash. The crowd were not to be disappointed for long. After playing this eccentric bowling with great
care for an over or two, Steerforth went down on one knee to
crack a long-hop into the crowd at square leg. That took his score
into the seventies. The next ball was even worse, a half-volley at
least a foot outside the leg stump. Steerforth aimed a mighty blow
at it which, if it had connected properly, must seriously have
endangered the pavilion clock. But as often happens in cricket, it
was the worst ball that induced the false stroke. Steerforth had
played the shot too early and it was the leading edge of the bat
rather than the middle that met the ball. Such was the violence of
the stroke that even partial contact produced a spectacular hit.
Spinning like a top, the ball spiralled into the outfield near the
square-leg boundary. It looked for all the world like that oddity
of cricket, a mishit for six. But there, racing from long-leg to the

square boundary, was a lone figure. His eye was fastened on the ball as it spiralled in the upper air. His feet pounded the turf. His head upturned, his hands cupped at his breastbone, Inayat Khan ran forty yards round the legside boundary to make a spectacular running catch. There was a moment's silence, then the crowd erupted. It was an act of great skill and daring, almost as hard to conceive as to execute. Augustus Steerforth was out, robbed of his century. As he walked past Inayat Khan he first beat his bat against his gloved hand in salutation, then raised the bat in mock attack.

When the match was over I met the two boys for the first time in the cricket pavilion, that same pavilion where Steerforth's name was to be inscribed in so many rolls of honour in later years. I congratulated Steerforth on his innings and asked him which team he would play for during the school holidays. Good schoolboy players need to keep playing after the end of the summer term, or they develop at only half the speed they might.

'I'm not sure whether I'll play this summer,' he replied. 'My family is rather keen on tennis. In some ways I prefer it too.' Having played such a remarkable innings he might have been suspected of false modesty with such a casual comment, but in his open smiling face I could see no sign of such dubious motives.

'Well Steerforth,' I replied, 'I have of course never seen you play tennis, so I cannot judge of that. But I know a good deal about cricket and I can tell you that one day, if you wish to, you could play for England.' Then I walked away before he could dissent.

Inayat Khan was surrounded by admirers congratulating him on his bowling and his wonderful catch. I thought perhaps he might look up from his orange squash and catch my eye, but he did not do so. I was not entirely surprised. I had been standing very close to the boundary when Khan brought off his remarkable catch. I had heard his pounding feet, his gasping breath, had seen how he grasped the ball and clutched it happily to his breast. I had received the impression (no more) that in that moment when his hands seized the ball from the air, his foot had also crossed the white-painted boundary line. According to the rules of cricket such a catch is deemed to have been taken outside the field of play, and so is no catch. It counts as a six. By convention any fielder making such a false catch indicates the fact to the umpire, who at once signals the six. Knowingly to do otherwise is to cheat. If Khan's foot was over the line, it was only by a few inches. His next stride took him swerving back into the field of play. Did he cross the boundary line? If so, did he swerve back inside the line before or after receiving the ball? I could not tell. But I knew the question burned in his mind too, for when at last I did catch his eye I saw in it a raging doubt about the fairness of the catch, and yet an even fiercer need to have made the catch and to be the hero and to have overthrown Steerforth. What is the significance of these recollections? Why bother with a boy's cricket match a generation and more ago? Does it matter whether the catch was a fair one? I still believe it does. Steerforth now laughs at me when I say so, calls me an old-fashioned duffer, but I honestly believe that a man who cheats at cricket is capable of any enormity.

For me the translation from senior English master at a school in the centre of London to housemaster at one on the north-western fringes of the city meant much more than professional and material advancement. The move meant first that I exchanged the stately but monochromatic environs of the city for the more varied hues of the green and pleasant land in which my new school was established.

A visitor to the school important enough to enter it at the main entrance would walk round a large semi-circular drive looping a monumental arch. He would enter at once a large and spacious rotunda under a glass dome. Straight in front of him the visitor would see the crowning glory of the school, a neo-classical portico facing over the valley. But by now he would also have sensed a pair of vigilant eyes trained upon him. For he would have come under the appraisal of the school porter, Mr Steele, who spent a good deal of his time in a small, glass-fronted box near the main entrance. Steele was a pleasant fellow, then in his prime, with a career in the Royal Navy behind him. To left and right as the visitor stands on the portico spread spacious gardens. Below him lie grassy terraces punctuated by wooden staircases leading down to the first XV rugby pitch known as Top Field. To one's left as one gazes across the valley stands a group of huge cedar trees which shadow the windows of the school buildings. These are great and ancient trees which must be far older than the house itself. Although the cedars are tall, they seem nevertheless to express themselves in a basically lateral movement, their huge boughs seeming to float outwards from the central bole as on a lake of air. Up from the deep well of unconscious rumination came one evening the perfect lines to describe the terrace by the old portico:

But O, that deep romantic chasm that slanted
Down the green hill athwart a cedarn cover!

Was the quotation appropriate? My scholar's mind brooded for some time upon this question. There was no chasm, but a green hill and most assuredly a cedarn cover. On the whole it seemed a permissible extension of Coleridge's vision.

It was at any rate while walking upon this terrace late one summer evening that I had my second memorable encounter with Inayat Khan some two or three years after that cricket match in which he bowled so fast. I was, I remember, vexed with a problem connected with petty pilfering in the kitchens. But in the midst of these internal concerns I was suddenly stopped short by a strange and inexplicably sinister sight.

From the terrace one had a very good view of the studies along the main corridor of School House. Unless the curtains were drawn the persons in the studies were clearly visible to anyone on the terrace, while the watcher himself might go unobserved in the shadow of the cedars. I have always found that persons observed in a lighted room take on a curiously significant air, as if they are characters in a play. The scene being enacted in study number eight was of a sufficiently dramatic appearance to drive from my mind all thought of the missing consumables.

The curtains of study number eight were open and so was the window. The electric lights in the room were switched off, but the room was dimly and somewhat eerily lighted as if with a torch or a candle. In the centre of the room facing outwards towards me stood a boy whom I could not yet recognise. For a moment I thought he was alone, but then I realised that there was also another person in the room, seated with his back to the window. I took a step or two forward, utterly unable to imagine what was going on in study number eight or to remember who its occupants were. From closer range I could see that the person seated with his back to the window was sitting at a table and that the light in the room came from two candles in holders placed upon the table. The seated person's head and shoulders were now clearly silhouetted against the light of the candles. It also seemed to me that the boy standing up in the candlelight was holding in his hands a thick old book like a family Bible or a Greek lexicon, and reading from it to the seated person. I had the strong impression that the seated person was listening with particular avidity to what was being read out. For a moment I was tempted to walk away and forget the whole business. No doubt there was some perfectly logical explanation for the scene in the candlelight: perhaps the two boys were rehearsing a sketch for the end of term smoker. But the next moment a curious wave of emotion swept over me, compounded equally of curiosity and alarm. I was responsible for everything that happened in School House. I could not simply walk away and forget it.

The standing boy now closed the great book and laid it gently down on the table. He leaned forward to do so, bringing his head downwards towards the light and towards his companion's face. For a moment that made my heart turn cold, it almost seemed that he had leaned forward to kiss the person in the chair. But then he stood erect again and seemed to speak to his companion. He listened, presumably while the other replied. Then he shook his head emphatically. After that, what I can only describe as a ritual began to be enacted.

First the standing boy reached out both his hands and picked up a candle-holder in each. As he did so I could see that these two candles were the only ones in the room. Each was set in the kind of old-fashioned enamelled holder that one rarely sees today. The boy lifted his hands until his arms were horizontal. He stood for a moment in this cruciform position, the lighted candles at each extremity. Then slowly he began to move his hands inward towards his face, bending his elbows. At last each candle was only a few inches from his face. The light flickered round his cheeks and eyes with a weird and sinister glow. It was still not bright enough for me to recognise the boy. The light also reflected upon the hair of the boy seated at the table, which seemed to me to glimmer like dark gold. Slowly he extended his arms again until they were at full stretch. He held them there for a long moment, then moved them inwards again until they brought the candles back on either side of his face. Then he slowly set the candles down on the table and spoke some words to his companion, who nodded his head as if in agreement. The standing person then took up the candles again, but this time with both the looped metal handles of the holders in the same hand, so that the two candles burned as close together as he could make them. He stood for a moment gazing at the candle flames, waiting for them to steady after being moved. Then he slowly raised both candles to his face, for all the world like someone raising a glass to drink. As the standing boy raised the light to his face, the combined flames seemed for some reason to give a better light than the two burning apart. I was instantly able to recognise the standing boy. The seated boy seemed to throw his hands in the air in elation or despair. It almost seemed that I heard his voice cry out in the still summer air. His hands were raised and silhouetted in the light. His companion, around whose clearly visible features the light seemed to flicker and writhe, was Inayat Khan.

I cannot pretend that what I had seen made any sense to me at the moment I saw it. Should I simply ignore whatever schoolboy game they were playing, or was it my schoolmasterly duty to investigate? I decided simply to walk back at my normal speed to the house and to intervene only if the curious business was still in progress when I passed by. A few minutes later I stood outside the door of study number eight. The candlelight still flickered. I opened the study door.

'Good evening sir,' said Steerforth. At once I realised that I should have recognised his hair when the candlelight glinted on it.

'Mr Hawkesworth?' said Khan. 'Is everything all right sir?'

'I am not sure, Khan,' I replied. 'I was slightly intrigued by this game you have been playing with these candles. Are your electric lights out of order?'

'No sir, the lights are working perfectly. We have been conducting a scientific experiment,' said Steerforth with a smile.

'An experiment, Steerforth?'

'Yes sir.'

'With what scientific objective in mind?'

'Khan has found a theory in some old book that the flames of two candles held together produce more light than those of two candles held apart. I said that was ridiculous. Each candle produces a given amount of light, a given volume of photons. How can two candles stimulate each other to produce more?'

'What have you to say for yourself, Khan?' I asked. I had the uneasy feeling that I, the wielder of authority and the would-be detector of sins, was being cleverly and rather easily manipulated by this son of an English peer.

'I can't really explain why it should be so, sir,' said Khan, 'but may I ask at what stage in the proceedings you were able to recognise me?'

'Yes,' I answered without thinking, 'it was when you held the candles to your face together.'

'You see, Steerforth?' said Khan at once. 'It was not just your impression that the theory is valid. Mr Hawkesworth here is our impartial observer and he confirms that the flames of two candles held together give a much stronger light than both of them separate. I think that's pretty conclusive, don't you?'

'I wonder if the photons replicate?' muttered Steerforth. I had meant to turn on the electric light at once, but had been put off my stroke. Only at this point did I flick the switch and leave all three of us blinking in the light.

'May I enquire which old book contains this interesting theory?' I asked as Steerforth put out the candles. The thick volume from which Khan had been reading and which I had seen him set down on the table beside him was no longer to be seen, but he answered promptly without it.

'The book is one you may have read yourself, sir,' he replied. 'It is Joseph Priestley's book *The History and Present State of Discoveries relating to Vision, Light and Colours.*'

'Is it indeed?' said I, not knowing how to respond to such a specific answer. 'What year?' Even Steerforth smiled at this, as I was obviously clutching at straws.

'1772 sir,' answered Khan at once. But he did not offer to fetch the book from wherever he had put it. Even at the time it struck me as odd that since the book was presumably to hand somewhere in the study, Khan did not produce it for my inspection. Perhaps he wanted me to know about the book and its author only as much as he chose to disclose. I gave them a mild rebuke about the folly of playing with naked flames in a house where nearly a hundred boys were fast asleep. They listened in silence and expressed their regret if they had caused me any concern. At length I packed them off to their beds.

'In future perhaps you might limit your scientific experiments to the science block.'

When they had gone and the house was silent, I went slowly and for some reason reluctantly to my own quarters. I felt restless and uneasy. In my mind's eye I still saw the figure of Khan with the candles in his hands. For some reason what I had seen seemed far more portentous than a mere scientific experiment, though it would have been absurd to disbelieve what Khan had said. And I was haunted too by the thought that I had read somewhere before about the light of two candles joined, though I was sure I had not read Priestley's book for twenty years or more. I sat for some time in my quarters and at last went to bed. I expected to lie awake for hours, but fell at once into a deep and troubled sleep. I had a dream of unparalleled vividness. I was standing with Khan and Steerforth on the deck of a ship, an old-fashioned sailboat. The ship was motionless, the sails limp. The moon was very bright and caused the ship to throw a dark shadow on the sea. Beyond this shadow, where the moonlight gleamed, great water snakes were turning over and over in the bright waters, their backs throwing up silvery flakes as they broke the surface. From my right, where a makeshift cabin had been erected, a voice was muttering. At first I could not make out the words, but then I heard a reference to the light of two candles held together. I sat up sharply in my bed, seeming at once to know that Khan had set me some kind of riddle in his reference to Priestley's book, dropped (so to speak) a clue in a mystery the nature of which was yet far from clear, and that the solution to the riddle lay just below the conscious level of my mind. Then an owl hooted and the whole image dissolved. Confused and baffled, I slipped back into sleep. It was to be over thirty years later that the solution was recaptured.

꩜   ꩜

Several terms came and went before I had any special reason to think of Steerforth or Khan again.

'I say sir, Steerforth has broken his ankle,' said a boy as I passed along the school house corridor. And so it transpired. He had fallen awkwardly while making a tackle in a game of rugby and so broken the bone. I climbed the stairs to the sick room and found him there, propped up in bed with pillows, being tended by the matron and with Khan in attendance. They were waiting for the doctor to arrive and determine whether the ankle required a plaster cast or simply bandage and sticking plaster. After a time I went downstairs to my study to call his parents. Lady Steerforth's secretary answered first but soon connected me to herself. I explained his mishap.

'Oh the poor dear,' she murmured. 'Is he in pain?'

'It seems not. He is sitting up in bed, drinking tea and waiting for the doctor.'

'That's a relief, Mr Hawkesworth. But the end of term is only a few days away. Will you allow him to come home when the doctor has seen him? I should like to look after him myself.' I explained that the final decision on such a matter must rest with the headmaster, but that I felt sure no unnecessary obstacle would be placed in the way of the victim's early homecoming.

'But how is he to travel? Lord Steerforth is away on business and will not be back for a week. He has taken the driver with him. My secretary and I are immersed in charity work for the next few days. Could the school arrange an ambulance?

I explained that an ambulance might seem too grave a response to Steerforth's minor affliction.

'The other boys might think we were molly-coddling him,' I suggested, 'and his life would become intolerable.' At once Lady Steerforth saw the point and so it was agreed that I would drive young Steerforth home in my own car, a service I would be glad to perform in return for a glimpse of the Steerforth family in its natural habitat, which I understood to be of some grandeur. It was agreed that Steerforth and I would be expected at tea-time on the following day, unless the headmaster raised an objection.

No such demur being forthcoming on either medical or pedagogic grounds, I prepared immediately after luncheon the next day to drive Steerforth the fifty or sixty miles that separated the school from his home. His immediate requirements were packed in a suitcase and placed in the boot, the rest of his effects to follow in the trunk courtesy of Messrs Carter and Paterson. Steerforth himself was to be installed in the rear seat, surrounded once more with pillows and blankets. But during the process of getting him prepared for departure, while the matron and Mr Steele were vying to outdo each other in solicitousness, up ran Inayat Khan to see his friend off. The three of us stood just inside the entrance while the luggage and bedding were disposed, Steerforth leaning on his friend's shoulder.

'Well,' said I, 'it looks as if they are ready for us.'

'Have a good holiday, Steerforth,' said Khan, extending his hand. As their hands touched, there was an unusually loud discharge of static electricity between them, loud enough to be heard and strong enough to make the two of them flinch for a moment. The weather was cold and dry, favouring the build-up of static. But it was still a strange thing to see the two of them, one golden-haired but lame and the other dark and nimble, touch and jump and then laugh. By the time we had manhandled Steerforth into the car, the incident was forgotten and their usual banter resumed.

'Are you sure you won't break en route? We could always wrap you like a little dolly in cotton wool,' said Khan eyeing Steerforth's copious wrappings.

'Oh have you got some cotton wool?' answered Steerforth. 'Then why not pad your mouth with it?' Khan feigned climbing in the window of the car to extract vengeance for this insult. A small group of boys had already gathered in the area behind the memorial arch to witness Steerforth's departure, an area to which they were forbidden access in normal times. Before more unseemliness could ensue, I released the hand-brake, engaged the clutch and drove off, leaving matron unkissed by Steerforth and Steele untipped by me. Driving off, I glanced at Steerforth in the rear view mirror. He was wrapped – almost engulfed – in his overcoat and his blankets and wore a school scarf coiled about his neck. From his pillowed nest his face gleamed with interest and pleasure as though he and I were setting off on the greatest adventure in the world. His blue eyes scanned everything we passed – people, houses, shops, dogs and prams. If only Khan were with us, his eyes seemed to hint, what a time we should have then!

I drove westward towards Edgware and turned north on to the old Roman road at Watling Street. Presently we were in the open country beyond the suburban fringe, bowling along the country roads in the mild autumn sunshine. In those days, almost thirty years ago, the farmland closely girded the northern periphery of London, bringing to places such as Barnet, Elstree and Cockfosters cattle, horses and farm dogs that ran to bark at passing motors.

'I'm sorry that I deprived you of your afternoon walk sir,' said Steerforth suddenly.

'My afternoon walk?'

'I know that you usually go for a walk after luncheon, sir. One or two of us have observed you, coming and going, and have envied you the freedom.'

'I suppose that even poor enslaved schoolboys may go for a walk if they choose. I have seen them doing so.'

'Ah, we may go for a walk, sir. But walking is one thing and paying visits another. There are places we may not visit that we might like to visit. Places that masters might visit but pupils not.' He did not elaborate on this somewhat cryptic remark but quickly changed the subject. For a while we talked of other matters.

'I am sorry to be a nuisance, sir,' said Steerforth at last, 'but my legs are becoming somewhat cramped in the back here and I would greatly appreciate the chance to stretch them. The severity of my injury may be increased by stiffness. Rather than hobble about in the gutter, we might step into one of these places.' He waved his hand at a pub as we passed by.

'Indeed?' said I. 'What a suggestion! Does your father take you into pubs, Steerforth?' I gave him a stern look in the rear view mirror.

'Of course,' he answered simply. 'The pubs on the estate are where he meets the tenants and finds out what is what. Naturally he takes me along, since one day I shall have to deal with them, or with their sons.' A boy like Steerforth, once he has made up his mind to convince you of something, can be very determined. At last I was persuaded that we might stop for twenty minutes, that Steerforth might stretch his cramped legs and drink half a pint (no more!) of bitter or stout upon condition that this excursion should be kept secret both at home and at school.

The bar was crowded, but a seat was soon found for Steerforth as he hobbled in, clutching my arm for support. By the time I had fetched the beer he was already engaged in conversation with a young farm hand and a pensioner, explaining how he came by his injury.

'Quite a jolly place, eh?' he remarked as he raised his glass. 'What a joke it would be if the Headmaster were to walk in here now!' I could not entirely share Steerforth's opinion about such a possibility or its potential as a source of merriment: but luckily my sense of humour was not put to the test.

'It's a pity that your friend Khan isn't with us,' I remarked. 'Do you think he would enjoy himself here?'

'I'm sure he would. He likes to get about and mix with all sorts. He has a great interest in England and wants to see everything as fast as he can. This vacation I believe he must go and stay with his aunt in Paris, but next vacation I hope he may come and stay with us for a while. What a fellow! When you consider the things he's suffered and seen his family suffer. . . .'

'And do you trust him?' I asked.

'Trust? I'd trust him with my life. Why do you ask, sir?'

'No particular reason, just curiosity,' I answered, but in my mind's eye I saw Inayat Khan once more swooping round the boundary to pull off that spectacular and doubtful catch. Yet I could not bring myself to mention my doubts.

Some distance north of St Albans we turned east and passed through the small town of Bain Brook, which was almost the fiefdom of the Steerforth family. We passed a point where the road was built up to bisect two ponds – or rather two halves of the same pond. We were now within the boundaries of the Steerforth estate and could see on either side of the road the smallholdings of the tenants and the cottages of the farm workers.

Near a cluster of such buildings we swung to the right, passed another collection of ponds with rather odd names such as Leg of Lamb pond and the Cookpot, and came within sight of a massive oak tree.

'The last Prior of Bain Brook was hanged from that tree,' remarked Steerforth just as we came in sight of the house itself.

Bain Brook Priory is one of the loveliest buildings in England. Its name is really a misnomer, since the present edifice has never been used for monastic purposes, the twelfth century priory having been long ago demolished.

'We Steerforths have never been renowned either for our piety or our courage,' I had heard Steerforth tell Khan. 'One of my ancestors got a bit jittery at the time of the Plague and decided to treat Bain Brook as his personal funkhole. He brought his missus and a great tribe of children up here to get away from London and deposited himself and his dependants upon some poor unfortunate cousin, whose only offence was to own a large if wholly dilapidated country mansion, once a seat of piety. Just think, but for the foolish hospitality of that cousin the tribe of Steerforth might have vanished from the earth!'

It was this fugitive from London, who must have made his way north with far less ease than Steerforth and I had done, who had turned Bain Brook Priory into a family seat. Not much of the original seventeenth century building, erected on the even earlier priory site, was left standing. What is now seen by the visitor skirting the Leg of Lamb pond and the Cookpot dates almost entirely from the middle of the eighteenth century. The west front with its imposing pediment and ducal crest is what most people think of when they think of Bain Brook.

The Steerforth title, though you would not know it to judge from Steerforth's easy and unpretentious manner, is much older than the fabric of the house. The first Earl was a boy of fifteen when Shakespeare was born. By the end of the seventeenth century the earldom had been transformed to a dukedom. The family tree contained the usual mix of spendthrifts and shrewd investors, gamblers and pedants, aesthetes and politicians. Steerforth's father, the thirteenth duke, employed an expert farm manager to run the estate (under the vigilant supervision of Lady Steerforth) and devoted himself almost exclusively to the management of his large and vastly profitable publishing business. Given the artistic treasures of Bain Brook and the sole proprietorship of the business, the Duke must have been many times over a millionaire.

'Mr Hawkesworth,' said Her Grace, when Steerforth himself had been almost carried into the house and half buried in a tide of pillows, blankets and dogs, 'I cannot tell you how grateful I am to you for bringing Augustus home. It is so kind of you. I could have hired a driver, of course, but heaven knows what escapades Augustus might have got up to on the way. Knowing him and his father's terrible example, he probably would have insisted on taking lunch in a pub!' I indicated appropriate horror. No trace of a smile touched her lips, but in her clear and level gaze was something that taught me a simple lesson. After our visit to the pub, Steerforth ought to have sucked a peppermint before he kissed his mother.

I did not dare look at Steerforth lest we both betray our guilt. I simply shuffled my boots and muttered until the arrival of tea rescued me.

Later, when her son had hobbled off on the arm of a servant to supervise the unpacking of his belongings, she and I sat alone in the library of Bain Brook Priory while the dusk descended over Leg of Lamb pond, the Cookpot and the tree where the last Prior had met his untimely end.

'Mr Hawkesworth,' said Lady Steerforth, 'you are an honest and serious-minded man. I want to ask you an important question. Do you know Augustus's friend Inayat Khan?'

'Yes I do,' I answered. 'In fact he is another of my pupils in School House.'

'Augustus has asked his father and me whether he might invite Inayat here for the vacation. What is your opinion of such a possibility?'

'I believe that Augustus and he are very good friends. It would be a real kindness to welcome Khan into your home. Do you know anything of his terrible family history?'

'Only a little,' she answered. 'I gather that he is more or less alone in the world, and that most of his close relations died in the most horrible way. . . . But I know no details.'

'He has an aunt in Paris who was responsible for getting him out of India on a Pakistani passport when his parents died, and who sent him to school here in England. He will spend his vacations with her, unless he is lucky enough to be invited elsewhere. Otherwise he has no one.' When Augustus came downstairs, his effects unpacked to his satisfaction, he was told that whenever Inayat was not expected in the Avenue de Suffren, he might be invited to visit Bain Brook. He glanced at me, as if guessing that my approval for the arrangement had been sought. Dusk had fallen by the time I set off for London.

CHAPTER 2

A Silent Joy

It is time now to recapture the thread of the conversation I had with Steerforth on that November evening in 1980 concerning Inayat Khan. He turned next to the bonds that linked them in friendship during their days as schoolboys.

'I recall,' said Steerforth, 'with extraordinary vividness the early days of my friendship with Khan. We were both interested in a number of things in common such as cricket, the House Society and such like matters. Khan having (as we then believed) no real family of his own except for his aged aunt in Paris, my parents became a kind of substitute family for him. On several occasions he came to stay with us at Bain Brook. On one of his visits, his mysterious uncle also turned up to see him.'

It is perfectly true that despite his apparent lack of any relatives other than his aged aunt it did transpire that Khan had an uncle. The gentleman turned up first on a visit to the school, much to the surprise of his nephew. Later he appeared equally unannounced at Bain Brook. Of these two visits I will later give an account. For the moment I will return to Steerforth's story.

'The one thing that united Khan and myself more than anything else was – guess what? – science. Inayat was later to become a physicist and a very good one at that, while I was to become a rather mediocre mathematician. To that extent our paths later diverged. But during the earlier, less specialised years our shared discovery of science was like a common adventure. The greatest excitement of all was in Khan's area – in physics. Khan has an amazing ability to understand physics intuitively. He doesn't have to think about things, they just seem obvious. It must have been an unnerving business for the physics master to teach Inayat Khan but it was an inspiring business studying with him, a little like being number two on a bob sleigh. Khan could always move much faster than I, particularly when we left the field of classical Newtonian physics and moved into the modern era. That was a fantastic challenge. Sometimes Khan would get so far ahead of me that I'd lose sight of him on the trail. But if I stuck at it, I always found that he would reappear ahead of me, call out some more or less intelligible account of his detour and beckon me to follow him as he surged onward and upward.'

As Steerforth spoke of his intellectual adventures with Khan, I had the clearest possible mental picture of the two boys at work. My own domain of School House had been joined by a covered loggia to the main classroom block. The classrooms were arranged on two floors between the ridge road on the one hand and the school quadrangle on the other. Beyond the quadrangle, in lonely majesty, stood the science block. From their study in School House to the classrooms and thence to the science block Khan and Steerforth would wander, books in hand and eyes wide-opened. Even as a poor English master I had been able to appreciate that these two boys, each stimulated and encouraged by the other, had quite literally fallen in love with the mysteries of the physical universe. The climax of this process was to come, as Steerforth now explained, when the concept of relativity was introduced to Khan.

'Perhaps you know the famous paradox of the light on the train? No? Well, Einstein used it to illustrate one of the problems his theory was designed to resolve. One of the precepts of the theory is that the speed of light is a limiting factor in the universe. Nothing can exceed it. But the precept creates problems. Imagine a lamp shining in the night. At what speed do the photons leave the lamp? Why, at the speed of light, naturally. Suppose you are on board a train travelling at a hundred miles an hour. You throw a pebble forward from the train with a speed relative to the train of ten miles per hour. At what speed does the pebble travel? At one hundred and ten miles per hour – at least until the resistance of the air begins to slow it down. Suppose you now fit the lamp to the front of the train and the train is still travelling at the same speed. At what speed do the photons travel? At the speed of light plus the speed of the train? But in Einstein's universe, that's illegal. So do the photons shout, "Hold on chaps we're being asked to break the speed limit. Let's slow down –" and reduce their speed relative to the lamp by the precise speed of the train? Now I've explained Einstein's paradox rather poorly, but Mr Hughes made it seem an unbearable mystery. We were all quite stimulated by it. But when I glanced at Khan he was absolutely transfixed. His eyes shone, his lip trembled and his hands turned white as they gripped the desk.' Steerforth paused for a moment.

'Forgive me,' I said at last, when the silence had lasted for what seemed an eternity. 'Forgive an old English scholar who can barely do a long division. . . . But what is the answer to the paradox?'

'The paradox is less bizarre than it seems,' he replied, smiling broadly. 'The speed of any moving object can really be defined only relative to some assumed point at rest. If you are travelling at a hundred kilometres an hour in a car and a man is running towards you at ten kilometres per hour, what speed is the man actually doing? Is it related to your speed in the car? Not really. It's a bit confusing to muddle the two things up.' Steerforth grinned as he explained this to me: not for the first time I reflected that being on the receiving end of one of Steerforth's grins was at once an agreeable and an unnerving experience, for his features were both pugnacious and cordial, like those of a friendly but powerful dog.

'There are some things about Khan that are rather hard to accept,' he continued. 'They include such matters as his sources of knowledge. When the time comes I will try my best to explain them to you, but you will have to understand that at first you'll think I have gone crazy. One of the most important things to bear in mind is Khan's affinity for physics. Mr Hughes, the physics master, used to find that Khan knew things almost before he had been told them. Perhaps Inayat Khan was destined to come to terms with the ultimate riddle of the universe. Perhaps he also knew that, right from the start. Perhaps it was also intended that I should be around to do his sums for him. He always found maths a bit boring. So at least these things sometimes appear to me.'

At this point Steerforth tried to explain to me, scientific ignoramus that I am, the nature of the problem Khan was trying to solve. He made some sketch diagrams on a few sheets of college notepaper. I have them before me as I write.

'You, Hawkesworth, are interested in the past, in Chaucer and his contemporaries. Very naturally, you think of time like the ever-rolling stream of the hymn. Yesterday, today and tomorrow in an ordered sequence. Actually, that's rot. To make it clear, let's stage an imaginary experiment. Two men – as they're scientists, we'll call them Michelson and Morley – go out one day in rowing boats. Although they do not know it, the surface of the river on which they are rowing is moving from west to east at a rate of four feet per second. They decide that, in order to calculate the speed of flow, Michelson will row north ninety feet, then south the same distance. Morley will row east ninety feet, then west the same distance. It looks like this.' He made the following diagram.

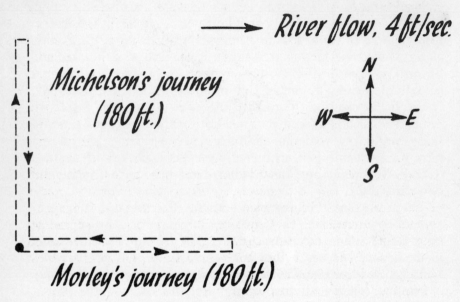

River flow, 4ft/sec.

Michelson's journey (180ft.)

N
W ← → E
S

Morley's journey (180ft.)

'For the purpose of the experiment, we'll assume that both row over the surface of the water at precisely five feet per second. And that they can turn round instantaneously. Now the stream will force Michelson sideways on both legs of his trip. It will accelerate Morley on his outward leg, but slow him down on the way back. Agreed?'

'Agreed,' said I. Even to me, the explanation was adequate so far.

'Now we can easily calculate the time required for Morley's journey. Outward bound he travels at five feet per second plus four feet per second for the speed of the water. He reaches the turn in 10 seconds. Homeward bound he travels at five feet per second minus four, and takes 90 seconds. In total he takes 100 seconds. Michelson's journey is more complicated to time. Let's draw it like this.'

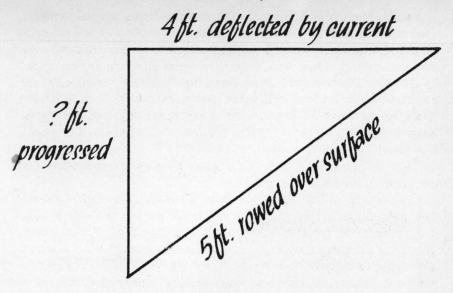

'For every second he rows he advances five feet over the water but is deflected four feet sideways. Fortunately Pythagoras comes to our assistance. The distance actually progressed is the square root of 5 squared minus 4 squared, or three feet. So Michelson takes 60 seconds to cover the course. If they did not know the speed of the flow of the water, they could use stop watches to time their journeys and thus deduce the rate of flow from their times. Yes?'

I nodded agreement once again.

'Good,' said Steerforth. 'Suppose that they repeated their experiment and found that their stop watches gave the same time for both journeys? Let us say, 36 seconds?'

'Why then . . .' I said slowly, 'from that we could deduce that the surface of the water had no effect upon their speed, and that the water was motionless.'

'Exactly,' said Steerforth. 'The surface of the water is motionless with respect to them. Let us now suppose, however, that you yourself, Hawkesworth, are observing this experiment. The boats are floating on a vast lake, the shores shrouded in mist. To the men in the boats it merely seems that the water is motionless. Hovering above them, you perceive that in fact the water is moving eastwards at four feet per second. You expect them to take respectively 100 seconds and 60 seconds. But because the water is motionless to them, they both take 36 seconds. Their stop watches are wrong!'

'Then who is right?' I asked. 'Is the water motionless or not?'

'It is motionless to Michelson and Morley, but not to you.'

'If they are satisfied with their results, then who cares what I observe?'

'Very good,' laughed Steerforth. 'But if the water actually is moving and they are merely ignorant of the fact, how would you chart their progress against, let's say, the muddy bottom of the lake? Do they in fact travel the distance they think at the speed they think? Or if not, what?'

'Then their clocks are correct for them, but mine is correct for me?' said I, somewhat aghast.

'Precisely,' said Steerforth. 'We now know that we cannot regard time as an absolute thing. It is an attribute of the world in which it happens to be measured. Time like an ever-rolling stream turns out to be precisely the wrong way of looking at it. We have our own clocks and our own measuring rods. We think of them as absolute, because we think of our world as stationary. This is a total delusion. Minkowski said: "From now onwards space and time sink to the position of mere shadows. . . ." He was right. These are the mysteries that Khan, from his childhood, felt destined to unravel.'

It is now time to explain the matter of Khan's uncle. One afternoon in the summer of 1952 a taxi arrived at the main entrance of the school. As I remember, it was one of those summer days that sometimes descend like a magical spell upon a boys' boarding school towards the end of the summer term – or at any rate did so in that now long-forgotten era. Great clouds of warm air, tangible and almost visible, seemed to come billowing in off the open land to the north. If such a day chanced to fall on a Sunday, chapel services had to be held with the doors wide open. Under the floating boughs of the cedar trees, a tense and heady silence seemed to lurk as though something rather menacing were somehow trapped there. The inhabitants of School House had mostly deserted its baking corridors, common rooms and studies to seek refuge at the swimming pool. I sat alone in my study, going through the motions of marking some sixth form essays, watching and listening as summer droned endlessly across the valley.

As the distant clock on the cricket pavilion struck three, the visitor arrived. Mr Steele, the lodge porter, was slumbering in his little office by the main entrance. He roused himself, straightened his black tie with a firm, nautical hand and hurried down the steps to open the door of the taxi for the visitor. He found himself face to face with a distinguished-looking Asian gentleman with gleaming black hair and piercing black eyes. At first sight he seemed to be in his middle thirties, though a closer inspection might have served to reduce the estimate by two or three years. His features were regular, but his nose was fiercely hooked. He was squarely built, and dressed in a suit of rather rough blue material with dull metal buttons. All in all his appearance hinted at some alien quality, some other-worldliness that was very hard to identify or describe. When the taxi had been paid off and had chugged off down the road towards Edgware, the visitor made himself known to Mr Steele.

'I am here to see Inayat Khan, who I believe is studying here,' said the stranger.

'Who shall I say is asking for him?' asked Mr Steele politely.

'Say it is his uncle,' was the reply. Now Mr Steele was very surprised by this reply, because he thought (like everyone else) that the old aunt in Paris was Khan's only surviving relative. In fact he felt certain that on the last occasion Khan had set off to spend his holidays in the apartment in the Avenue de Suffren where his aunt lived, Khan had confirmed the fact. However it was not for Mr Steele to argue with this important-seeming Asian gentleman who was at least convinced in his own mind that he was Inayat Khan's uncle. The visitor was given a chair and a newspaper, a kitchen maid was summoned to make him a cup of tea after his journey, and Mr Steele himself went off to hunt for young Inayat. Now Mr Steele was by way of being a friend of mine and might, when his duties were not too pressing, be persuaded to take a glass of whisky in a lonely housemaster's study. He later confided in me that when Khan at last was found and summoned to meet his uncle, his behaviour was not at all what might have been hoped for by a relative who had, it was assumed, travelled from some remote part of the globe to visit him.

'Uncle?' said Khan. 'What do you mean? I have no uncle.'

Naturally enough, Steele could only insist that the gentleman waiting for Khan had presented himself as an uncle. Khan frowned, then agreed to come and meet his visitor. He walked slowly down the length of the School House corridor with the studies on his right hand and the common rooms on his left. He stopped to leave his towel and swimming costume in his study, then stepped out under the glass dome of the rotunda to meet his uncle. For a moment Mr Steele thought he would faint, as he stumbled and caught his breath. Mr Steele claimed that in all his years at the school, and in all his nautical years, he had never seen anyone look so 'shook up'. Khan's uncle rose swiftly to his feet and came to meet Inayat. They did not shake hands at once but stood looking at each other. Khan's eyes were wide, his skin had taken on a greyish tinge and his breath was ragged.

'You were expecting me, weren't you?' said Khan's uncle rather urgently. 'Please think about it. You must have known that I would come. I had to come . . . about the papers. How could I not?'

'Yes,' said Khan slowly. 'I must have known that you would come. As you say, how could you not? Forgive me anyway. It was a shock.'

'Of course. If anyone understands, it is I. It's a shock for me too. So long, you know. Shall we shake hands?' Below the terrace where the cedars grew lay the school first team rugby pitch, and beyond that ran a footpath skirting the touchline where a number of benches stood. Here in the shadow of some large horse-chestnut trees that rained conkers in the autumn was one of the quietest and most peaceful spots in the school grounds. Only an occasional boy passing by on his way to the cricket nets infringed the privacy of this area. It was to this place that Khan led his uncle on that long-ago afternoon, that they might sit and talk of whatever concerned them. As I have mentioned, I was working in my room and looking out from time to time at the cedars and beyond. Perhaps some instinct prompted me to step over to the window and look down the green hill, athwart the cedarn cover to the place where they sat, a man and a boy talking together on a hot afternoon. They were, I suppose, at least fifty yards from my study window – maybe sixty or seventy. There was no question of my overhearing any word of their conversation. But from their attitudes I could see that Inayat Khan was mostly silent, while his uncle did most of the talking. The man was leaning forward with a piece of paper in his hand, speaking very earnestly and gazing at Inayat every once in a while. The boy's attention was fixed upon what his uncle was saying, as if his very life depended upon understanding and remembering it all. For some reason the picture of the man and the boy seated under the horse-chestnut trees, the sunlight falling dappled by the leaves upon their faces, hands and clothes – for some reason that picture burned itself sharply and permanently into my memory. In my mind's eye I see it as I write. Khan's uncle was a handsome, slightly florid man, in whom the family resemblance to his nephew was quite marked. His suit was of a slightly unusual cut, though it was hard to pick out exactly how it differed from the usual. He radiated a slight but unmistakable aura of the outlandish, of otherness, as if he had just arrived in something of a hurry from some foreign country, which for all I knew he might well have done. But I also supposed, for some reason, that he might not spend much time either in his native land. After some further discussion, Khan's uncle carefully folded the piece of paper he had been holding and placed it in an envelope. He handed the envelope to Khan and laid a hand upon his sleeve as if to impress upon him the importance of its safekeeping. As I witnessed these events I felt a blush of shame, as if I were intruding from the furtive privacy of my study window upon some intensely private exchange between the man and boy. The envelope might contain some private memento of Khan's parents and of his other dead relatives. Perhaps this unexpected visitor was himself a survivor of that massacre in which all the rest of Khan's family had so cruelly died. What if Khan had escaped into the forest leaving his uncle for dead among the other corpses? Such a possibility would at least explain the shock which Mr Steele had observed when the boy first set eyes upon his uncle. No doubt the earnest words which his uncle had poured into Khan's ears were a plea to uphold the unity of the family and the survival of its traditions, now resting entirely and perhaps precariously in the hands of the uncle, the nephew and the old lady in the Avenue de Suffren. When I had indulged these fantasies to a point which sated even my own somewhat excessively morbid tastes, I went back to my desk and to the essays I was marking.

However weighty the matters he had come to discuss, they were apparently not numerous. For only an hour and a half after Khan had been summoned to meet him, the uncle was walking rather quickly up the drive on to the ridge road in the direction of the public telephone box, whence (it was supposed) he might call his taxi back. He went with the air of a man who has discharged an important piece of business, as it later transpired an accurate impression.

By the time of his uncle's visit both Khan and Steerforth had graduated to the school first XI at cricket. Steerforth, as might be expected of a future English player, was in the process of rewriting almost every batting record in the school's history. He was certainly the only boy ever to score a double century for the school, and he also scored eight separate centuries in one season. Khan was still a very fast bowler by schoolboy standards, but it was clear by now that a Blue at Oxford or Cambridge or a county cap was likely to be beyond him. In any case he lacked real interest in the game. It was, apparently, while the two boys were packing the first XI bag for an away match one morning that the subject of Khan's uncle came up.

'I say, Khan,' said Steerforth, 'aren't you going to tell me about your visitor?'

'What visitor?' said Khan in a rather surly fashion.

'I gathered that one of your relatives turned up out of the blue. If you weren't expecting him it must have been quite a shock.'

'Why do you suppose I wasn't expecting him?' said Khan, now with open irritability.

'Only because you have never spoken of him. We had all supposed that your aunt in Paris was your only surviving relative. I could have sworn you told me that yourself.'

'Then you were all wrong, weren't you?' said Khan coolly.

'Apparently so,' agreed Steerforth with cheery persistence. 'Where does he live?'

'Abroad,' said Khan vaguely. 'He's in business overseas.'

'Will he invite you to visit him, wherever he is?' asked Steerforth. To his surprise Khan laughed outright at this suggestion.

'I suppose he might invite me to visit him,' he said. 'But I don't think I'll accept. I might find it hard to get back.' Unclear what was meant by this remark, Steerforth set off on another tack.

'He's your uncle, I believe. Is he your father's brother or your mother's?' At this, Khan laid down the pair of batting gloves he was preparing to pack, and looked Steerforth squarely in the eye. He seemed determined to close once and for all this uncongenial line of conversation.

'Now look here, Steerforth,' he said, 'just because you English aristocrats take such a fanatical delight in displaying your family trees on every conceivable occasion, please don't think that everyone else in the world has the same obsession with genealogy. My family is my own affair and I prefer to keep it that way. Now would you mind if we leave the subject of my uncle alone?' Steerforth could tell that unless he wanted to finish packing the cricket bag alone, he might as well respect Khan's wishes. Later on, as they carried the bag from the pavilion to the bus, Khan seemed to repent a little of the severity with which he had spoken to his friend.

'Anyway,' he said, 'in my country such relationships are not so scrupulously defined. Practically everyone I knew in my village was a cousin or an aunt or an uncle.'

In those days of the 1950s the admission of undergraduates to the colleges of Oxford and Cambridge was a much less highly organised business than it is today. Much depended then upon long-standing connections between particular colleges and schools and upon performance in certain examinations. There was such a connection between our school and a certain Oxford college, the result of many admissions over the years. Both Khan and Steerforth (and I myself, though not as an undergraduate) were eventually to benefit from this relationship. Particular emphasis was also placed on the results of academic competitions held within those schools which had favoured connections with the colleges. At our school there were two such competitions. The winner of the school's music prize traditionally became a music scholar and – provided his skills lay in the appropriate area – chapel organist at a certain Cambridge college. The winner of the school physics prize was traditionally elected to a scholarship in physics at a certain Oxford college, an arrangement which, while not in such concrete a form as a closed scholarship, was reputed to date back to a gentleman's agreement over the terms of an endowment in the sixteenth century. Such arrangements have now of course given place to more open and democratic measures, though whether the new regime results in pupils finding their way more or less frequently to the most suitable college is largely a matter for conjecture.

For this reason the school physics prize was much sought after. In the summer term during which Khan received the visit from his uncle, there were two outstanding candidates for the prize. One was a slightly older boy named Ralston who had already won a place at another Oxford college but who would nevertheless welcome the extra kudos that a scholarship would bring. The other was Khan himself. In total, including those who were believed to have little chance of success, there were some six to eight candidates. It was customary at important school prize examinations that the invigilator should always be a master whose knowledge and discipline equipped him in not the slightest degree to help or hinder any candidate, a tradition perhaps dating back to some long-forgotten attempt at favouritism. By chance when an invigilator was chosen for the physics examination the lot fell upon me. Of all the arts masters I was perhaps the most qualified, for my ignorance of physics was almost perfect.

On that day the school gymnasium was turned over to the purpose of an examination room. To avoid damaging its smoothly boarded floors the candidates were required to wear plimsolls. I remember most vividly that when I invited them to troop into the room and to take their seats at their widely spaced desks, each with a name card, their rubber shoes squeaked on the wooden floor in a manner calculated even further to strain nerves already tense. Each candidate found himself confronted by a pile of foolscap paper and the examination paper itself, placed face down upon the desk. The day was warm and the gymnasium was stuffy, the faint odour of boyish sweat and embrocation in the air. I decided for the time being at least to leave the door open. A milk trolley with clanking bottles passed by on the ridge road. In the nearby chapel a choir practice was in progress, though precious little progress seemed to be made for some time as the choir struggled again and again with the same apparently insuperable passage of an anthem. How many times they repeated that passage I cannot say, yet the repetition seemed endless.

'Gentlemen,' I announced, using the term of address customary for sixth formers, and proceeded to drone my way through the examination rules. At length I finished. 'And now,' I said, 'you may turn over the paper and begin.'

The whispered sussuration of eight papers. A moment's silence. A cough. The almost physical excitement of a high-grade academic examination crackles in the air. One by one the candidates all begin to write.

Something was wrong. Something about what had happened was not as it should be. What was it? No one was using a crib, or looking at notes handily inscribed on his shirtsleeve cuff. No one had looked at the questions and walked out of the room, as a boy once did in a Roman history examination which I supervised. For a split second it seemed that I might be able to concretise (as the French say) this fleeting impression of something amiss. Then it was gone, winging away from me at the speed of light like the lamp on the front of Einstein's train. The feeling, the knowledge that something was not as it should be was as real, as clear-cut, as persistent in my mind as my recollection of the squeaking plimsolls, the clanking milk bottles, the endless repetitions of the choral passage in the chapel. Yet if I had been obliged on pain of death to say exactly what was wrong, then I should have had to face the firing squad without demur.

The end of the summer term in a boys' boarding school is a heady, drowsy and ecstatic time. Once the examinations are over, the impetus of academic study drops to a minimum. The school cricket season comes to an end; those who are fated to win their colours sport their new ties and blazers. The rest try to mask their bitter disappointment, which is also good practice for later life. We masters spend the dying days of the academic year trying to prepare our departing charges among the older boys for university life, church, business or the armed services, as their various inclinations and abilities have befitted them. I have never known a boy, however tough or cynical, to remain unaffected by these wild, sad days at the end of his school career. Whatever he may have suffered or achieved, he feels – he knows – that these are the last days of his boyhood. Those not yet leaving the school (including Khan and Steerforth) we masters would attempt to divert with projects of a more or less serious kind. Khan and Steerforth were never a problem: they had their love affair with science to keep them occupied.

Exceedingly few people ever knew what then passed for the full story of Khan and the physics prize, and even fewer now know what actually happened. Only Mr Hughes (who had the task of marking the papers), the Headmaster and I in my capacity as Khan's housemaster were involved in the first place. The three of us met in the Head's study and Mr Hughes, who had requested the meeting, explained his difficulty.

'May I ask you to look at these pages,' he said, neatly laying out on the Headmaster's desk the dozen or so numbered sheets of Khan's examination script. It was indeed an exceptional or even a unique paper. During my life as a schoolmaster and a don I suppose I have seen thousands, or perhaps tens of thousands, of examination scripts. Some have been brilliant and some appalling, many middling. I do not recall that I ever saw one quite like Khan's. Typically a candidate's handwriting changes quite markedly during the course of an examination. As he tries to write faster in the last hour, so his writing becomes smaller and more cramped. Spelling errors and the use of abbreviations become more frequent. Deletions and corrections become more common, as the pen outruns the mind. Unless the paper on which he is writing is lined, the candidate's ability to write a level line is often degraded by haste and tiredness. None of these faults was present in Khan's paper. At first sight it seemed as if the handwriting throughout was as neat, as ordered and as leisurely as on the first page of the script. There were not above three or four deletions, insertions or corrections from first page to last. And though the paper was unlined Khan's script was very level throughout.

'Perhaps you find me a suspicious old curmudgeon,' said Mr Hughes. 'But I am bound to admit that I find this paper far beyond the bounds of normal excellence. Since neither of you is a physics graduate, I had better tell you that the content is as admirable as the presentation. This paper is the sort you see in books of model answers. Apart from the old examiner's rule that perfection is unattainable, I can see little reason not to mark it one hundred per cent. Yet it worries me.'

'Have you shown it to any other physicist?' asked the Head.

'I showed it to my wife,' said Mr Hughes, who had married a kindred academic spirit. 'She also was worried.'

'Let me ask you a difficult question,' said the Headmaster. 'What are the chances that such a perfect paper could be produced by any pupil relying on his own unaided efforts, forgetting for the moment that the pupil in question is Khan?'

'Well, Headmaster,' answered Mr Hughes slowly, 'bearing in mind that the school prize competition is set not against any fixed and limited syllabus but against a broad knowledge of physics at university entrance level, then I would say the chance is less than one in a hundred. Perhaps less than one in a thousand.' The silence in the Headmaster's study was a deafening torrent of accusation.

'Now Mr Hughes,' said the Headmaster, 'I am afraid I must ask you an even more difficult question.' He did not need to put it into words.

'I truly cannot believe that Khan cheated in the exam,' said Mr Hughes. 'Quite apart from the question whether he would, I don't see how he could. I prepared the papers myself and my wife typed out the copies. I kept them under lock and key until the day of the examination. I gave them to Mr Hawkesworth in a sealed envelope after lunch that day.'

'And I could swear upon my life,' I added, 'that Khan used no crib or notes during the exam itself.' So there was the riddle. A paper so perfect that no one could believe it was the result of honest endeavour, versus precautions so thorough that cheating seemed to be out of the question. There seemed to be no logical possibility of an explanation. Mr Hughes summed it all up.

'If Khan is a cheat,' he said, 'he is a jolly poor one. A decent cheat would have made one or two errors to make the whole thing less suspicious. And if he is a genius he's a jolly odd one. A typical genius would have done some of the things his own way and covered three or four more pages with barely decipherable calculations of his own. . . .' Even in the grim circumstances of this inquisition into Khan's honesty, the Headmaster and I could not resist a moment's laughter, for Mr Hughes's propensity for long, straggling and barely legible equations was a legend in the school. But the point was a valid one for all that it had personal relevance.

'Gentlemen,' said the Headmaster at length, 'I require your advice. The matter is not a light one. The nomination to this prize is normally followed by election to a scholarship at Oxford. It is a signal honour, one which should not at any price be conferred upon a cheat. Yet although we have our suspicions, we have not a shred of evidence and indeed cannot even guess how Khan might have cheated. I believe we have three choices. We may stifle our suspicions and award the prize to Khan. Or we may disqualify Khan and award the prize to the second-best candidate, which I imagine means Ralston. Or invite Khan to come and see us and openly challenge him to prove how he came to produce such a perfect paper. I will feel happier, gentlemen, if our choice of course is unanimous.'

And unanimous it was, after a period of very serious debate. Courteously and kindly, in this as in all other matters, the Headmaster thanked us for sharing with him this unpalatable task. But just as Mr Hughes and I were leaving the study, he asked me to stay behind for a moment. When Mr Hughes had withdrawn, the Head sat facing me with his hands folded on the leather of his desk top.

'Hawkesworth, my friend,' he began, 'you have been with us now for only four years. And you are still a relatively young man – you are not yet fifty years old? My friends at Oxford have written to me about you. They have had their eye on you for some time. They have been much impressed with your published articles on Chaucer and the Italian poets. Did you know that you had such distinguished admirers of your work?'

'No Headmaster,' I replied quite truthfully. What on earth was coming next?

'In October of next year,' he continued, 'there will be a vacancy for a fellow in English literature at the college. The stipend is not great, but a university lectureship can also be made available. Together the two stipends make a decent salary. A course in Chaucer and Dante is required. You would have a year's notice of the appointment, so that you might think ahead a little. The place is to be offered to you, Hawkesworth. I have said that I think you will accept. Will you make a liar of me?'

'No Headmaster,' I faltered. I knew that he had sacrificed the convenience of the school for my interests, since a new house-master would now have to be found. How easily he could have diverted the college's attention towards another candidate! I cannot deny that as I left his study, my heart was pounding and my head whirling. Four years ago I had been contented enough in my routine in the city. The job at my new school had come out of the blue. But Oxford! I could hardly believe it. Visions of pro-fessorships falling into my lap with equal facility had to be swiftly and consciously dispelled. If I am candid I must admit that the question of the physics prize and of Khan's performance in the examination was also driven from my mind by the teeming pros-pects of the new life I was to undertake.

All too soon the agreeable days at the end of the summer term had drawn almost to a close, and Founder's Day was upon us. This was the great occasion of the year, a festival and a memorial rolled into one. It was also the day on which the prizes were awarded. A marquee was erected in a field adjoining the rugby pitch. A public address system was rigged up and hundreds of folding chairs set out on the quadrangle. The weather was perfect. Parents soon began to arrive. At two o'clock precisely the Governors took their places and the prize-giving began. I could see Khan and Steerforth in the audience, with Steerforth's parents seated beside them. All through the prize list went the Headmaster, from Greek verse composition to English poetry, from sixth form classics to junior chemistry. At last only two prizes remained to be announced. The music prize was awarded to a very popular boy. He walked up to shake hands with the Headmaster and receive his inscribed book to (as the school magazine was later somewhat archly to put it) 'a chorus of approval'. School magazines think nothing of such atrocities.

'Finally,' said the Headmaster, 'the school's premier academic prize, the annual award for physics, is this year awarded to Inayat Khan.' At this Steerforth belted his friend so hard across the back that he seemed for a moment to have winded him. Lady Steerforth was wide-eyed, and had a handkerchief pressed to her mouth as if it were Augustus himself who had won the prize. Amidst tu-multuous applause (for Khan also was a popular figure) Inayat stepped forth into the sunlit passage between the blocks of chairs and turned towards the dais where the Headmaster stood. As he did so, a photograph was taken which was later to appear in the school magazine. His head is held high, his eye gleams as he steps out in his elegant morning suit as if to fulfill a destiny. His teeth gleam brilliantly against his dark skin as he grips the Headmaster's hand. The inscribed volume is handed over, and with it by custom and practice goes an open scholarship at one of Oxford's oldest and finest colleges. The ceremony was complete.

Two final memories seal my recollection of that remote and magical period of the past. Steerforth later told me that Khan had very carefully preserved his copy of the question paper from the physics prize examination and had even sealed it up in an envelope before locking it away in his tuck-box. This puzzled Steerforth a little, since Khan was usually the sort of person who travelled through life lightly encumbered, not much given to the retention of memorabilia. Khan seemed faintly irritated when Steerforth was moved to comment on the matter.

At the very end of term came the final chapel service of the year, a rather emotion-laden occasion for all present but most particularly so for those boys who were leaving school the next day. There is a traditional order of service for this occasion which is designed to bring a tear to the eye of all but the most insensitive of those who have spent five years of their young lives learning and playing in that pleasant place. I was carried away into a reverie once more, reflecting that the next time I heard this order of service I too would be preparing to leave this place – albeit as a grown man and a teacher rather than as a mere schoolboy, I too would be seeking my fortune in a wider world, in the rarified atmosphere of an Oxford college. I suppose I was once again slipping into vainglorious dreams about what I might achieve in that palace of learning when suddenly the choir launched itself into the second and final anthem of the service. Just after the opening bars of the anthem came the very passage which the choir had been rehearsing so repeatedly while I was invigilating the physics examination in the gymnasium. The long repetitions had done their work. This time the awkward passage was negotiated without (at least as far as my untutored ear might discern) undue difficulty. But more to the point, the link of that music in my ears seemed somehow to transport me in time to the day of the examination. I could sense once more the heat gusting in through the open door of the gymnasium, as real and tangible as the music itself. I heard once more the nerve-twisting squeak of the candidates' plimsolls on the polished wooden floor as they filed in. I heard my own voice, solemn and sonorous, reading out the examination rules. And once again, just as on the first occasion, I had a deep yet imprecise feeling that as the examination began something was wrong – something was not as it should be.

I closed my eyes and let the music and the young voices flood over me and through me. I strove to pluck that impression up from the deep well of unconscious thought, concentrating all my mental powers upon its retrieval. And in a trice I had it.

Realisation opened my eyes with an almost physical jolt. I found myself staring into a pair of eyes equally alert and equally stimulated, it seemed, by the recollection that this was the same music we had heard in the gym during the physics exam. In Khan's eyes I saw the self-same look that I had seen when he took the doubtful catch to dismiss Steerforth, a look of raging doubt but of utter hunger to have at any price the thing so desired. And I saw that he knew some deeper knowledge had come to me of him and of his ways. What I had suddenly recalled I never shared with Mr Hughes or the Headmaster, for what was done was done. Khan had his prize and his scholarship and the whole school had applauded him in his triumph. But I knew for a certainty – not thought, or half-believed or recalled but *knew* – that though Inayat Khan had turned over the paper containing the examination questions at the same time as all the other candidates, he had cast only a cursory eye over the paper as if to confirm that the questions he knew would be there were in fact on the paper. He had begun at once to write out his oh-so-perfect answer without even reading the rubric, let alone the text.

⤞ CHAPTER 3 ⤝

Ancestral Voices

At this point in our recollections, Steerforth and I were interrupted by a knock at my study door. It was the same young man from the porter's lodge who had first announced Steerforth's arrival, but now he was bidden by the Warden of the college himself to enquire with great respect whether Lord Steerforth was to dine with the Warden and Fellows in hall?

'Oh Lord,' said Steerforth, 'I should have told the old boy I was coming and paid my respects. Now he's miffed that I'm here unannounced. The trouble with being a college benefactor, Hawkesworth, is that you are never free to come and go as you please like any other visitor but must check in and out more religiously than the humblest commoner!'

In the end the youth was dispatched with a note carefully written out by Steerforth on headed college paper to the effect that his visit was only a fleeting one and that his dinner tonight was looked after for him in London but if the invitation were still open when he could pay a more prolonged visit. . .? It was clear that Steerforth wanted our discussion to go on. So when the boy had delivered Steerforth's note and returned to express the Warden's appreciation, etc. I sent him over to the Lamb and Flag for sandwiches and gherkins and opened a bottle of a rather fine Château Beauséjour I had saved for some such reunion.

And then, with the food and wine spread out on my desk, with more coals heaped on the fire and with the old oaken door occasionally shaking in the winter wind as if it yearned to wrench itself off its hinges and fly about the college, we went on.

Inayat Khan's election to an open scholarship in physics at

Oxford followed on in due course from his victory in the prize competition. Although I was still puzzled by my clear recollection that Khan had begun to write before reading the question paper, I had not mentioned the fact to the Headmaster or to Mr Hughes. I simply could not see what useful end would be served by reopening this question. Any lingering disquiet I felt about the possible unfairness to Ralston, the other leading candidate for the prize, was dispelled when he too (at the second attempt) won an open scholarship at another college.

There was another area of uncertainty about Khan that worried me. It had to do with money. With most of the pupils in the school I had a fairly clear idea of the family circumstances surrounding each one's plans for a university career. For the children of the wealthy, such as Steerforth, there was obviously little difficulty in financing their university careers. At the other extreme, for the handful of scholarship boys that the school took and who were in the main very clever children from working-class homes, there was equally no real problem. For they would qualify for the whole of the approved student grant which, though not lavish, was enough to keep a prudent undergraduate alive at Oxford or Cambridge. The problems could arise for the middle-range parents, those not well enough off to sneeze at the expense of keeping a son at Oxford for three or four years yet too well placed to qualify for the full grant. Thus it was, for instance, the manager of the local bank branch and the not-too-successful doctor in general practice who fell into this category. It concerned me that in the case of Inayat Khan I had no idea at all how he might be placed to survive at university: I was not even sure if he was aware of the expenses he would meet. His scholarship brought great prestige but little cash. And as a foreign national I did not know whether he would be eligible for support from the local education authority. This uncertainty led me to resolve that I would raise the matter with him when an occasion should present itself. And so it did at Lord's cricket ground where Khan and I were present to witness one of Steerforth's adventures.

The annual cricket match between the Public Schools team and the Combined Services team was in those days one of the major events of the amateur cricket calendar. Khan and I were seated side by side in the members' enclosure watching the earlier batsmen of the school side discomforted by the combined team's bowlers. At last it was Steerforth's turn to bat and he clattered down the steps of the pavilion, capless and golden-headed in the sun.

'Good luck, Steerforth!' called Inayat Khan. Steerforth turned and scanned the crowd for us, then raised his head in mock surprise as if familiar faces and friendly good wishes were the last things he had expected to find in the daunting environment of Lord's. Steerforth's greatest weakness as a cricketer was a tendency to become over-confident or perhaps even casual and to play an injudicious stroke at a critical moment. On this occasion he seemed determined to restrain himself and make a big score. So he progressed, passing his half-century just after lunch and his century just after tea. Soon afterwards he was out, caught and bowled by a wily old artilleryman off a fiercely struck drive that nearly drilled a hole through his military midriff. He came in, as the saying is, tired but happy to an enthusiastic reception from his admirers – with Khan and myself in the vanguard.

When the excitement had subsided and Khan and I had settled down, I raised with him the question that was worrying me.

'Now that your scholarship at Oxford is secure, Khan, how shall you manage for money? The expenses of life at Oxford are much greater than those at the school, you know. And then you have the vacations to consider. I don't mean to pry, but I have no idea how your family finances are arranged.'

He nodded and glanced keenly at me as if trying to assess the degree of business acumen with which the question was posed, since the answer to be provided might vary accordingly. The sun flashed on his almost blue-black hair as he dipped his head and carefully weighed my question.

'There is no difficulty, sir,' he replied at length. 'There are family funds available as a result of some rather prudent actions taken by my father before partition. This money is now controlled by my aunt who, as you know, lives most of the year in Paris. She is a surprisingly capable manager of the family's money, considering that she was quite old when she came to live in the west.' He paused for a moment, and I could not help but feel that he was tempted to tell me something he felt he should really keep to himself.

'And then again,' he said slowly, 'there is my uncle. He always seems to be able to get his hands on some cash if necessary. He has helped my aunt once or twice already and has promised to do so on a more substantial scale if that should prove necessary.'

'Well that's good news,' I said with a cheeriness that I only partly felt. Somehow I felt that my enquiry had been an example of occidental gaucherie, a violation of some code of gentlemanliness too English to be attainable by the English.

'That's excellent news. I'll stop worrying myself on that score then. Shall we go and see if Steerforth has cooled off enough to receive our homage?'

Later that evening I sat with Khan and Steerforth in the bar at Lord's while a number of passers-by stopped to murmur their congratulations on Steerforth's innings. He had just been invited for the first time to play for Middlesex in a county match.

'Well Steerforth,' I said, 'I suppose you recognise one of the consequences of your exploits today?'

'What's that, sir?'

'The admissions tutors of all the colleges in Oxford and Cambridge will be lining up to invite you to their exams, and vying with each other to offer you the most congenial terms. You can take your pick of any college you like.' Steerforth smiled and nodded and sipped his beer, as if he could not dispute the truth of what I had said but didn't quite see its relevance to his own case.

'Perhaps that would be too easy,' suggested Khan suddenly.

'What do you mean?' said Steerforth.

'Winning an easy admission on the strength of your sporting ability might not satisfy your intellectual aspirations,' said Khan.

'I suppose it might not,' admitted Steerforth.

'The lofty academic standards adopted by Steerforth,' said Khan to me in a loud stage-whisper, 'would not be satisfied by admission granted for cricketing prowess. Steerforth prefers to take a more intellectually respectable route. . . . Am I right?'

'Well what's wrong with that, Khan?' said Steerforth suddenly. 'I imagine you're not the only person in the world who might aspire to academic respectability.'

And so that autumn Augustus Steerforth, already by then a county cricketer and a desirable entrant for any college, packed his bags and set out for the misty and numinous towers and passages of Oxford.

'Well, blockhead, how did you manage?' said Khan when Steerforth returned. 'Did you even get an interview?'

'Yes I got an interview,' replied Steerforth. 'Actually they seemed to think there were so many illiterate savages contriving to win open scholarships nowadays that it would make quite a change to have a normal Englishman in the place. Hence I'm not sure if I still want to go.'

My own preparations to uproot myself from the life of a schoolmaster and install myself as a don in Oxford – albeit as a junior and apprehensive don – were also gathering pace. I had, of course, all the normal work of a housemaster to perform and had no complaints against the school on that account. But I was also deeply involved in the preparation of my lecture series for Oxford and I encountered in this task a problem I had already met once or twice before in my life; I applied myself to it with such excessive zeal and diligence that it all began to go wrong. I was ploughing through Chaucer, Boccaccio and Dante at breakneck speed and sparing myself no effort to verify every reference and citation, turning to texts and dictionaries to check things I was very nearly sure of. And then I found that I was actually checking things I was sure of! I found myself checking the spelling of words I had known for twenty years or more. I believe that if I had gone on working at the same pace I should have found myself checking the spelling of the name of Chaucer himself, or perhaps of my own.

Fortunately destiny created a diversion. One morning I was sitting in my study just before breakfast time. I was supposed to be cleaning my shoes and was sat with a shoe in one hand and the brush in the other. But my attention was caught by the pattern of the ice and snow on the boughs of the cedar outside my window, small needles of snow having fallen and covered the branches as if they were sprinkled all over with dust. So many of these tiny needles had fallen that they lay as they had fallen crossed over one another and looked very like a cobweb on the tree. The sun was shining and the branch nearest my window was in shade, so that the snow sparkled as bright as diamonds. It seemed to me that I should recognise, were not my mind so exclusively encumbered with Chaucer and the Italians, some reference in literature to these needles of ice . . . but then there was a tap at my door and a boy with a grin that nearly sheared off the top of his head burst into my room with a letter in his hand. He tried to thrust the letter into my hands, only to find the way barred by shoe and brush.

'Steerforth, what is it?' I gasped. 'Is it from Oxford?'

'Yes sir. Oh read it, please!' So I set down my brush and my shoe and sat in socked feet to read Steerforth's letter, which was from the Warden of the same college for which Khan was destined and where I was soon to be installed as a don. The Warden's handwriting was rather shaky but the message of the letter was unmistakable. Steerforth had been elected to an open major scholarship in mathematics at the college.

'There was a case,' said Khan later, 'which occurred in Germany in the late eighteenth century of a totally uneducated servant girl – in fact I think she was illiterate – who in the delirium of fever recited whole passages of Latin, Greek and Hebrew verbatim. It transpired that she had lived as a child in the house of an old scholar and had heard him recite these texts and had unwittingly memorised them. Something of the same sort must have happened with Steerforth's scholarship, don't you think, sir?'

During the assembly at which the Headmaster congratulated Steerforth, I fell to musing about Khan's story of the illiterate German girl with her perfectly memorised passages of classical literature. I knew I had heard of that story somewhere before: but where? Once or twice before, Khan had produced these little nuggets of general knowledge that seemed familiar, yet which I couldn't trace. It was so infuriating. How did the boy do it? So engrossed had I become in these reflections that I missed my turn to make my exit from the Assembly. To the titters of the lower forms, one of the other masters had to turn back and tap my shoulder before I remembered where I was and what I was at. But that wretched German girl with her Homer and Virgil continued to haunt me for weeks. Then she was swept away again on the tide of my preparations for Oxford, and I can honestly say that I did not think of her again for a quarter of a century.

At some time during the period in 1954 when Khan and Steerforth were finishing their days as schoolboys and waiting to go to Oxford – and just for once Steerforth's memory was imprecise as to whether it was the spring vacation or the summer – Khan was invited to spend a few weeks at the Steerforth home at Bain Brook Priory. In Steerforth's account of this visit considerable emphasis was placed upon such characteristically summer pursuits as tennis: I think it more likely that the visit took place in July or August, when Khan and Steerforth had both left school, rather than the April preceding their final term. He had visited the family once or twice before and was a welcome and popular guest at the house, valued not least for his skill at tennis.

The tennis courts at Bain Brook were congenial to Khan from many points of view, not least since they were enclosed by a wire mesh fence that guaranteed the exclusion of dogs. That summer of 1954 Khan and Steerforth played a good deal of tennis whenever Steerforth's cricketing engagements permitted. They were both quite reasonable players, though Steerforth was inclined to be over-ambitious and to try to make every shot a decisive winner.

Khan was more deliberate in his approach to the game and there-fore in a singles game against Steerforth he usually won. As I recall it, the two of them also found doubles partners that summer in the daughter of the local vicar, who was killing time before entering a college of education, and Lord Steerforth's secretary, who was similarly underoccupied while her employer was engaged on one of his periodic tours of all the publishing company's offices around the world. Apart from managing his diary and acknow-ledging his correspondence, there was little that this young lady could do while Lord Steerforth was away. But once he returned she would make up for this period of ease with a string of sixteen-hour days and six-day weeks. Her London flat and the head office of the firm being somewhat hot and stuffy during the summer, she had been invited to spend as much time as she wished at Bain Brook.

An invitation to Bain Brook was a passport to a different world. Apart from the sheer grandeur of the place, the great staircase rising without visible means of support to the ducal passage and the endless rows of portraits of ancestors gazing down in earnest disapproval as such lowly creatures as oneself passed by, there was also a more lofty style of life followed at Bain Brook in the time of Steerforth's father. When Lord Steerforth was at home, for example, everyone was expected to put on black tie for dinner. Lady Steerforth was less meticulous in her observation of these matters and during her husband's absence would encourage a more relaxed and informal style of life. Personally I always found, on the occasions that I was invited to Bain Brook, that the spectacle of all the young people dressed up in the evening was a most agreeable one.

'Tell me, Inayat,' said Lady Steerforth one evening when she and the two young men were gathered before dinner, 'what do you propose to do at Oxford? I can't remember whether you play cricket, like Augustus, or whether you are going to work all the time and be fearfully academic as I rather suspect Augustus's father was in his time.'

'I have played cricket, of course,' answered Khan. 'In fact it was pretty well compulsory at school. But I have never shown the talent for it that Steerforth has, and I doubt if I will play at Oxford.'

'That is actually nonsense,' said Steerforth. 'Khan is by far the fastest bowler at any school in England and could easily get a blue at Oxford if he could be bothered. In fact he'll probably swot all the time and end up as Professor of Physics, or win a Nobel Prize or something.'

'Do you think there are still great discoveries to be made?' Lady Steerforth addressed her question to both the young men. 'I remember reading somewhere that towards the end of the nineteenth century a young man was going up to Oxford and a friend advised his father not to let him read physics, as all the great discoveries had been made. How wrong he was! But how is it now, do you think?'

'Between now and the end of the century,' said Inayat Khan, 'a period of forty-six years, there will be the greatest expansion of human knowledge in the physical sciences that the world has ever known. The new discoveries will arise in every branch of physics from the nuclear level to the cosmic. There are about eight – or perhaps ten – sciences which are potentially architectonic in their own right, meaning that each of them could in isolation from all other sciences transform the life of humanity. Taken in combination, they create a future world which is incredibly dynamic, even volatile, a world in which the only thing you can say is really impossible is for the old world-order to remain unchanged.'

'What do you think they are, these architectonic sciences?' asked Lady Steerforth. Inayat Khan ticked them off on his fingers.

'Nuclear engineering, including both fission and fusion processes, genetics, digital computer science, interplanetary travel, deep space astronomy and cosmology, molecular biology, space–time field theory. . . .'

'Oh enough, enough,' cried Lady Steerforth. 'Where do you plan to make your own contribution?' Khan seemed tongue-tied for a moment as if nonplussed by the very directness of the question and its ready assumption that on the roll of scientific honour beneath the names of Faraday, Newton, Einstein and Fermi was a space waiting to be inscribed with Khan's name. Steerforth jumped in and told his mother something of the study Khan had made of the work of Einstein and how he was trying to understand the very fabric of the universe. At the end of Steerforth's explanation, his mother smiled and shook her head in wonderment.

'When I was a child,' she said, 'there was an old tenant on my uncle's land who was supposed to have fought in the First Afghan War. How quickly everything seems to happen in the world. And what will be the sum total of all this change and all this new knowledge, Inayat? Do you think the total volume of human satisfaction and fulfillment will be increased in proportion to all this new scientific knowledge?' Khan pondered on this question for a moment, as if wondering how best to attempt to answer it.

'I think the knowledge itself is just a tool,' he began at length. 'What matters is how the knowledge is applied and what results are achieved. Applications of nuclear engineering include the provision of abundant light and heat for the world, and the total destruction of the world. You can have whichever applications you want – or rather whatever you deserve and earn.'

'And what kind of applications do you think we shall deserve?'

'That depends. Our current ways of determining such choices are such that the worst decisions are likely to be taken. But that need not always be the case. At present we appoint a set of people who apparently know nothing about science and who often seem proud of the fact to take scientific decisions on our behalf. Their only qualification is that they can pull the wool over the eyes of millions of other people whose scientific ignorance is even more profound than their own. These government leaders' – he gestured vaguely and rather contemptuously towards the south, where lay London and the centres of the government he was about to vilify – 'are advised by civil servants whose training equips them to over-simplify every issue to a straight choice: will it help or hinder the political leaders to win the next beauty contest? This is the process by which we are deciding how to apply science's revolutionary upheavals to our national life. No wonder it fails to produce the right answers!'

'And what is your solution, Inayat?' asked Lady Steerforth. Just at that moment it was announced that dinner was ready. Khan laughed happily that he had been saved from the task of proposing an alternative to Parliament, which was just as well because he didn't really have one to propose.

'But I am sure,' he said as they entered the dining room, 'that the future of mankind is too hazardous to leave under such hit-and-miss control. I know that something better must be possible, or all the benefits of science will turn to dross in our hands.'

Coffee after dinner was taken in Lady Steerforth's favourite room, a refectory with walls covered in tiny seashells, part of the original seventeenth century fabric of the house. An arched recess was filled with flowers. Thousands of seashells adorned the walls around this recess, surrounding the figures of dolphins, mermaids and sea monsters in stucco. The floor was covered in large tiles of yellow and pale brown, and the whole room adorned with

Davenport plate. In summer this refectory was a cool, airy and pleasant place for Lady Steerforth to entertain her guests. When the coffee was served and the staff departed, she turned again to Khan with a serious expression.

'What relatives do you have in the world, Inayat?' she asked.

'I have some in Pakistan,' replied Khan, 'odd cousins and such. Everyone is related to everyone else in a place like that, you know.' And he laughed uneasily, as if inviting Lady Steerforth to pass on without further ado from such a trivial, or even risible, subject of conversation.

'And in the West,' she persisted gruffly. 'What relatives have you living in the West?'

'Only my aunt,' replied Khan quickly. 'An old lady with a rather seedy apartment in the Avenue de Suffren in Paris. But she has been very kind to me and looks after me when I am not lucky enough to receive invitations such as yours, Lady Steerforth.'

'Have I been misinformed?' said Lady Steerforth sharply with a glance at her son. 'I could have sworn that Augustus said you also had an uncle who had come to visit you at school. Was he wrong or have I misremembered?'

'Oh my uncle,' said Khan. 'I am surprised you remember him. I had almost forgotten him myself. He only came to visit me once at school, on a matter of urgent family business, and I hardly count him as a near relative.'

'Where does he live?' asked Lady Steerforth. Khan paused for a long moment, his forehead furrowed and his eyebrows lowered over his burning eyes.

'He has a base in the Far East,' he replied at length. 'But he travels a great deal, wherever and whenever his business takes him. He is a great businessman. All his attention is devoted to his business.'

'And what is his business?' asked Lady Steerforth with the kind of directness that is tolerable only in aristocrats or the closest of friends.

'Exports and imports,' said Khan vaguely: then added, as if trying to be helpful, that he had heard his uncle once described as 'trading in futures', though neither Steerforth nor the Duchess had much idea what was involved in such activities.

'Your parents died at partition, then?' asked Lady Steerforth. Khan looked evenly into her eyes, smiled and nodded, as if she had asked whether he took sugar in his coffee. And as she drew breath to ask another question he quickly looked away.

'I say, Steerforth, are we playing tennis tomorrow?' he asked. The subject of Khan's family in general and of his parents' demise in particular seemed as firmly closed in the face of the Duchess's enquiries as to any other inquisitor.

Perhaps Steerforth drank too much coffee that evening in the refectory. At any rate when the party adjourned to bed, sleep eluded him. He sat up in bed and read a book. At last he put on his dressing-gown and began to wander through the house, listening in the darkness to the tiny creaks and groans of the ancient structure. In the hall, one of the dogs was asleep on the hearthrug. It raised its head, growled gently and, catching sight of Steerforth, fell back into its dreams. Standing at the French window and winding his wristwatch, which told him it was after three o'clock in the morning, Steerforth looked out over the moist and silent lawns of Bain Brook. The moon was shining brightly from a cloudless sky and the trees and bushes were unruffled by any breath of wind.

Suddenly he saw a figure moving slowly and silently across the lawn, leaving dark footprints on the silvery grass. At first he thought it was the shape of some ghostly cleric dressed in the habit of a monastic order, perhaps even that of the last Prior of Bain Brook who had ended his days swinging from a rope under the tree by Leg of Lamb pond. Then he realised that it was a living person dressed in night clothes but wrapped in a dark-coloured blanket. At length he recognised the face above the blanket and was on the point of tapping on the window to attract Khan's attention. His hand was raised and his mouth open to speak when he paused. Khan looked up as he passed by the window and gazed directly at the moon. And as the light of the moon fell directly upon his face, Steerforth saw that Khan's cheeks were covered with tears that glittered bright as diamonds, or like needles of ice under a winter sun. All at once Steerforth fell silent, and his hand dropped to his side. He stood by the French window while Khan let himself into the house and slowly made his way upstairs to his room. Fortunately the dog did not stir.

The next day, however, the resilience of youth had apparently worked to the benefit of both Steerforth and Khan. Both were recovered from their respective maladies enough to play three sets of very active and noisy tennis with the vicar's daughter and Lord Steerforth's secretary, during which it may be supposed that collisions between the male and female members of each team were more frequent than is usually the case and that such collisions obliged the male players to support the females in their arms more often than usual. The game, in short, was keenly enjoyed both as a sporting occasion and a social encounter.

While the game was still in progress a train arrived at Bain Brook Station and a passenger alighted there. The newcomer seemed to have a pretty good idea of the station layout and made at once for the less frequented exit that faced towards Bain Brook Priory. He was a dark, almost swarthy man of middling height with glossy black hair and a slightly fleshy face. His eyes burned darkly as he exhibited his return ticket to the collector and set off down the road toward the Priory. He was, the staff later agreed, undoubtedly a foreigner of some description. No one had much idea where he might have come from, or (if he was indeed headed for the Priory) what his reception among the gentry there might be. Someone remembered that there was a foreign boy staying at the Priory this summer. Some affinity was guessed to exist between the foreign boy and the visitor. Once again the most outlandish thing about the visitor was his clothes, for he was wearing the same blue suit of light twill as he had worn at the school. The effect was to combine the appearance of a French workman's overall and a cowboy's trail clothes. If the station staff had been more familiar with Inayat Khan, they could have been more certain of the link between his presence and the visitor's arrival, for the family resemblance was instantly noticeable to anyone who knew Khan. The same almost blue-black hair, the same huge brown eyes and the same brown and slightly creamy skin were noticeable in both. The visitor was of about the same height as Inayat but much more heavily built, about the build that Inayat might be in ten or twenty years. The other instantly noticeable difference, if one saw the two of them together, was that Khan's nose was straight and rather fine in shape, whereas his uncle had a distinct hook in his nose. It was what the English call a Roman nose, though if you examine Roman statuary you will find that hooked noses were far from common among the Romans. Khan's uncle had a rather fiercely angled specimen, as if it bore testimony to some bruising encounter in the boxing ring.

On foot it takes nearly an hour to reach the Priory from Bain Brook station, and by the time the visitor had reached the house Steerforth, Khan and the two young women had finished their game, enjoyed a cold drink and fixed a day for their next game. Khan was soaking in the bath when one of the servants tapped at the door to tell him that his uncle had arrived and was waiting for him below.

With no more than normal haste, Khan appeared downstairs to meet his uncle for the second time. He seemed far less shaken than on the first occasion, shaking hands with his relative and briefly introducing him to Steerforth. When Lady Steerforth also put in an appearance, tea was asked for and a pleasant little tea-party held, during most of which Khan sat in silence: he did not seem nervous but slightly withdrawn.

'Inayat has told us little about you, Mr Khan,' said Lady Steerforth. 'I believe he enjoys investing his family with an air of mystery.'

'There is little enough to tell, Lady Steerforth,' answered Mr Khan. 'I am a businessman, buying and selling various commodities and products around the world. My work is highly seasonal and I must be in the right place at the right time to make a deal. So I have no real home to speak of. I know England quite well, but no better than half a dozen other countries.'

'And your own country?'

'Pakistan? I know that least of all. I left it when I was a child.'

'When it was still part of India . . .' murmured Lady Steerforth. For a moment Khan's uncle looked uncertain how to reply to this remark, true as it undoubtedly was. Then he simply glanced at his nephew, smiled and nodded.

He seemed a man without either roots or background. Apart from Inayat he seemed to have no family attachments. He mentioned no business associates, no friends, no property and no home. It was as if he was the embodiment of a fiction, some genie periodically released from his bottle only to be corked up again before he could develop any of the appurtenances common to human existence. Even when Lady Steerforth tried, in her gentle yet persistent way, to draw him on the details of his current project he seemed to deflect her interest with calculated vagueness.

He did manifest great interest, however, when the conversation turned to current affairs. What did people think of President Eisenhower? When would Sir Anthony Eden become Prime Minister? He would undoubtedly be a most experienced man for the job, particularly in the area of foreign affairs. At one point in the afternoon the radio was switched on for the news bulletin, and Mr Khan sat and listened in rapt silence. He was particularly interested in the progress of the French military campaign in Indo-China and in the reports on the recent opening of Soviet Russia's first nuclear-powered electricity generator. Later on a daily news-paper was produced and he studied it carefully as if he had been out of touch with the news for an uncomfortable period of time. When Lord Steerforth's daily telephone call was announced, he seemed very interested in the business activities of the Steerforth company and even cross-questioned Lady Steerforth on her hus-band's plans. He seemed very interested too in the fact that Steer-forth & Sons had recently declined to publish the first novel of a female Oxford philosophy tutor. Lord Steerforth himself had wished to accept the book, since he was convinced that it showed definite promise. His professional editors had insisted, however, that the book was too complex, too literary and far too bookish for modern readers.

'Besides,' one of them had remarked, 'you know what these dons are like. We could spend a fortune on promoting this one book, then find that she produces nothing more for twenty years. You can't rely on dons like professional authors.' Sadly Lord Steerforth had deferred to his professional staff, consoled only by the fact that the philosopher-authoress had found a more receptive response with another publisher.

'How would Lord Steerforth feel if the lady turned out to be immensely popular and terribly prolific?' asked Mr Khan.

'I think he would feel glad that he had been proven right against those clever experts in popular literary taste, and sorry that the benefit of his being right had gone to another publishing house.' And there the subject of that donnish lady's literary ambitions was left, though Lady Steerforth was naturally inclined to reflect upon it in later years when the writer in question produced a string of best-sellers.

The two young men later walked with Mr Khan in the garden of Bain Brook, while Lady Steerforth occupied herself with the affairs of the house. Steerforth regaled his guests with some highly coloured yarns about his ancestors, one of whom was executed in the seventeenth century for allegedly plotting against the monarch.

'Six years later,' he explained, gesturing vaguely towards the house and its grounds, 'we got all this in blood money. William and Mary decided my poor ancestor was too stupid to plot against anyone. A Royal Pardon was granted, the Dukedom bestowed and a hefty cash settlement made in lieu of any bad feelings. His sister, by the way, died in childhood after eating some berries from a bush over by Leg of Lamb pond. What an accident-prone

bunch they were! It's a miracle that any of us survived at all.'
They turned towards the house again and as they did so caught
sight of one of the labradors bounding zestfully across the lawn
towards them.

'Oh Lord,' groaned Steerforth, 'one of the wretched dogs has
escaped from the yard. Inayat is rather allergic to dogs, you know.'
He ran forward ten or fifteen yards to head off the animal, which
was making for the little group of humans with all the instinctive
conviviality of an animal that simply can't conceive what it is to
be disliked.

'But as I stepped forward,' Steerforth later told me, 'the most
uncanny thing happened. I knew all about Inayat's hatred and
fear of dogs. The rest of us had rather cruelly joked about it at
school, though I don't suppose that it's the slightest bit funny if
you happen to suffer from it. But as I turned to Inayat's uncle to
explain how things stood between Inayat and the dogs – why, I
saw the self-same look of horror and terror on his face as on
Inayat's. I grabbed hold of the beast and wrestled him indoors as
quickly as I could. But what do you think of that, Hawkesworth?
Did you think that cynophobia ran in families?'

Just as I had watched Khan and his uncle talking together under
the horse-chestnut trees at school, so Steerforth watched them
from the French window at Bain Brook, the middle-aged man in
his strange workman's garb and the dark slender figure of Inayat
Khan strolling side by side over the ancient lawns.

'Mr Khan, you are staying to dinner,' said Lady Steerforth when
the two Pakistanis returned to the house.

'You will appreciate, Mr Khan,' said Steerforth, 'that my mother
does not issue invitations. She delivers ultimatums.'

'But I have no suitable clothes,' said Mr Khan.

'That is not important,' replied Lady Steerforth. 'We worry
about such matters only when my husband is at home. The suit
you are wearing will be perfectly adequate. In fact it makes the
rest of us look rather scruffy.'

At this point Lady Steerforth laid a hand upon Mr Khan's arm
as if by this friendly gesture to dispel any question about the
suitability of his clothes. Steerforth knew his mother well enough
to guess that she was also taking the opportunity to assay the
texture of his unusual suit. It was, she later told her son, a kind of
close-textured twill which she vaguely remembered was known in
France as *serge de Nim* and which was indeed widely used there to
make workmen's *surtouts*. Suitable or not, it was all that Mr Khan

had with him and there was no alternative but that he should wear it to dinner. The meal apparently passed in a rather awkward manner, Inayat seeming rather tongue-tied in his uncle's presence.

Next morning everyone was up early to see Mr Khan off. Khan and Steerforth ate breakfast with him in the morning room, then the farewell party was joined by Lady Steerforth in the front entrance.

'My visit here was not entirely for pleasure,' said Mr Khan. 'Although it certainly has been agreeable, I had a definite aim in mind in coming here.'

'Is it a family matter?' asked Lady Steerforth. 'Would you like us to leave you alone for a moment?'

'Not at all,' said Mr Khan. 'In fact my mission has to do with Augustus here, rather than with Inayat.' At this point he reached inside his jacket of *serge de Nim* and took out a white envelope, which he stood for a moment holding in his hand. The envelope was quite ordinary in appearance, rather long and slim, but it was sealed with a hefty blob of old-fashioned sealing wax which looked strangely out of place. It was addressed in neat block letters to Augustus Steerforth Esquire.

'I want to hand you this envelope,' said Mr Khan, 'with rather precise instructions on what to do with it. May I do that?'

'Of course,' said Steerforth with a rather puzzled smile.

'What I would like you to do is to keep the envelope in your possession until I tell you to open it. It may be some time before that happens, but I want you to keep the letter with you wherever you go and, however tempted you may be, not to open it until I say so.'

'Then you're sure that you and I will meet again, are you, Mr Khan?'

'As certain as I am of anything,' smiled Mr Khan. 'So will you do as I ask you?'

'Yes of course I will,' replied Steerforth, 'though I would be grateful for some hint of what it is I'm looking after so carefully.'

'Think of it as a message,' said Mr Khan. 'Like many messages, it would be totally meaningless if you were just to wait until I've gone, then tear the envelope open and read it today. It wouldn't make any sort of sense. At the appropriate time and place it will be very significant indeed. But you'll have to trust me to tell you when that time is and where that place is. Will you trust me that far, Augustus Steerforth?' And so saying he placed the envelope in Steerforth's hands. For a moment Steerforth held the letter up to the sun as if to try to glimpse its contents, then he placed the envelope carefully in his inside pocket.

Mr Khan was very profuse in his thanks for Lady Steerforth's hospitality, hands were shaken all round and Mr Khan set off in the direction of Bain Brook station. They stood and watched him, a shortish and slightly alien-looking figure in his blue workman's suit heading back to the mysterious business activities that seemed so to absorb him, leaving an equally mysterious message not to be opened until some future meeting.

'Your uncle,' said Steerforth to Khan a few days later, 'is as odd a cove as I've met in many a long day. Funny workmen's clothes and mysterious envelopes . . . what do you think he's up to?'

Inayat Khan shook his head and smiled in mystification. He did not feel much like talking, for his face was swathed in sticking plaster and bandages and his head still ached abominably. What's more he felt a total idiot. At the end of the three sets of tennis, showing off in front of the girls as he had ruefully to admit, he had vaulted the net to celebrate his victory. Much to Steerforth's amusement Khan had caught his toe in the net and gone sprawling. Worse still, he had got his racket caught in his legs as he fell and had failed to put out a hand to break his fall. He had landed right on his face and had broken his nose and his cheekbone on the asphalt court. A minor operation had been needed to prevent his cheek from being permanently indented.

'I've done as much as I can to straighten the nose too,' said the surgeon, 'but I'm afraid there will always be something of a kink in it.'

'I say, Khan,' Steerforth went on, 'has it occurred to you that you'll look even more like that peculiar uncle of yours if your conk is as crooked as his?' Khan did not comment on this observation but on either side of the sticking tape and lint around his nose, from a face darkened by bruising, his eyes blazed at Steerforth.

꙳ ꙳

'What time is it, my dear chap?' said Steerforth, suddenly bringing me back from the summer of 1954 to the winter of 1980. It was nearly two o'clock in the morning. The wind had dropped somewhat, and a still cold chill had descended over the college. But we were stiff and stuffy from sitting so long by the fire and so when Steerforth suggested that we should take a turn around the college grounds I readily agreed. By now his coat and hat had dried out completely. I found my own and we ventured forth into a night of moonlight, ragged clouds and pale swirling mists of snow like white shadows across the dark quadrangle. We walked slowly round the quad under the shadow of the college chapel, our footsteps ringing dully on the icy flagstones. Far off to the west towards Cumnor a train hooted faintly.

'You know, Hawkesworth, I have a recurring nightmare which comes to me sometimes at Bain Brook, sometimes at my flat in London and sometimes when I'm travelling abroad. In it I find myself here in the college. I have lots of urgent work to do. Finals are only a few weeks away and I'm badly underprepared. But I simply cannot remember where in the college my rooms are. . . . I rush from one staircase to another, flinging open the doors of rooms. And all in vain. . . . I usually wake up in a cold sweat, then almost faint with relief to find it's just a dream.' We walked on for a time in silence.

'Am I keeping you up too late?' asked Steerforth suddenly. 'If you have a busy day tomorrow – or rather today – then I can only apologise for keeping you so late.'

'It's probably ten years since I stayed up so late,' I replied. 'I feel ten years younger for it. Tomorrow I must be up at the crack of noon to meet a young lady. That is my only obligation.'

'A young lady?'

'A postgraduate student from America who suffers under the name of Edwina May McGrath. She is to study here for a time and perhaps to take some undergraduate classes if she proves able. Tomorrow is our first encounter and we are to lunch together. That is not too exacting a schedule for a senile Chaucer scholar. We need not yet hasten to shovel these old bones into their bed.'

Under the shelter of the chapel entrance Steerforth paused to light his pipe. Then as we walked on he whistled a few bars of church music and in a flash I was transported back to the spring of 1955, as he had intended that I should be.

'*Te Deum Patrem colimus . . .*' I murmured.

'Just so,' said Steerforth, releasing a cloud of scented tobacco smoke into the frosty air. We walked on for a while in silence, my mind hovering between the recollection of that May morning a quarter of a century earlier and the more immediate consideration of my graduate student.

I was still fast asleep when Steerforth tapped at my door on the

morning of the first of May in the year 1955. It was just after five
o'clock on a cool and breezy morning. When I peered out of my
window across North Parks Road and down the paths that Ruskin
was reputed to have walked each day, I saw no one about. 'Are
you sure this is a good idea, Steerforth?' I asked, for even then
you must remember that I was a man of over fifty for whom
getting up before dawn for a champagne breakfast was something
of an effort.

'Yes of course, sir, you know what your beloved Chaucer would
have said to such a question.'

'I do, Steerforth, but are you seriously asking me to believe that
you do too?'

'The sesoun,' quoted Steerforth, 'priketh every gentil herte, And
maketh him out of his sleep to sterte, And seith, "Arys, and do
thyn observaunce."'

'Top marks, Steerforth,' I exclaimed. Even his accent was almost
tolerable.

'So please hurry. Khan is coming with the hamper and the
porter has been told to open the college gate for us. Without you,
I doubt if he would agree to let us out at this time.' We put on
coats, for although the sun was up and the pale shafts of light
were already creeping across the lawn toward the chapel wall,
there was still a very distinct nip in the air. We found Khan by the
college notice-board, chatting with the sleepy porter. The man
soon unlocked the college gate for us and we stepped outside,
Khan carrying the large wicker hamper that Steerforth had mentioned. We set off down Parks Road, the boughs of the trees
nodding merrily over the walls of the colleges on either side and
birds of all varieties whistling their heads off for the first of May.
I looked at Khan and Steerforth bustling along on either side of
me, and my heart rose up in me to be up and about on this of all
days. I thought of Palamon and Arcite in their prison-tower
looking down into the garden and seeing Emily there, whom
Chaucer can only fitly describe as being as beautiful as the dawn
on the first of May.

The hamper must have been heavy but Khan strode along
effortlessly with it. Just before half past five we crossed the end of
Broad Street, where the heads of the Roman Emperors by Bodley's
Library seemed to stare with even more than their usual severity
at the little groups of people heading for the river. What an out-
rageous spectacle for students and even a few dons to make of
themselves at such an hour! The light gleamed like gold on the

dome of Radcliffe's Camera, like a helmet on its plinth, or some huge flying object waiting to soar over the turrets of Brasenose or All Souls. Steerforth now took a turn carrying the hamper as we emerged into the High Street, the sunlight now streaming down the road past the Schools and Univ. Other groups of early morning celebrants could be seen emerging from the lanes leading down to Teddy Hall, New College and the southern colleges such as Oriel and the House. College scarfs abounded in the bright chilly sunshine. As the daylight grew brighter the hushed voices of the dawn-time grew in confidence; an occasional shout of laughter echoed down the High. In duffle-coats and corduroy trousers the young and a few of the not-so-young of Oxford converged on Magdalen Tower.

The boatman, as arranged, had one of the college punts waiting for us in the shadow of the bridge, and handed over the long pole with its striped tip in return for a battels chit which Steerforth signed, and a few coins discreetly added to the value of the trans-action. Khan began to busy himself with the breakfast hamper while Steerforth expertly poled us out into the middle of the stream. The pop of the champagne cork and the clunk of the punt pole on the gravelly water-bottom sounded together. A few more strokes and we were in the desired position, just under the bank opposite the Great Tower. Steerforth found a good parking spot for the punt and secured it against the bank by sticking the pole in the muddy river-bottom and wedging the punt against the bank. Khan handed round thick sandwiches of egg and crisp bacon, fruit and flutes of champagne. All around us, from the punts that lined the riverbank and the people lining the bridge and thronging the base of the tower, voices fell silent as six o'clock struck and the voices of the choir rose in the Hymnus Eucharisticus: *te Deum Patrem colimus.* . . . The sounds of the voices and the words of the hymn rose like jewels into the spring sky. In the silence at the end of the hymn only the lapping waters of the river could be heard. Then an early bus trundling along the High towards Cowley and the distant reality of the motor factory broke the silence. In the punt next to ours a young woman sighed and turned to her companion.

'How perfect . . .' we heard her murmur. 'How absolutely per-fect. . . .' Suddenly the silence was broken again, as Khan's voice cut through the cool morning air like a silver knife.

'What rot,' he said rather loudly. 'What absolute rot.'

'What is?' asked Steerforth, taking up the glass and sandwich he had decorously laid down during the singing of the hymn.

'All this business of spring rituals and Latin hymns. You wealthy people send your sons here to learn the ways of mastery, then you pretend the training you're getting is all to do with pretty hymns on May morning. What hypocrisy!' I was amazed, and I think Steerforth was too, to see Khan so incensed by the ritual. What harm could it do to sing a Latin hymn on May morning?

'Well Khan,' said Steerforth at length with an agreeable smile, 'I am very sorry that you didn't enjoy the hymn. But I'm pleased that whatever the shortcomings of an Oxford education, you appear to be enjoying it.' And he nodded towards the river, the sunlight, the champagne and the pretty girl in the next punt – as if all were part and parcel of the life Khan had decried.

'Oh I accept all of this,' said Khan at once. 'But I am honest about it all. I'll tell you this, Steerforth, and don't you forget it, for it may be useful one day to remember it. Your parents sent you here and I daresay they told you that you're here to learn to serve. Eh? To serve your country, your family, your friends . . . that rings a bell, I suppose? To give and not to count the cost. But I have no family to sell me such a story. Oh you will learn well how to serve and you will add to your family's riches by serving others. And if you hadn't a title to begin with, you would end up with one. That too is part of your reward for service. But I'm not here to learn to serve. I am here to learn to rule. Perhaps it's because my people have been servants long enough. Make no mistake about it, anyway. I'm here to learn how to get power, and how to use it!'

We finished our champagne breakfast in silence, then Steerforth poled us down the river a while, gliding under the canopy of leaves and through the dappled patches of bright sunlight. Those sunny spots of greenery dissolved Khan's evil spirits and by the time we returned to college for hot coffee and toast just after eight o'clock he had recovered himself.

'What an irritable fellow you are when you feel like it!' remarked Steerforth, making as if to hurl the empty bottle at him. Khan made as if to throw the hamper back at Steerforth, with a grin on his face, but I felt all the same that somehow when he spoke of learning how to get power and how to use it, he spoke the literal truth.

By the time Steerforth and I had walked twice round the quadrangle, and had talked of the May morning of 1955 and of Khan's sour reaction to the singing of the hymn on the Great Tower, we were both frozen to the marrow and happy enough to get back to the fireside in my rooms. Piping hot coffee was the order of the day.

'During the whole of this time,' Steerforth continued as soon as the influence of the hot coffee had worked upon us, 'Khan and I were both involved in the exploration of those new worlds of knowledge that were being opened up to us. I found the mathematics fascinating and rewarding. Khan had an interest in the physics that was almost obsessive. At that time, if you can recall, the expansion of our knowledge of the physical universe was absolutely spectacular. After Einstein's theories a sudden flood of knowledge had been let loose, ranging from elementary particles to deep space and radio astronomy. And it was in a particularly mysterious area of research that Khan found his real fascination.' At this point Steerforth glanced first at his watch, then at my bedroom door and finally at me, as if trying to assess my ability and willingness to remain awake for a further instalment of Inayat Khan's story. Evidently, though to my surprise, he must have decided that my aged frame would stand the strain. With the coffee inside us, we both felt that another glass of malt whisky was called for. Thus fortified, Steerforth went on with his story.

'Do you remember my Michelson and Morley diagrams? How they illustrated that time and motion are really relative concepts that depend upon the point of view of the observer? The basic idea of "Time like an ever-rolling stream" was shot to pieces once those experiments were completed and, for the sake of certainty, replicated in other forms. It's surprising how much of our latter-day knowledge goes back a long way. Because, you see, the other thread in Khan's work was predicted in theory as long ago as 1798 by a scientist called Laplace.'

Steerforth suddenly rose and, beckoning me to follow him, drew back the curtain of my study and looked out on to the deserted quadrangle. 'Look up there,' he said, pointing upwards to the wintry sky. Beyond the clouds and swirling mists of snow we glimpsed the odd star like a jewel behind a veil.

'What do you suppose is going on out there?' said Steerforth, but hastened on before I could answer him. 'Even now stars are still being formed from the clouds of hydrogen gas and tiny specks of graphite or sand in the interstellar gulfs. We can see such clouds in the spiral arms that radiate outwards from the galactic centre, masking the stars we know just as these snow-clouds are doing now. Sometimes these clouds are excited by stellar energy and we can see them glowing in the abyss, the raw material of future stars that may one day have planetary systems and nurture intelligent life.' He drew the curtain again and we resumed our places by the fire.

'Consider for a moment the life of a star. It's born from such a cloud as I've described. At first its radiation is in the infra-red or radio part of the magnetic spectrum. Later it emits visible light. Now the light and heat radiated by a star are a colossal drain on its resources of energy and mass. Our own star, good old reliable Sol, loses around four million tons a second. As far as we know, he's still got plenty of mass left to keep going for a while, at least long enough to see the human race out. But the process is a very powerful one. Basically the sun is a thermonuclear power station fusing the nuclei of lighter elements to form heavier ones, accompanied by a massive conversion of material into energy. So a star begins its life with lots of hydrogen and gradually builds up the heavier elements such as helium, carbon, oxygen and nitrogen. At last, perhaps having nurtured planets and civilisations, having shone on kings and beggars, saints and miscreants, the star begins to run short of thermonuclear fuel – lighter elements. At this stage many alternatives face the star, depending upon its size and density. Some stars simply explode. We call it the Nova state, because when it was named it was not recognised as the death of a star, but thought to be its birth. The death of stars in a Nova is one of the few such events that is visible with the naked eye from Earth. In 1054 the people of China and America witnessed a supernova explosion that was visible even in daylight and that may have been the origins of the Crab nebula. But that's just one fate that lies in store for dying stars. Others which are heavier compress their atoms so that the electrons and nuclei are fused. Thus the star is composed of a whole mass of neutrally charged objects – a neutron star.' Steerforth took up his pipe again, carefully packed it with tobacco, lit it and stared for a moment into the fire, still holding the matchbox in his hand.

'Neutron stars are both rare and very, very heavy,' he went on, seeming to test the weight of the matchbox in his hand. 'In fact if this matchbox were full of the stuff of a neutron star, it would weigh about a million tons. But the strangest fate of all that can await a dying star is neither to go Nova nor to become a neutron star. Have you ever climbed Everest, Hawkesworth?' Little to his surprise, I shook my head. 'It must be a hell of a struggle, but you do have one minor factor in your favour. As you get further away from the centre of the earth, so the gravitational pull of the earth grows slightly less powerful. It's a fact that at the top of Everest gravity is distinctly if slightly less strong than at ground level. The converse is also true, so that as the outward energy of a star declines and its surface gets nearer its centre, the gravitational pull on the surface gets stronger and stronger. If you were on the surface of such a collapsing star, it would take a progressively more powerful rocket to lift you off its surface. When the escape velocity needed to lift any object, even a photon, off the surface of the collapsing star reaches the speed of light – then you have a black hole, an object from which nothing, not even light itself, can escape. It was this strange theoretical object, invisible yet perhaps inescapable, that began to fascinate Khan.' He paused again, and seemed to shift in his seat. Perhaps he was thinking of the scale of the cosmic processes he had described and felt himself inadequate to communicate them to a layman.

'The critical size of a black hole, the deadly sphere within which nothing that goes in can ever escape, is known as the Schwarschild radius after the man who calculated it in 1917. Just to give you an idea of the compression of the material within a black hole, if the Earth itself were one its Schwarschild radius would be about one centimetre. Two other regions around a black hole are also of great significance. The point at which you can go no closer to the black hole without being engulfed is known as the event horizon. To all intents and purposes the traveller who passes the event horizon of a black hole can say goodbye to all he holds dear. The second region, of importance to Khan's experiments, is one which occurs in the case of rotating black holes. As the black hole grows smaller and denser it rotates faster and faster. The size of the star can freeze outside the event horizon. The area between this outer limit and the event horizon is known as the ergosphere. And in the ergosphere time dilation effects occur. If one traveller were suspended inside the ergosphere of a black hole and the other just outside it, they would age at vastly different rates. Time can actually be said to pass at different speeds within and without the ergosphere. An object accelerated to great speed would pass through the ergosphere, perhaps (if it were energetic enough) even through the event horizon itself and could emerge in a different timescale, past or future. Such phenomena seem incredible to us of course. Objects popping out of existence in one timescale, zipping through a black hole and out into another timeframe. But a lot of current radio-astronomy suggests that visible matter is in a minority in the universe. There are seventy-three galaxies in

Virgo, for instance. They seem to contain fifty times more invisible matter than visible. In the cluster that's known as NGC4486 only two per cent of the matter is visible. Maybe it is our funny little solar system that's out of step. Perhaps a world of visible matter and constant timescales is really the freak, while the real universe is riddled with black holes. What price time like an ever-rolling stream then, you may well ask yourself.' And Steerforth held up his pipe in triumph, smiling broadly, as if the mysterious universe he had just described were his own personal creation.

'As you know,' Steerforth went on, 'Khan and I graduated in the same year, 1957. A year later Khan was conducting certain very limited experiments on the nuclear particle accelerator here in Oxford. Atomic particles are accelerated up to very high speeds, and then guided through a bubble chamber so that their paths can be traced. Once he had mastered the techniques of particle tracing, Khan was asked to carry out some much more ambitious projects. I'll tell you more about them later. I went to see the particle accelerator once or twice with Khan, and to examine the tracings from the bubble chamber. Odd to see those spidery, uncertain lines and to reflect that they are the signature of the infinitesimal. One morning very early we were working in Khan's rooms. Even as the most junior of junior fellows, they were better than our undergraduate quarters had been. Both of us were very busy and we'd worked through the night. Suddenly Khan broke off and made a casual remark that I was to remember very clearly later on.

"Would you think, Steerforth, that a black hole would be very hard to find, if you only knew for sure that it was there?"

"I imagine it would," I answered. "Since no visible light can be emitted from a black hole it stands to reason that you can't see it. So it must be the hardest thing in the universe to find."

"That's true enough. But there's another respect in which the black hole is very easy to find. Imagine that a space vehicle is approaching a black hole at a speed of one hundred thousand miles an hour. Imagine that the black hole has an event horizon of just half a mile. Can you guess by how much the space vehicle would have to be missing the black hole in order not to be sucked into it?"

I tried a few rough calculations but soon gave up.

"About fifty thousand miles," said Khan. "Black holes are quite attractive objects, aren't they? If you go anywhere near one you're quite likely to end up inside it, even if it's rather small." I made some fatuous joke about the size a person would have to shrink to under those circumstances, and promptly forgot about the inside of a black hole for several months. Later, when Khan asked me to join him in his great and secret project, I was to remember very clearly that seemingly insignificant remark.'

One day in 1958, just over a year after they had both graduated, Steerforth received a visit from Inayat Khan. After taking tea together in the Senior Common Room (to which as junior fellows they were now admitted), Khan suggested that they should take a stroll round the Parks. It was a fine if slightly chilly day. The university cricket team was struggling to hold its own against one of the better county sides, and a few hundred spectators were scattered around the boundary rope witnessing this somewhat daunting spectacle. Inayat Khan began to speak with an unusual degree of earnestness.

'I want to talk to you about the project I am working on,' he said. 'But first of all I need your solemn undertaking that everything I say will be treated by you as utterly confidential. The project is of the utmost secrecy and, whether you decide to take the matter further or not, you must guarantee to keep quiet about it. The project team reports direct to the PM, to give you some idea of its potential significance.' Steerforth hastened to assure Khan that everything he might say would be treated with the utmost discretion. Khan glanced quickly round the field, as if he half-suspected the spectators of being alien spies or perhaps was looking out for a traitor among the fielders or umpires.

'You know the broad areas in which I have worked in recent years,' said Khan, and Steerforth nodded. 'Relativity, very fast particles, black holes, time dilation effects and so on. Ever since Einstein we have known that time travel was a theoretical possibility. Now I'm convinced that it's a practical possibility. What's more, so is the British government. And they are prepared to set up a pilot project to test the hypothesis. I've been asked to accept the job of chief physicist on the project and to recruit a chief mathematician. The initial experiments will be done here in Oxford. Later on we may have to go to the USA or perhaps Switzerland. Well, how does it all sound?'

'It sounds incredible,' said Steerforth. 'What are the experimental objectives?'

'I'll tell you that in a minute,' said Khan. 'But in the meantime here's a practical question. Can you come to London on Wednesday morning? The Prime Minister wants to vet personally all the top people in the project team. We're requested to be at Downing Street by eleven o'clock.'

'Yes, that's fine,' said Steerforth. 'But won't I need some kind of security clearance before then?'

'You've already got it. Otherwise I wouldn't be allowed to tell you about the existence of the Magus project, let alone invite you to join in. Aren't you interested in the terms and conditions of the job?'

Amidst a rather languid shout of appeal and to the accompaniment of sad but resigned applause, another of the university batsmen was caught. Steerforth frowned with irritation, and then turned back to Khan for more information about the Magus project.

The next week Augustus Steerforth went with Khan to Ten Downing Street and was appointed chief mathematician to the Magus project. The appointment was officially gazetted as 'Senior Adviser (Science), Ministry of Defence – Temporary Appointment'.

'Let me now try to explain the true nature of Khan's discovery,' Steerforth continued, 'which is certainly as important a scientific achievement as any in the history of mankind.' Steerforth rose again from his chair and paced about the room for a while as if to order his thoughts. I heard the college clock strike the hour, but so absorbed was I by Steerforth's tale that I could not swear if it struck three or four o'clock.

'The true nature of space and time,' he continued, 'is best explained by an analogy. Consider for a moment a two-dimensional world – a world, say, that is confined to the surface of a large, flat sheet of glass. There is no up or down. Only north–south and east–west. For convenience we'll call east–west the x axis and north–south the y axis. Now you'll agree that the geographic location of any point in the Flatworld can be precisely indicated by its x and y coordinates? Good. Let's now move on to the more familiar world of three dimensions. If there were a universe, Hawkesworth, bounded by the walls of this room' – and here Steerforth sprang to his feet and began to pace out the dimensions of the room – 'then you could fix any point in it by its coordinates on the door-to-fireplace axis, the window-to-bedroom wall axis and the floor-to-ceiling axis. Yes?' I nodded my agreement. 'Now we have already seen from the experiments of Michelson and Morley how time and space get muddled up. If the world of an observer is moving sufficiently fast in relation to the world of the observed, then what one measures in time alone, the other will measure partly in space and partly in time. Remember the clocks recording different times? Thus we are forced to conclude that the universe we inhabit is based on at least four dimensions, three spatial and one temporal, or (more accurately) upon a single continuum called space–time.

'You and I, Hawkesworth, live in a world of limited velocities. In cosmic terms we can scarcely break out of a crawl. So we have no problems in agreeing time and distance axes and jointly creating the illusion of time as an ever-rolling stream. But the distinction between space and time which we share would not be at all obvious to the inhabitants of a Beta particle streaking through our universe at close to the speed of light.' He sat down again and clenched his hands in front of his face, as if the effort of clarifying his thoughts were almost a physical one.

'What then do I mean when I speak of the events of my life? I mean a collection of events forming a time-section of the universe as perceived by me. Another observer might object and claim that these events did not occur in the sequence I claimed or that they were much more widely separated than I stated. Although the examples in the Michelson–Morley experiments were differentiated in seconds, there is no reason why they should not be differentiated in centuries or even millennia. Fred Hoyle has employed a useful analogy; he says that reality is like a set of pigeon-holes lit up in sequence by an array of spotlights. But the sequence in which the lights come on and go off is not fixed. There is no absolute before and after, only before and after as perceived by an observer or as agreed by a group of observers. History is a conspiracy.'

'Let's return for a moment to our two-dimensional world on the surface of the glass – Flatland. Suppose this world is inhabited by a two-dimensional creature we'll call a flatipus. The flatipus crawls around on the surface of the glass never looking up or down, never dreaming that it is possible to jump off the glass or bore into it. Now you could, if you chose, represent the flatipus nevertheless as inhabiting a three-dimensional world; two dimensions being concerned with space and one, corresponding with the up–down of our world, being concerned with time. Thus the position of the flatipus in its universe is given at any point in its history by the references x, y and t – east–west, north–south and time since zero hour. Conceive if you like the flatipus moving about on the floor of this room. Its movements leave a traced line on the floor as it progresses. Use the up–down axis to record time, and his tracery will gradually spiral up from floor to ceiling, representing the whole life of the flatipus from birth to death. We call this, in Minkowski's terminology, the *world-line* of the flatipus. If he had brothers or sisters, uncles, aunts and cousins, their world-lines would also trace the room. On every occasion that they met him, their world-lines would cross his. The sum of all these lines, the delicate mesh of traceries now filling your study, Hawkesworth, is the space–time universe of the flatipus species.'

'Now we cannot easily depict the four-dimensional space–time universe of mankind in a diagram, any more than the flatipus can conceive of the vertical t axis we have assigned to time in his universe. But we also have world-lines in our universe, and these cross with other world-lines to represent events in our universe. Given that the sequence of events in the universe is not fixed but is in part a function of the observer, you can understand that it is theoretically possible for world-lines to be discontinuous. The world-line of the flatipus could end at one point, break for a while and then resume. Or it could run along the same course twice, or cross itself.'

'Conceive if you will a break in the world-line of a flatipus. It stops at a given point, resumes elsewhere in the flatipus space-time continuum and persists there – or perhaps returns later to its old position. All this is theoretically possible, actually rather easy to conceive. Khan proved that it can also be done in practice. To the observer of the flatipus, it seems that at a certain point in time –the observer's time – the flatipus ceases to exist, and at another point it begins again to exist. I have seen experiments designed to demonstrate this phenomenon successfully conducted, Hawkesworth, both with animals and with men.'

'And has Khan travelled into the past or the future?'

'He has,' said Steerforth. 'And I too. I have travelled into the past and returned to the present.' He paused for a moment to allow me to absorb this statement.

'Now perhaps you can see why the British government was so interested in Khan's experiments. Let us suppose, Hawkesworth, that all mankind's worst fears are realised and a nuclear war takes place. Can you imagine what would be the deterrent effect of a Magus machine on a sufficiently large scale? You could make your own weapons disappear from that part of the space–time continuum after the aggressor had launched his attack, and reappear a day or an hour before the attack. His weapons systems and his cities could be destroyed before he could attack, but the counter-attack could be delayed until after he attacked, thus making a mistaken retaliation impossible. Magus is the ultimate and insuperable defensive weapon.'

'And it exists?' I asked in a whisper.

'It exists somewhere – or rather somewhen,' answered Steerforth. 'But just how to find it is quite another matter.' He went on to explain as best he could how the Magus project had been designed.

'Imagine if you can a large tube, circular in cross-section, bent round to meet itself in a circle. It would look like a very large doughnut, would it not? This is the shape of the particle accelerator that scientists call a Torus. All the way round the perimeter of the Torus are high-powered magnets which can be adjusted to squirt the particles faster and faster round the Torus, until they are moving at speeds about ninety per cent of the speed of light itself. Then the matter in the Torus is magnetically deflected into a plasma chamber, where even more powerful magnets are at work. Inside the plasma chamber the matter is subjected to vast gravitational pressure. What happens next is an artificial and temporary gravitational collapse. A black hole of microscopic size is created. As I explained, the event horizon of a black hole is much greater than the hole itself. By adjusting the magnetic pressures, you can determine not only the size of the event horizon but also its shape. Every material object within the horizon is sucked into the black hole and emerges elsewhere and elsewhen. The flatipus raises his head above Flatland. As you can imagine, the biggest problem in conducting such experiments is to find an adequate power source. The first experiments were carried out here in Oxford, working with subatomic particles. But for the larger experiments we needed a bigger power source.'

I have no doubt in my mind that Steerforth went on to tell me more about the Torus and the Magus and all the rest of the mind-boggling stuff that he and Khan had been involved with. But I have a sad confession to make. The reader can imagine that I was anything but bored – rather the reverse. But old age and malt whisky have a combined effect that is irresistible, and I must confess that Steerforth's voice began to drift away from me. Two or three times I pulled myself together and focused my eyes upon him. But at last exhaustion engulfed me and I slept. I know that Steerforth carried me to my bedroom – light burden in his strong arms – removed my outer clothes and put me to bed. But I cannot honestly say that I remember it. I remembered nothing until the next morning, when my American postgraduate student was to arrive and find her new professor flat out at midday amidst a confusion of dirty glasses and cups and half-drunk whisky bottles, with a peer of the realm comatose on the sofa.

And yet I cannot close this recollection of the Oxford years without describing one other episode and introducing one other character who was to play a critical role in everything else that was to happen. And though I cannot remember the precise moment at which Steerforth and I spoke of Abigail during that long and sometimes rambling remembrance, I think that at some point we did. Or perhaps she rose up, angry at her exclusion from the story so far, and swept down from her hiding-place in time straight into my dreams. Perhaps indeed I did dream of Abigail.

> The mountain people rise at dawn
> They rise and sing their songs at dawn
> Their songs rise to the mountain top
> And please the Emperor God.

Khan and Steerforth had gone off late that afternoon to meet the train from London. As I recall, two of the girls from Steerforth's family and business circles had been invited to the college ball, perhaps the same two with whom they played tennis at Bain Brook. I had also invited a partner, an old friend, a modern languages tutor from one of the women's colleges.

It was a fine and lustrous evening in summer, the quadrangle beginning to gather in its shadowed corners those purpled dark zones that are so characteristic of the dusk in Oxford. Already students, their well-scrubbed cheeks pink under the lights and their jowels shaven with microscopic zeal, were beginning to make their way a trifle self-consciously through the college grounds to meet their guests. The college looked very splendid that evening, with a marquee erected in the main quadrangle, coloured lights strung up along the walks, and potted plants and flowers glowing under the lamps. When my guest had arrived, and had been shown the decorations and expressed herself duly impressed (to the gratification of the secretary of the ball committee), we made our way to my rooms where it had been arranged that drinks would be served.

Now although the room in which the drinks were to be served was (for convenience) mine, the party was very much Steerforth's. The first thing I noticed on entering the room was that the white-jacketed steward dispensing the drinks was not, as I had expected, the gloomy young fellow from the porter's lodge, but a figure from a more distant period of the past.

'Steele?' I gasped, extending my hand as if in truly urgent need of a drink.

'Dr Hawkesworth? It's wonderful to see you again!' And he seized my hand and pumped it enthusiastically. It seemed that Mr Steele had recently retired from his duties as porter at the school. He had his pension and his little country home but, his wife having died some years earlier and his only son emigrated, he had little in the way of family ties. Steerforth had been looking for a personal aide, something between a valet, a chauffeur and a factotum. For a year or two at least it seemed that these duties would not be too onerous for Mr Steele. When at last he proved ready for true retirement, the country home would still be there. The first of his new-found duties was to dispense the drinks at this little gathering and to ferry people to and from the station in Lord Steerforth's Rolls-Royce, commandeered for the evening by his son. So the first thing that seized my eye was the presence of my old friend. The second was that the numbers were unbalanced, there being one lady too few. During the afternoon, I was told, the young lady who was to have been partner to Khan had met with some domestic accident, emptying a pan of hot water or milk over her own foot as I recall. All attempts to summon up a suitable substitute having failed, she had been unable to do more than apologise.

Everyone seemed to resolve that the absence of Khan's partner should not be allowed to ruin the evening. I must say that if any of the ladies in company with other men had had the chance to say, privately and without embarrassment, whether they would be willing to exchange their partner for Khan – then I do not think he would long have remained alone. For he looked better in a dinner jacket than almost any man I have ever seen. The blackness of the material makes many Englishmen look a trifle pallid or even unhealthy. It made Khan's skin glow like dark gold. His perfect teeth, revealed in a dazzling smile, his dark hair gleaming with almost blue highlights, were set off perfectly by the formal black and white of his attire.

By now the music had begun to play in the quadrangle below and so, champagne glasses in hand, we all made our first sortie of inspection. In the main quadrangle, within the large marquee, was what I think could still at that time properly be called a dance band. It played the waltz, foxtrot and tango, as well as some of the less overtly manic popular songs. Such musical emanations were, at the time, within my sphere of knowledge; my own efforts at dancing were therefore confined to the large marquee. We discovered as we continued our tour, from time to time summoning Steele with further refreshments, that the more remote parts of the college offered more exotic musical fare. In one of the minor quads was a group of musicians using guitars, a double bass, a piano and (believe it or not) an ordinary domestic washboard. Their music seemed American in origin and was much concerned with gaols, freight trains, chain gangs and mountains. Khan, Steerforth and the young lady accompanying the latter all seemed conversant with this type of music, and some dancing was done to it. From the garden behind the oldest part of the college came the sounds of another unfamiliar musical strain. When we rounded the building we saw why. High on a dais above the lawns, under the light of a dozen or more gas flares, a group of black men were striking music miraculously with bare hands from the bottom of inverted petrol drums! Forgive me if this sounds ridiculous. In later years even I came to know the characteristic rhythm of the steel band and the calypso. But at that time I had never seen or heard such a band before and I was deeply impressed.

So too was everyone in our little party. The echoing sound of the steel band swirled around those ancient English walls and the jewelled hands of the players glinted in the coloured lights, and their accents lent an exotic charm to their songs. At length stepped up another figure from the shadows below the dais, a woman singer tall and slender and swathed in cloth of gold. She sparkled as she stood there and took the microphone in her gold-ringed hands. Her hair was made up into a mass of individual tiny plaits, each one decorated with gold threads and tiny gold beads. Her face was thin, eyes somewhat slanted. Her skin was not just black but gleaming like anthracite. She sang three or four songs to a soft and shuffling rhythm, which none of us had ever heard before. No one in England had heard it then, though it was to become famous in later years as the rhythm of the reggae.

'Ladies and gentlemen,' said the leader of the band, 'please let's have a nice round of applause for our singer Abigail!' The applause was indeed loud and long. It seemed to me that during the evening more and more people heard about the magical black music and the beautiful black singer in the gardens. That reggae music that we heard for the first time that evening is irresistibly kinetic and soon nearly all the young people were dancing to it. I noticed that Inayat Khan made no attempt to dance. His face was entranced as he watched Abigail sing her songs. Her black plaited hair, the style that Coleridge called 'witch-locks', falling about her head, her thin and saintly face raised to the sky – the overall appearance she presented was of a creature not entirely human.

At length she finished her songs, for the present at least. As she walked from the dais, she moved with that slightly drooping elegance that African women sometimes have but that other black women merely strive for. And as she stepped past us and her colleagues resumed their instrumental music, Inayat Khan stepped forward.

'Madam,' he said, 'will you dine with us?' She turned to look at him, and then her eyes took in all of us in turn, lingering a moment as her gaze passed over Augustus Steerforth. She raised a finger and laid it upon Khan's black-clad chest, just above the heart.

'You?' she asked.

'Inayat Khan. Born in Pakistan.' The interrogatory finger swung back to her own gold-clad breast.

'Abigail. Ethiopia. Yes Mr Khan, I will be pleased to dine with you and your friends. If you are ready now, so much the better. Singing gives me a great appetite. And I must be back in one hour to sing again.' And so Inayat Khan and she led the way to dinner, the tall black singer and the talented physicist. We discovered over dinner that she came from Abuya Myeda, a mountain district about a hundred and fifty miles north of Addis Ababa.

She came of a particular religious sect that regarded Ras Tafari, Haile Selassie, Emperor of Ethiopia, not just as a secular leader but as a god, come to rescue the black people of the world from oppression. With the benefit of nearly thirty years of hindsight, the reader will have recognised the cult to which Abigail belonged as a precursor of the worldwide Rastafarian movement which has since come to command much support in the West Indies and among the black people of Britain and America. I must admit that her beliefs sounded at first blush a trifle comical. What sounded anything but comical – in fact, if you please, majestic – was the song she sang after our dinner together. It was the song she had written herself in tribute to Haile Selassie, her emperor and her god, and as a parting gift to her people when she left them to come to Britain, the song of Mount Abuya. She sang it alone, accompanying herself on an Ethiopian stringed instrument resembling a zither and called (she told us) a kissar. She sang in deep, strong, crooning tones like the mother of a nation weeping for her children.

The mountain people rise at dawn
They rise and sing their songs at dawn
Their songs rise to the mountain top
And please the Emperor God.

Perhaps indeed I dreamed of Abigail as I slept in my bed that night and the following morning, and as Steerforth slumbered on the sofa. Both of us had drunk far too much whisky. Ill-omened dreams can be occasioned by such over-indulgence. All I know for sure is that when Edwina May McGrath knocked at the door of my rooms expecting her first induction into this great university, and found instead a peer of the realm and a professor of the university sleeping off an excess of drink, she was mightily displeased. And having arrived late, been obliged to pay through the nose for a taxi and then found her new professor in such a disgraceful state of unreadiness – who could blame her?

CHAPTER 4

Something One and Indivisible

'I feel, Miss McGrath –' began Steerforth in a rather shamefaced tone but he was at once interrupted.

'*Doctor* McGrath, in fact,' she said icily, peering at him over her spectacles.

'Ah, my apologies. I feel, Dr McGrath, that since I was really responsible for keeping Professor Hawkesworth up so late that he has overslept and is unprepared for your visit, it is only just that you should give me the opportunity to redeem myself.'

'What do you propose?' she asked, still glacial.

'That I might invite both you and the Professor to join me for lunch. You will talk as much literary shop as you need or care to, and I shall eat and drink and be silent and feel that I have made some small amends for my selfishness. Is that acceptable?' Dr McGrath looked from Steerforth to me, as if for guidance. I smiled and nodded my agreement.

'Very well, Mr Steerforth, I shall be pleased to accept.'

'Excellent. Oh, by the way. . . .'

'Yes?'

'It's *Lord* Steerforth, in fact,' he said, with mock acidity. For a moment Edwina May McGrath's face registered an amazing mixture of emotions, among them disbelief, irritation and, naturally enough, a sense of being impressed: not every man you wake on a sofa turns out to be a peer of the realm. Then all those feelings melted into laughter, as she took Steerforth's hand.

We strolled down to the Randolph Hotel for lunch, and the first half of the meal was devoted very seriously to a discussion of Edwina May's project. Her plan was to carry out a comparative study of a number of Romantic poets, including Byron, Coleridge, Keats, Shelley and Wordsworth.

'Do you realise,' she said to Steerforth over her aperitif, 'that in the year 1800 all those poets were alive? Talk about an *annus mirabilis*. Admittedly not all were active. Keats was only a child, and at twenty-eight Coleridge had already written all his best poetry – at least we think he had. But it was still quite a year.' Edwina May was proposing to take as her starting point one poem by each author and first analyse their unique qualitites. Her review of the works would be quite lengthy, and would be both literary and historical. Finally she would try to thread all the different elements into a single picture of a poetic age.

'Not a movement, you understand. No spurious affinities. Just a picture of that time. What it might have seemed like to a poetry-loving contemporary.'

'Perhaps some contemporary illustrations?' suggested Steerforth, violating (as I had known he must) his self-imposed exclusion from the discussion of literary affairs. I could see from the gleam in his publisher's eye that he was becoming quite interested in Edwina May's project, and when I told her that he was the chairman of a major publishing company I also detected a reciprocal quickening in her interest. After some talk of the poets we turned our attention to the food, and to doing our best to dissuade Edwina May from ordering a steak, since Britain could not offer what she might expect.

'What was it that kept you two gentlemen up so late?' asked Edwina May. 'It must have been rather fascinating, whatever it was.'

'It was a story about a friend of ours. Perhaps you have heard of Inayat Khan, the famous Pakistani physicist. He has been mentioned once or twice as a possible winner of the Nobel Prize. He's still in his middle forties, so he still has time to win it one day. Anyway he has come up with a rather shattering invention, and we were discussing it. Forgive me if I don't go into details. That part of the story is covered by the Official Secrets Act.' Edwina May nodded and smiled. But her eyes flickered towards me for a moment, as if to ask what security clearance I enjoyed that I might know what she might not. After that, however, no more was said of Khan and Magus until the meal was finished, the bill paid and Edwina May departed for her lodgings. Steerforth and I then ordered further supplies of coffee in the lounge, and between lunch and tea he told me the rest of Khan's story.

There had been a particle accelerator in the nuclear physics laboratory at Oxford for some years. It was called PEPR. Some limited additional equipment was also made available, including a tiny plasma chamber. Given the rather limited magnetic forces at their command, Khan had calculated that only a displacement of a few nanoseconds was feasible.

On the back of yet another menu – which I have not retained, as it happens – Steerforth showed me what a successful Magus experiment would look like on PEPR. The fine lines of the sub-atomic particles are photographed as traces in a bubble chamber. When the Magus experiment succeeded, either a line would be discontinued (indicating that the particle had momentarily jumped forward in time) or it would be duplicated for part of its course (indicating that it had gone back in time and, as it were, accompanied itself across the chamber).

'That's a bizarre notion,' said Steerforth, when Khan first explained what they would be looking for with PEPR. 'Do you mean to say that there are two different versions of the same particle side by side?'

'Of course,' replied Khan. 'That is logically inescapable.' The equipment was in use for other experiments at other times. Not even the security status of the Magus project nor the personal interest of the Prime Minister could suddenly cancel all other high energy projects in the laboratory. Another difficulty was that PEPR itself and the ancillary equipment used in the experiments consumed an inordinate amount of power, which simply was not available at peak periods without risking the sudden blacking out of the univeristy, the city and the nearby motor factories. For all these reasons most of the early experimentation was carried out at night.

The power supply problem was acute. They overcame it with an ingenious system, converting power to kinetic energy slowly then reconverting it quickly. A metal flywheel some fifteen feet in diameter was mounted on a steel frame. The flywheel was beautifully balanced and rotated in an almost frictionless fashion. A series of electric motors was used to power the wheel and it was gradually accelerated over a period of several hours. When the linear speed of the wheel's surface was about three hundred miles an hour, a clutch mechanism engaged and a massive pulse of energy was drawn from the hurtling wheel. This pulse was used to power both the final acceleration of the PEPR material and also the magnets around the plasma chamber. When the big flywheel was first installed, it was a frightening thing to use.

'The surface of it was moving so fast it seemed to shimmer. Then the clutch mechanism would suddenly engage and all hell was let loose. A gigantic pulse of power would run all round the lab. And then we would look at the particle traces to see what had happened. And the answer was always the same. Nothing.' Steerforth smiled as he recalled those long and disappointing nights in north Oxford.

'Once when the flywheel was rotating at top speed, Khan asked me if I'd ever worked out what would happen if it jumped out of its mountings. I hadn't, but by the next night I'd done the sums. It didn't seem to me that there was much that would stop the wheel before it got to London, provided it stuck to the A40 and didn't run into a traffic jam at Hanger Lane. It certainly generated a lot of power very effectively. The one thing it totally failed to do was to shift a particle one iota upstream or downstream in time. After two years no progress had been achieved. The theoretical argument in favour of time shifts was overwhelming, but the practical problems of making them happen seemed no nearer to a solution.'

The pressure from other projects to use more of the limited facilities of the laboratory increased again. Steerforth began to play cricket more regularly and to aim more seriously at an England cap. And two years after work on Magus began, Khan had (as previously narrated) met the beautiful black singer Abigail.

At this time Khan, no longer entitled to rooms in college, had a small apartment in north Oxford, within walking distance of the high energy laboratory. For a time Steerforth also slept in Khan's spare room when he was in Oxford to work on Magus. But presently that became more rare. One morning when Steerforth was in a hurry, the bathroom door was locked.

'Come on Khan, get a move on!' shouted Steerforth, rattling the doorknob energetically. The bathroom door opened at once and a long, black and (even without make-up) beautiful face appeared, gazing from the folds of Khan's dressing-gown.

'It's not Khan, it's me. I won't be long.' But she was. Thereafter Steerforth usually stayed at the Randolph, making up the difference between the room charge and his Ministry of Defence allowance out of his own pocket.

Abigail and Khan were an impressive couple. Both physically very attractive, they were also both outstanding in their own fields. Since the Magus project had begun, with its necessary veil of secrecy, Khan's reputation as a scientist had been at something of a standstill. But he was still widely regarded as one of the best five or six young physicists in Britain and still received plenty of invitations to give papers at international physics conferences, the yardstick of academic respectability. Abigail's career as a singer was also beginning to flourish. She received more offers of work than she could accept and had about eight or ten different musicians whom she used in various permutations to accompany her. She could no doubt have earned a great deal more money by adapting her style to the fashions of the day, for these were the first great years of popular music in Britain when young men and women far less gifted and appealing than Abigail became overnight sensations and instant millionaires. Abigail continued to sing in her own subtle and quiet way, weaving the complex patterns of her reggae rhythms long before the world was ready for them. She also continued her studies of the Rastafarian philosophy, corresponding with other scholars and believers in the West Indies and many African countries. In 1958 she attended a meeting of over three thousand Rastafari in Kingston, Jamaica. The cult was catching on.

🙢　🙠

'If we look objectively at what we have achieved so far,' said Khan, 'it is precious little. We have set up a test-bed environment that should work. We have become experts at bubble chamber technique. But we have not been able to conduct a successful experiment.'

Steerforth nodded gloomily. In the background the huge flywheel was slowly turning, in the early stages of building up momentum for yet another super-pulse and yet another magnetic squeeze destined to end in failure.

'There is one possibility that might be worth investigating,' said Steerforth at last. 'Nearly all the work we've done so far has been analytical, trying to calculate the precise particle speeds and the precise magnetic field strengths we need.'

'Yes that's right,' said Khan. 'Is there an alternative?'

'We could use one of the big government computer centres to try to simulate the experiment, to build a mathematical model and simply play with it until we get it right.' Khan reflected on this for a moment.

'Or do we simply accept that it can't be done?' asked Steerforth.

'Perhaps we should just report to the Prime Minister that Magus is a beautiful dream and nothing more.'

'No,' said Khan. 'We can't do that. Believe me, Steerforth, that's the one thing we can't do.' He paused for a moment, gazing beyond Steerforth's shoulder to where the magnets and the accelerator track awaited their brief but mighty burst of activity. 'We do find a solution to this problem, you know. We do find it.' Steerforth was struck by the oddity of Khan's expression.

It was decided that Steerforth would try to construct a computer model of the Magus experiment. He spent a couple of weeks poring over a thick manual devoted to Fortran and quickly turned himself into a competent computer programmer.

'My God, the people who write these manuals ought to be tortured as they torture English,' he grumbled. But he stuck to his task. For a whole week he spent each evening at Khan's apartment, going again and again through the complex formulae that described what was supposed to happen inside the Magus.

'The big advantage of this simulation lark,' he announced at last, 'is that it makes you think very hard about every aspect of your problem. If you have to attach a value to everything, you have to think rather carefully about what it is you're trying to describe.' He sucked the end of his pencil for a moment and gazed into space. Then he ran his hand across his eyes and added, 'But the trouble is with thinking rather carefully about things, that it hurts one's head after a while.'

At length the design of the mathematical model seemed complete, and all the complex interrelations taken into account. Steerforth had written out the program instructions on special coding sheets, ready for an operator to convert them into punched cards which the computer could accept. The parameters were likewise written out in a carefully formatted pattern: they too would be transferred on to cards and fed to the machine.

'The model is designed to set up and test an almost infinite series of combinations of particle speed, mass, energy and magnetic compression within the plasma chamber,' explained Steerforth. 'What we measure is the probability that in each combination of factors a time shift can take place.'

'And that probability can vary from very close to one to very close to zero?' asked Khan. Steerforth nodded, and began to pack his pages of program code and data into his briefcase. He was off to the computer centre the next morning. Khan asked him to call later and let him know how the simulation had gone. When the call came at about nine o'clock that evening Steerforth sounded suitably chastened.

'I haven't actually got the computer program set up yet,' he admitted. 'I made some mistakes in the layout of the program, silly things like putting a comma in the wrong place or opening a bracket and forgetting to close it. But I'll get those right tonight and try to get a shot on the machine tomorrow.' Steerforth had a lot to learn about life in a computer centre. When his program was correctly punched, it found that some of the data was not in the form it expected and rejected that. When the data was correct, he found a number of minor (and again silly) logical errors that stopped the program from running on the computer. And when his program was correct, the data in the right format and the logical errors eliminated, the manager of the computer centre decided that it was time to run the monthly salaries and wages programs for a huge government department and Steerforth had to cool his heels while the computer cranked out thousands upon thousands of payslips and cheques. If these people knew that their silly payroll was obstructing the invention of time travel, thought Steerforth, they'd happily do without their wages for a month . . . or would they?

Steerforth went back to his London flat that night for a good sleep. There was nothing he could do until the computer was available. Steele was expecting him and served him a light dinner in front of the fire. After dinner Steerforth sat by the fire and dozed. He telephoned Khan to put him in the picture and took a shower and an early night. Next morning at eight thirty the telephone rang. It was the computer centre manager.

'The night shift ran out of work,' he said. 'Some of the payroll data didn't balance so they couldn't go on. They've run your little job. You can collect it when you like.'

Steerforth shouted a message to Steele, and raced from the flat amidst Steele's grumbles about wasted breakfasts. The London traffic seemed heavier than usual so Steerforth left his car behind and headed for the nearest underground station. It took him nearly an hour to get to the computer centre on the north fringe of the city. Once there he flashed his temporary security pass, raced into the computer output area and stood in feverish anticipation while the payroll clerks collected their huge bundles of print-out. Steerforth's dozen or so pages seemed trivial in comparison. He sat down in one of the tiny horseboxes provided for the staff who used the computer centre and scanned the results. Then he ran to the telephone and, with trembling hand, dialled Khan's number.

'Listen carefully, Inayat,' he said when he was connected. 'There are a huge range of very high probabilities, which suggests that many different kinds of Magus could be built. But nearly all of the good values lie outside the capability of the equipment we now have. But this is the main point. There are one or two high probabilities of time-shift which are just about within our capacity right now, provided we're prepared to spin that blasted wheel as fast as ever we can and then smash the clutch in. What do you think?'

'Yes,' said Khan after a momentary pause. 'Yes of course, that's what we do.'

Steerforth returned to Oxford the next day but a further week was to pass before Khan could arrange for PEPR to be made available to them, and then only in the depths of the night.

'Just as well, really,' muttered Khan. 'If that overgrown bike wheel jumps its moorings and heads off down the road for London, the fewer people there are about the better.'

That night Khan and Steerforth set off to walk the short distance from Khan's flat to the high energy nuclear laboratory with Steerforth's computer print-out nestling in his briefcase like a secret weapon. It was a fine, dry evening in early April in the year 1964. They both knew that for the Magus project as a whole, tonight's work was probably the last chance. There was no doubt in the minds of the two scientists that tonight was critical. There was, however, a doubt in the mind of Steerforth whether the effort would succeed. Was his simulation accurate? How reliable were the results? Would the wheel fly off its mounts and literally tear the laboratory and the Magus machine to pieces? Could the equipment handle the power required to generate a time-shift? Steerforth's mind was in a turmoil. Khan in contrast seemed utterly calm and utterly sure that the experiment would succeed.

'You seem pretty confident, old man. Do you have an exaggerated respect for the output of computers, or do you know something that I don't?' asked Steerforth.

'I expect I know something that you don't,' replied Khan. 'Tonight's experiment works. I promise you it does. It simply has to. There really isn't any option.'

They reached the laboratory and turned on the lights. They had built up a complicated procedure for checking that all the equipment was in working order before they started to use it, similar to the pilot's checklist on an aircraft. Despite their urgent wish to get on with the experiment, they disciplined themselves to go through the tests – and were rewarded for their patience by finding a faulty bearing on one of the plasma chamber magnets. Khan worked silently and calmly at the task of refitting it. At length all the tests were satisfactorily completed: as far as they could tell, the Magus machine was ready to go. The power was switched on and the huge flywheel began ponderously to roll. At first it moved so slowly that it seemed the motors must have failed. Then it slowly gathered speed, its surface gleaming under the lights. For a while Khan and Steerforth stood and watched it turn. Then, since there was nothing to be done until the wheel reached maximum speed, Steerforth went out to buy sandwiches and bottled beer to sustain them through the night. Khan settled down at the rather ancient desk in the laboratory and began to examine the probability tables generated by Steerforth's computer model: he was already looking ahead to a bigger and better Magus and was trying to learn all he could from the printed tables. Steerforth returned, the two of them shared a simple meal. Afterwards Khan seemed eager to return to his calculations, and Steerforth had to content himself with lying in an armchair with his eyes closed. Naturally he told himself that sleep was impossible. And so, as sometimes happens, he was in the deepest of sleeps when Khan shook him, handed him a coffee and told him to stand by.

The flywheel was now moving faster than ever before and still accelerating. Every once in a while a tremor would pass through the metal frame on which the wheel rested, though there was as yet no sign of the harmonic effects that could tear down the metal structure and the whole laboratory.

'Give me that print-out, will you?' said Khan and pointed to a set of figures he had circled in red. 'These are not the lowest set of values we could try with some chance of success, but they are only a couple of percentage points above the lowest and give a much better probability of a shift. The power required is only slightly more, but the Schwarschild radius is twice as great. So here we go!'

The two scientists watched in silence for another hour as the wheel continued to accelerate. Its metal surface now was a blur. It was giving off a high-pitched whining note like a jet engine. The tremors in the metal legs supporting the wheel were becoming ominously frequent and noticeable. Steerforth thought he could detect a faint puff of concrete dust in the air where the massive metal bolts fastened the mounting to the laboratory floor.

'Bring the accelerator up to maximum normal power,' called Khan. 'We'll take a shot at it in twenty minutes.'

The next twenty minutes seemed to last ten years. As the particle accelerator boosted the sub-atomic fragments towards the highest linear speed it could attain, the flywheel seemed to be bounding in its mountings like some terrifying animal determined to break free. Steerforth gazed as the wheel now seemed to blaze and shimmer under the lights, the violence of its motion clearly far beyond anything that he and Khan could control. The scream of the flywheel was deafening, and must have been heard the length and breadth of north Oxford. But what the hell, thought Steerforth wildly, if that thing bounds through the wall of the lab in a minute or two then the neighbours will have more than a bit of whistling to complain about!

What Khan cried out as he pressed the button that engaged the clutch was swept away in the ensuing chaos. As Steerforth gazed in horror, the clutch mechanism crashed into place, engaged, held for a few clangorous and explosive moments and then disintegrated in a shower of flying shrapnel. It was a miracle that neither he nor Khan was injured or killed by the metal components of the clutch assembly ripping across the laboratory as it broke up. The mountings of the flywheel turned red hot, then white, then seemed certain to melt and fuse and rip the building apart. But then the wheel ran free and began to decelerate. The whistle faded away. Steerforth turned to Khan. On his friend's face he saw an expression of mystical joy.

'We got the pulse. I'm sure we got the pulse,' shouted Khan. Ten minutes more were to pass before they had the first of the photographs from the automatic camera in the bubble chamber. At first sight it was no different from any other PEPR photograph. Then Khan slotted it into a viewing frame and Steerforth's heart just stopped. From left to right across the picture ran the trace of an elementary particle, perhaps an electron. Three or four inches from the edge of the plate the trace ceased. Two inches further on towards the centre of the plate, the trace reappeared. A particle of matter in our universe had flickered out of existence at one instant of time, entered a microscopic black hole and reappeared at a future instant of time.

'What do you think the displacement is?' said Steerforth. 'Surely it's not more than six or seven nanoseconds.'

'Who cares?' answered Khan. 'When the Wright brothers flew,

their wheels hardly left the ground. But they'd proved the thing *possible.*'

They cleaned up the laboratory as best they could, though some of the windows and walls had been badly damaged by the flying fragments of the clutch mechanism. They turned off the power and the lights, put out their empty beer bottles and emerged into the pallid light of a spring dawn.

'I'll tell you what, Steerforth. . . .'

'What?'

'I'll stand you breakfast on this of all mornings. How about that?' The offer was accepted and they set off down Parks Road, turning right at the Camera towards the market. An early morning breakfast stall for the market porters was already doing a brisk business in bulging egg and bacon sandwiches and pint mugs of piping hot tea. Khan stood with his sandwich in one hand and his mug of tea in the other and grinned rather foolishly.

'We'll have to get our report in as fast as we can,' he said. 'It would be nice to get the next block of money approved before the general election.'

'The Civil Service will want time to check everything first,' said Steerforth. 'It may have been just a trick of the light, or a fault in the camera that made the particle seem to disappear.'

'We can easily replicate that experiment with a bigger and better Magus machine,' replied Khan. Steerforth was seized with hysterical laughter at the idea of anyone trying to do anything more with the existing Magus equipment.

In a file which Khan kept at the time of the first Magus experiments, Steerforth later found a sheet of paper with a message written in Khan's hand.

My mind feels (said the note) as if it ached to behold and know something great – something *one and indivisible* – and it is only in the faith of this that rocks or waterfalls, mountains or caves give me the sense of sublimity or majesty! – But in this faith *all things* counterfeit infinity!

For some time neither Steerforth nor I could with certainty identify the author of this sentiment, though the use of the word 'sublimity' seemed oddly evocative. It is taken from a letter by Samuel Taylor Coleridge.

Khan wrote up a report to the Minister on the success of the Magus experiment, including all Steerforth's statistical simulations as one of the major appendices. The report was superbly presented. Khan wangled enough out of his Defence funding to have it properly printed and typeset with lots of photographic illustrations. One of the things that Khan intuitively understood was how to present his results to someone he wished to impress. His performance in the physics prize examination all those years ago had first proved that he enjoyed this talent. Steerforth was right about one thing. The report, detailed as it was and carefully presented as it was, created uproar both in Westminster and Whitehall. Many people thought that the results of the experiments were inconclusive: some even hinted at deception in the presentation of the results.

'Very convenient for this Pakistani fellow, isn't it? He achieves his spectacular result in one final experiment that just happens to wreck the lab equipment. Difficult to prove him a liar under those circumstances, isn't it? Rather hard to ask him to repeat his experiment and replicate his results. Pity about that. . . .' So said one or two of Khan's critics among the very limited number who were allowed to know of the Magus results. The presence of Steerforth at the experiments and the fact that he was co-signatory to the report were both advantages to Khan: it was difficult for any critic to suggest that a member of a premier ducal family had lent his name to something that, if not a triumph, could only be a fraud. In the end, with the change of government in the autumn of 1964, the final decision on the future of Magus had to be taken by the incoming Defence Minister and the appropriate cabinet committee. Still in circumstances of the most closely guarded secrecy (Khan later joked that Magus was just about the only secret that this leak-prone government didn't spill) the committee met and authorised the next stage in the project.

In the late spring of 1965 Khan was told that his appropriation was in order and that he could start making arrangements to use the big Torus in Switzerland for the next round of experiments. Neither Steerforth nor I ever knew the precise amounts of money earmarked for the task of converting Magus from an experimental rig to a practical time-travel vehicle, for by now a fully fledged accounting and project control apparatus was set up. The way in which these no doubt essential arrangements were made was a perfect example of official cack-handedness.

One afternoon Khan asked Steerforth to meet him in the physics laboratory. When Steerforth arrived he was first introduced to a small and rather dapper gentleman in his early fifties.

'Steerforth, this is our new Project Director, Major Tolson.'

'Project Director?' asked Steerforth, then added with a touch of characteristic bluntness, 'I thought running the project was your job, Khan.'

'From a scientific point of view no one wishes to interfere with Mr Khan and yourself at all,' said Major Tolson rather swiftly, as if he had practised that line and was happy to have the chance to use it so promptly. 'My task is concerned purely with the administrative aspects of the Magus project, those and the security aspects, I should say. I'm here to make sure that whatever you gentlemen need to get done, it gets done quickly and smoothly.'

So that was the picture. What had started off as a hare-brained experiment run by two young scientists on a shoe-string budget in the dead of night had now become a fully fledged government project with a soldier to command it. It also had (though Khan and Steerforth found out about it only later) a pukka Whitehall steering committee and a tame psychiatrist whose job was to make sure that Khan and Steerforth didn't go crackers and tell the Russians all about Magus. Truly the something one and indivisible of Samuel Taylor Coleridge's letter was in danger of becoming a bureaucracy in which the roles of the two real originators of Magus were rather unimportant.

The Torus was situated in a valley with wooded hills all around it. These hills were firmly closed to the public, fenced off with a wire mesh and patrolled by armed guards with German shepherd dogs. Thus it was hard to get an impression of the size of the Torus. But where a part of the track could be seen running between some bushes and into the trees, it looked like a part of a decent-sized tubular railway system.

'It makes PEPR look like a toy,' murmured Steerforth as they drove up and parked their hired car at the blockhouse, ready to submit themselves to a very thorough security check before being admitted. Once their identities were firmly established and their credentials examined in every detail, Khan and Steerforth were asked to collect their luggage from the car.

'We will return the car to the hire office in Geneva,' said the young civilian security man who had supervised their examination. 'While you are here on the Torus site transport will be provided for you. The expense of keeping your own car is unnecessary.' Khan nodded his thanks. The argument based on reduced expense was final in its appeal to the Swiss mentality: but Khan thought the real reason for the free transport was so that the Torus authorities would always know where the British scientists were and what they were doing.

They got a better idea of the size of the Torus once they and their belongings had been loaded in a Mercedes limousine driven by a uniformed chauffeur, and while they were being conveyed to their lodgings. There was a reasonable-sized town built within the circuit of the Torus, and in places where the two scientists could see both a part of the Torus and that part which seemed to be diametrically opposite they judged its diameter to be about five or six kilometres. When they found their lodgings, they were in a pleasant bungalow some way from the main gate.

'The Director of the Torus Centre would like to speak with you. Would it be convenient for you to unpack your things and prepare yourselves in half an hour?'

'Of course,' said Khan. The driver used his car radio to contact his base. It was all well organised, efficient and slightly chilling. As Khan and Steerforth began to unpack their belongings, the driver went off on some other errand. Or perhaps he just thought that waiting round the corner would be more tactful than waiting outside the house. In any event, when Khan and Steerforth stepped from the door exactly a half hour later the Mercedes was just gliding to a halt beside the spotless sidewalk.

'Good afternoon gentlemen, and welcome to the Torus Centre. My name is Konrad Dubendorf and I am the Director of the Centre. If there is anything – anything at all – that we can do to make your work here more fruitful or to make your environment more congenial, please don't hesitate to let me know. My staff and I are here to serve you.' Dr Dubendorf eased his small and very dapper frame into a chair and gazed earnestly at the British scientists through highly polished rimless spectacles.

For about twenty minutes Dr Dubendorf guided them, with infinite zeal, through the details of the Torus Centre and how it was run. He had site maps, restaurant timetables, lists of relevant officers for different facilities and passes of every kind to issue to the visitors. When all the administration was finished, he turned to more important matters.

'For security purposes,' he said, 'your project has been accorded our highest grade of confidentiality. This means that the only people here that know anything about the Magus project are myself and four of the top scientists and security men. There are no exceptions. I must urge you very strongly to cooperate in this matter, since it is clearly in your own government's interests. Please do not speak to anyone about Magus at all unless he is one of the five cleared officers on this list,' and he handed over the names of the Torus officials cleared for knowledge of Magus.

'There is also one other security matter for us to discuss,' he continued. 'Something that you do not yet know about the facilities here at the Torus Centre and which you must undertake not to discuss with anyone not on that list. Is that understood?' Khan and Steerforth nodded their agreement, and Dr Dubendorf politely thanked them.

'From the point of view of the Magus project,' he said, 'one of the most important elements in the success of the experiment is, as I understand it, the power source. You need a very powerful surge of energy to bring the material in the Torus up to its final speed and to power the magnets that create the collapsar effect to build the black hole in which the time dilation effect occurs. Is that right? Yes, good. Well now I must tell you that we have here in Switzerland a very efficient source of energy. As you doubtless know, Switzerland has very little natural carbon fuel. And our hydro-electric schemes are rather vulnerable to saboteurs, if a crisis should come along. So we have put a lot of effort into alternative sources of energy. Nuclear fission has of course been of great interest to us, but it has certain disadvantages from an economic and environmental point of view – matters I needn't elaborate for you two gentlemen. Within the Magus experiment you employ, as I understand it, a plasma chamber within which to make the big crunch that generates the gravity collapse. Yes? Well we also use a plasma chamber here at the Torus Centre. But for a different purpose. Within our chamber the elementary particles of atoms are fused by the external pressure of the plasma envelope. Some particles are left over from the fusion process and are converted to energy. As a fuel. . . .' he smiled shyly, as if wishing to avoid overstatement, 'it beats coal.'

So at last the Swiss had perfected in secret the technique that scientists had been wondering about for almost fifty years. Within the powerful grip of the plasma envelope they could quite literally explode a hydrogen bomb in a controlled fashion, and tap the resultant power at any rate they liked. For Magus experiments, the power available at the Torus Centre would be virtually unlimited. Steerforth felt more than a little ashamed as he recollected that great clumsy wheel whizzing round on its frame. All the time these Swiss engineers had had a star in a bottle as their energy source! Yet still it had taken the ingenuity of Khan to design the Magus experiment and the mathematical ability of Steerforth to see how it could be made to work. So perhaps they weren't so useless after all. As if he read Steerforth's thoughts, the little Swiss raised a hand in modest self-effacement.

'I mention this facility not to compare it in any sense with your accomplishment, gentlemen,' he said. 'What we have achieved is a modest engineering triumph, something that someone was sure to get right one day. But the impact of the Khan effect on human life is on a different scale. Without a joke, perhaps I can say on another dimension. No, I mention this new power source only because I think it can make your task much easier and because it is still very, very secret. As secret for different reasons as Magus itself. If the knowledge of cheap and safe thermonuclear energy were to be suddenly unleashed on the world, imagine the political and economic consequences, especially in the Middle East. Our power source is a blessing but also a bombshell. So we keep it for the moment from the eyes of the world.'

So there it was. Steerforth and Khan went back to their rooms and began to rethink their experimental strategy in the light of having infinite power available instantly and cheaply.

'One of the things Inayat has that a great inventor needs,' said Steerforth, 'is the ability to be lucky at the right moment. He got the government interested in Magus at just the right moment. He had me around to do the maths and prove that we could get an experimental result. And then the two greatest strokes of luck of all – he got a worthwhile result from a last desperate gamble that wrecked the equipment – and then the Swiss gave him plasma-contained thermonuclear energy on a plate! What a series of lucky breaks, one after another. And all the time he just sailed on quite serenely, as if he always knew that everything would fall into place just when he needed it to.'

The optimum design for a Magus machine employing one plasma chamber to generate thermonuclear power and one to create the collapsar effect turned out fairly quickly to resemble the layout of the Swiss Torus – the circular track enclosing the rest of the works.

Since the Torus track and the energy plant already existed and could be used, work began straightaway on the design and construction of the gravity pressure generator. Much more powerful magnets were to be used in this model, so as to exploit the extra power available from the thermonuclear generator, and so as to create potentially massive time-shifts. For much of this work it was not necessary that both Khan and Steerforth should be in Switzerland at the same time. So Steerforth spent a good deal of the time in England, while Khan supervised the building in Switzerland. In the summers of 1965 and 1966, as Wisden shows, Steerforth played virtually a complete season's professional cricket – though he did not even approach regaining his England place.

In the autumn of 1966 Khan sent a letter to Steerforth at his London flat, which also contained about fifty very high quality bubble chamber photographs.

'With this equipment,' wrote Khan, 'it is laughably easy to replicate the results we achieved with PEPR. There is no lengthy wait for that frightful wheel to build up speed and no fearful clash of mechanical gears as you engage the clutch. If you wanted you could set up dozens or even hundreds of experiments and just have them carried out sequentially under computer control. It turns out to be more fun to do the experiments one at a time and so to have the pleasure of observing the results. But it is unquestionably a less efficient way of proceeding.'

Khan had carried out dozens of different experiments, and the photographs (cross-referenced to the tables of values in Steerforth's simulation) showed how regularly the time-shift phenomenon had occurred. Idly flipping from one set of photos to the next, Steerforth could casually notice a trace that he and Khan would have given anything to see during those long and disappointing nights in north Oxford. Partly out of a scientist's preference for walking before running, and partly because he wanted Steerforth to be present before any further progress was made, Khan restricted himself to the particle experiments. But it was obvious that more ambitious tasks were now feasible, and so Steerforth hastened to make arrangements which would permit him to make another extended visit to Switzerland. And Steerforth had the feeling that this would be the visit, more than any other, that would mark the successful development of a usable Magus machine.

The Swiss are great respecters of success in every walk of life, and the success of the Magus experiments obviously had an effect on how Steerforth and Khan were treated. A uniformed driver was at Geneva airport to whisk Steerforth in speedy luxury to the Torus Centre, the formalities at the blockhouse though no less thorough were much more quickly completed, and Steerforth then discovered that he and Khan now qualified for more opulent lodgings much nearer to Dr Dubendorf's own quarters.

'Congratulations, Khan,' cried Steerforth when they met. He grasped Khan's hand and put his arm round his friend's shoulder.

'Those results must be the most spectacularly accurate experimental results in the whole history of science!' Khan smiled with unfeigned delight.

'Don't you mean the simulation results were the most uncannily close forecast of what would actually happen?' he asked. Khan looked fit and happy, and Steerforth guessed that the Swiss mountain air had given him an appetite, for he seemed to have gained a few pounds in weight.

Dr Dubendorf greeted Steerforth warmly and spoke with great enthusiasm about the results of the first round of experiments.

'When your results can at last be made public,' he said, 'we hope that some minor credit will also be granted to the Torus Centre.' Khan and Steerforth hastened to assure Dr Dubendorf that the invaluable assistance of the Swiss would naturally be fully acknowledged. He seemed delighted with the whole business and, after shaking their hands again and bowing his dapper little form courteously to each, he left them to plan their next experiments.

A few weeks later Khan and Steerforth were seated at the controls of the Torus Centre, ready for the first time-shift with a living subject. As Khan had said, the whole set-up was very different from the Magus rig in north Oxford. They sat on comfortable chairs at an electronic console, with four visual display screens facing each of them. Each had an electronic keyboard with a full alpha-numeric keyset and a large array of function keys. Attached to the console was a powerful minicomputer which allowed one or a whole series of experiments to be set up in advance and executed under automatic control.

'I think we need to project a mass equivalent to the mouse and the cage,' said Khan. 'If we just project the little beggar, he might move at the critical point. Then we might neatly slice him in two, with half of him in one time zone and half in another.'

When all the parameters had been fed into the computer, Khan left the control room for a moment and returned with a wire cage in which sat a small and apparently rather frightened white mouse. Khan opened the cage and took the mouse out for a moment, stroking it with a finger tip to calm it.

'Come on, little chap,' he murmured. 'You are going down in history, if you did but know it.' He keyed in a further code to the computer, which automatically opened a panel in the side of the plasma chamber. Carefully Khan inserted the mouse in its cage in the chamber. A further code keyed in to the machine served to seal the hatch.

Khan was right. Compared with the experiments in Oxford, the Swiss Torus was downright anti-climactic in operation. For a few seconds tables of values were exhibited on two of the screens, monitoring the build-up in power. Then a soft tone sounded and the screens all showed the message, 'Final Hold'. This was a fail-safe point at which the experiment could be subjected to final Go/ No go decision. On a closed circuit television screen they could see the mouse in his cage inside the plasma chamber.

'Ready?' said Khan and Steerforth nodded. Khan pressed a function button marked GO and the mouse obeyed. Without fuss or bother or loud bangs or bright flashes, the Magus machine catapulted the mouse and his cage into the future. The screens began to fill up again with dozens of readings taken during the few nanoseconds it had taken to conduct the test.

'How long?' asked Steerforth.

'Two minutes,' answered Khan. Those one hundred and twenty seconds seemed like centuries but as the computer chirped and displayed a message to the effect that the time was up, the TV screen remained obstinately blank.

'What's happened?' asked Steerforth.

'We appear to have overshot the runway, so to speak,' answered Khan. He typed in a lot of questions and examined the computer's answers. At last he shook his head. 'I'm afraid we've lost him somewhere in the future,' he said.

'I'm afraid I just haven't a clue at present where or when he is. I'll have to look very carefully at the figures.' In another room off the control centre, a high-speed printer began to produce a detailed log of all the facts and figures relating to the mouse's mysterious journey into the future.

'I told you he'd go down in history didn't I?' said Khan. 'I just didn't realise how far down. I'm rather glad, Steerforth, that neither you nor I was the star of that particular experiment.'

A week later Khan found an error in the computer program that controlled the cut-off of power at the end of a Magus pinch. As far as any one could tell the mouse might have been projected forward into the very far distant future of the universe or even into infinity itself.

'If you know anyone who leads a sufficiently blameless life to be tolerably certain of getting a good seat on Judgement Day,' said Khan, 'tell him to keep a sharp look-out. I've a feeling that a mouse in a cage may suddenly appear at God's elbow.' A week after that a less unfortunate mouse was catapulted 120 seconds into the future and this time returned on cue. Khan and Steerforth ran the recorded film of the experiment several times, then handed over the Torus to a team of German scientists and walked out of the Centre carrying the universe's first successful time traveller in his cage.

That night a waitress in a bar in St Julien, just over the border into France, was surprised to see two young men in dinner jackets take seats at a table and place between them on a table-top a small white mouse in a cage.

'A bottle of Bollinger for us and a piece of Gruyère for our friend,' said the dark-skinned, handsome one.

Later that evening, after Khan and Steerforth had bought several bottles of champagne to share with the club hostesses, a photographer appeared at their table.

'This is the sort of place where one gives a false name,' said Steerforth as Khan prepared to sign an order form for the photographs. Khan squinted at him through a champagne haze, and then nodded knowingly.

Steerforth had kept a copy of one of the photographs from that rather hectic evening. It showed Khan with one arm round the waist of one of the young ladies, a glass raised high in his other hand. On the back was a scrawled message. 'From your one true friend,' it read, 'Nehemiah Higginbottom.'

'Was that the alias that Khan used to order the pictures?' I asked, and Steerforth nodded. I had a feeling that I knew the name as that of a fictitious character, but could not recall from where.

By now evening had begun to fall over Oxford. The lights in the windows of the Ashmolean Museum gleamed brightly through the dusk. The teapot being long since cold, Steerforth and I agreed that a glass of dry sherry might be in order, though we also agreed that it should not presage such a late night as yesterday.

The Magus effects that had so far been achieved were strictly one-way journeys. A mouse could be projected a few minutes into the future, and would turn up on schedule. A mouse could be projected into the past: it would appear on the table as if to prove, so to speak, that it had been dispatched in an hour's time. Khan now turned his attention to building a mouse-sized time machine with sufficiently powerful fuel cells to make a return journey. The mouse could then, in theory at least, travel to the time of Shakespeare or Julius Caesar and observe the scene from the safety of its cage. The on-board computer on the modified vehicle would, after the appropriate delay, project the cage and its occupant back up the time stream to its start point or to another set of space–time coordinates. While Khan tackled the engineering and computer control problems involved in making the Magus controllable, Steerforth spent a good deal of time in Oxford and London preparing the draft project report. Provided what Khan called the problems of steering the Magus could be overcome, they would be in a position to recommend the development of manned time travel. Otherwise there seemed little point in hopping about in such a narrow segment of the continuum.

At this stage of the project also, a minor disappointment occurred. Konrad Dubendorf, the director of the Torus Centre, invited Khan to his office one morning.

'I regret to say that I shall be leaving the Centre in the very near future,' said Dubendorf. 'The fact is that the chair of physics at the University of Zurich has been offered me. It has always been my hope that one day I could return, in triumph as it were, to the city of my birth. My family is also there, you understand.'

'Dr Dubendorf, I thank you from the bottom of my heart for all your help,' said Khan. 'Without that help, Magus would have remained a laboratory experiment. With it, I believe we are on the verge of manned timeflight.' No doubt the new director, when he was introduced to Khan and told about his work, thought that Dubendorf was pulling his leg. But support for the Magus project continued smoothly enough after Dubendorf's departure. No one could then have known what a crucial role the Swiss scientist was to play in subsequent stages of the drama.

One day Steerforth received an urgent message from Khan by telegram. It read simply, 'Magus return tickets available. Book now.' He took the next flight to Switzerland and within hours was in the Torus Centre. On the laboratory table was a metal box about the size of a briefcase. Mounted on top of the box was a turret like that of a tiny submarine, in which a mouse could be seen through thick glass windows.

'All the power and control equipment is in the case?' asked Steerforth. Khan nodded.

'Does it work?'

'Don't know yet. I wanted you to be here when I tried it.' Khan and Steerforth took up their places at the control panel.

'I've set the controls for six hours from now,' said Khan. 'Shall we try it?' He pressed the GO button and the mouse and its box disappeared.

'What do you call the new vehicle?' asked Steerforth.

'The Time Travel Module or TTM,' said Khan. The vehicle was absent for three minutes as planned and then returned.

'Well, at least we know it comes back,' said Steerforth. They went out to lunch, rested in Khan's room and returned to the laboratory in good time.

'Ten seconds to go,' said Khan, watch in hand. 'Five, four, three, two, one, zero.' Right on time the TTM materialised on the table. It remained on the table for three minutes, then vanished. The two men embraced; controlled time travel was a reality.

It might have been imagined that a manned time trip would follow on fairly quickly from the development of the TTM and its successful operation. In fact nearly three years elapsed between the first trip by a mouse and the first by a human. The engineering problems took only a fraction of this period to resolve. The rest of the time was taken up in seemingly endless discussion with government Ministers and their top officials. Suddenly those few people who were in the know about Magus were confronted by the near-certainty that it would work, and felt the urgent need for what they called 'a coherent policy towards Magus'. This involved all kinds of questions that were not of the slightest interest to Khan or Steerforth. Would Magus be shared with the Americans? Or with NATO? Would the Russians be told about it? They must be. What's the point of the ultimate deterrent if your likely enemy doesn't know about it? Would a demonstration be staged to convince the Russians that Magus worked? If so, could they then figure out how it worked?

'The Prime Minister,' remarked Steerforth one evening, as he and Khan walked along Downing Street in the pouring rain, 'serves remarkably good sandwiches but execrable coffee.'

'I wish he would make up his blasted mind what he wants us to do,' grumbled Khan. 'I am a scientist not a politician. If I can have a decision out of him, I'll do without his coffee and his sandwiches.'

At last the official approvals were all given, though if clear policies were adopted on all the questions raised in the debate, they were not conveyed to Khan and Steerforth. In late 1970 they were back in Geneva preparing for the greatest experiment of all – manned time travel.

'You will make the first journey yourself, Inayat?' asked Steerforth. Khan nodded. Somehow, ever since the possibility of time travel had first been mentioned, Steerforth had known in his heart that the first journey would be reserved for Khan. No one else was as qualified as Khan to earn the unique distinction of being the first human voyager in time. Only if the Magus machine malfunctioned was there any risk, and apparently Khan was prepared to endure that risk for the honour of making the trip.

'I want you alone to operate the console, too,' said Khan. 'It doesn't really need two people to do the job and you are the only person I would trust to react fast enough if anything did go wrong.'

'What are the coordinates of the first trip?' asked Steerforth. 'Do you feel like witnessing the discovery of America? Or the crucifixion? Or would you rather attend a New Year Party for the year 2000?'

'I've worked out six separate experimental loci,' said Khan, 'and I want to try them all in one sequence. But I'll set up the parameters myself if you don't mind.'

'You'd prefer me not to know where and when you're going?' said Steerforth in a rather miffed tone.

'Not at all. But I want to demonstrate to you in my own way that Magus works. And that will be easier if I set up the apparatus myself.'

So Steerforth went off to make some telephone calls, to have dinner and to take an early night in preparation for the next day's experiments. Khan was sat at the console when Steerforth left him, tapping in data and verifying it on the screens. When Steerforth went to bed he tossed and turned for an hour or so before he could sleep, and was then tormented by wild dreams of his friend Khan witnessing the murder of Julius Caesar or the birth of Christ.

In the middle of the night the telephone rang, hauling Steerforth out of the bottomless pit of his uneasy sleep. The switchboard operator told him that there was a call for him from England.

'Augustus?' It was Lady Steerforth on the line.

'Mother? What is it?'

'Augustus, prepare yourself.'

'Yes,' he said, but he knew what it was.

'Your father is dead. In New York, of a heart attack. He was working at the time, of course, trying to set up a film deal for one of his authors. You are the Duke now, Augustus.' There was a long moment's silence.

'Are you going to New York to collect him, Mother?'

'Yes.'

'May I come with you?'

'Of course.'

'I'll leave here tomorrow afternoon. I'll come to London first.'
He rang off, and sat up in bed for a moment thinking of his father
and of the strange thing that his father had passed on to him with
his dying hand. Then Khan tapped at his door, awoken too by the
shrilling telephone. Steerforth told him what had happened.

'Do you want to go in the morning? We could postpone the
experiment.' But Steerforth shook his head.

'It means so much to both of us. I'm sure my mother will understand that.'

For an hour or so Khan and Steerforth sat up together. Khan
rang the cafeteria of the Torus Centre, and in spite of the late
hour persuaded the staff to deliver some tea and biscuits. Steerforth did not seem anxious to talk about his father or to indulge in
any display of grief, but somehow Khan sensed that he would
prefer not to be left alone. At last, however, Steerforth lay down
in his dressing-gown and fell asleep. Khan turned out the lights
and left him. For him too the next day was to be a taxing one.

Khan and Steerforth had both slept badly but next morning
they were first into the restaurant of the Torus Centre, and both
looked sharp and eager for the coming adventure. They collected
their breakfasts at the counter of brilliant stainless steel and took
seats at one of the tables near a window. The sun was still rising.
Patches of sunlight and shadow alternated in the woods around
the Torus Centre. As they ate, Steerforth glanced at Khan. He
looked calm and relaxed, his hair combed sharply back from his
forehead and his eyes bright and clear. Khan was wearing a blue
denim suit and an open-necked shirt. As he finished his breakfast
and walked across to the disposal with his tray, a shaft of sunlight
burst through the early-morning mist and lit up the breakfast
room. Even at that moment, and with the mixture of conflicting
emotions within him, Steerforth felt that there was some unique
quality in his vision of Khan that would never be repeated.

He felt somehow that the success or failure of this day's experiments would change both his relationship with Khan and the
history of mankind, that in a few hours when the first journeys
into the past and the future had been made the Khan he knew
would in reality have ceased to exist. That rather handsome but
otherwise quite ordinary-looking man unstacking his dirty
crockery in a Swiss canteen would be replaced with some other
creature, immensely more powerful, unknowable and dangerous.
What messages Khan could bring back from his journeys in time,
Steerforth could only guess.

'Well then,' said Khan when both had disposed of their breakfast dishes, 'shall we go and rewrite the laws of the universe?'

They left the cafeteria and took the elevator down to the level of the Torus control room. They produced their security passes and signed in for the use of the Torus. Under the heading that indicated the purpose of the experiment, Khan limited himself to writing 'Program Test'. They let themselves into the control room and powered up the Torus. The human-sized Time Travel Module looked rather like a heavy-duty invalid car.

'Will you give me a moment to validate my data?' asked Khan. Steerforth went to the far side of the control room and busied himself with some pointless task while Khan paged through the contents of the computer's memory. At length Khan was satisfied. He keyed in the code that opened up the plate in the Time Travel Module – this time a man-sized plate instead of a mouse-sized one – and prepared to take his place inside it.

'Good luck, Khan,' said Steerforth. So overcome with the moment was Khan that he could not even reply. He simply nodded, grasped Steerforth's hand and then turned from him and stooped under the lintel of the Time Travel Module. Steerforth entered the code that closed the entrance and then switched on the closed-circuit television. He watched Inayat Khan carefully seat himself in the large metal chair which was now built into the chamber. He waited patiently as Khan fastened a belt about his waist and earphones on his head.

'Can you hear me, Steerforth?' said Khan.

'Perfectly,' answered Steerforth.

'As soon as you are quite ready,' said Khan, 'you may begin the Magus sequence.' He was clearly visible on Steerforth's television screen, his eyes closed and his hands gripping the arms of the chair.

'Good luck,' said Steerforth and pressed the console button marked GO. And Inayat Khan obeyed. Without fuss or bother or loud bangs or bright flashes, the Magus machine catapulted Khan into the past. Though Steerforth anxiously scanned the visual display screens no meaningful data was shown about Khan's trajectory in time. Clearly Khan had ordered the computer to suppress any such revelations. Steerforth had no idea how long Khan was scheduled to be absent. He could only watch the screen in silent terror while it was empty. It was somehow terrifying to think of his friend, who had been with him moments ago, walking alone somewhere and somewhen in space and time. Then the Time

Travel Module materialised as abruptly as it had vanished. Khan sat for a moment, then opened his eyes and rolled his head from side to side. After about five minutes the closed-circuit television screen again became empty. Khan was off on another Magus journey, all under the control of the Torus computer. Again he returned and again departed. In all Steerforth counted six trips, though he had no idea of the space–time loci, before Khan unfastened the seatbelt and the earphones and eased himself out of the chair. He opened the module door and emerged.

'Well?' asked Steerforth as soon as Khan had disentangled himself from the cockpit of the Magus. 'Did it work?'

'It worked, it certainly worked,' answered Khan – and even he seemed momentarily stunned by the experience of time travel.

'Where have you been? Or rather *when?*'

'Hang on a second. My body has aged physiologically by about forty hours in the last half-hour of your time. So apart from anything else, I'm rather tired and hungry. Anyway I want you to do something while I'm ordering a sandwich.'

'Of course. What do you want me to do?'

'Do you remember all those years ago at Bain Brook when you and I were there together and my uncle paid us a visit?'

'Yes of course I remember,' said Steerforth. 'But what on earth does that have to do with the Magus? I hoped you'd bring back a Shakespeare manuscript or a splinter from the Cross. Can't you prove that the Magus worked?'

'Listen. Do you recall that my uncle gave you a note when he left Bain Brook?'

'Yes of course. A note in an envelope sealed with sealing wax. What of it?'

'Where is it now?'

'It's in my room. Your uncle said that I was to keep it in my possession always until he told me to open it.'

'Do you also recall what he said was in it?'

'He said it was a message, but that if I opened the envelope at the wrong time I would find the message quite devoid of meaning. Do you mean to tell me that you know what is in that envelope, Inayat?'

'I think I do. But would you please go and fetch the envelope here, while I order us some food and drink?' By the time Steerforth had hurried upstairs to his room, retrieved the envelope from his briefcase, passed once more through the security checks and returned to the Torus room, Inayat Khan had already made a healthy dent in a plate of ham and cheese sandwiches and a stainless steel flagon of steaming coffee. But Steerforth was too excited to eat.

'Here,' he said, 'here's the wretched envelope, what do you want me to do with it?'

'Open it,' said Khan in a cool and level voice.

'I can't,' answered Steerforth. 'You were there yourself. You heard your uncle tell me quite plainly not to open the envelope until he told me to do so. I've respected his wishes for over twenty-five years. Why should I violate them now?'

'Steerforth, please open the envelope,' said Khan quite sharply. 'Will you please accept my word that by opening the envelope now, you will not be acting against my uncle's wishes?'

'How can that be?'

'He might just as well have told you that you were to open the envelope only when I told you to do so. I think that's really what he meant to convey.'

At last Steerforth was persuaded to open the ancient envelope, picking the sealing wax from it with a knife from the luncheon tray. Khan stood and watched as Steerforth picked away at the seal, a slight smile on his face.

'I don't understand,' said Steerforth at last when he had extracted from the envelope a single sheet of paper. 'This can't possibly be the same letter that your uncle gave to me at Bain Brook all those years ago.'

'Do you suppose,' asked Khan, 'that someone has got into your room and substituted an identical envelope for the one you have kept? Why should anyone do such a thing? And wasn't your briefcase locked?'

Steerforth felt a momentary surge of something very much like panic. He would have to leave soon to catch the flight back to England, to face the ordeal of his father's funeral and his own succession to the title, to being introduced at the House of Lords and to all the paraphernalia of his new rank. He looked hard at the piece of paper in his hand, but his eyes and mind refused to accept what he saw there.

'Tell me what you see,' said Khan gently, as if he had known what Steerforth was thinking.

'I see a letter written in your hand on the headed paper of the Torus centre dated yesterday and wishing us good fortune in our experiment. For good measure you have added a few details relating to yesterday, such as the temperature, the snow conditions on the slopes, the value of the Swiss franc against the pound and the share value of the Ciba Geigy company.'

'Information which my uncle would have found hard to predict in the 1950s.'

'Certainly. The Torus centre didn't even exist then. Nor did Ciba Geigy for the matter of that. And the statistical information would have been totally unguessable.'

'So where do you suppose my uncle got this knowledge?'

'You gave it to him. You, Inayat, went back to the Bain Brook of the 1950s and gave your uncle this information? And then he passed it on to me?'

'Nearly, Steerforth, nearly right. One small detail is wrong.' A terrifying silence hung like a cloud in the room. Momentarily the paper shook in Steerforth's hand like a leaf in a gale. Then he regained control of himself.

'Steerforth,' said Khan quietly but distinctly. 'I have no uncle. Less than an hour ago in my physiological time I handed you that letter myself. But you were a lad of eighteen and the year was 1954.'

Steerforth sat gazing out of the window of the Randolph Hotel into the gathering dusk of the Oxford evening. Between his fingertips he held the luncheon menu card upon which he had sketched for me what a successful Magus experiment had been expected to look like. I could see how he had drawn the tiny filigree lines of the sub-atomic particles as traces in the bubble chamber, and how, if a Magus experiment were to succeed, the line would either be discontinuous or duplicated. If a particle went back in time it was inevitable that it would accompany itself, so to speak, across the chamber.

'Whenever the world-line of the flatipus crosses the world-line of another flatipus, we understand that two flatipi are meeting at a given location,' said Steerforth. 'But once the flatipus can move up and down the vertical axis we call time, then his world-line may bisect *itself*. The flatipus will then encounter himself at different stages of his physiological age. If you think about it in relation to sub-atomic particles or flatipi, it seems obvious and quite logically inescapable. But if you think about it in relation to people, it's rather spooky. I remembered at once, of course, my mother's comments about Inayat's uncle's clothes. In the 1950s it was an eccentricity for anyone in England to wear a suit made of *serge de Nim*. In 1970 Inayat's blue denims were perfectly commonplace. Of course Inayat Khan had to break his nose playing tennis and end up looking even more like a younger version of his crook-nosed uncle. If Inayat hadn't broken his nose playing tennis, then his uncle wouldn't have had a crooked nose.'

'Good heavens!' I cried, and sat bolt upright in my chair, nearly tipping out the remnants of my dry sherry in the process. 'Now I understand about the physics paper!'

'What physics paper?' asked Steerforth. I told him about Khan's amazingly good – suspiciously good – performance in the physics prize paper and how Mr Hughes had sought some honourable way of finding out if Khan's paper was honestly done. And I went on to explain how I'd felt there was something unaccountably wrong about what had happened in the exam, but couldn't for the life of me tell what it was.

'Then by chance something reminded me of the scene in the gymnasium. I remembered all at once what was wrong. Inayat Khan had started to write his answer to the first essay question without even reading the paper properly. He just glanced at it to make sure that it was just as he had remembered it, and then started to write.'

'Exactly so,' said Steerforth. 'I'm certain that he kept the paper all those years and then, when the Magus was available, took it back and gave it to the teenage Khan.' So it must have been, perhaps on that very day when I had seen the two of them (if such a term had any meaning) talking together under the horse-chestnut trees. I seemed to recall that Khan the elder had taken from his pocket some paper or an envelope and handed it with great ser-iousness of purpose to Khan the younger. Here is the crib to the physics exam which you must win to go to Oxford, because if you don't go to Oxford you will not work on PEPR and invent the Magus, and if you don't invent the Magus then how can you travel back in time to the 1950s with the crib to the physics exam? My brain reeled at the implications of it all.

'And of course,' added Steerforth, 'cynophobia doesn't run in families, or at least not necessarily so. The fact that Khan's uncle was as frightened of dogs as Khan himself becomes rather unsurprising when you realise that Khan's uncle is Khan him-self.'

Later that afternoon Steerforth had left Geneva and flown back to his bereaved mother in London, en route to fetch his father's body from America. Khan had already sent Lady Steerforth some flowers which she much appreciated. As he unpacked his bags from Switzerland and repacked them for America, Steerforth could not but wonder whether the flowers had been delivered in the normal way or whether Khan had dropped them in himself, arriving in London before Steerforth in spite of departing from Geneva in the middle of the following week. Apart from his visit to Bain Brook, Khan never accounted for any of his six time trips. It seemed possible later that he already knew he was laying his plans for the future – or rather for a new past.

CHAPTER 5

A Magnifying Power

Sometimes when I lie in bed in my quarters in the college I feel a tremor of panic pass through my ancient limbs. I am a teacher of English, a specialist in Chaucer, a mild and contemplative man. If ever I were to have undertaken any rash adventures, the time to have done so was when I was a young man just after the Great War. It was a war, indeed, in which I was only just too young to serve. At the age of seventy-six, what am I doing with space and time travel, with sub-atomic particles and Magus machines and gravity collapses? Surely I can forget the whole thing and turn back to Chaucer and the Italian poets, to Edwina May McGrath's thesis and to my pupils' essays? The most catastrophic of my pupils had never plunged me into the same turmoil as Steerforth and his Magus.

But whenever I am tempted to turn my back on Steerforth, to plead my advanced years as an excuse for withdrawing from him such slender help and support as I can offer, I see again his tense and anxious face as he tells me the story of the Magus. He has no one else. His parents by now are both dead and his former wife is six thousand miles away in California. He has told the full story of the Magus experiments and of Khan's disappearance to no one but me. His attempts to gain official notice for his views have failed: the government view is now that the results of the Magus experiments were not conclusive and perhaps not valid. They are halfway towards persuading themselves that Magus was never invented, and that Khan's disappearance is tantamount to an admission that the whole thing was a hoax. Steerforth has the air of a man carrying around a load of guilt and despair, so that even if

I wished to abandon him I doubt if I could bring myself to do so. Sometimes when the two of us are together with Dr McGrath I have a feeling that Steerforth is about to take her into his confidence, for she has a sympathetic and understanding manner. After getting off on the wrong foot, when she found him asleep in my rooms at midday, Dr McGrath and Steerforth have been getting along quite well together and have almost become friends.

The story of Khan and Magus from the moment of the first time voyages up to the disappearance of Khan was never told to me as a consecutive narrative, as was the account of the invention of the Magus machine. Instead I pieced it together from various bits of information gleaned from conversations with Steerforth at different times and from examining one or two of Steerforth's notebooks which he has lent me.

After Steerforth had returned to London for the funeral of his father and the ritual of Ducal investiture, Khan stayed on in Geneva to write up his results in a report. Now the precise status of that report is a matter of some uncertainty, and the passage of the years has not clarified the issue. A few things are certain. Within a few months of the successful time journeys a summary of the report stating that human time travel had been accomplished found its way through the labyrinth of official scepticism and on to the Prime Minister's desk. The effects of this information upon the Prime Minister were very marked indeed, as will later be made clear. But for several months, such was the degree of disbelief among the senior civil servants who surround the Prime Minister, neither Khan nor Steerforth was invited to give a personal account of the Magus journeys. When Khan had almost completed his report he telephoned Steerforth to discuss the next steps. They considered the possibility of staging some really spectacular coup to demonstrate the power of time travel. Perhaps Napoleon could be kidnapped from his exile and transported to the twentieth century. He and Khan might suddenly materialise in the middle of a cabinet meeting at Downing Street. Or perhaps one of the television channels might welcome some colour footage of a notable historic event – say the Crucifixion or the battle of Marathon? Wisely no doubt they resolved for the time being to eschew such blatant gimmickry. It was tentatively agreed between them that in the near future Steerforth himself would have the opportunity to make a Magus journey, but that it would be as cautiously discreet as those that Khan had made, devoid of impact on the broad course of history. The talk of intervening in the course of history raised obvious questions in both their minds. If a television camera crew were to be present at the Crucifixion, why do the Gospels not mention the fact? And if such a crew were inserted by Magus into the fabric of space and time, would the text of the Gospels suddenly change in all the millions of Bibles already printed? Or would the Crucifixion witnessed by the TV team be in some sense a different event from that recorded in the Testament? And perhaps the humanity that its victim came to redeem a different humanity?

'Perhaps there are an infinity of different universes in which the Crucifixion is filmed or not filmed, concluded or cancelled, described or forgotten. Perhaps our intervention simply shifts us from one universe to another like the points on a railway line.' The faint background hum of the international telephone line seemed deafening in the silence that followed these speculations of Khan's.

'Anyway Steerforth,' said Khan in a more practical tone of voice, 'you had better give some thought to when and where you want your Magus trip to take you.'

'I have an idea about that,' answered Steerforth. 'But you may think it a little childish and vain.'

'What's the point of inventing time travel if you can't indulge your whims?' asked Khan.

Before Steerforth made his own journey in time, however, another event occurred that was later to take on significance in the story of the Magus project. Steerforth and Khan had met in the physics laboratory at Oxford to discuss and record certain details of the remaining experiments. They did their work. They put the files away in a safe, of which only Khan and Steerforth knew the combination, and left the laboratory in darkness. That evening Khan was to go to Cambridge while Steerforth would dine in college. It was only just before the dinner bell when Steerforth remembered that he had left his academic gown in the physics laboratory. Without it he would be improperly dressed for dinner. He just had time to walk quickly back to the laboratory and fetch it.

'What the devil. . .?' said Steerforth aloud to himself as he opened the door. Everything else in the room was normal, but the door of the safe was open. Steerforth felt quite certain that he had closed the safe when the files were last put back there. Had Khan been back to the laboratory for some reason? Had he left the safe door open? It seemed most unlikely. All the Magus files were present and correct, as far as Steerforth could tell. He closed and locked the safe door, and tested that it could not swing open again. He left the laboratory quickly, his gown under his arm. And as he did so, he saw a figure walking away from him in the dim light of the street lamps that instantly attracted his attention. The man was of medium height and solid build, wearing a dark overcoat and hurrying down the road away from Steerforth. When the man was almost out of sight, Steerforth thought he glanced back over his shoulder towards the physics laboratory. But at that range his face was invisible. There was something about his appearance that struck Steerforth as very familiar. But beyond that he could not go.

'Come on you idiot,' he said to himself. 'You'll be late for dinner!' He promptly forgot the passer-by in the street.

Some further experiments were necessary to fill out the Magus report, though none of them appeared to involve further manned time travel. For these experiments Khan and Steerforth returned to Switzerland.

'While we are at the Torus Centre,' said Khan. 'I think it would be appropriate to carry out one private and wholly unofficial experiment of our own.'

'What's that?' asked Steerforth, his heart thumping.

'That, my dear Steerforth, is your first Magus journey. You have amply deserved a trip. Have you given any thought to when and where you want to go?'

'Yes I have,' said Steerforth. 'I want to go to Sydney, Australia, in 1964. Can you guess why?'

'Of course,' said Khan with a soft and knowing smile.

While they were in Switzerland for these experiments, they also had a certain amount of time to kill, since the Torus was now heavily loaded with other experiments and it was far from easy to schedule their time. They visited Dr Konrad Dubendorf, the former Director of the Torus Centre, who had done so much to make their work possible. He was now well established as professor of physics at Zurich University. Despite his outwardly cool and reserved air, Dubendorf was a man of great human warmth. He and his wife arranged a superb beef *fondue* for Khan and Steerforth at their home. Afterwards as they sat nursing the pear liqueur of the region, Konrad Dubendorf smiled and made a heavily charged remark.

'I have no access now to Magus material,' he said, 'I have no need-to-know status and no security clearance. Therefore I would not dream of asking you about the success of the Magus project. And I would be gravely worried about the security of the project if you gentlemen were to volunteer any information unasked. Whether it has proved possible to make manned Magus journeys is not for me to speculate and not for you to tell. But it is nice to see you back in Switzerland and to assume – I use no stronger word – that the facilities of the Torus Centre are still being put to good use.' Konrad Dubendorf smiled as he spoke these words and if it is possible for a man to have a mischievous glint on the lenses of his spectacles, then Dr Dubendorf had such a glint. Inayat Khan smiled and patted Dr Dubendorf's arm.

'You seem to assume, Konrad, that we would not be here in Switzerland consuming the valuable time and resources of the Torus Centre unless we have been able to achieve the targets of the original plan. All I can say is that as the former Torus Centre Director, it would be surprising if your judgement of such a policy issue were too far adrift.'

On days when there was little else to do Khan and Steerforth arranged for a car from the Torus Centre to take them on sight-seeing tours around Lyons, Mulhouse or Bern. At Bern they discovered to their delight the outdoor chess boards in the cathedral close, with their four or five foot chess pieces that have to be lifted bodily around the board. Khan remarked that walking in and out among the pieces gave the whole game a more spatial feel.

'Yes,' said Steerforth. 'And it makes the loss of a piece much more traumatic. A pawn you've walked around and carried in your arms is like an old friend.'

'Have you considered,' asked Khan as they sat relaxing in the cathedral gardens after their game, 'what kind of reaction the Magus reports are likely to trigger off in the minds of our political masters, once they have had a few weeks to bend their little minds around the fact that Magus works?'

'I imagine that about half will be utterly terrified by the whole thing. I don't really blame them,' admitted Steerforth, 'for to be quite honest it sometimes frightens me.' Khan professed himself devoid of any such fears.

'And how do you think the rest of the politicians will react?' he asked. 'Those who are not terrified, how will they respond?'

'There will be a great temptation,' said Steerforth quite slowly and softly. 'They will be tempted, as the Americans were when they alone had nuclear weapons in 1945. The Americans could have blackmailed the world into disarmament if they had wished.

A trial explosion in the Sea of Okhotsk or the Laptev Sea would have convinced the Soviets that they meant business. The arms race and the cold war might never have taken place. Eastern Europe might have remained free. The American economy would have been infinitely stronger, since only a few weapons would be needed to back up the threat of nuclear attack.' It seemed utterly incongruous to talk about the survival or destruction of nations here in this quiet and ancient cathedral close, where two old Bernese had taken over from Khan and Steerforth with the man-sized chess pieces, shuffling them slowly from square to square in the pale sunlight.

'With Magus,' said Steerforth, 'Britain is in much the same position as the Americans in 1945, except the opportunity is much vaster. If the government wants to, it can exploit Magus quite ruthlessly. Every moment of history past, present and future can be interfered with. The infant Hitler could be strangled in his pram. Gandhi could have been assassinated twenty years earlier, so that India remained British. There is no limit to our ability to shape history to our own ends.'

'But do you consider such a course to be morally defensible? Is the British government the right instrument to wield such enormous power?' asked Khan.

'I have my doubts,' said Steerforth, his brow wrinkled. 'I am not sure that any authority on earth is fit to wield such power. Perhaps the ebb and flow of history, the turning and twisting of evolution, perhaps these are better guides to where we should go?'

'The best of all histories in the best of all possible worlds?' asked Khan with a wry grin. 'The only thing I feel sure of is that a government served by such people as Tolson is quite unfitted to wield the power of the Magus. Almost any solution to the problem is preferable to placing the Magus in hands like those.'

A few days later Khan and Steerforth made their way once more through the security checks and into the Torus centre. They took the elevator down to the Torus control room and signed on for the period they had been allocated on the Torus itself. They let themselves into the Torus control room and took over from the German team which had conducted the earlier experiments.

Together Khan and Steerforth had worked out the time and space coordinates for Steerforth's Magus journey. As a safety measure both of them entered the coordinates at the computer keyboard. Then the machine was asked to compare the two sets of data. It found them identical. The code which opened the door to the Time Travel Module was entered, but this time it was Steerforth who stepped inside and fastened the seatbelt round his waist and the earphones to his head.

'Let me know when you're settled and ready,' he heard Khan's voice say in his ear. Steerforth closed his eyes and gripped the arms of his chair.

'Ready,' he said, and in the next instant his every sense seemed to miss a second or two. He seemed weightless and bodiless, with a momentary hint of the kind of nausea one feels at the peak of a roller-coaster ride. The space beyond the Time Travel Module seemed colourless and remote. There was a moment of silence. Then Steerforth suddenly found that the Module was in bright sunshine. He had arrived in a remote corner of the Royal Agricultural Society Show Ground. As far as he could tell, the arrival of the Time Travel Module had been unobserved. He emerged, locked the door and set off for the adjoining Sydney Cricket Ground. He spent the next two and a half hours seated as inconspicuously as possible in the Brewongle stand. It was a world cricket first that Wisden was never to record.

After Steerforth's Magus journey to see a Test Match in which he himself had scored a fifty, he and Khan returned to London to await the political decision about the future of the project. The weeks dragged by. Steerforth was kept busy by the task of managing the publishing house and Bain Brook, both of which he had inherited from his father at the time of the first Magus voyage. The problems of arranging his late father's affairs in such a way as to avoid bankrupting the company and crippling the estates with death duties were urgent and absorbing. For Khan there was no such compelling distraction, except on evenings when he might accompany Abigail to one of her concerts. And even at those he felt a little ill at ease among the musicians, the technicians and the innumerable other hangers-on.

For all these reasons Khan began to grow irritable and ill at ease whenever the subject of the Magus experiments and the government's reaction was mentioned.

Abigail proposed to Steerforth that an expedition to the Lake District should be mounted, in order to provide a distraction from the fretful business of waiting for the government decision. The idea was appealing, but the date proved inconvenient for Steerforth. Khan and Abigail went alone. They sent Steerforth a colour photograph in the manner of a postcard. The card, which Steerforth happened to keep, showed a large, rectangular house with a rounded wing. The house was not identified. On the reverse, Khan had written a message: 'A house of such prospect that if impressions and ideas constitute our being, one might have a tendency to become a God there.'

Major Tolson inhabited an office in London. Neither Khan nor Steerforth had ever been there. Neither knew the address, perhaps itself a secret, though both had a telephone number where Major Tolson could be contacted, sometimes in person. Both were accustomed to receiving telephone calls from the Major.

In this instance, not long after Khan's visit to the Lake District, it was Steerforth who received a call.

'Have you made a time trip in the Magus?' asked Major Tolson.

'Yes I have,' answered Steerforth.

'Did you clear your time and space coordinates with my office?' asked Tolson sharply.

'No, of course not,' answered Steerforth in an equally spirited fashion. 'We have never got security clearance for the details of Magus experiments. We would never agree to do so.'

'Why is your trip not described in the official report?' asked Major Tolson.

'It's not necessary,' answered Steerforth. 'The report describes some of the trips made by Khan, which adequately substantiate our claims on behalf of Magus. That is all the report sets out to achieve.'

'The security on this project has been appallingly slack,' said Tolson. 'My hands were tied. You two young geniuses had to have everything you needed without time to tie up the loose ends. Now the inevitable consequences have followed.'

'What are you talking about?' asked Steerforth rather testily.

'I'm talking about the integrity of the project,' answered Major Tolson. 'Now you admit that you have made unauthorised and unrecorded Magus trips. . . .'

'Unauthorised? By whom?' shouted Steerforth. But the major ignored his anger.

'Have you an equally lax attitude towards the project's property?' asked Major Tolson, a sudden and cunning tone coming into his voice. 'Do you know anything about missing materials?'

'What materials?' asked Steerforth. It transpired that Major Tolson had uncovered some quite serious shortages in the Magus project's inventory both in Oxford and in Geneva. As a general rule, for each component of the Magus machine a number of spares had been produced and taken at least to the semi-finished stage. This was standard practice, designed to avoid unnecessary delay if a component were damaged or lost. From what Major Tolson suggested – though he would not be explicit about what was missing – it seemed that some of these spares and some of the spare materials had been found to be missing from stores.

'But the whole matter of indents and stock control is so slack, I may never be able to trace exactly where everything has gone.'

It was too much to expect that Tolson would openly express his confidence in Augustus Steerforth. At length however Steerforth got the impression that he was not exactly high on Tolson's suspect list, and that his role was to point the finger of suspicion at someone else. He could think of little to say that might be useful. Not much later, Major Tolson rang off. Steerforth was plagued by the suspicion that Khan might know something about the missing components and materials. He could not decide whether to speak to Khan about it. If Khan knew as little about any shortages as Steerforth himself, he would be puzzled and perhaps offended that his friend might think it worth checking. But if he had taken the parts – perhaps to support some perfectly legitimate variant on the Magus experiments that Steerforth knew nothing of – then surely he should be warned about the sinister interpretation Tolson was putting on the shortages? Steerforth immediately telephoned Khan's apartment. Khan was not at home nor at the laboratory.

'To hell with the whole business,' muttered Steerforth as he slammed the receiver down. 'I'll leave the security to Tolson. The little wretch revels in it anyway!' But all the same he felt over-shadowed with anxiety and guilt, as if any indiscretion of which Khan was guilty was partially his own responsibility, or as if he should have established Khan's innocence as effectively as he seemed to have done his own. It was several days before he could put out of his mind the lingering taste of disquiet that Tolson had stirred. After his first impulsive effort to contact Khan, he preferred to leave matters alone: he even went out of his way a little to avoid contact with Khan. There were no more calls from Tolson on the subject of the missing stores. Steerforth imagined the security man silently beavering away behind the scenes, poring over stores issues and other scraps of paper.

Steerforth's turn to pore over scraps of paper was yet to come. After Khan's disappearance he would spend hours, even days, in a vain hunt for some clue. From the laboratory and the apartment he would glean a few faint scraps of evidence. But they seemed more likely to reflect Khan's state of mind during this crucial episode than to suggest some specific place and time as his destination. On one such scrap of paper Steerforth found what he later identified as a passage from the *Republic* laboriously copied out in Khan's inexpert Greek hand:

Οὐκοῦν ἵνα καὶ ὁ τοιοῦτος ὑπὸ ὁμοίου ἄρχηται οἷουπερ ὁ βέλ-
d τιστος, δοῦλον αὐτόν φαμεν δεῖν εἶναι ἐκείνου τοῦ βελτίστου
καὶ ἔχοντος ἐν αὑτῷ τὸ θεῖον ἄρχον, οὐκ ἐπὶ βλάβῃ τῇ τοῦ δούλου
οἰόμενοι δεῖν ἄρχεσθαι αὐτόν, ὥσπερ Θρασύμαχος ᾤετο τους
ἀρχομένους, ἀλλ᾽ ὡς ἄμεινον ὂν παντὶ ὑπὸ θείου καὶ φρονίμου
ἄρχεσθαι, μάλιστα μὲν οἰκεῖον ἔχοντος ἐν αὐτῷ, εἰ δὲ μή, ἔξωθεν
5 ἐφεστῶτος, ἵνα εἰς δύναμιν πάντες ὅμοιοι ὦμεν καὶ φίλοι, τῷ
αὐτῷ κυβερνώμενοι;

(*Platonis Res Publica,* 590c8 to 590d6)

And below this was set out Khan's somewhat awkward translation of the Greek, annotated with numerous references to Liddell & Scott's Lexicon:

'In order therefore that such a man may be ruled by the same principle by which the best is ruled, do we then state that he must be the slave of the best? Not thinking (like Thrasymachus) that it must be to the detriment of the slave to be so ruled, but that it is better for everyone to be ruled by the man of vision and sanity — especially if he has either within himself or imposed from without the ability to ensure that we are all as far as possible equal and dear, governed alike – is that what we state?'

In the original Greek text and in his own translation, Khan had underlined the words describing the man of vision and sanity. He had also underlined the words 'imposed from without', as if concerned with what sources of inspiration the man of vision and sanity might enjoy, other than his inherent wisdom.

The passage Khan had copied from the Republic was familiar to Steerforth. He had heard it described as the central core of the whole masterwork. Was it truly the responsibility of those with knowledge and power to use them for the good of their inferiors? Or was it overweening pride for anyone to consider himself 'a man of vision and sanity'? The British government had not exactly impressed Steerforth and Khan with the clarity of its own vision. Perhaps the Magus machine was just the kind of external source of power that a man of vision and sanity needed, something that would both enable and qualify him to rule the universe. The nobility of the Greek language masked the brutality of Plato's sentiment. In the end he had opted for an intellectual oligarchy as the best form of government. Khan had expressed the same sentiment more bluntly at Magdalen Bridge: 'I'm not here to learn to serve. I am here to learn to rule. . . . My people have been servants long enough. Make no mistake about it. . . . I'm here to get power and to learn how to use it!' Steerforth wondered vaguely what Sokrates would have made of the Magus machine, then realised with a shock that Khan could easily have gone back to Athens and asked him. Perhaps he had. It seemed likely that Sokrates, Plato's mentor, would approve of the sovereignty of the man of vision and sanity. But what if Khan's vision and sanity were Steerforth's blindness and madness? Who then would resolve that dispute?

The government machine, though moving slowly, proved that it had not totally stalled. One evening in the autumn of the year 1972, some fourteen years after they had started work on the Magus project, Khan and Steerforth were together in Oxford. They dined at a small French restaurant in the High and walked slowly back to Khan's apartment in north Oxford. It was a damp and chilly evening and the wind blew unpleasantly off the Parks. Almost as soon as they reached the apartment, before they had even taken off their coats, the telephone rang. It was Major Tolson and as usual he wasted little time on social niceties.

'Downing Street tomorrow at eight thirty,' he announced. 'The Prime Minister wants to see you both for morning coffee.' The line went dead. Presumably when the Prime Minister issued an invitation its acceptance was taken for granted.

Next morning at six Khan was already up and about by the time Steerforth arrived in the Rolls-Royce to pick him up. Mr Steele was driving the car on this occasion, so that Khan and Steerforth could sit in the back and decide how to handle the Prime Minister and his staff. Five minutes before the appointed hour they presented themselves at Downing Street and were whisked into the Prime Minister's presence. A young man with a notebook and a flying pencil was the only other person present.

'At first hand,' said Steerforth later, 'the Prime Minister is somewhat smaller than he looks on televison, and rather tougher-looking. His famous blue eyes are absolutely rivetting.' At first he said, he had found the contents of Khan's report utterly unbelievable. He had found it necessary to read the report several times and let its implications gradually sink into his mind. It was for this reason that his meeting with Khan and Steerforth had been delayed.

'Now gentlemen,' he said, 'I am ready to believe that time travel is a reality. I am less ready to announce to the House of Commons or the world's pressmen that it is so. I think they would be as stupefied as I was at first. It is a hard thing to accept, you know.' He glanced at them both keenly, as if to assess how well they understood this difficulty or recognised their own responsibility in creating the problem.

'But sooner or later it must be announced,' he went on. 'In a country like ours there is no such thing as absolute secrecy. You have to be prepared to silence people for ever if you want that. Once a few people know about Magus, the secret is bound to leak out.' Steerforth doubted if Major Tolson would relish the Prime Minister's gloomy view of security arrangements.

'The question of what we are to do with Magus is therefore of some urgency. We can't keep it secret indefinitely and we can't make a proper announcement until we know what we will do with it. What is your opinion, gentlemen?'

'The use of the Magus as an instrument of national policy is a political question of the first order,' said Inayat Khan softly. 'Are you asking us for suggestions on that question, Prime Minister?' The Prime Minister said nothing but merely nodded and smiled slightly.

'In that case,' said Khan carefully, 'you may not be surprised to know that Steerforth and I do not necessarily agree on every detail.'

'It would be rather surprising if you did,' commented the Prime Minister.

'Perhaps it would be best if Steerforth spoke first,' said Khan. Steerforth nodded, took a deep breath and began to speak.

'The existence of Magus,' he said, 'takes us into uncharted waters in much the same way as the nuclear bombs did. When they were first developed no one knew for certain that the explosion of a single bomb might not ignite the atmosphere and destroy all life on earth. In the same way Magus gives us the ability to eliminate those events or people in history that we find uncongenial. Hitler, Napoleon, Judas Iscariot – they could all be removed from history like weeds from a garden. But what of the history we know? There are millions of history books that refer to Napoleon. Do they just flicker out of existence? There are tens of millions of Bibles that refer to Judas Iscariot. Do they instantaneously modify themselves to delete all reference to him? From a purely practical point of view we don't understand the implications of using Magus in anything but the most passive of ways, as undetected observers. We may go and watch the infant

Hitler at play. But if we try to arrange his accidental death we risk much more than we can gain.' Steerforth paused and glanced around the opulent drawing room in which the three men sat, as if the very fabric of Downing Street might suddenly melt away in some unknown universe to which Magus might transport them.

'From a philosophical point of view also,' said Steerforth, 'I find that to use Magus to intervene decisively in history is unacceptable. What does any one individual or group of people really know about the longer-term destiny of mankind? The twists and turns of history baffle us. We can't make the judgement that the Second World War was in any absolute sense an evil thing. Of course it led to the death of millions of people. But it also led to the unification of Western Europe, the liberation of the British Empire, the foundation of the state of Israel and the discovery of rocket motors. Without that war, awful as it was, your people' – and Steerforth looked hard at Inayat Khan as he spoke – 'might still be under colonial rule. It is an act of fearful and overweening pride to think that we can judge the best interests of mankind and intervene accordingly in its history. It is the sin the Greeks called *hubris*, when men play God. It is savagely punished and never forgiven.'

'In what way would you use Magus, if at all, Lord Steerforth?' asked the Prime Minister.

'I would retain it as a weapon of final resort,' said Steerforth. 'If ever I had complete and convincing evidence of a first strike nuclear attack against this country or its allies, I would use Magus to go back in time and destroy the enemy's nuclear capability in the past. As a deterrent, I would make sure the world knew I had this capability. I would permit limited use of Magus as a research tool, where time travellers can observe the past or the future without attempting to influence events. There is evidence in the past history of the world that suggests we do, in fact, sanction such experiments.'

'What evidence?' asked the Prime Minister sharply.

'What do we think ghosts are?' said Steerforth. 'They appear unaccountably throughout history, they see and are sometimes seen, they hear and are sometimes heard. But they never intervene directly in man's affairs. People are often scared by a ghost, but when did you ever hear of anyone being attacked or killed by a ghost? Ghosts behave just like well-trained Magus observers.'

There was a moment's silence. Then the Prime Minister glanced at Inayat Khan.

'The history of mankind is a succession of forward leaps and backward slides,' said Khan. 'Of course there are desirable side-effects from catastrophic causes. I agree with Steerforth about that. But the whole point of Magus is that if we think carefully enough about what we want, we can have all the desirable effects *without* the disasters. It's no longer necessary to accept that history is too complex and unpredictable to be managed. We can intervene at whatever level of detail is needed. We can begin to engineer man's history in the same way as we have engineered the environment – except that with Magus it's much easier to put right any mistakes we make. As for Steerforth's assertion that we can't judge what's right and wrong, I think that's unnecessarily defeatist. We could make a quick shopping list of Magus projects that might command quite widespread support. Abolish war. Abolish hunger. Abolish disease. Abolish crime. Not too many people would oppose those aims.'

As Khan was speaking, the Prime Minister's eyes seemed to burn with interest. Was it the idealist in him burning with zeal to pursue these noble goals? Or was it the politician lusting after the place in history that such achievements might earn him? If it was the latter, thought Steerforth, he might well reflect that in the era of Magus an enduring place in the history books might be a thing beyond attainment.

'You gentlemen do not simply represent a marginally varying opinion on the future of the Magus project,' said the Prime Minister at length. 'You are at opposite poles of the spectrum in basic philosophy. Those are the contrasting views that I must try to reconcile.' The discussion went on for another ten or fifteen minutes. One valid point that Khan made, though Steerforth could not remember exactly when, was that there was a glaring inconsistency in Steerforth's view of when and why Magus might be used. He was willing to contemplate using Magus in the future if it were the only way of forestalling a nuclear attack. Fine. Under those circumstances almost anyone would agree that Magus should be used. But once again the historical consequences of such an action would also be unknowable. The destruction of Britain by a nuclear weapon might also be an instrument of the force of destiny, pursuing good ends through disastrous means. The only difference was that the Second World War (which Steerforth would not agree to prevent) was in the past, and the nuclear attack (which he would prevent) was in the future.

'And if there is one thing that Magus has done,' said Khan, 'it is to establish that the distinction between past, present and future is a wholly man-made fiction.' Logically Steerforth felt that Khan had presented a much more compelling case to the Prime Minister. But he also sensed that even the sharp and resilient mind of a professional politician veered away in alarm from the implications of Khan's advice.

'I think he sees the point,' said Khan as they waited in the lobby for Mr Steele to come and pick them up. 'The question is whether he feels powerful enough to embrace it.'

Khan seemed somewhat cheered by the encounter with the Prime Minister. But Steerforth felt restless and depressed. He had never seen so clearly before the difference, indeed the gulf, between his own opinion on how Magus should be used and that of its co-inventor. He could understand the cold, relentless logic of Khan's argument but he found it chilling and not a little repellent. It seemed that the hideous experiences of Khan's early life had somehow crushed some vital spark of compassion and sympathy, some sense of how awesome the sum of human things might be, and left him only with his cold but passionate pursuit of power. Now the ideal tool to grasp that power lay in his hands. He seemed unable to feel anything but bafflement towards anyone who hesitated to make unrestricted use of the tool – bafflement tinged with contempt. Steerforth had a strong and unwelcome presentiment that the Prime Minister would be more deeply impressed with Khan's realism and greed for power than with Steerforth's pallid fears. For some reason he was reminded of the cricket match in which he had played against Khan so many years ago when they were schoolboys. On that day Steerforth had felt determined, capable and ready to do battle. He had triumphed over Khan for a time, facing his fastest bowling with assurance and even hooking him for six. But in the end Khan had overcome him, racing round the boundary to grab an improbable catch out of the air. In the end perhaps Khan would always produce some spectacular, even miraculous, *tour de force* to overcome Steerforth and get his way.

During the next few weeks, while Khan and Steerforth were anxiously awaiting the outcome of the meeting with the Prime Minister and while Steerforth became more and more convinced that the politician's opportunism would triumph over the statesman's restraint, Major Tolson had been diligently delving into the records of the Magus project. One day he telephoned Steerforth at his office.

'I have now completed my audit of the stores and supplies of the Magus project,' said Major Tolson. 'It has taken a long time and involved a good deal of effort. I had to get some help from the Treasury to get it done at all. I didn't fancy that, I can tell you. It's a damned sight easier to get those types involved in something than it is to get them out again.'

'The situation is much worse even than I feared,' reported Tolson. 'The Magus spares inventory has been systematically depleted over the past two years. So much has gone that if the original Magus were to become inoperative for any reason, it's highly doubtful if another could be built from existing components. Of course it's hard to tell without a complete engineering test set-up which electronic circuits are which. But the total number of circuits and printed circuit boards is only about a fifth of what it should be. But that's not the whole story. The power consumption for Magus experiments is much greater than it should be. I know a few extra journeys have been made, your own included. But the excess is far more than that. I believe about twenty other Magus trips have been made over and above those we can account for and those we know unofficially about. And on top of that the Swiss authorities have reported a serious shortage of fusion material from the Torus store.'

Despite his customary scepticism, Steerforth was both impressed and alarmed by the extent of the losses.

'Can you prove all this?' he asked.

'Everything is documented and cross-checked. All the figures have been authenticated by the Treasury experts. There's no longer any room for doubt. The Swiss are absolutely stunned. Their security arrangements at the Torus are absolutely watertight. But material has been disappearing from under their noses in Geneva just as it has in Oxford.' A long silence ensued.

'It seems clear to me that someone is deliberately trying to sabotage the Magus project,' said Tolson at last. 'But I can't for the life of me imagine who it could be. You and Mr Khan are the creators of the thing. Why should you want to destroy your own work? Dr Dubendorf's successor, the new Director of the Torus Centre, might have been able to manipulate the security arrangements in Geneva. But how could he have arranged to have stuff stolen from Oxford?' It seemed to Steerforth that Tolson had something more on his mind but was hesitant to discuss it.

'Do you suspect Khan of sabotaging the Magus project?' asked Steerforth. 'As you said yourself, why should he do that? He is one of its originators. Why would he destroy his own work?'

'I have worked in security for a long time,' answered Tolson gloomily. 'Nothing much surprises me any longer.' But Steerforth remained unconvinced. Whoever might be the saboteur he knew it was not Khan.

Steerforth presumed that Khan must have had some similar interviews with Major Tolson in which his (Steerforth's loyalty was also put under inspection. Is Steerforth one of those odd aristocrats who expunge a sense of guilt arising from their privileged position by betraying their country to the Communists? Has he over-indulged the traditional pastimes of the noble – gambling, drinking, womanising? Is his estranged wife draining his wealth away through California-style alimony? Is the upkeep of Bain Brook cripplingly expensive? Would Steerforth's pride take such a convoluted form that he might be willing to preserve his heritage with treacherous gold?

Whatever the substance of the speculations Major Tolson might fabricate about him, Steerforth did not discuss them with Khan. Indeed the disappearance of the inventory items and the fusion material was never really discussed at all between the two. One evening in a restaurant in Oxford just as Abigail, Khan and Steerforth were sitting down to dinner, Steerforth did manage to blurt something out.

'Tolson thinks that someone is trying to sabotage the project. He thinks for some reason that the saboteur might be you or me. I've told him that's impossible. Do you agree?'

'Are you asking, Steerforth, whether I am sabotaging the Magus? Or whether I believe that you are? In either case the answer is no. I know that I am not sabotaging the project and I am as certain as I can be that you are not.' He smiled brilliantly at Steerforth and Abigail, then turned his attention to the wine list. Steerforth was later to discover that what Khan had said was the literal truth. But it was not the literal truth, as Khan perhaps intended to convey, that he knew nothing of the disappearance of the stores.

One of the things that Khan and Steerforth learned from the Magus project was that one could never guess how government was going to communicate a decision to them. They might have guessed that the Prime Minister would call them to Downing Street again to tell them what (if anything) he planned to do about Magus. Or perhaps one of Major Tolson's telephone calls might be the preferred method. Or they might have simply read in the newspaper that the Prime Minister had announced the invention of time travel in the House. What neither could have guessed is what actually happened, and what seemed to typify official response to Magus. Neither Khan nor Steerforth ever heard anything definite at all. The government's response (if the expression is not too active) was never communicated to the inventors of Magus. The truth filtered through a little at a time.

First Khan and Steerforth each received a formal letter from the Torus Centre in Geneva informing them that Magus had been reclassified. It was now no longer an active project, but a stand-by one. There was a procedure for reactivating such a class of projects, should the sponsor government ever decide it wished to do so. For a time Khan and Steerforth were uncertain what this change of status signified.

'Do you think it's just an automatic procedure?' suggested Steerforth. 'Perhaps every project of a certain age is moved to this category, just to stimulate the sponsor government to think carefully about it.' But Khan seemed doubtful.

'I suspect that this letter is the first indication of the British government's decision,' he said. 'I think your view has prevailed, Steerforth. Magus is going to be used only as a last resort to avert nuclear destruction. But I doubt if its very existence is to be revealed to the Russians.'

Suspecting that his view had after all prevailed, Steerforth felt an odd mixture of emotions. Predominantly he felt relief that the frightening risks of standing history on its head would be avoided. Inevitably, however, he felt a sense of anti-climax that Magus was not to be exploited to the full. And he had a totally irrational sense of guilt towards Khan, as if he had somehow robbed his friend of his triumph. This sentiment was plainly absurd, since Steerforth had a right and a duty to express his apprehensions as clearly as he could. But still the feeling lingered. Odd snippets of information passed through Geneva or the Oxford laboratories, chance remarks made by Major Tolson and the mere passage of time without any firm announcement to the contrary all confirmed that Khan was right. Only the most limited use of Magus was being contemplated by the authorities. Any pleasure that Steerforth might have felt at having his view accepted was eclipsed by Khan's obvious disappointment and frustration, and by the piecemeal and almost furtive way in which the decision was made known. On a number of occasions Steerforth caught sight of the Prime Minister on television, spouting away with every sign of confidence on economics, foreign policy or defence.

'You idiot!' thought Steerforth. 'What right have you got to pontificate in this way when you can't even decide what you want to do with Magus, or let us know clearly one way or the other? How can such a ditherer be fit to run the country?'

In the spring of 1973, fifteen years after they had begun work on the Magus project and nine years after the first successful experiment with PEPR and the flywheel, Khan and Steerforth faced the abandonment of their work. From one or two hints that Major Tolson had thrown out it seemed that not everyone in the highest circles was convinced that Magus could be made to work as claimed. The official mind was just too inflexible to be wrapped round a concept as shattering as Magus.

'It's almost as if they had somehow *disinvented* the whole thing,' said Inayat Khan.

At about this time I was assailed with a minor illness of some kind. I was obliged for a week or two to stay in my rooms, and I remember Khan and Steerforth coming to visit me there. They stayed for an hour or so, then walked together round the quadrangle a few times. I remember watching them from my window. I felt a surge of affection as I watched them, now grown men in their late thirties, whom I had known and nurtured since their boyhood. Perhaps on that very day while I watched them stroll around the college they were having their final argument about Magus. I learned later from Steerforth that it took place in the college, though he could not recall precisely the occasion.

'However the decision was reached,' said Steerforth, 'and however churlishly we have been treated, we must accept the position. Perhaps the authorities are right. Magus is too hot to let loose on the world. Perhaps the authorities are the ones who have been sabotaging the project. At any rate their view is not so important. You and I know what we did. We don't need Tolson's approval.' But even as he spoke Steerforth knew his argument was to no avail. Khan would never accept that anyone knew better than he what should be done with Magus.

It was perhaps two months later when I next met Steerforth. I was restored to health and had walked into the newspaper shop in Cornmarket Street to buy a magazine. I saw Steerforth buying a copy of a magazine about popular music, and mildly chaffed him for his unusual taste.

'Look at this, Hawkesworth,' he said, showing me the front cover of the paper. It contained a large photograph of Abigail, and a news story about her. Seemingly she had cancelled a number of concerts which had been arranged for her and had also post-poned 'indefinitely' a series of recording sessions. The magazine was indignant on behalf of her admirers. What was most interest-ing was the reason given for her sudden cancellation of all the arrange-ments made for her: she was reported to be planning 'an extended absence overseas on business with her fiancé.'

'Do you suppose that means Khan?' I asked.

'I don't know,' answered Steerforth. 'I haven't seen Khan for a week or two. But then I didn't really expect to. He's told me nothing about a trip abroad.'

'It might be extremely inconvenient if he is going abroad,' I said. 'He is due to give a talk at the Royal Society next month. I put his name forward. If he cannot fulfill the engagement, I ought to let them know at once.'

At that time, Steerforth told me nothing of the Magus project. He was thus relieved to learn that I had a reason for trying to find out whether Khan was planning a protracted absence.

Together we went out to Khan's apartment in north Oxford. There was no sign of him. Inside the door we glimpsed a pile of post gathering dust. A few discreet enquiries soon gained us the name and address of the company that owned the apartment. They were cagey at first, obviously reasoning that if we were friends of Khan as we claimed then he would have left us his new address. At the laboratory the same picture emerged. No one knew where Khan was. Eventually by dint of persuasion and (who knows) perhaps a little bribery, Steerforth got hold of a key to Khan's apartment. Within a week of his disappearance we went to the place a second time, and this time let ourselves in. The furniture was still in place: wherever Khan had gone, he had no need of that. Most of the books were gone. A few papers still were to be found in the drawers of Khan's old desk.

'Shall we look through the post?' suggested Steerforth. Soon the two of us were sat at Khan's dining table with a pile of envelopes before us. A few of the letters were addressed to Abigail. Those we opened last. There was little of any significance in either her mail or Khan's. There was a letter from the company that owned the flat, confirming that Khan had terminated his tenancy and paid what he owed. Khan appeared to have closed down his bank savings and current accounts and drawn out the balance in cash. Khan's tailor had written to remind him that it was a year since he last ordered a suit. His dentist had issued a similar notice with regard to his teeth. At whatever cost to his appearance or his oral health, Khan would never acknowledge either warning. It was clear that his departure had been neither sudden nor precipitate. He had carefully and secretly planned his disappearance, together with Abigail.

I cancelled Khan's lecture, with suitable apologies to the Royal Society. For a while Steerforth was too busy with the affairs of his publishing company to give much more attention to the question of Khan's departure. When he had time to think about it, he often invented some plausible and harmless explanation. Perhaps after thirteen years of close friendship Khan and Abigail had finally decided to marry and had gone off on their own to do so. Perhaps they had gone to Africa so that Khan might meet her relations on the slopes of Mount Abuya. There were a thousand possible explanations, all of which might be wholly innocent. Yet the fear that haunted Steerforth would not entirely go away, the fear that Inayat Khan's disappearance had somehow some link with what Major Tolson regarded as an attempt to sabotage the Magus.

The tendency for the authorities quietly to bury Magus, to act as if it had never been invented and to avoid any specific decision about it, naturally gathered momentum with the departure of Khan from the scene. Somehow the authorities couldn't quite believe that Khan would have turned his back on something as historic as Magus – unless of course the whole thing was a bit of a hoax.

'There was, however, one fact which I never drew to the attention of the authorities,' confessed Steerforth to me in the privacy of my college rooms. 'And that was what I discovered when I went through the project files at the Oxford laboratory. I don't know what I expected to find. I didn't even look at the files for several months after Khan had disappeared. I felt no sense of urgency about them. I was just hoping for some clue to Khan's whereabouts.' He sat for a while in silence, a glass of sherry in his hand and a pipe in his mouth.

'Even when I discovered the truth,' he went on, 'it came as no great revelation to me. I felt just a dull, aching certainty. It was almost as if I had known in my heart what Khan was doing, but had just refused to face the fact. Most of the ancillary files were still intact as far as I could tell. But there were three main files containing the basic records of the Magus project. One was on the theoretical side, one on the physics and one on the electronic design. Together these three files amounted to the blueprint for Magus. All three were empty. It was at once obvious to me that with the one and only Magus in the world under the control of a government that didn't believe it worked, with many of the spare parts and the materials for the project now missing and – the final blow – the design files now unaccountably removed from the safe, the Magus project was to all intents and purposes dead. It did not take long to work out who had taken the files and who, therefore, had been guilty of the theft of the spares. Tolson had mistaken the purpose of the theft. Khan had not sabotaged Magus. He had stolen it. Somewhere Khan had built a new Magus machine and disappeared with it.'

Later as darkness crept across the quadrangle I left the room unlighted. We sat gazing out at the Oxford sky. 'You couldn't really blame him. Not really. Magus was his life's work. The officials wanted to stop it. I was cautious . . . too cautious. Khan couldn't contemplate Magus being suppressed, least of all for such unintelligent reasons. He was the man of sanity and vision, the one by whose principles the republic must be ruled. Imagine what Sokrates would have thought of the Magus! Khan had to have the chance to put Magus to work, even if that attempt imperilled the future of the universe.'

How long had Khan planned to steal the time-machine? Did he make an unauthorised trip into the future to see what the Prime Minister's decision would be? There was no way of knowing. While Khan and Abigail were in the Lake District his plans must have been in place, many of the necessary components already spirited away. Abigail must have known already of their impending departure.

'What a fool I'd been,' said Steerforth, suddenly bitter. 'I had known Inayat Khan for over twenty-five years. It just never occurred to me that he would deceive me. Perhaps it was the influence of Abigail. I never wholly trusted her. At any rate there it was: Khan had gone and taken Magus with him. I had to decide what to do.'

Whatever plans Inayat Khan might have made for the private exploitation of the Magus machine, life had to continue in its accustomed way for Steerforth and for me. Steerforth had his publishing business to run, Bain Brook to maintain (in the face of soaring costs and increasingly detailed interference by the local authority) and periodic trips to make to the United States to visit his ex-wife and his children. The daily and weekly round of activities often so absorbed him that he would go whole months without a thought of Khan and the Magus. But then a long rail journey, or a trip by car with Mr Steele at the wheel, would afford him leisure to reflect on the power of Magus and its potential menace to the continuity of our universe. And by the time he arrived at his destination Steerforth would have worked himself again into an agony of apprehension and frustration: surely he alone, as co-inventor of the space-time device, might be expected to make some effort to combat whatever plans Khan might make. But how? Without a clue as to where (or when) Khan had planned to make his base in space and time, Steerforth had nowhere to begin his own campaign. The whole of space and time were at Khan's disposal: the task of tracking him down made the proverbial needle in the haystack seem ridiculously easy to find. At least there was only one haystack, and it existed in the commonsensical world of the here-and-now. Khan and Abigail might still be in the twentieth century, possibly settled in her native Ethiopia or his native Pakistan. But they could as easily be living among the swamps and jungles of the primeval world – or living quietly among the colonists of Mars. As far as Steerforth could see, Khan would have no special reason to favour one age or region over any other. Once the Magus was built, he would have access to modern or indeed future technology whenever and wherever he needed it.

Steerforth's inner agony was made more intense because he could not share it. More than once in the years that followed Khan's disappearance he seriously considered unfolding his story to someone. Major Tolson (until one day Steerforth spotted his obituary in *The Times*), Dr Dubendorf and I were all considered. Yet it was not until his visit to my college rooms in 1980 that he communicated all his fears to any other human being: and even then I fear that an aged professor of English literature was but a frail and faltering ally to him in his great task. Some mornings he awoke with a great dread upon him. Would this be the day the known universe would in one moment flicker out of existence, when ten thousand years of recorded history would suddenly cease to be valid? And if so, would there be a single searing moment when all that is was fused with what might have been? Not even Steerforth's personality, as solid and rocklike as it was, could endure unchanged the years of solitary misery and fear. He carried out his work in a cold and mechanistic fashion. To his friends he became cooler and less amenable. His attendances at the House of Lords became rarer. He absented himself increasingly from state and royal occasions to which the antiquity of his title would readily admit him. By nature an active and participative man, he withdrew more and more into his private world. He declined an invitation to act as assistant manager of an England overseas cricket tour: he could not bear to think of his inward anxieties bringing unexplained despondency to a team of young and eager sportsmen. Pacing alone about the halls and passages of Bain Brook (for his mother had not long survived his father), he sometimes considered abandoning his work at the publishing house, perhaps even selling the famous old Steerforth imprimatur to an American house, to concentrate all his powers and energies on the battle. But what could he achieve? And where might he begin? By now he had come to think of Khan only with bitterness and resentment.

In his London flat he sat one evening for an hour at a time holding in his hand the photograph of Khan and himself taken in the nightclub in St Julien on the day they projected a mouse into the future. From time to time he reread the curious inscription in Khan's handwriting: 'from Nehemiah Higginbottom'. Was this a clue? He had no way of knowing. Once in the Concorde passengers' lounge at New York airport he felt his heart race and then almost stop at the sight of a tall and elegant black woman with a slender figure, a strikingly beautiful face and long hair plaited into tails. A moment later she was swallowed up in the crowds of passengers and friends. *Could* it have been Abigail? Certainly it looked like her. But by the late 1970s the Rastafarian dreadlocks she alone had worn fifteen years earlier had become commonplace. And tall, beautiful black women are not exactly rare in the public places of America. Everywhere he heard the curious, stumbling lilt of the reggae music she had played and sung: if she were still performing she might have been a millionairess by now. The Rasta cult too had spread throughout the Caribbean and black America. As an Ethiopian she might herself have claimed a key role in the unfolding of that mystical lore, perhaps only second to the Emperor-God himself. The mantle that had fallen upon the shoulders of the singer-poet of Trenchtown, Bob Marley, might have hung instead from her spare and elegant frame. More than once, sitting alone in his flat, mocked by the old photographs of cricket teams hung on his walls, Steerforth bowed his head and wept.

In 1980, prompted as much by loneliness and despair as by any expectation of actual assistance, he sought me out in my Oxford rooms and told me his sad and magical story in the terms I have recounted. Despite all my frailties I really believe that it helped him greatly to have a confidant. And soon, for reasons that neither of us could then foresee, he was to have another partner in his great venture – one of unbounded youthful zest and energy, of unlimited sympathy and affection and (even more than these) with the knowledge painstakingly gained by years of careful study to unlock the mystery of Khan's plans. For deeply buried in the history of Khan's childhood and youth, so intimately shared with Steerforth, lay all the clues and hints that would lead us over centuries of time and continents of space to confront Khan in his base. The flames of two candles, the old house in the Lake District, the unlettered servant girl who nevertheless spoke fluently in Latin, Greek and Hebrew, the alias of Nehemiah Higginbottom . . . all were pointers carefully or casually planted by Khan in the texture of his thirty-year friendship with Steerforth. I doubt if they were truly accidental. Khan (as I now perceive) perhaps relished the challenge represented by Steerforth's resistance to his planned empire of time. This man of sanity and vision (as he styled himself) needed a worthy adversary simply to prove his superiority. Yet the challenge necessary to the accomplishment of his dream was not to be too easily taken up: unless his adversary could detect and interpret the clues, he was not worthy to take up Khan's challenge. This alone, I believe, explains how deeply buried the clues lay, like a few fragments of pottery in a desert of sand and stones that tell to a knowledgeable eye the whole story of a civilisation. What Steerforth and I might all too easily have overlooked, the falcon's eyes of Edwina May McGrath would light upon and fix forever as the true pointers to Khan's imperial strategy.

For several years before he came to see me in my Oxford rooms Steerforth had been scanning the press for any reports of news or incidents that might lead him to Khan. What was he looking for? In truth he could not accurately say, but perhaps some apparently inexplicable event might be reported, a mystery to which Magus alone might provide an explanation. When such a clue arrived at length from America, it served only to confirm suspicions already well formed in Steerforth's mind.

Steerforth was not to know, but the saga of Magus was still unfolding three thousand miles away. The small town of Ogunquit, Maine, was beginning in the spring of 1981 to prepare itself for the annual invasion of summer tourists. The town boasts a line of attractive beaches, excellent seafood (clams and lobsters are the specialities) – though the visitor will find the ocean water too cool for swimming. Most of the tourists who pass through Ogunquit stay for a few days en route for the more northerly resorts of Bar Harbor and the Acadia National Park. But there were two visitors that year who had arrived early and stayed for several months in the town, a tall and elegant black lady with high cheekbones and dreadlocked hair and an Asian gentleman of distinguished appearance. They had booked a chalet beside the sea for several weeks, an old-fashioned New England place with a wood-burning stove in the lounge. In the first part of their visit the stove was a very necessary comfort, for until the spring arrives Ogunquit is bitterly cold. The Asian gentleman received a great deal of mail, which he took each day to the library in the town centre. He and the black lady were registered at the chalet as Mr and Mrs S. T. Comberbache, though the cleaner noticed that Mrs Comberbache wore no wedding ring. Most weeks Mr Comberbache hired a car and drove himself out of town towards the north, to some unidentified destination. It was believed that he had some business interest somewhere up near Bar Harbor. A good deal of his mail came from there. While he was away Mrs Comberbache kept herself very much to herself, walking on the beach in good weather and staying in her room in bad. She owned a kind of zither and was sometimes to be heard playing and crooning gently to herself during the husband's absences. Every week Mr Comberbache paid his bill for the chalet rental in new dollar bills. He never used credit cards or traveller's cheques.

The local police in Ogunquit Maine can tell you that as spring approaches it brings with it not only the tourists from New Jersey and New York State but also a regiment of less welcome guests. The living in Maine in good weather is as easy as it is hard in bad and thus attracts from the less congenial areas further south a fair number of travelling folk – or, as the local police would call them, panhandlers and bums. They hang around the towns cadging drinks or cigarettes from the tourists, spinning their complex yarns of injustice and ill-fortune to melt the hearts of the chilliest New Yorker, sleeping on the beach until they are moved on. One of the panhandlers who regularly passed through Ogunquit was Jake Harper, a man of some sixty years and of a distinctly disreputable appearance. His eyes lit up with interest when he saw the Asian gentleman and his black lady in a café in downtown Ogunquit. They were obviously tourists.

'Hey mister,' he said, 'can you spare a couple of dollars for a poor Yankee?' He felt slightly ill at ease as the financial transaction was completed, one dollar only being forthcoming. The black lady fastened her sombre gaze upon him as he waited for the man to get out his money-clip. Jake had the uneasy sensation, under the gaze of the beautiful black woman, that he understood what it was like to be a bug under the microscope. He still felt her black eyes boring into him as he pocketed the dollar and headed for the door of the café.

That was the last Jake saw of the Asian and his wife, until a remarkable evening a few weeks later when he had left Ogunquit and reached Bar Harbor on Mount Desert Island. From patient investigation it has been possible to reconstruct most of what happened. Like most travelling people Old Jake believed himself to be a basically honest man, and it was certainly true that he was asked to move on by the police far more often than he was questioned or arrested. But he held the view that a lot of ordinary folk had a lot more money than they rightly knew what to do with, and that they often became criminally careless with their unwanted wealth.

So when a few weeks after his encounter with Khan and Abigail he noticed that a young tourist with a pretty wife and two small children had wandered off and left his money-clip barely covered over with a towel, Jake reckoned that here for certain was a man with so much money he had no need to take proper care of it. As he trudged along the beach he paused only for a moment as if to tie the lace of his old sneakers, and the money-clip was in his pocket. The bushes above the beach turned out luckily for Jake to contain no hidden policemen with binoculars. The young man was still down at the water's edge with his adorable family. It would be another twenty minutes before he discovered his loss. In the shade of the bushes Jake discovered that his haul amounted to nearly two hundred dollars. He stuffed the money into his pockets and buried the money-clip in the dry sand. Unless the young man knew the serial numbers of his notes, Jake was in the clear. He left the beach and took a bus up into the National Park area, where he could hide out in the forest for a week or more. By then he hoped the young man would have forgotten all about his two hundred dollars and the local police all about Old Jake. Near the bus stop he converted some of his new wealth into those few consumables he would need to stay alive and well in the forest. The food items were optional, but the carton of cigarettes and the three bottles of best bourbon whiskey were essentials.

West from Bar Harbor the bus headed towards the shore of Eagle Lake. The bus was crowded with happy, sunburned tourists. Old Jake crouched among them with his arms wrapped round his provisions. He was dying to take a drink from one of his bottles, but the healthy and decent people thronging so close round him stopped him doing so. Near the lake, the bus turned on to one of the Acadia Park roads heading south towards Seal and Northeast Harbors. Near Bubble Pond, between the trees that fringe Eagle Lake and the first slopes of Mount Cadillac, Jake got down from the bus. Here on the slopes of Cadillac, Champlain and Penobscot Mountains he would hide out for as long as the two hundred bucks lasted. Then he might head back to the mainland and on inland towards New Hampshire and Vermont, to find his way in the fall back to New York State and thence by winter to Massachusetts and his home town.

Up into the foothills of Mount Cadillac Old Jake climbed. His way led between huge conifers, maple, oak and birch trees. To a more practised eye then Jake's, the trail would have yielded evidence of the deer, beaver and raccoon who were to be his neighbours for the next few days. Halfway to the summit of the mountain he found a sheltered spot with a cover of ferns and a bed of maple leaves. He lay himself down, took a swig of whiskey and lit a cigarette. He felt as if his two hundred dollars might last him till the end of time. He settled down to drink and to sleep. By the time the stars rushed out into the black night of Acadia National Park, he was fast asleep. Every once in a while that chilly night, Old Jake would wake and stir himself. But he never found any problem in his sleepy little hollow on the mountainside that a swift pull at his bottle would not solve.

For two more nights he stayed where he was. Then he moved higher up the slope. He thought he had heard dogs barking down the hillside somewhere. Probably they belonged to some tourists. But he preferred to play it safe. Two or three hundred feet below the peak of the mountains he found another spot to rest. Here he was on the highest ground for miles around, and when he came out of his little shelter he could see clean across the valley to Pemetic Mountain in the south and up to Dorr Mountain in the north. But it was right beside him on Mount Cadillac that he found the most unusual thing. Near the peak of the mountain it seemed that some kind of construction project had recently been going on. A rough road had been hacked out of the mountainside, road which Old Jake had never seen before. And at the mountainpeak itself it seemed that tunnels had been drilled into the mountain at regular intervals around its circumference. It was just as if someone had decided to carry out a big mining operation on the top of Mount Cadillac.

Once or twice Old Jake thought he heard people moving about on the paths near the top of Mount Cadillac. Once he woke with a start, and saw a large packing case – nearly as high as a man – on the path above him. He could have sworn that no truck had passed by in the night. But how else could it have got there? He slept again and when he woke the packing case had disappeared. And then he *did* see someone – and it was someone he had seen before. It was the Asian man he had seen in the café in Ogunquit, who had been with the black lady whose burning gaze had so disturbed Old Jake. The man was quite tall, well built and with very dark, almost blue-black, hair. He was wearing a denim suit and he seemed for a moment to have emerged from one of the tunnels drilled into the rock. Was he actually living inside the mountain? After half an hour or so Jake saw that the man did in fact take a last look round at the rocks and ferns, then turn and make his way down one of the tunnels into the heart of the mountain. Jake scratched his head. He could not imagine why anyone would want to live inside a mountain. He took a drink and fell back into unconsciousness.

The police record of Jake's case, which Steerforth later examined, showed that the old man ran and staggered the five miles back to Bar Harbor, arriving at the police station at two thirty in the morning. He had begged to be allowed to spend the night in the cells. He was willing to confess to the theft of two hundred dollars from a tourist in Ogunquit. He seemed to be in a state of near hysteria. When questioned all he could offer as an explanation was that someone had 'blowed the top off Mount Cadillac'.

At the same time the defence computers of the USA registered an unusual charge of energy somewhere in the area of the Maine coastline. It was momentary and unrepeated. It could have been a meteorite impact – or even a computer error. It was classified as an unresolved incident.

When Jake dried out enough to give a halfway coherent account of his story, he claimed that he had woken suddenly because the ground he was lying on began to tremble. Then, as he later told Augustus Steerforth, the whole top of the mountain seemed to melt into light.

'Just for a moment I seemed to see the rock melt into a new shape. It was like a flat block or slab with a dome on the top.' Steerforth sketched out a few designs for Jake to approve or reject. They ended up with a shape not unlike that of St Paul's Cathedral or the Taj Mahal, though somewhat more horizontally extended. The new figure of the rock was outlined for no more than a moment or two, according to Jake. Then it was gone. The strange Asian man with his tunnels and his packing cases had 'blowed the top off Mount Cadillac'.

The local police had indeed heard of a construction project going on at the mountain for the previous year or more. As far as they knew, all the local building regulations had been observed. There was no suggestion that the project had been linked with any criminal activities. There had been no reason for them to investigate the movement of materials and labourers in and out of the area. When they went to investigate Jake's story they found that it was all too literally true. The top of the mountain had been neatly and cleanly lopped off like the top of an egg. The rock surface where the mountain peak had been removed was as smooth as a mirror. Several hundred or even thousand tons of rock had been removed. No one would ever know what technology, stolen from future centuries, Khan had used to carve his Magus machine out of the mountain peak.

Later on, an English Lord of some kind arrived and took a great interest in Old Jake and his story. He examined the police records and seemed to find nothing surprising. He went to Cadillac and examined the truncated mountain top and its glazed surface. At last he tracked Old Jake down in a bar in Boston and heard his full story. Although he told none of the Americans the truth, Steerforth knew that Jake had witnessed the departure of Khan's Magus machine for a remote destination in space and time. At length Steerforth closed his file and turned to go.

'Oh just one more thing sir,' said Jake. 'Can you spare ten dollars for a poor Yankee?' To his surprise, he got the full ten. He wished he had asked for twenty.

✎ CHAPTER 6 ✎

Some Infinitely Superior Being

Shortly after his return from the Acadia National Park Steerforth began consciously to make plans for the future, and to think seriously about some form of resistance to Inayat Khan. For the story of the exploding mountain, which had led him to Old Jake and the launching point of Khan's Magus, he was indebted to a combination of circumstances. By sheer chance, one of Edwina May McGrath's cousins, who came from the same town on the island of Martha's Vineyard, had taken a job as a guide in the Acadia Park and sent a local newspaper cutting about the incident.

Less fortuitously, a further search of Inayat Khan's mail (including some letters which had arrived since his departure) yielded evidence of some kind of building project in Maine, for which he had paid out very considerable sums of money over the past two years. The correspondence was conducted under the cover of a pseudonym, that of Silas Tomkyn Comberbache, a name that had a curiously familiar ring to it. We established that Khan and Comberbache were one and the same person by examining the latter's signature on legal and accounting documents. The writing was clearly Khan's.

How had he obtained the money? Several million dollars had been spent on building materials and works, in addition to all the valuable equipment and components missing from the Magus stores. Obviously the unauthorized use of the Magus machine in Geneva would permit Khan to enter and leave unseen the vaults of any bank or gem store in the world. And as a gambler Khan, with a copy of tomorrow's newspaper to help him, would be a bookmaker's nightmare. So access to funds was no problem.

The clues in the letters had already half-disposed Steerforth to think that Khan's point of departure might lie in North America, and perhaps in the state of Maine. The press story (half-dramatic, half-incredulous) about the decapitation of the mountain instantly intrigued him. He left for Boston the day after he saw the press clipping and returned a week later certain that he knew whence Khan had gone. But whither was another matter, and one about which all of us were still in the dark.

One thing that seemed obvious from Old Jake's description of the Magus departure and from the surface of the mountain was that Khan's new machine was much more powerful than the old machine at Geneva. A machine literally carved from the top of a mountain could be the equivalent of a time-travelling fortress, with space for dozens of travellers and their equipment. It was difficult to conjecture what or whom Khan might have taken with him. We were both tolerably certain, Steerforth and I, that wherever and whenever Khan might set up his base, Abigail would be there at his side. Indeed, Steerforth was half convinced that Abigail was a sort of evil genius to Khan, urging him on to more and more grandiose plans. I was not so sure. There had always been a touch of excessive ambition about Khan, as the incident in the cricket match had shown. I was not sure that Abigail had led Khan. More likely she only confirmed him in his path.

'It seems clear to me,' said Steerforth, 'that if Khan has fled into the past then our best hope of finding him is by finding in the history of the world some kind of anomaly which his presence alone might explain.'

'Something like a prehistoric helicopter?' I ventured.

'Exactly,' answered Steerforth. 'Of course if on the other hand he has made his base in the future, then I have no idea how we could track him down.' For some weeks Steerforth immersed himself in a great deal of the rather cranky literature which concerns itself with very advanced technology cropping up in the ancient world. He found nothing, as far as I know, which excited him in the slightest.

For a few weeks also in that wet and sunless summer I had my own problems to occupy me, and I must admit that they were such as to drive Khan and Magus wholly out of my thoughts for a time. I was working as hard as ever, despite having attained an age at which most men have been retired for a decade or more. I felt that my teaching capability and my critical faculties were as sharp as ever, though I no longer felt the enthusiasm to undertake new work for publication or to extend my horizon to include new authors. With Chaucer, Shakespeare and Milton I had a lifetime's familiarity. Sometimes they seemed to me to be more real than the colleagues with whom I worked or the students whose work I supervised. But though my mental powers were, in my own opinion, quite adequate to deal with the everyday demands of my college work, I became conscious that summer of a slow but steady decline in my physical condition. Let me not mislead the reader: I was not suddenly or dramatically struck down. But one or two people commented on my loss of appetite. My body weight declined by a few pounds. For many years I had been accustomed to take a nap after lunch. Now I began to find that unless I set my alarm clock I would sleep on into the afternoon. One day I was in the Parks watching the university cricket team giving a rather inadequate account of itself. One minute I was making some doubtless ill-advised comment on the fielding of the team. The next I was lying on the grass with a lady's handbag propping up my head and someone's blanket covering my limbs. An ambulance was summoned and I was taken to hospital. In the ambulance I was conscious for the first time of a considerable degree of pain. Later that evening Edwina May McGrath came to visit me in the hospital. Steerforth, summoned with exaggerated urgency from London, arrived part way through the visiting hour. They left together, the English peer and the American scholar. The next day they took me into the operating theatre and carried out what was described as an 'exploratory operation'. That is to say they opened me up, took a look and closed me up again. I was told that I would be supplied with some tablets to dull the senses a little and presently turned loose on the university once more. Before I left the hospital I had a discussion with the chief surgeon, during which I am pleased to say he treated me with the candour due to a mature person. After a week or two of further recuperation I was able to resume my normal life in most of its details. It was not in any case a particularly energetic life, involving for the most part only limited movement around the college and a periodic visit to the town. I took the tablets the doctor had given me and tried to forget about my internal condition.

One of the first social events I attended after the convalescence was a small gathering organised in my honour by my college friends and among whom the college chaplain was the prime mover. It was restricted to the college teaching staff and one or two friends such as Steerforth and Dr McGrath. As the weather was not too bad, the event was held in the open air. As I made my way to the rendezvous, nothing was further from my mind than the possibility that we might track down Inayat Khan as a result of a chance remark at this drinks party. The sky was blue, with fleecy white clouds overhead but darker and more menacing prospects becoming evident in the west. The total of guests for this minor celebration was between a dozen and twenty people, as I recall. One of the last to arrive was Steerforth himself, driven down from London for the day. I watched him make his way across the turf with his nimble, rather springy walk, to where I stood under a tree with Edwina May McGrath. The party proceeded with all due conviviality until the chaplain expressed fears about the weather. As if on cue a distant mutter of thunder was heard from the direction of the darkening clouds: it began to look as if a storm might be girding its loins over Port Meadow in preparation for an invasion of the city.

'At least we have had a little sunshine for your return to health, Hawkesworth,' said the chaplain, 'but I fear it would be imprudent to presume further. Shall we retire to the Senior Common Room while we still have time for an orderly retreat?' His suggestion was acceptable to all.

'Where in the United States is your home, Dr McGrath?' asked Steerforth as we were transporting our supplies and ourselves indoors.

'I was born in a small town in Massachusetts called Oak Bluffs. Have you ever heard of it?' Steerforth admitted his ignorance.

'I'm not surprised,' said Dr McGrath cheerfully enough. 'Most people even in the United States haven't heard of it either. It's on the island of Martha's Vineyard, and most people are familiar only with the more notorious parts of the island such as Chappaquiddick.' We were soon settled in the Senior Common Room, in time to watch (to the infinite gratification of the chaplain) a storm of rain burst over the chapel and the gardens. Steerforth and Dr McGrath continued to discuss the United States and its similarities to and differences from Great Britain, while I became involved in some desultory chat about college affairs. At length I managed to extricate myself from these academic musings, and returned to Steerforth and Dr McGrath just in time to hear him ask about the progress of her thesis.

'It's taken a long time to get the structure right,' she said. 'But at last I think I've got that done. Now I'm faced with a new problem.'

'Which is. . . ?'

'The problem of determining a truly contemporary view of the poetry. As you know the theme of the paper is the amazing flowering of English romantic verse around the end of the eighteenth century and the beginning of the nineteenth. But we now *know* what we think of Byron, of Coleridge, of Keats, of Shelley, of Wordsworth. What was it like to be an ordinary educated person in 1820? Did they *know* they were among giants? It's hard to peel back the layers of subsequent commentary and get at the contemporary reaction.' Edwina May McGrath was now launched into the subject that fascinated her most. Her spectacles slipped unnoticed to the end of her nose, her eyes sparkled and her rather small hands fluttered in excitement as she spoke. In all my life I never saw a woman whose lips moved more prettily when she spoke than Dr McGrath. Steerforth's eyes shone with an almost equal lustre and never for a moment left her face.

'I say,' said the chaplain, pointing out of the window of the Senior Common Room. 'Just look at that!'

Just over against the chapel, arched between heaven and earth like an extravagant monument in the sunshine and the rain, was a truly magnificent rainbow. It was mentioned in the Oxford newspaper the next day: I doubt if many people have seen a finer rainbow than the one we saw then. It seemed unbelievable that it should lack material substance.

'"The sun paints rainbows on vast waves,"' quoted Edwina May McGrath, speaking more to herself than to us. As the beauty of the rainbow began to fade a little, the large group by the big window broke up. Steerforth, Edwina May and I were standing alone.

'"*Paints* rainbows,"' repeated Steerforth.

'Yes, it's nice, isn't it? Do you know who wrote it?' asked Dr McGrath, somewhat teasing him.

'It has the ring of Priestley,' guessed Steerforth. 'Is it from *The History and Present State of Discoveries relating to Vision, Light and Colours*? The book of Priestley's that we usually call *The Opticks*?'

'That is an extraordinarily good guess, Lord Steerforth,' said Dr Edwina May McGrath. 'At least I imagine it's a guess, since it is in fact wrong. Actually the quote is from Father Bourzes: the *Letters of a Missionary Jesuit* is the source and Coleridge quotes it in his notes. But Priestley's *Opticks* was an excellent shot in the dark. Are you familiar with it?'

'A little. I have a friend – or perhaps had a friend – who got interested in Priestley and the *Opticks* many years ago when we were at school together. Professor Hawkesworth here was our housemaster at the time. My friend and I tried to repeat one or two of Priestley's experiments with light. One of them misfired a little and frightened the life out of poor Hawkesworth.'

'Which one?' asked Dr McGrath with a smile at me. Steerforth explained how he and Khan had found in Priestley the assertion that the flames of two candles held together gave a stronger light than that of the two held apart, how they had tried to repeat Priestley's experiment to test the assertion, and how their silly housemaster seeing them from the terrace had felt obliged to investigate the experiment, even to deliver a warning against the fire hazards inherent in such a project. During this explanation, which was accompanied by a good deal of laughter on Steerforth's part (enough indeed for both of us) Dr McGrath listened with good humour but some impatience.

'That's nice,' she said at last. 'But,' with some finality, 'that's not from Priestley either.' Steerforth's face at that moment was a vivid illustration of his conflicting emotions. Faced with the certitude in Edwina May McGrath's voice, he hesitated to challenge her assertion. Yet I knew very well that he and Khan had looked up the passage in Priestley all those years ago, and he was not a man to cry content to something he did not believe to be true. At last it was Dr McGrath who broke the deadlock.

'You seem unconvinced,' she said.

'I have the clearest possible recollection of having verified the reference to Priestley. That's all.' The effect of this comment on Dr McGrath, mild though its implicit challenge might be, was marked. Her eyes lit up behind her spectacles, her mouth tightened, and she took up a leather shopping bag that she had deposited on a table when we came in from the garden. Her manner was playful, but at the same time she was clearly convinced that she was right and Steerforth wrong, and she was utterly determined to make her point. If anyone had any doubts about the single-mindedness that had led her, at such a young age, to a rather senior position in the academic world, their doubts were about to be resolved.

From her leather bag she extracted a rather unusual-looking object. It was a sort of primitive book, fashioned by fastening together with string some hundred photocopied pages. The dark text of the original manuscript was heavily annotated with red, blue and green ink notes all in the hand of Edwina May McGrath.

'I happen to be working on this right now,' said Dr McGrath, setting down the volume on the table and turning the pages.

'What is it?' said Steerforth, a little testily I thought.

'I'll tell you in a minute,' said Dr McGrath. 'First listen to this.' She held the book firmly down on the table and began to read aloud:

'The flames of two Candles joined give a much stronger Light than both of them separate – evid. by a person holding the two Candles near his Face, first separate, and then joined in one.'

'Wouldn't you say that was it?' she asked, her nose giving a little triumphant twitch.

'It seems to be,' confessed Steerforth, decently enough. 'But what is that source?'

'Can you guess, Professor Hawkesworth?' she asked mischievously, pushing the seemingly disordered heap of papers across to me. I turned the pages of the homemade book. Since all the pages had been copied on to modern paper it was not possible to judge the quality of the original medium. The somewhat grainy quality of some entries suggested that they were made in pencil. Quite a few were in Latin or Greek, though none I noticed were in any modern foreign language. The script was spidery but fluent, and somehow suggested the early nineteenth century. As I turned the pages at random, one or two entries caught my eye.

'Matted hair – deemed Witch-locks,' reminded me for some reason of Abigail and her dreadlocks. But I still could not guess who was the author. Then I spotted an entry that gave me a clue.

'People starved into War – over an enlisting place in Bristol a quarter of Lamb and piece of Beef hung up –'

'That was the method of recruitment used in the late 1790s to find soldiers to fight France,' I said. 'The author was anti-war, presumably young, living at the time in Bristol or its surrounds.'

'Exactly,' said Edwina May McGrath.

'Perhaps he himself had signed up as a soldier in a mood of despair when life at Cambridge University got too expensive and too complicated for him?' I ventured. 'But did he then prove to be England's worst cavalryman, and decide after all to return to Cambridge?'

'Exactly,' said Edwina May McGrath.

'Samuel Taylor Coleridge,' said Steerforth.

'Exactly,' said Edwina May McGrath.

'So Coleridge is the source of the assertion about the flames of two candles?' asked Steerforth.

'It seems so,' answered Dr McGrath.

'But what if he is not the prime source? I'm quite certain that Khan and I looked up the reference in Priestley's *Opticks*.'

'Is there a copy of the *Opticks* in the college library?' asked Dr McGrath. No one knew, but it seemed worth a try. By now the party was beginning to break up. I thanked the chaplain for his kindness in arranging the little celebration, Dr McGrath stuffed her pages of Coleridge back into her shopping bag, and the three of us set off to acquire the key to the library from a distinctly suspicious porter.

We clattered up the steps and opened the library door. Myself I rarely enter the college library, since I find its atmosphere dull, stuffy and oppressive. For all my time at Oxford I have preferred to work in my rooms, or in the Radcliffe Camera or the Ashmolean. It took some time, therefore, for me to determine from the index cards that there was indeed a copy of the *Opticks* on the shelf. And as I held the card in my hand it was Dr McGrath herself who pointed to the publication date.

'The *Opticks* came out in 1772,' she remarked, 'while that entry in Coleridge's notebook was probably made in 1795. So it's at least possible that Coleridge had read Priestley and got the theory about the two candles from him.' If Steerforth was tempted to gloat he resisted the impulse. Presently we had the book out on a table, a ponderous old quarto volume so thick with dust that you might think Samuel Taylor Coleridge himself had been the last to look at it – if this were Cambridge.

'I have a feeling that the reference is towards the back of the book,' said Steerforth, 'though after all these years it's impossible to be certain.' So there we were for half an hour or more, an aged professor, a peer of the realm and a brilliant young American scholar hunting for a needle in an eight-hundred-page haystack. In all truth we had no right to find it and might easily have been forgiven for abandoning the hunt. But suddenly, when we had reached the very last page of the huge book, Edwina May's finger darted forward like a striking snake.

'There it is!' she cried, in a voice that seemed shockingly loud in the quiet of the library.

'Dr Franklin shewed me,' we read, 'that the flames of two candles joined together give a much stronger light than both of them separate; as is made very evident by a person holding the two candles near his face first separate, and then joined in one.'

'So it was Benjamin Franklin who demonstrated the trick to Priestley,' exclaimed Dr McGrath. She might in fact have known this, for I later discovered that the copy of the *Opticks* in the Harvard College Library, where she had studied for her doctorate, was presented to the library by Dr Franklin himself. But no one can know everything that he or she might.

We sat down at the table and looked at each other. What did we know? Khan had got the story of the flames of two candles from Priestley. So apparently had Coleridge – unless he too had it directly or indirectly from Benjamin Franklin, with whom it appeared to originate. Our minds all seemed to be working in the same direction for Steerforth suddenly asked if there was any other evidence that Coleridge had read the *Opticks*. Neither Dr McGrath nor I could help. We sat for a moment longer in silence. Idly I turned the pages of the great old book. Steerforth was about to speak when I suddenly uttered a screech even louder than Dr McGrath's, and pointed to a passage that seemed to jump off the printed page.

It spoke of fishes which 'in swimming, left so luminous a track behind them, that both their size and species might be distinguished by it'.

'That is pure Coleridge!' I exclaimed, but with her special knowledge of the poet Dr McGrath had the exact parallel to hand. Softly and excitedly she murmured:

> 'Beyond the shadow of the ship,
> I watched the water snakes:
> They moved in tracks of shining white,
> And when they reared, the elfish light
> Fell off in hoary flakes.'

'Well,' I said, 'we seem to have established that Coleridge knew Priestley's book and used it as a source. And that means that Dr McGrath has done us the service of identifying the original version of the flames of two candles.' We returned the book to its shelf, wondering how much dust it would gather before it was consulted again. We walked down the steps more slowly than we had mounted them, still radiant with the thrill that even a minor piece of successful academic sleuthing brings in its wake. As we walked through the quadrangle to return the key to the porter's lodge, I was struck by another curious recollection.

'It's a remarkable illustration of the way the unconscious mind works,' I said. 'Steerforth, do you recall the night that I saw you and Khan conducting the experiment with the flames of two candles? Well that night I dreamed of water snakes. I'm sure I didn't consciously recollect reading the passage from the *Opticks* about the flames of two candles, or link it with the passage about the fish, but in my subconscious mind the link must have been made. It must have been twenty years since I last read any Priestley but it must have stuck in my mind.'

'Is your friend's name really Khan?' asked Dr McGrath. Steerforth indicated that it was.

'Then perhaps he is a secret Esteesian,' she remarked enigmatically. We asked for an explanation.

'In his notes and letters Coleridge always refers to himself as STC. Somewhere along the way the adjective Esteesian got coined to describe anything perculiarly apt to STC. Nowadays we Coleridge scholars describe ourselves as Esteesians. It's just a little inside joke. But as your friend has an Esteesian name – or surname – I thought he might have got the candles story from STC and used Priestley as a cover.'

'Hiding his light under a bushel?' said Steerforth, and there for a moment the matter was left to rest. But it was not to be long before we were back on the Esteesian trail.

'Look here, Hawkesworth,' said Steerforth one day, 'I want to ask your advice on an important matter.' We were standing under a tree in the University Parks, waiting for a shower of rain to pass overhead and hoping that the cricket team might resume play after not too tedious an interval.

'I was very struck with the way Dr McGrath followed up that clue about the *Opticks*, weren't you?' I indicated assent. 'We are looking for a needle in an n-dimensional haystack, aren't we?' Again dissent was impossible. 'I must say that I believe Dr McGrath would be a useful ally in our hunt. I am seriously inclined to take her into my confidence and tell her everything about Khan, the Magus and the whole story. What do you think?'

I certainly had no objection to his suggestion: if the tracing of literary clues could help us find Khan, then her young and agile mind would be far more valuable than my old and slow-moving one.

'My only doubt,' said Steerforth, as the passing shower turned into a steady downpour and the cricket journalists began to leave the Parks, 'is whether I can persuade her to believe the whole fantastic business. Sometimes I almost disbelieve it myself.' It was agreed that Steerforth would invite Edwina May McGrath to dine with him on some suitable occasion and would try to convince her over dinner of the truth of his story. And so it turned out. However immovable the force of Dr McGrath's scepticism, the force of Steerforth's patent truthfulness was irresistible. By the next time I saw them together, she knew as much as I about the history of the Magus project. Perhaps more.

Unlike Steerforth and myself she had never met Khan. She was therefore quite devoid of any personal inclination to favour, or even consider, the philosophical basis of his actions. She was outraged by his theft of the Magus. She shuddered with horror when Steerforth handed to her the passage from the *Republic* Khan had copied out.

'"Do we then state that such a man must be the slave of the best?"' she read. '"It is better for everyone to be ruled by the man of vision and sanity. . . ."' She glanced at Steerforth, eyes glaring and lips narrowed. 'This man is a menace to humanity!' she cried. 'He must at all costs be found and stopped or he will enslave the world.'

It needed perhaps a person who had never known Khan, had never experienced the warmth of his friendship, to see the issue as starkly as that and to draw out the battle lines so clearly. Khan must at all costs be stopped. Perhaps women are better at such judgements, at least as far as men are concerned. I feel certain now that the advice Abigail had given to Khan would have been just as stern and uncompromising on his side as Dr McGrath's was on ours. I suspected even then that she would turn out to be a redoubtable ally and a dangerous enemy, this slender and softly spoken girl from Oak Bluffs, with her delicate hands and her fund of Esteesian knowledge. It said a good deal for Steerforth's judgement of people that he had so quickly identified her value as a comrade in arms.

'Your friend was doubtless amused by the game of planting Esteesian clues,' said Dr McGrath, 'partly because a famous Khan also appears in STC's opiated dreams.'

'How did Coleridge get hold of the legend of Kubla Khan?' asked Steerforth.

'From a book of travel stories called "Purchas's Pilgrimage", as a matter of fact,' said Dr McGrath. 'Would you be interested in knowing precisely how?' Steerforth nodded, and once again she reached into her apparently bottomless shopping bag to extract a copy of Coleridge's poems. We were sitting, I recall, on a bench in the college gardens. In her quiet and precise way Dr McGrath read out loud the poet's account of how that strange and mysterious fragment of a masterwork was given to him.

' "The following fragment is here published at the request of a poet of great and deserved celebrity (Lord Byron) and, as far as the Author's own opinions are concerned, rather as a psychological curiosity, than on any grounds of supposed *poetic* merits.

' "In the summer of the year 1797, the Author, then in ill health, had retired to a lonely farm-house between Porlock and Linton, on the Exmoor confines of Somerset and Devonshire. In consequence of a slight indisposition, an anodyne had been prescribed, from the effects of which he fell asleep in his chair at the moment that he was reading the following sentence, or words of the same substance, in 'Purchas's Pilgrimage': 'Here the Khan Kubla commanded a palace to be built, and a stately garden thereunto. And thus ten miles of fertile ground were inclosed with a wall.' The Author continued for about three hours in a profound sleep, at least of the external senses, during which time he has the most vivid confidence, that he could not have composed less than from two to three hundred lines; if that indeed can be called composition in which all the images rose up before him as things with a parallel production of the corresponding expressions, without any sensation or consciousness of effort. On awaking he appeared to himself to have a distinct recollection of the whole, and taking his pen, ink and paper, instantly and eagerly wrote down the lines that are here preserved. At this moment he was unfortunately called out by a person on business from Porlock, and detained by him above an hour, and on his return to his room, found, to his no small surprise and mortification, that though he still retained some vague and dim recollection of the general purport of the vision, yet with the exception of some eight or ten scattered lines and images, all the rest had passed away like images on the surface of a stream into which a stone has been cast, but, alas! without the after restoration of the latter." '

Steerforth and I gazed blankly at each other.

'And that,' concluded Dr McGrath, 'is practically all we know from the lips of Coleridge himself. There are a few other things we can conjecture. The date may be wrong. It was probably the next year, 1798, that 'Kubla Khan' was written – the year after 'The Ancient Mariner'. The confusion over the date is not as surprising in the case of Coleridge as it would be with most people: he often gets dates wrong. He seems to have had a rather confused idea of the passage of time.'

'What was the anodyne?' asked Steerforth.

'Probably laudanum, tincture of opium,' answered Dr McGrath. 'On a manuscript of the poem, which is now on display in the British Museum, Coleridge gives a slightly different account. "This fragment," he writes, "with a good deal more, not recoverable, composed in a sort of Reverie brought on by two grains of Opium, taken to check a dysentery, at a Farm House between Porlock & Linton, a quarter of a mile from Culbone Church, in the fall of the year, 1797." We know that STC took opium even while he was an undergraduate at Cambridge. He says he took it as a painkiller to relieve his swollen joints. Certainly as time passed, he became a real addict. Just how far the drug affected his poetic output is a matter of intense and long-lasting academic dispute. I don't expect the dispute to be settled in my lifetime.'

'But at least we know that Kubla Khan was a product of a drug-induced sleep?' asked Steerforth.

'Not really that,' answered Dr McGrath. 'Coleridge says that he wrote the poem in 1797 or, as we now suspect, 1798. But it was never published until 1816, when Lord Byron advised Coleridge to publish it. By 1816 there was a morbid public interest in the habits of the "opium-eaters" and money to be made out of scandalous confessions about drugs. Some scholars have suggested the poem was actually written in 1816 and that the story about the dream and the vision and the person from Porlock is just a lot of hokum.'

From the Senior Common Room we could hear the clatter of cups and catch the scent of recently infused tea. We left our bench and strolled gently across the lawn.

'What were Purchas's sources for the story of the pleasure dome?' asked Steerforth suddenly.

'I can give you the *ipsissima verba* from Purchas, if you are interested,' answered Dr McGrath. Once we were settled in the Common Room and provided with tea, she did so.

' "In Xamdu did Cublai Can build a stately Pallace, encompassing sixteene miles of plaine ground with a wall, wherein are fertile Meddowes, pleasant Springs, delightfull Streames, and all sorts of beasts of chase and game, and in the middest thereof a sumptuous house of pleasure, which may be removed from place to place." The sources are pretty consistent. Xanadu or Xamdu or Shang-tu was the reputed site of a mediaeval palace in China built by a Mongol prince called Kubla or Kubilai. The common elements are always the same: beautiful walled gardens, lovely fountains and a miraculous palace where magic is possible. But various writers add their own frills to the basic picture, like Coleridge's Abyssinian maid. But there is also one puzzle about the origins of the story.'

'What's that?'

'There is a thirteenth century Arabic version of the story of Kubla Khan which was not translated into any European language until much later than Coleridge's time. And despite Coleridge's undoubted status as a polymath, a library cormorant with a tenacious and systematising memory as he described himself, there is no evidence that he ever spared the week or two it might have taken him to gain a working knowledge of Arabic. So we know that he didn't use it as a source. But it describes the pleasure dome like this: "On the eastern side of that city a karsi or palace was built ... after a plan which the Kaan had seen in a dream and retained in his memory." According to this ancient Arab tradition the blueprint of the palace was given to its builder in a dream, just as Coleridge said the poem was given to him in a dream. No one has ever explained that riddle.'

Silence fell upon us as we brooded upon the mystery of the mediaeval prince and the ancient Arabic text, the poet's dream and the lost lines of the great poem. One of the college servants came from the kitchen to refill our teacups and, like the person from Porlock, she disturbed our reveries.

'I must go,' said Dr McGrath, gathering up her papers and her leather bag. 'Professor Hawkesworth my supervisor is a very demanding taskmaster and if Professor Hawkesworth my friend prevents me from preparing next week's work on Keats, I may irritate the former and lose the latter.'

'Just before you leave us,' said Steerforth, 'may I beg one favour? Would you please be kind enough to read us the text of Coleridge's poem?' Dr McGrath agreed at once, but instead of opening the volume of poems she closed her eyes and recited the text from memory. Her face was small and tender, her voice low and resonant. Her accent lent new charm to the familiar lines.

ALLAH'S
DESCRIPTION
OF
PARADISE

In Xanadu did Kubla Khan
    A stately pleasure-dome decree:
Where Alph, the sacred river, ran
Through caverns measureless to man
    Down to a sunless sea.
So twice five miles of fertile ground
With walls and towers were girdled round:
And there were gardens bright with sinuous rills
Where blossomed many an incense-bearing tree;
And here were forests ancient as the hills,
Enfolding sunny spots of greenery.

But O, that deep romantic chasm which slanted
Down the green hill athwart a cedarn cover!
A savage place! as holy and enchanted
As e'er beneath a waning moon was haunted
By woman wailing for her demon-lover!
And from this chasm, with ceaseless turmoil seething,
As if this earth in fast thick pants were breathing,
A mighty fountain momently was forced;
Amid whose swift half-intermitted burst
Huge fragments vaulted like rebounding hail,
Or chaffy grain beneath the thresher's flail:
And 'mid these dancing rocks at once and ever
It flung up momently the sacred river.
Five miles meandering with a mazy motion
Through wood and dale the sacred river ran,
Then reached the caverns measureless to man,
And sank in tumult to a lifeless ocean:
And 'mid this tumult Kubla heard from far
Ancestral voices prophesying war!

The shadow of the dome of pleasure
    Floated midway on the waves;
Where was heard the mingled measure
    From the fountain and the caves.
It was a miracle of rare device,
A sunny pleasure-dome with caves of ice!

A damsel with a dulcimer
    In a vision once I saw:
It was an Abyssinian maid,
    And on her dulcimer she played,

Singing of Mount Abora.
Could I revive within me,
Her symphony and song,
To such a deep delight 'twould win me,
That with music loud and long,
I would build that dome in air,
That sunny dome! those caves of ice!
And all who heard should see them there,
And all should cry, Beware! Beware!
His flashing eyes, his floating hair!
Weave a circle round him thrice,
And close your eyes with holy dread,
For he on honey-dew hath fed,
And drunk the milk of Paradise.

My only misgiving about Dr McGrath's reading was that her American pronunciation of the word 'fertile' destroyed the internal assonance with 'twice five miles'. But I reflected later that it also created an assonance with 'girdled' in the next line, which left me wondering how Coleridge said 'fertile'.

For a week or two after we discovered the first hints of an Esteesian dimension to our mystery, the three of us had little opportunity to discuss the matter further. Dr McGrath naturally became increasingly concerned about her thesis, while Steerforth had his business affairs to attend to. For my part I found during those days a further deterioration in my health set in and I was obliged to rest a good deal during the day. At length, however, I received a telephone call from Steerforth.

'For some reason I feel rather convinced that Dr McGrath is on a useful trail with her theory of a Coleridge dimension,' he said. 'I can imagine Khan carefully planting clues over the years, as a sort of test of our ingenuity. I would quite like to know which others he planted, if any.' He went on to suggest that the three of us might meet up somewhere outside Oxford for a weekend, to put such evidence as we had under scrutiny and see what other clues we could identify. Finally it was agreed that we would spend the weekend at the pleasant little town of Broadway.

'Would you like me to ask Dr McGrath if that arrangement is convenient for her?' I asked.

'Well actually I've already checked,' answered Steerforth. 'And it is.'

'Well, Hawkesworth,' said Steerforth, as Mr Steele led the way to the reception desk of the rather antiquated hotel we had chosen for our retreat, 'I hope you have brought all your wits with you for this weekend. If there are any real hints about Khan's plans buried in the past, I want to dig them out.' Over dinner that first night we talked in a desultory fashion of the schooldays Khan and Steerforth had shared, and of their early times at Oxford. Nothing seemed to emerge of any significance, and I had the feeling that none of us really expected much of that first evening. Everyone was rather tired and we all went off early to our beds. We spent the next day walking in the vicinity and visiting one or two attractive Cotswold churches. After dinner we sat in the deep club armchairs in the lounge and directed our minds seriously to the matter in hand. It was a chilly evening, cold enough for the hotel staff to have lighted a fire in the lounge. We secured three brandy balloons and asked the waiter to leave with us the bottle of Remy Martin. Watching Steerforth settle himself by the fire and carefully light his pipe, I was reminded of the night he had turned up unexpectedly in my rooms wanting to talk about Inayat Khan. There was one great difference now. Then there had been just the two of us: now we had a lively and intelligent woman as our companion and ally.

'Let us first take stock of what we know,' said Steerforth. 'Khan stole the secret of the Magus and disappeared somewhere in space and time. We don't know where or when, present, past or future. We think Abigail is with him, but we can't be sure. We believe his philosophy is such as to lead him to launch a takeover bid for the whole of human history, but we don't know how or where or when. Playing perhaps on the coincidence of his name with that of a mediaeval prince, he seems to have used Coleridge as a source of clever clues – and then to have covered them up. But we still don't know what we're looking for, so it's hard to evaluate the clues.'

'We know of only one clue so far, don't we?' said I, and Steerforth agreed.

'What does your Khan look like?' asked Dr McGrath suddenly, as if a physical description might aid her spiritual recognition. After offering a catalogue of Khan's height, weight and other features, Steerforth suddenly remembered that he had in his briefcase a photograph of Inayat Khan.

'I'm afraid it's rather a disreputable picture,' said Steerforth sheepishly. 'It was taken in a nightclub in St Julien, just over the French border from Switzerland, on the night that Khan and I first transported a mouse in time. We were celebrating, you understand.' As Steerforth handed the picture to Edwina May McGrath I caught a glimpse of Khan's grinning face, his arm around the waist of the nightclub hostess and a glass of Bollinger raised high as he saluted the photographer.

'So this is Inayat Khan, is it?' she murmured, and gazed for some time at the picture before turning it casually over to glance at the back. I looked over her shoulder at the inscription: 'From your one true friend, Nehemiah Higginbottom,' it read.

'Did Khan write that?' asked Dr McGrath, with what seemed to me to be more than a passing interest. Steerforth answered yes.

'Why did he use that pseudonym?' she asked again.

'He said it was the sort of place where one gave a false name,' explained Steerforth. 'From the appearance of the nightclub hostesses, you can see why.'

'Yes but why that particular name rather than any other? Had he to the best of your knowledge ever used it before?' she asked sharply.

'I've no idea,' admitted Steerforth. 'Has it any significance? I seem to recall that a lot of the other guests had signed in as Donald Duck or Mickey Mouse.'

'Taken in isolation the name might not be important,' answered Dr McGrath. 'But taken in conjunction with the flames of two candles, it may be significant.' She gazed at Steerforth as she spoke, a triumphant light burning in her eye. Even before she explained, it was clear that she had found another clue.

'In late 1797 Coleridge was waiting in some trepidation for the playwright Sheridan to give his opinion on Coleridge's tragedy *Osorio*. It was a jittery and depressing time for him. To pass the time, he wrote a collection of parodies entitled *Sonnets attempted in the Manner of Contemporary Writers*. Among the poets satirised were Lamb, Lloyd and Southey, all of whom were at least acquaintances of Coleridge. To avoid overtly upsetting them, STC published the parodies under a *nom de plume*. It was Nehemiah Higginbottom.'

We sat in silence. There before us was another link between Inayat Khan and Samuel Taylor Coleridge. It seemed to have been deliberately if cryptically woven into the history of the Magus project, so that if anyone with sufficient determination and knowledge were to study that history then the link to the poet would become manifest. And the *nom de plume* of Nehemiah Higginbottom was not the last such link we found that evening.

'Did your friend Inayat Khan ever use any other pseudonyms?' asked Edwina May.

'Not that I can recall,' said Steerforth.

'Ah but he did,' said I. 'The building works on Mount Desert Island in Maine, they were carried out under an alias, were they not? What was it?'

'Of course they were!' exclaimed Steerforth. 'It was an odd name, deliberately archaic. Cumberland? Comberland?'

'Comberbache,' suggested Edwina May, with a quiet, triumphant smile. 'Silas Tomkyn Comberbache, if I am not mistaken.'

'Yes, that was it,' said Steerforth. 'How did you know?'

'It's another Esteesian clue,' said Edwina May. 'You know that in December 1793, in despair at ever getting his life organised at university, Coleridge enrolled as a Dragoon? Clearly he could not enroll in his own name, so he needed a pseudonym. But his freedom of choice was limited. He was too hard up to buy a complete new set of underwear, and his real initials were embroidered on his clothes. So he needed a name that matched STC. He chose Silas and Tomkyn as two of the stupidest names he could think of, suitable for his future role. He took the surname Comberbache, he later admitted, off some lawyer's shingle in Lincoln's Inn. Somehow the absurdity of the name is all of a piece with the incident itself.'

It was not all plain sailing, though this narrative may make it seem so. Among the other papers Steerforth had brought with him were some press cuttings about Abigail and a handful of other photographs from Khan's past. One of the press reports quoted the words of Abigail's Rastafarian song, and Edwina May McGrath read out the verse in a soft and wondering tone:

> The mountain people rise at dawn
> They rise and sing their songs at dawn
> The songs rise to the mountain top
> And please the Emperor God.

'I wonder if that is a clue too?' she said. Neither Steerforth nor I could guess what, if anything, it signified. In fact the song proved to be unconnected with the hunt, just one of a number of red herrings that we pursued for a while. But among the photographs was another that now commanded Edwina May's attention. It was the picture of the house that Khan had sent to Steerforth from the Lake District.

'Did Khan send this?' she asked.

'He did,' answered Steerforth. 'Is it significant?'

'The house is called Greta Hall,' said Edwina May. 'It is in Keswick. Coleridge lived there from June 1800. This is his study window, up here on the first floor.' She turned over the photograph and examined the inscription.

'Oh my God,' she laughed. 'Your friend has quite a sense of humour. He writes, "a house of such prospect that if impressions and ideas constitute our being, one might have a tendency to become a God. . . ." Those are pretty well the exact words in which Coleridge described the house in a letter to Godwin. He must have known that.'

'Something else I remember Khan saying which I think may have had a Coleridgean connection,' I remarked, 'concerned an illiterate serving girl in Germany who in the grip of a fever recited whole passages of ancient languages. I remember Khan telling that story with particular fervour, don't you, Steerforth?'

'Yes, with the intention of comically disparaging my attempt to win an Oxford scholarship,' smiled Steerforth. After a speedy reference to her notes Dr McGrath was able to confirm that there was a reference to such a case in the *Biographia Literaria*, though for all she knew it might also crop up elsewhere in nineteenth century literature.

'What then do we know?' said Steerforth. 'We have the flames of two candles, the illiterate serving maid, the house in Keswick and the pseudonyms of Nehemiah Higginbottom and Silas Tomkyn Comberbache. All are definite links to Samuel Taylor Coleridge. All are hints actually given by Khan to one or both of us. It is exactly like a game of hares and hounds – all the clues are there if you care to follow them. But why, why, why?'

Steerforth topped up our brandy glasses again and we all sat gazing intently into the fire.

'Clearly the trail is there to be followed. But it is not to be made too easy. Khan went out of his way to emphasise that the theory about the flames of two candles came from Priestley. Unless we had chanced to meet a Coleridge scholar, perhaps we might never have tracked down the reference in the Notebook.'

I felt obliged to agree, though I was somewhat mortified that as a literary man I had missed the Esteesian connections. I could only console myself with the belief that if they had related to my own specialist subject of Chaucer, I would certainly have spotted them at once. I did not recall that I had the excuse that the volume to which Edwina May McGrath had referred was published in German before an English text was generally available. For a proper English edition the world had had to wait until 1957.

It was a curiosity to me, still unexplained to this day, that on the night that Khan and Steerforth tried to experiment with the two candles I had dreamed of water snakes just like those in 'The Ancient Mariner'. Was it just a coincidence? Or was my subconscious mind aware of the link? I sat and gazed at the fire, glancing from time to time at Steerforth. My friend was looking with a fixed intensity into the fire, as I had seen him do before. His eye glittered with almost fanatical brightness. Now that STC was in the air, I was reminded of what John Sterling wrote of the poet: 'It is painful to observe in Coleridge, that with all the kindness and glorious far-seeing intelligence of his eye, there is a glare in it, a light half unearthly, half morbid. It is the glittering eye of the Ancient Mariner.' Outside in the gardens of the hotel a peacock cried its plaintive wail, so like a cry for help.

'And then,' said Dr McGrath at last, 'there is the coincidence that one of Coleridge's best-known poems is actually about a Khan. In fact about the Khan of Khans. Do you think Inayat's imagination might be stirred in that way?'

'Perhaps,' said Steerforth, looking up from the fire at Dr McGrath. 'He might feel that he was in some way the spiritual heir of the Khans, a latter-day Khan of Khans.'

'Might he even wish to model his empire to some extent on the great Empire of the Khans?' I asked. Both Steerforth and Dr McGrath nodded vigorously at that, as if it embraced most clearly all our suspicions.

'So what do we know of Kubla Khan himself, other than what we have learned from Coleridge and Purchas?' I asked.

'Not a great deal,' answered Dr McGrath. 'The total number of Europeans who passed that way was few enough – perhaps only a dozen or so. And of those only a few left any description of the city. Marco Polo was one, Father John of Montecorvino was another and Friar Odoric of Pordenone was a third. All of them got as far as Xanadu or Shang-tu, though I can't be certain whether they were there in the time of Kubla Khan. Marco Polo commented on the way the Khans used staged runners to create a kind of postal system. At the time these Europeans made their visits, between 1250 and 1300 AD, Xanadu itself must have been a most impressive place with huge barracks where the Khan's soldiers lived, a beautiful palace, huge earthworks and wonderful hunting grounds. If your friend is a romantic I can understand how he might be tempted to model his empire on Xanadu.'

Even as we reviewed the knowledge we had of Kubla Khan and his great kingdom, I had a strange intuition. There was something in what I had heard about Xanadu that rang a deeper and more significant note than we had yet recognised. Something that Dr McGrath had said, or something she had read out from a book in her bottomless bag, had been more vital a clue than we had known. But what was it? It was just a vague intellectual itch on the skin of my mind: I did not even attempt to put it into words. If it signified, it would surface. We sat in silence for some time, brooding upon our mystery. It crossed my mind to wonder what Khan was doing at that moment, while we were so engrossed in trying to unravel his secrets. But then I almost burst out laughing when the absurdity of the phrase 'at that moment' impressed itself upon me.

'Is it your belief,' said Dr McGrath at last, 'that Khan's friend Abigail went with him wherever and whenever he has gone?'

'We believe so,' said Steerforth. 'They had lived together for some years almost as man and wife.'

'Almost?' asked Dr McGrath with a quizzical smile.

'You must remember that Abigail was a popular musician, quite a famous one actually. Her work took her away a good deal. She and Khan might have been closer otherwise.'

'Yes,' said Dr McGrath. 'I have been doing some homework. She was almost the inventor of reggae music, wasn't she? With her dreadlocks and her zither she must have been an impressive performer.'

'Was it a zither?' said Steerforth.

'A *kissar* actually,' I replied. 'A kind of ancient Abyssinian instrument, I believe.' And poor, stupid creatures that we were at that moment with the secret of Khan's empire staring us in the face, we utterly failed to grasp it.

The real key was Abigail's musical instrument, her *kissar*, but for the moment we were too stupid to see it. Or perhaps we were too tired. It was now well after two o'clock in the morning and the Remy Martin was vastly depleted. We prised ourselves up from our chairs and collected our keys from the night porter with many a stifled yawn.

Yet tired as I was, I found it impossible to sleep. The mystery of Khan's disappearance and all the strange Esteesian clues kept buzzing round in my mind. What reason might Inayat Khan have for basing his empire of time upon the empire of an obscure prince from mediaeval China who simply happened to have attracted the attention of the poet Coleridge? For an hour or more I lay awake pondering upon the mystery of it all, then fell at last into a shallow and troubled sleep. It must have been four or five o'clock in the morning when I suddenly awoke with the key to the whole thing in my mind. How idiotic we had been! Abigail and the Magus were the keys to the whole mystery, Abigail with her zither and the Magus with its capacity to travel in time and space. I rose from my bed and, as quickly as my trembling fingers would permit, I put on my dressing-gown. I stumbled along the corridor to the room I knew to be Steerforth's, having heard the number when we collected our keys. I knocked at the door and, hearing only a muffled grunt, opened it and went inside.

'Steerforth!' I called out. 'For heaven's sake wake up! I've got the answer to the whole thing. It's all to do with Abigail and the Magus. . . .'

'Abigail and the Magus. . . .?' repeated Steerforth in a thick and sleepy voice. I sat down on the edge of the bed and tried to explain.

'Abigail came from Ethiopia, did she not? She played a zither. Do you remember the song she sang at the college ball all those years ago? Do you remember what it was about?'

'It was about a place she came from in Ethiopia,' answered Steerforth. 'What was it called? Abuya Mountain, I think.'

'If you were an eighteenth century poet and you heard or read a description of Abigail, how would you describe her?'

'An Ethiopian maiden?' said Steerforth. 'No, of course not, Ethiopia is a modern name.'

'An *Abyssinian* maid,' said Dr McGrath, sitting bolt upright all of a sudden. 'And on her dulcimer she played, singing of Mount Abora.'

'My God,' said Steerforth. 'Do you mean to say that there is a description of Abigail in the poem "Kubla Khan"?'

'Of course,' said Dr McGrath. 'It's perfectly obvious now. A zither could easily be mistaken for a dulcimer, and Mount Abora for Mount Abuya.'

'But what does it mean?' asked Steerforth.

'Hold your horses, Steerforth,' I replied. 'There is another clue we totally underexploited. Do you recall the exact words that

Purchas used in his *Pilgrimage* to describe the palace of Kubla Khan?'

'I do,' volunteered Edwina May McGrath, and recited them from memory. ' "In Xamdu did Cublai Can build a stately Pallace, encompassing sixteene miles of plaine ground with a wall, wherein are fertile Meddowes, pleasant Springs, delightfull Streames, and all sorts of beasts of chase and game, and in the middest thereof a sumptuous house of pleasure, which may be removed from place to place." '

'Exactly,' I said. ' "Which may be removed from place to place." Now Coleridge doesn't mention the fact that the palace was mobile. Perhaps he didn't read Purchas as carefully as he might have done, or perhaps he also had at least one other source. He must have had such a source, actually, since he mentions things that Purchas seems to have known nothing about, like the Abyssinian maid and Mount Abora or Abuya. But the main point is this. Kubla Khan's magical palace could move around by itself, and in it there lived a beautiful Ethiopian girl who played the zither – who sounds in fact amazingly similar to Abigail. Steerforth, don't you see? Khan did not model his empire on that of Kubla Khan. He *is* Kubla Khan!'

There was a moment's stupefied silence as the true import of my explanation dawned upon them. Inayat Khan was born in India in 1936, came to school in England in 1948 and built the palace at Xanadu that Marco Polo saw in the thirteenth century. It was fantastic, but no more so than Khan bringing himself the answers to a physics exam when the question paper had not even been printed. No wonder the travellers who saw Xanadu were impressed. They were looking at twentieth century (or later) science and technology with thirteenth century eyes. No wonder they wrote miraculous accounts of the pleasure dome, which Coleridge among others used as source material for poems. And there, of course, lay the significance of Coleridge in Khan's scheme of things. One of the greatest poems in the English language was actually *about* Khan and his empire of time. It was only natural that he should show a marked interest in the poem's author. Wondering upon all this but convinced nevertheless that I had solved the mystery of Khan's disappearance – he had taken himself off to ancient China to found the legendary kingdom of Xanadu about which Coleridge would write his wonderful poem some five hundred years later – I left Steerforth's room and slowly wandered back to my own. Only when I was safely tucked up again did a further thought crowd in upon my mind: Steerforth and Dr McGrath had been sleeping in the same bed!

చా   ఇ

At breakfast next morning we tried to review what we knew of Xanadu. Naturally Edwina May McGrath was handicapped because she had not brought to the hotel a full library of Coleridge books. But what we could recall between us was a start.

'I have a vague recollection,' said Dr McGrath, 'of some kind of defensive arrangement mentioned in the Notebooks. But what it is I really can't remember.' Later however the precise recollection came to mind. In several places Coleridge referred to a species of deadly tree known as the Upas, which could strike dead any living creature that came within a certain distance of it.

'Yes I think that's a clue,' said Dr McGrath, pushing her spectacles up her nose as seriously as if she were at a tutorial. 'Somewhere in the Notebooks STC describes a Tartarean Forest all of Upas trees. I think a fair translation of Tartarean is "hellish". And although Coleridge himself never tells us what a Upas tree is, Erasmus Darwin does. It's a tree within fifteen or eighteen miles of which no living creature can survive.'

'What do we suppose is the significance of Alph the sacred river?' said Steerforth.

'It runs through caverns measureless to man, down to a sunless sea,' said Dr McGrath with a wry smile. 'Oh, and it sinks in tumult to a lifeless ocean. That's about all.'

'The Magus machine might produce a fair amount of radioactive waste,' said Steerforth. 'Perhaps the poem is just describing a waste disposal mechanism.'

'My God, that's about the least romantic explanation of the mysteries of Kubla Khan that I've ever heard!' said Edwina May McGrath. We all laughed, but at the same time we were all overburdened with the weight of the secret we had unravelled. To think of Khan establishing his kingdom hidden in the depths of mediaeval Chinese history! Later that day Edwina May McGrath read us out a further passage from STC's notebook that might have been written with Inayat Khan in mind: ' "It surely is not impossible that to some infinitely superior being the whole universe may be one plain, the distances between planet and planet only the pores that exist in any grain of sand – and the distances between system and system no greater than the distance between one grain and the grain adjacent. . . " '

From that morning onwards too another important matter was made open and clear: Augustus Steerforth and Edwina May McGrath were lovers. What motives had made them secretive before, I do not know. But now they walked hand in hand or arm in arm as the mood took them, and called each other by the usual terms of endearment. In his lover's presence Steerforth seemed more relaxed and natural than he had been for some time. Edwina May, or EM as Steerforth began to call her, was for almost all the time unchanged – as sharp and clever as any man and twice as independent. But every once in a while her face would melt into a smile, she would lay her hand on Steerforth's arm and look at him in adoration. I tried to give them a little time together during that weekend in Broadway, using my illness as an excuse for going off alone to rest. Nor was the excuse entirely fabricated, for I was tiring more and more easily as the illness progressed. At the end of the stay in Broadway we drove back to Oxford in pensive mood, wishing a little perhaps that we had not so incontrovertibly exposed Khan's secret. For now we three alone shared the certain knowledge that Khan's empire of time had found a permanent base, and that he could make his incursions into the fabric of history wherever and whenever he liked. The danger was all around us. Nothing of the past history of the world was safe, nothing in the future. Not even the survival of the universe was assured. Under grey skies and with these momentous thoughts in mind we were driven back to Oxford by Mr Steele. I said goodbye to my friends outside the college and, feeling exhausted, went straight to bed without eating dinner.

For two weeks or so after the weekend at Broadway, I heard no more of Steerforth's plans. I tried to concentrate my own mind upon my college work and also to focus Dr McGrath's attention upon hers. My efforts were hindered by my declining health, Dr McGrath's perhaps by her new-found romantic attachment to Steerforth. But we both did our best to overcome our disabilities. And our respite from the Magus affair was fairly brief. Within a fortnight Steerforth was back in the hunt, and trying to enthuse us with his determination.

'We have to do something about Khan,' he said firmly one day. 'But the question is what?'

'We have to stop Khan from dismantling history and reassembling it to suit himself,' said Dr McGrath.

'How do we know that he isn't already doing so?' I asked.

'Because if he were,' said Steerforth, 'we wouldn't be talking here. We probably wouldn't exist in Khan's reassembled universe. We would be the first thing he would unhappen.' It seemed a rather frightening idea that any second we might cease not only to exist, but to have ever existed.

'So let's unhappen him before he unhappens us. Why don't we mount an expedition back to the world of Kubla Khan and somehow prevent him from launching his attack?' asked Dr McGrath.

'How?' asked Steerforth in turn.

'Perhaps we could sabotage his Magus machine and leave him stranded in thirteenth century China. Or perhaps we could hijack it and send it into the infinite. There must be some way to hog-tie him!'

'But if we use the Magus technology to intervene in Khan's affairs, aren't we then guilty of just the same overweening pride as he is? Aren't we then agreeing with Khan that it is better for all men to be ruled by the man of vision and sanity? The only difference is that now I am the man of vision and sanity, not Khan. In that case, Khan has won the argument and we might as well pack up and go home.'

'No, Augustus,' said Edwina May McGrath, 'the motive defines the act. Khan wants to use the Magus to enslave mankind. You should use it to prevent Khan from doing so. That's equivalent to using it to liberate mankind. There is all the difference in the world.'

Thus was born the idea of some kind of expedition in time to nip Khan's plans in the bud. At first it was just a hazy notion, something rather agreeable to reflect upon but not likely to be put into operation. Then it became more familiar to us and we began to speculate about minor details of such a plan – which somehow made us feel that the broad concept had been accepted.

'But how would we build our own Magus?' said Steerforth. 'As I have no copy of the plans, we would have to rework all the physics, which is Khan's department. Whom could we ask to help us? Who is the best physicist in the world after Inayat Khan?' The real answer to this problem was in fact to lie in quite another direction.

'Whom would you invite to join the expedition?' asked Edwina May McGrath.

'You of course, EM,' said Steerforth. 'I would not care to venture into the dangers of the remote past without you at my side.'

'And then I would invite Hawkesworth,' continued Steerforth.

'Although he is not in the first flush of youth, his experience would be invaluable.'

'You are a splendid fellow, Steerforth,' said I. 'If I were forty years younger, or even twenty, then nothing in the world would prevent me from joining you to chase Inayat Khan back to Xanadu, back to Eden itself if need be. But I should just be a burden to you both. Even old Steele is a sprightly youngster next to me.' But they began at once to say that such an expedition would be unthinkable without me. And there for the moment we left the matter.

A week or two after our initial discussion of a possible expedition against Khan, Steerforth told us that he had to be away for a few days. He did not explain his absence to me, nor I think to Dr McGrath. We later discovered, however, that he had gone to Switzerland for a meeting with the former Director of the Torus centre, Dr Konrad Dubendorf, now a professor of physics at the University of Zurich. They had a long meeting the next day. As a result of these discussions, the University of Zurich made a formal request to test the workability of some equipment which had been established at the Torus Centre while Dr Dubendorf was its Director. Why should the university be interested in this obsolete equipment installed at the Torus Centre? Only because Dr Dubendorf was to publish a learned paper connected with the work he had done at the Torus Centre and needed to check the respectability of some of his particle experiments. As a great favour between two leading Swiss institutions the Torus Centre scheduled a one-day slot for the university. On the day in question Dr Dubendorf and his team arrived at the Torus Centre and began to reassemble the component parts of the Swiss Magus. It was to serve for two more time trips before it was utterly forgotten. By night the old Magus was fully reassembled and Steerforth was ready to go. He and Dubendorf carefully set up the coordinates, he settled himself in the Time Travel Module, closed his eyes and found himself in north Oxford in the year 1971.

He was in the University Parks, where he had so often played cricket for Oxford: but now it was night-time and cold. His time of arrival had been very carefully planned. He set off at once for the physics laboratory. Ever since he had worked in the laboratory, Steerforth had kept his key to the main entrance. For a moment he found himself hoping that the key still fitted the lock after all these years: then he recalled that it was 1971 and that he, Steerforth (or a younger version of him) still worked most days in the laboratory. Of course the key would fit. He found the laboratory in darkness, let himself in and groped his way down the once-familiar corridors to the room he had shared with Khan. On the same keyring he found the door key to the office and the key to the safe where the Magus plans were kept. He opened the files and began to photograph the pages, using a pocket camera. The light from the table lamp was good, the camera worked perfectly, and he had plenty of time. He had checked in an old diary that Khan was away at a conference in Cambridge on this particular day, while he (Steerforth) was in Oxford but had dined in Hall that evening. It was close to seven o'clock when Steerforth photographed the last page of the Magus files. He glanced around the little office, which he remembered quite well after all these years. He glanced through one or two letters that lay on Khan's desk, and was tempted to write some message from the future on one of them. Then he realised that he mustn't, because he hadn't ... so to speak. Hanging on a peg by the door was his old college scarf, and his gown. Gown?

'Oh my God,' muttered Steerforth, 'my gown is here. How can I be having dinner in college if my gown is here?' At that precise moment a footfall sounded in the passageway. Someone was making for Khan and Steerforth's office. Quickly he bundled up the files and crammed them into the safe. But the footfall was now right outside the door. He had no time to close the safe. He turned off the light and took up a position just where the open door would hide him.

The man came into the room and switched on the light. He caught sight of the open safe.

'What the devil ...?' he said, and advanced a few steps into the room. In a moment he was kneeling beside the safe and examining the files, as if to check that none had been stolen. Steerforth stepped silently round the edge of the door and into the passage. He tiptoed to the end of the passage, then ran helter-skelter to the laboratory door. He felt the camera bouncing in his overcoat pocket. Once in the street he forced himself to walk slowly and casually towards the centre of Oxford. But he could not resist looking back once, to see a figure emerge from the physics laboratory and look rather wildly up and down the street. Steerforth quickly looked round, and walked on. The lines came to his mind:

> Like one, that on a lonesome road
> Doth walk in fear and dread,

And having once turned round walks on.
And turns no more his head;
Because he knows, a frightful fiend
Doth close behind him tread.

It is one thing to watch one's own self score a half-century in a Test Match. Steerforth had found that experience only slightly eerie, an extension perhaps of watching oneself on film or on television. But to be almost apprehended by oneself in the act of copying secret documents, that was another experience. He felt a profound sense of relief when he was back in his own physiological time zone of 1981. And most important of all he now had a photographic copy of the Magus plans and the scientific calculations upon which Magus was based. And with that plan, and some further materials he soon acquired in the twentieth century, Steerforth was to make (with the active help of Konrad Dubendorf) his very last trip on the Swiss Magus machine. It delivered him to a destination in time and space that was so secret that not even Dr McGrath and I knew it. Later we came to learn that it was in the future of mankind rather than its past, for reasons which will become plain. But the most remarkable thing about this Magus trip was that, although the Time Travel Module returned in due course to the Torus Centre, it returned without a human passenger. Steerforth deliberately stranded himself in time; if his plan failed to work, he was cut off forever from the century of his birth. As far as the Torus Centre was concerned, it was left with a security puzzle: a British postgraduate student authorised by the University of Zurich had gone into the Torus Centre, used the Torus and some equipment of his own, and simply disappeared. Dr Dubendorf invented some comfortable lie, no doubt, to explain Steerforth's disappearance. But any further difficulties were avoided when a telephone call to Lord Steerforth's home in England revealed that he was safe and well and in good spirits, though a little tired after his journey.

A few days after he had left for Geneva, Steerforth called me by telephone and asked if I would go to Bain Brook on urgent business. Dr McGrath was also invited, and had agreed to drop everything and set off as soon as Steele arrived to pick us up. I had a feeling that Steerforth's voice sounded a little unusual, a little softer and thinner than usual. But otherwise I noticed nothing amiss. The journey passed off uneventfully enough, though Mr Steele seemed rather more sombre than usual. Dr McGrath was a delightful travelling companion, so that Steele's dark humours troubled me little. When we arrived at Bain Brook we were shown into the library. Presently one of the staff came in, switched on the lights and drew the curtains closed. A few minutes later someone came into the room and quickly turned off the lights, plunging the room into darkness.

'Hawkesworth? Edwina May? Are you there?' It was Steerforth's voice but hearing it directly made me think even more that there was something changed about it.

'I am sorry about the amateur dramatics,' said Steerforth. 'I want to explain one or two things to you first, before you see me in the light. . . .' Edwina May gasped and half-rose to her feet.

'No, please,' said Steerforth urgently, 'don't worry too much. I've not disfigured myself in some fearful road accident or anything like that.' She settled again and in a moment Steerforth began to speak.

'I was finally persuaded that we simply had to take drastic action to stop Khan's plans for the conquest of time, and that using the Magus was the only way to do so. God knows if that makes me as great a tyrant as Khan. I gave up trying to puzzle out the morality of it all. But I knew I had to take action. As you know I have been to Switzerland to see Dr Dubendorf and to ask for his assistance. I needed his help to gain access to the old Magus machine just once more. I had no option but to tell him the whole story. I could tell he believed me. He is a good judge of character and had already summed Inayat up as a man of infinite ambition. At last I had to explain to him what I wanted to do. Even Dubendorf, that great and good friend, was stunned. He asked for twenty-four hours to think it over and perhaps to pray for guidance. He is a very pious man, is Konrad Dubendorf. Next day I returned and he told me that his conscience would trouble him if he agreed to my request, but that it would torment him like hellfires if he refused me. He is a man I would trust with my life.' Here he paused for a moment. I remember that Edwina May McGrath shifted a little in her chair, and I suddenly appreciated what torture it was for her to sit in darkness listening to some fearful mystery from the lips of the man she loved when she must have yearned only to run across the darkened room and take him in her arms.

'I made two journeys with Dubendorf's assistance,' continued Steerforth. 'The first was to the nuclear physics laboratory in Oxford at the time when Khan and I perfected the design of the

Magus. I took a pocket camera with me and photographed all the files that Khan was later to steal. That meant that all the physics and maths I needed to build a Magus machine were at my disposal. My next journey was a different kind of trip. I went into the future – which century and which country doesn't really matter. I cut myself off from the people. I had as little impact on the history of that period as I could. I was dreading taking some action that might disrupt the course of history in that future age. God knows what the consequences might be! But I was just an eccentric foreigner living the life of a recluse and working on the construction of some highly specialised flying machine in a factory he had rented. I had no staff. At that point in the future robots are commonplace. But I did pay one price for building my own Magus. The physiological time I spent in that century was three years. When my Magus was completed I flew it back here to Bain Brook and 1981. But in the two weeks since I last saw you, this is what has happened to me.' And with that he walked across the room and switched on the lights. Steerforth had spent only three years in the future but they must have been hard and lonely years. His hair had greyed considerably. He had lost several pounds in weight, and his face looked gaunt and pallid. Just for a moment it was as if his father was standing there before us, not dead after all but aged as I remembered him. Edwina May McGrath uttered a low and ringing cry, and ran to Steerforth to embrace him.

'It is Khan that has made you suffer like this,' she said at last when he had calmed her and dried her tears. 'I have come to hate that man like no one else on earth. And that even though I have never met him.' I suppose that we should have asked to see the new Magus machine as soon as Steerforth told us about it. But we were both more concerned about the state of Steerforth's health than about the readiness of his machine.

'Whatever Dubendorf might ask of me in return,' said Steerforth, 'I shall remain for ever in his debt. I had no right to ask him what I did. But once he had consulted his Christian conscience, he risked his career without a second's hesitation. Never let anyone tell you the Swiss are unadventurous!'

'In that case,' said I, 'why not invite Dubendorf to make one of your expeditions? He sounds just the man!' For what seemed to me like several minutes, there was silence in the library at Bain Brook. Slowly, very slowly it seemed to me, the walls began to rotate and the floor to replace the ceiling. Steerforth tells me that in fact I fell to the floor like a dead man. All I can say is that I seemed to witness the whole thing as if in a slow-motion film. Then blackness slowly engulfed me until I awoke in hospital.

I remained in hospital for two weeks and was then conveyed back to my rooms in college. As before the effect of the rest was to bring about a temporary improvement in my condition. But my doctor told me that it could prove only temporary. One afternoon soon after my return I decided to try to clear up the few loose ends of my career. The first letter I wrote was to Edwina May McGrath. I have the text of it before me as I write.

Dear Edwina (it reads)
As you know I have not been well for the past few months. My doctor tells me that it is nothing serious, but just that I have been trying to do a little more than my age permits. Might I suggest in the circumstances that another Fellow might take on the supervision of your work? I will be glad to discuss with you who might be best. I am sure it will be better for you to be blessed with a less senile supervisor.

Yours etc.

The second letter, which I also have before me, was to my doctor. For reasons related to his professional practice he has asked me not to mention his name.

Dear Dr —
I am writing to thank you for your candour and kindness. I have no wish to undergo another round of operations merely in the hope of delaying the inevitable by a few weeks or months. I am not sufficiently afraid of death, nor of cancer, to want to ward either off vainly for such a short time. I have had a good life and a long one. I am ready to die whenever I am fated to do so.

There is, however, one matter on which I would welcome your advice. I have been asked to go on a potentially dangerous expedition with my friend Lord Steerforth. You will understand that the details of the proposed journey are confidential. Normally I would not dream of accepting Steerforth's invitation. I would rather leave such adventures to younger and fitter men. But on the other hand, what is there to lose? If my life is to end very soon in any case, why not enjoy one last perilous fling? In certain very hazardous circumstances there may be positive merit in having as a partner someone whose life is already forfeit. What is your opinion? Should I accept or not? I know it is a difficult and perhaps unfair question to ask you. But you have been so wonderfully honest about everything else that I know I can trust you to be honest about this.

Yours etc.

I placed the two letters in college envelopes, asked the porter to have them delivered by hand, then took myself to bed for my usual afternoon sleep. I believe that during that afternoon (not for the first time) I dreamed of Abigail and of Inayat Khan and of the palace at Xanadu that could move from place to place, and of Samuel Taylor Coleridge and his opium-induced trance. When I woke I had the feeling that I was not alone. I sat up on my bed and glanced about me. In the dim light of the late afternoon I could just make out the figure of Edwina May McGrath seated in the armchair near the foot of my bed. She must have quietly let herself into my rooms and sat waiting for me to awake. She was not crying, but her hands covered her face and every once in a while a sob would shake her. What new adversity, I thought, had come upon Steerforth so to distress her? I was tempted to lapse back into sleep before I learned her evil tidings, whatever they might be. But before I could lay my head down again on the pillow, my telephone rang. I reached for it, and saw Edwina May's eyes dart towards me in the gloom.

'Hawkesworth?' It was the voice of my doctor, to whom I had sent the note a couple of hours earlier. 'You *are* getting senile, you know. You have sent me a note today that was clearly intended for someone else. It's headed "Dear Edwina". Shall I return it to you?' When I had rung off, she came across to my bed with my letter to the doctor in her hand, and sat with her arms about me for some time. I think she wept again, silently and secretly. I know I did. Perhaps our tears mingled in the texture of the old dressing-gown I had had since I was housemaster to Steerforth and Khan. Neither of us spoke of the illness.

'You will come with us, won't you?' she said at last. 'We can't possibly go without you. Say you'll come.' I nodded silently and her arms tightened about me. For a brief time that sad day, by the merest of chances, I felt that perhaps I knew what it might be to have a beloved and loving daughter. She insisted on ringing Steerforth later when we had tea, to tell him that I would make one of their foolish expeditions to the past. I suppose she did it quickly so that I would lack the opportunity to withdraw my consent. But even so, I must admit that I was excited by the prospect of the journey. As I had pointed out to my doctor, what had a dying man to lose from any adventure, however outlandish?

Once I had agreed, nothing would do but that we should all assemble again at Bain Brook the next day. With the aid of my doctor I was easily able to cancel or postpone all my teaching appointments and to be ready when Mr Steele came to fetch us in the Rolls Royce. We passed the journey from Oxford to Bain Brook in a fever of imagination about what we should find when we arrived.

Once again we passed through the small town of Bain Brook, bisected the two halves of the pond and entered the Steerforth territory. We skirted Leg of Lamb pond and the Cookpot and at last came in sight of the old Priory. We passed under the branches of the famous oak tree from which the last Prior was hanged, and came to rest in front of the ornate doors of the old house.

Steerforth came out of the house to greet us, with a rapturous kiss and hug for Edwina May and a firm, strong handshake for me.

'I have a surprise in store for you,' announced Steerforth. He led the way into the library. And there, as large as life and twice as cheery, was Konrad Dubendorf himself. Summoned (as I had suggested before I fainted away) from Switzerland to hear for the first time the full plan for the Magus adventure, and to be invited to become one of our small force, he had accepted with untypical rashness.

'For too long I have been a respectable administrator and a university professor,' he said gleefully. 'Now it is necessary for me to become time traveller, crusader and soldier of fortune. Besides, if Khan is allowed to stand the history of the universe on its head, something unthinkable might happen.'

'What's that?' asked Edwina May McGrath.

'The Swiss might not come out on top,' answered Konrad Dubendorf. They made a good pair, this Swiss professor and the young woman from Oak Bluffs. They often sparred in the friendliest way possible, and shared the virtue of being instantly critical of whatever was presented to them – especially if it all sounded very plausible.

As soon as Mr Steele had transported our luggage to our rooms, we spent half an hour arranging ourselves and were in good time for a glass of dry sherry before dinner. When the meal was over, we sat for some time over the coffee and the port talking in a rather desultory way about everything but the Magus and our planned intervention in the fabric of history. At length Steerforth tapped his coffee spoon against his cup for silence and addressed a few words to his assembled troops – few as they were.

'EM and gentlemen,' he began. 'I have deliberately steered the conversation this evening away from the subject of the Magus machine and the task to which we must set our hand. I think it best that we should all get a good night's sleep and then turn our attention to our mission. The new time machine in which we shall make our journey is parked a couple of miles from here in an old aircraft hangar that my father built. Tomorrow I suggest that we take breakfast together at eight o'clock, then go straight to the old airfield and inspect the new timecraft.' Silence greeted his remarks. But I could tell from the faces of Dr Dubendorf and Edwina May that their souls trembled to contemplate the adventure that faced them. And I daresay my face showed the same, for Edwina May's eyes blazed with excitement as she returned my wondering gaze.

CHAPTER 7

A Miracle of Rare Device

I for one was up early the next morning. In fact I was bathed, shaved and dressed in my room a full hour before the breakfast time we had all agreed. I felt more like a jittery undergraduate on the day of an examination than like an aged professor suffering from a mortal illness. I took myself for a walk in the grounds of Bain Brook to pass the time. I walked for what seemed at least an hour, only to find that I had been out of the house for a mere twenty minutes. I tried to read the morning newspaper, but my mind kept wandering from the point. Soon I was joined by Konrad Dubendorf and a little later by Dr McGrath. It was only a little consolation that they too looked as fidgety as I felt. Precisely at eight, Steerforth appeared at the dining-room door. Formally and a little awkwardly, he kissed Edwina May's cheek and shook hands with Konrad and myself. Then we sat down to as little or as great a breakfast as each preferred, myself being content with fruit juice, tea and a slice of toast with butter and Oxford marmalade. Steerforth ate a full breakfast with eggs, bacon, tomatoes, mushrooms and black pudding: but I felt he had to force it down as a gesture of his imperturbability. He even smoked a pipe of tobacco, lingering over the newspaper to do so, before he could admit that it was time to set off for the disused airstrip.

We travelled in a small bus of the kind that hotels use to pick up travellers at airports. Mr Steele was in the driving seat. We sped through country lanes for about twenty minutes, heading in a generally easterly direction, before coming to a high wire fence. There was a gatehouse manned by a couple of tough-looking fellows in security uniforms. The one who opened the gate for us carefully strapped on a protective helmet before he left the gatehouse, and (though I suppose Steerforth was his employer) he checked a card which Steerforth showed him before he unlocked the gate and waved us through.

Once inside, the gate was locked behind us. The hangar itself was a few hundred yards from the gate. Mr Steele parked the bus on a concrete apron near the doors of the hangar, and Steerforth began to open the locks on a small door the right size for a person to go through. I wondered for a moment how the new Magus would get in and out of the hangar, without its huge main doors being rolled back. Then I kicked myself for an idiot. It would flicker in and out of existence inside the hangar without even a window being open. By now Steerforth had undone the last of the locks and held open the door. Mr Steele, who I gathered was to remain in the twentieth century while we travelled in time, stayed with the bus. Dr McGrath led the way, followed by Konrad and myself. Steerforth brought up the rear. Together we came into the presence of the most amazing human artifact that any of us had ever seen.

The shape of the new Magus machine was that of a discus with a central dome or conning tower, its size that of a modest modern house, rather than the huge, time-travelling castle that Khan had constructed. Conceive if you will a disc about five feet thick lying flat upon the ground and then place at the centre of that coin a hemisphere about the size of a small cottage – and that is the first impression we had of the shape of the new time machine. I suppose I had never considered before just how large a device would be needed to accommodate the five of us for a time journey of any duration. If I had thought of the size of the new machine at all, I had perhaps thought of something like the bus in which we had driven from Bain Brook. But the new Magus machine was somewhat larger. It must have measured over eighty feet from edge to edge. The other feature of the time machine which impressed us as soon as Steerforth switched on the hangar lights was the surface texture of the metal from which it was made. It looked silky and glittering, the light shimmering in different colours of the rainbow off its facets. It really did look smooth and polished enough to slip in and out of the texture of time and space without leaving a nasty hole behind.

'Darling,' said Edwina May McGrath, 'what a superb machine. If anything could be worth three years of one's life, then this would be it.' Dr Dubendorf and I added our congratulations, for the new Magus machine was indeed a stunning achievement.

As we walked round the perimeter of the timecraft, we looked up towards the central conning tower from which the time traveller would presumably look out on the worlds of the past or the future. On each side the tower was penetrated with windows, but the glass that covered them was no ordinary glass. It was (as we were subsequently to discover) a specially moulded plastic material with great resistance to heat or pressure, designed to prevent the windows of the timecraft from melting or bursting in almost any circumstances.

Inscribed on the conning tower just below the level of the windows was the name of the timecraft – The Magus III. The first timecraft had been the one that Khan and Steerforth had built together in Switzerland and which was now, to all intents and purposes, *hors de combat*. The second one was the one Khan had built secretly in the mountains of Maine and which (we supposed) had become the pleasure dome of Xanadu. This timecraft then was the world's third, which Steerforth had built in the remoteness of the future and brought back to us in the twentieth century.

'I can see the logic of the name,' said Edwina May, 'but it's misleading. You, Augustus, are the real Magus, the real magician. This machine is nothing but your creation.'

'Oh no, EM, I am merely the Magus's way of coming into existence,' said Steerforth solemnly, but the next instant burst out laughing and lifted Edwina May bodily in the air.

For a moment it seemed that the burden of his extra three years, those stolen from the middle of his life, fell from him. But when I looked again he was again a man of forty-six with a body of forty-nine. When we had walked a complete circuit of the Magus III, Steerforth decided that it was time to take us inside. He took from his pocket a small device like an electronic calculator and keyed in a code. At once two sections along the edge of the timecraft began to draw apart, creating a doorway into the time machine. At the same time bright lights came on in the interior of the timecraft.

'Come aboard everyone,' said Steerforth. The room we entered was shaped, as we later found all the rooms of the timecraft to be, like a slice of cake. At the middle of the ship was the core, with an elevator to the bridge and access doors to all the other rooms. But apart from the core, all the other rooms had been created by building radial bulkheads from the core to the perimeter.

'Close the door please, Magus,' said Steerforth and the door obediently closed.

'Voice-controlled?' asked Dubendorf, and Steerforth nodded.

'Voice recognition is very advanced in the era in which the Magus was built.'

The first room we entered was a storeroom. There were a number of tall metal lockers, which Steerforth opened. Inside were glistening plastic overalls, helmets and boots. The suitlockers stood in the middle of the storeroom. Down each side stood a row of vehicles unlike any we had seen before, three in each row making six in all. They looked a little like a conventional motorbike, if one looked only at the handlebars, the saddle and the rather large and stout-looking windscreen. But there the resemblance ended, for unlike any motorbike I have ever seen these had no wheels. Where the passenger would rest his feet, there was instead on each vehicle a metal apron or skirt resting on the ground. On closer inspection it also turned out that the machine had no petrol tanks but only a rather complicated battery of controls mounted on a box about the size of a transistor radio set.

'What on earth are they?' cried Edwina May McGrath.

'They're motorbikes,' answered Steerforth.

'But they haven't any wheels,' she pointed out.

'This thing here acts in lieu of wheels,' said Steerforth, pointing to the metal apron on one of the bikes. 'It's a ground effect machine or gem, which means that it moves like a hovercraft on a cushion of air. However uneven the surface you're travelling over, the bumps are smoothed out for you. Moreover you can't get a flat tyre because the gembike doesn't have any tyres.'

'When can we have a ride?' asked Dr McGrath.

'Later,' smiled Steerforth. 'Let's complete our tour of inspection first.'

We left the storeroom where the suits and the gembikes were kept by a door that led into the central core of the timecraft. The core was a vertical cylinder of which the upper part formed the interior of the central dome of the Magus III. Down below the core served as a central means of access to all the other compartments. The next segment after the gembike store, moving in an anti-clockwise direction, was the ship's arsenal. Carefully racked along the walls were a couple of dozen high-velocity rifles with telescopic sights. I took one down and balanced it in my hand. It was amazingly light and made of an alloy that I did not recognise. Perhaps it was a product of the technology of the future age where Steerforth had built his timecraft. In boxes along the walls there were also handguns and ammunition for the rifles.

There were also some weapons that were very definitely the products of future technology. They included hand-held laser cannon and a powerful-looking rocket launcher.

'What about water supplies?' asked Dr Dubendorf.

'We can top up from any convenient source or from the atmosphere when we have to,' answered Steerforth. 'But naturally the whole ship is a closed system where everything is recycled. Apart from what we lose when the doors are open to the world or what crew members expend outside, we keep and recycle everything.'

We re-entered the core and then went into the next segment of the ship, where the environment control equipment was installed and the maintenance spare parts were kept. In the next room, as we continued our exploration of the timecraft, we found only a number of anonymous-looking grey cabinets, linked by tiny filaments which Dr Dubendorf guessed were optical fibres capable of carrying as many signals as the thickest of ordinary cables.

'This is in a sense the most important room in the ship,' said Steerforth. 'These cabinets contain the Magus electronics, the computer hardware that builds and maintains the time-shift effect. The Magus hardware builds a field that is precisely the same size and shape as the ship itself. Thus the ship and its passengers slip through the time-shift together. If the computer malfunctioned we might find one half of the Magus in the twentieth century and the other half in the remote past or future. So these featureless cabinets hold the secret of our survival, my friends.' I gazed at the grey boxes. I could only hope they would work perfectly. If they needed any help from me with their task then we were all doomed. I dare say I am not the first layman to have thought as much about a computer.

'I see the cabinets where the Magus electronics are stored,' said Konrad Dubendorf, 'but does this craft also incorporate a Torus? Or have you found some other way of accelerating matter past the gravity collapse?'

'In a sense,' answered Steerforth with a smile, 'the Magus III *is* a Torus. The reason why it is built in the shape of a flying saucer is that beneath our feet, running round the entire perimeter of the timecraft, is a circular particle acceleration track. The Torus is actually built into the ship. I imagine the same is true of Khan's timecraft, since that is the logical shape for a timecraft to be.'

'And that in turn makes one reconsider all the persistent tales about flying saucers,' said Dr Dubendorf. 'Perhaps the people who claimed so earnestly to have seen flying saucers from another planet had merely seen Magus machines on a visit from the future.'

'That of course is a distinct possibility,' answered Steerforth with a frown. 'Nothing we yet know of the future as it currently exists suggests that time travel will ever become commonplace, but on the other hand very little that we currently know can be regarded as more than strictly provisional.'

We made our way in a somewhat sombre silence to the next room, which was a store for any consumables we would take on our journey to the past.

'I must emphasise,' said Steerforth, 'that the range of consumables on board the Magus will be strictly limited. The ship is designed to be a vehicle for transportation and a travelling armoury and workshop, not a place to reside for any length of time. At our target date we will live in the style of the contemporary population. We will eat their food and live in their habitations. Our stores will consist of medicines and emergency food and drink. There will be absolutely no modern luxuries such as tobacco or alcohol.'

The most impressive area of the ship remained to be explored. The rooms, as I have explained, radiated outward from a central core. At the lower level this core served as an access well to the different sections of the ship. In the floor of this well was an enormous hatch, some fifteen feet across, which would permit an engineer to descend into the bowels of the particle accelerator if ever that should be necessary. I am sure that I for one hoped that such an operation would never be needed. Built into the wall of the core well was a small lift which could take people, three at a time, up to the level of the conning tower at the centre of the Magus III, or – as we came to know it – the bridge. Standing in the bridge one could easily have forgiven Steerforth a sudden but serious attack of the sin of pride, for here of all places one could sense the power and elegance of the machine he had created. We sat in a number of high-backed leather chairs, with the Magus controls before us. An elaborate keyboard with a full range of alphabetic and numeric characters, plus a number of keys associated with special functions, was set before each chair. The windows of the timecraft were deployed to left and right. But the most impressive feature of the bridge was a gigantic screen which lay between the windows and which could be programmed to show the scene outside the Magus III, vital figures of any of the ship's operational functions, and an apparently infinite variety of other data in numbers, words or graphs. Truly the Magus III's bridge was the answer to a computer fiend's dreams. And while the keyboard was more convenient for some numerical operations, it was easy to control most functions by word of mouth. Seated before the bridge display of the Magus III, one felt oneself to be treading in the footsteps of some fictional hero from the pages of Jules Verne or Edgar Rice Burroughs. Once again I was impressed with the improbability of it all – that such adventures would fall so late in life to one whose days had been hitherto spent in scholarly and contemplative pursuits.

'While we are all gathered together,' said Steerforth, 'it might be as well to deal with the allocation of responsibilities. I have tried to match everyone's job with his or her abilities. Mr Steele will be the ship's quartermaster, checking the stores whenever we touch our home base. Somebody has to take overall control of the mission and be ultimately responsible for everything that happens on the ship. Since the whole thing was my mad idea in the first place, I suppose that had better be me.'

'Dr McGrath will be the Executive Officer,' said Steerforth. 'She will take over my responsibilities when I am ashore or when I am indisposed. She will be responsible to me for the good order and running of the ship and will resolve day-to-day problems on my behalf. But that is not her only responsibility. McGrath will also act as the ship's Chronogator.'

'Chronogator?' cried Edwina May. 'What in the world is that?'

'It's just the same as a navigator, but you steer in time as well as in space.'

'Holy cow!' shouted Edwina May. 'Do you guys want to end up lost in the upper reaches of infinity? I've never been good at math and I read maps like they were upside down. Thanks for the vote of confidence, Captain, but I think you should fire me now before I do any damage.'

'You will find that the Magus computers make the job an easy one from the mathematical point of view,' answered Steerforth with a smile. 'I am sure your mental alertness and memory for telling details will make you a most efficient Chronogator.'

Since Edwina May voiced no more protests, but merely shrugged her shoulders and rolled her eyes all round her spectacle lenses, she was confirmed in the jobs that the Commander had given her. I had a feeling that Steerforth had considered quite carefully the allocation of jobs to people, and would be less than interested in any conflicting opinions.

'Dr Dubendorf has one of the most exacting jobs, that of Chief Scientist to the ship. As you know, this ship was built from the original designs created by Khan and myself at Oxford. The maths included in those plans were mine, and I understand them very well. The physics belonged to Khan, and my comprehension of it is only partial. It was enough to build the ship, but not enough to understand fully how everything works. I want you, Konrad, to make yourself master of the Magus technology in every detail. We will all be much safer when you have done so.'

'I understand my task and will do my best,' answered Dubendorf with an even smile. It was difficult to imagine that anything could ever unsettle this placid but keen-minded man. By now I was beginning to wonder what task Steerforth might have reserved for me: I was not left for long in ignorance.

'Now Hawkesworth,' he said. 'Whatever we achieve or fail to achieve on this mission, we must remember that we are acting *sub specie aeternitatis*. It is for the good of mankind and the survival of the universe that we are venturing to attack Khan, not for any selfish ambition or desire for aggrandisement. We need to record what we do and why we do it. Whether or not such an account is ever published or read is another matter. If we fail, the kind of world in which books are freely published and read may disappear altogether. But we must make the effort to record our hopes and our actions now. If there is to be a posterity, let it know what we did and why we did it. Professor Hawkesworth is to be the ship's historian and to write the story of the Magus III.'

So it was agreed. Whether Steerforth truly believed that the history of our adventure was as essential as he said, or whether he simply created an apparently important task for the least physically active member of his crew, I cannot guess. But once I had accepted the task I turned my full attention to it in the hope and trust that it would prove as useful as possible. And that (for the benefit of any reader who has struggled through these pages thus far) is the genesis of this poor narrative, one which I know only palely reflects the great events it seeks to record. The faults of this account are not the result of a frivolous or casual interpretation of Steerforth's commission: I took him seriously when he said that we should look upon all we did in the light of eternity. No, the grave defects of this account are the result of its author's circumstances. Much that I would have liked to have written about at greater length, much that I would have wished to record of

Steerforth and Khan themselves, much that I would have wished to understand better and so to explain better about the science of time travel – I have been forced to omit. For like Marvell I seemed to hear, as I wrote these pages, 'time's winged chariot drawing near'. The task was entrusted to a sick old man. Let that be the answer to any critic who judges that the telling of the story does not match in grandeur the events thereof.

While we were still gathered together on the bridge, Steerforth asked us whether we had any questions about what we had been told and asked to do.

'I have a question,' I said. 'Why is there no provision for our intellectual refreshment? Why are there no books on board the Magus III?' Edwina May clapped a hand to her head as if she too should have noticed this grave deficiency. But Steerforth smiled gently.

'It is true that there are no books as such on the Magus III,' he confessed. 'But it's untrue that there is no literature. The trouble with books is that they are bulky and heavy, so that it becomes necessary to choose which books to bring and which to leave behind. What particular work interests you at the moment, Hawkesworth?'

'What about the poem that led us to our destination, Xanadu?'

'Very well. Magus, literature please. Coleridge's poem 'Kubla Khan'. Voice, text and manuscript versions. Begin.' What happened next was amazing. The elegant and cultured voice of the Magus computers began at once to read the familiar lines. At the same time the text of the poem appeared in one part of the huge display screen. The words appeared on the screen in a pleasant and unfussy type face and scrolled upwards as the voice advanced through the poem. But on another part of the screen, scrolling upwards at the same speed, was the manuscript version of the poem from the reading room at the British Museum – an accurate and beautifully displayed version of Coleridge's own script. A moment's silence followed the final line.

'How much of English literature is in the files?' I asked.

'Pretty well all of it,' answered Steerforth. I did not find that he exaggerated. Practically every known work of English literature was contained in the solid state magnetic memories of the Magus III computers, and wherever a manuscript version was extant in any of the world's libraries a facsimile copy of the document was also available. Critical works and scholarly journals were also included. I imagine that the source of this universal database (as it called itself) was some electronic library of that future age in which the Magus III had been constructed. I cannot think of any university of the contemporary era that could make such a literary compendium available to its readers. It was indeed a reassuring sign that the scholars of that future age valued the master works of the past enough to create such a database. There were two other characteristics of the universal database which, when I became aware of them, impressed me deeply. The first was that its range was not restricted to literature; it held files on physics, chemistry, mathematics, politics, economics, medical science – indeed on every branch of human knowledge. What a life the scholars of that future age must enjoy, able to range at will over the whole corpus of human knowledge! To them the polymaths of our own age such as Leonardo, Samuel Taylor Coleridge himself and Newton must appear as bumbling idiots grubbing about in the undergrowth of the world of knowledge, dependent upon the weak and fallible instrument of unaided human memory. Or do I place too much emphasis upon the value of the instruments of record and recall? Perhaps Coleridge's own memory, which he described as 'tenacious and systematising', was as subtle and powerful a tool as those millions of linked microcircuits that made up the Magus III system of intelligence. The second fact that became obvious to me as I used the Magus III files was that Steerforth had carefully excluded any references to material published after our own time. Or perhaps more likely he had just told the computers to do so. No material, and no reference to any material, after the year 1981 appeared on the screen in response to any enquiry, no matter how cunningly framed to elicit such a reply. Steerforth was obviously holding to his principle of interfering as little as possible with the workings of the future or the past.

It was lunchtime when we had finished our tour of inspection. Mr Steele met us with the small bus and in a quarter of an hour we were back at Bain Brook. I noticed as we left the disused hangar that there was only a simple bolt and padlock on the door. I could not help wondering what some simple country villain might make of things if he were to break open the lock in the hope of finding a few sacks of corn or a dozen chickens, only to find himself face to face with a timecraft built in the future. At the great house we were served with a simple luncheon of game pie, salad and fresh fruit. The only tribute to the special nature of the occasion was that (exceptionally we were assured) a bottle of

Bollinger was opened. After the meal copies of an instruction manual about the Magus were distributed to all crew members, and we were left for private study and reflection. I must confess that for my part after such revelations in the morning an afternoon sleep had become a necessity. Steerforth I think spent some time watching a Test Match between England and Australia which chanced to be shown on television, but most of the day answering questions from Drs Dubendorf and McGrath, who were taking their duties very seriously indeed. We were all informed that a week's serious training on the operation of the Magus III would begin in the morning. With his customary thoughtfulness Steerforth had provided some notebooks and an endless supply of pens and pencils so that I could, if I chose, make a start on my task as the project historian. He also informed me that all the papers he had kept from his years with Khan were available in the Bain Brook library and had also been copied into the Magus III files. I spent an hour or two making notes of dates and incidents I could remember from 1948 onwards, and compiling a list of questions to ask Steerforth about matters I had either forgotten or never known. Later in the same afternoon I learned that Konrad Dubendorf had returned to the old hangar to use the science sections of the universal database. By dinner time Dr McGrath had drawn up a schedule of activities for the remaining week, which she read out to us in her firm clear voice. At last the great adventure was about to begin in earnest.

The next morning, early, Mr Steele was dispatched to drive round the estate and make sure that no unwelcome intruders were about. As soon as Steele reported the coast reasonably clear of all but those who had a right to be there, we opened the hangar door and the gate to the gembike store and Steerforth rode one of the vehicles down into the sunshine. It rode about a foot above the ground and rose smoothly to compensate for any bumps it encountered. He brought it to a halt before us and it sank gently to the ground.

'Right, lady and gentlemen,' said Steerforth, 'lesson one on the gembike. It is a Ground Effect Machine – hence its name. Like a hovercraft it rides on a cushion of air which raises it above ground level. Unlike a hovercraft it has no propellers or jets for forward motion. The cushion of air itself is deflected to generate movement forward, backwards or from side to side. The controls are designed to resemble those of a conventional motorbike. There is a throttle to accelerate or decelerate, brakes to bring you to a halt and handlebars to turn left or right. All clear so far?' We indicated our assent.

'Good. The upper surface of the apron here' – he pointed to where the metal apron flared outwards, just where a normal motorbike has wheels – 'this surface is aerodynamically shaped to generate lift, like the upper surface of an aircraft's wing.'

'So the lift from the upper surface also accentuates the lift generated by the gem?' asked Dr Dubendorf.

'It does more than that,' said Steerforth. 'Above speeds of about 150 or 160 kilometres per hour, the lift of the aerofoil is actually enough to counter the weight of the bike and the rider. This means you can actually fly a gembike like a small aircraft.'

'At what height?' I asked timidly.

'In theory at any height we choose. In practice there is no point in flying at more than a few feet off the ground, since if you slow down you must revert to the gem to keep you airborne.'

Chosen as the first to try out the machine, Edwina May mounted the gembike and turned on the motor. At once a soft but powerful hum was audible.

'What powers this thing, anyhow?' she suddenly asked.

'It's a small nuclear motor,' said Steerforth. 'Nearly all the power units on the Magus III are based on fission or fusion.' Dr McGrath blanched a little.

'I want you to use the throttle to lift you off the ground, but use the brakes to stop you moving forward.' She followed his instructions and the gembike slowly lifted itself off the grass. The noise of the air blowers was not as loud as I had expected, and certainly much quieter than a conventional motorbike.

'What about balance? How likely am I to fall off?' asked Dr McGrath.

'I hesitate to say this, in case you regard it as a challenge,' said Steerforth. 'But the balance of the air cushion is adjusted by computer to compensate for the rider's movements. It is more or less impossible to overturn a gembike.' He showed her how to move the bike forward and backward with the throttle and how to turn gently to right or left. Soon she made a circuit of the field.

'Hey this is fun!' she cried, as she gently lowered the gembike to the ground. We all took turns to make a circuit. Mr Steele, who was a professional driver of cars, found the gembike very easy to control. So too (after our initial hesitations) did Dr Dubendorf and I. To my surprise I found the gembike one of the most congenial forms of transport I had ever tried. It was as easy to control as a pedal bicycle but as effortless as a powerful motor car. It was highly satisfactory to lean over into a turn and to feel the air cushion gently but firmly swing one back into the vertical. When we had completed the first training run, Steerforth proceeded to the next phase of our induction.

'You can all see that the gembike has a small computer control panel just where the fuel tank of a petrol-driven bike would be. That system has a number of features which I will now demonstrate.' Steerforth mounted the gembike and rode it away in a wide circle, turning at last to face the old hangar where the Magus III was parked. Without warning he accelerated the gembike towards the hangar. Silently but swiftly the machine hurtled towards the solid wall and Steerforth towards apparently certain death. By the time the machine and its rider were ten metres from the wall, they must have been moving at above 140 kilometres per hour. I noticed with horror that Steerforth had taken his hands off the controls of the gembike, as if to ensure that he made no effort to save himself. Equally suddenly, however, the bike veered to the left and shaved the corner of the hangar with a few inches to spare. Steerforth slowed down and turned the gembike back towards us, coming to rest gently on the ground.

'The gembike's computers and its sonar system won't let you ride into a wall,' he explained. 'Any solid object that represents a danger to the rider will be flown round or over. At the worst, the gembike simply does a U-turn and flies back the way it came. Now watch this.' Steerforth rode his gembike backwards into the Magus III and brought it to rest among the other bikes. He made an adjustment to the controls on his own machine, and as if by magic all the others rose into the air. He slowly rode out into the sunshine again. Equally slowly the other gembikes followed on in convoy. Once in the open air the five other gembikes took up an arrowhead formation on either side of Steerforth. As he moved out across the field the riderless gembikes moved in harmony, their speed and direction obviously controlled by Steerforth's machine. Once again Steerforth rode back towards the hangar at speed. But this time it was the gembike on the extreme right of the flying wedge that seemed destined to smash itself into the hangar wall. At the last moment it veered and slowed, tucking itself neatly in behind the bike on its left and skirting the hangar wall with a small but safe margin. As soon as it could, it resumed its proper place in the arrowhead formation.

The spare gembike of the six was returned to the store. The

remaining five were deployed so that Steerforth was at the point of the arrow with Dr McGrath on his right and Mr Steele outside her. For although Mr Steele was not to be a time traveller, Steerforth could not deny him the ride on a gembike. I was on Steerforth's left hand and Konrad Dubendorf on mine. We set off gently across the fields, then as we reached open land Steerforth increased our speed. In convoy we raced across the pastures and the arable land. We zipped through a herd of cattle, our sonar/computer systems ensuring that no collisions took place. The gembikes were so silent and our speed so great that I don't believe they even knew we had passed. As we headed towards a distant copse Steerforth increased our speed to over the critical point of 150 kilometres per hour and I felt my machine tremble slightly as the aerofoil began to operate. At a height of forty feet we sped silently over the treetops of Bain Brook, for all the world like a coven of witches on their broomsticks. I heard Edwina May's voice raised in excitement and exultation.

'That is the most fantastic machine!' she cried, when we had returned to the old hangar and dismounted. There was no one to argue with her. My own pulse was racing and my heart pounding. But my spirits were soaring like the gembike, and I felt more alive than I had for many years.

That evening we all gathered in the library – that same library where I had suffered my slow lapse into unconsciousness. When everyone was seated, Steerforth stood up and spoke.

'Lady and gentlemen, it now seems to me that we have done everything we can to prepare for the first part of our campaign. The Magus III is fully provisioned. Our course in space and time has been plotted and checked dozens of times and is now programmed into the Magus III computers. Konrad is gradually mastering the technical complexities of the timecraft and Hawkesworth has a good grasp of the facts leading up to our departure, which he can commit to his impeccable prose whenever he has leisure to do so. Let me tell you all now where and when we are going on our first intervention. Our first time trip will take us to Khan-Balik, the capital of the Mongol empire close to the site of modern Peking. You will find that then, as now, the city was populous and busy. It should be relatively easy for us to pass ourselves off as Frankish traders – Frankish in Mongol terms covering any kind of western European.'

Steerforth now turned to Edwina May.

'EM, I am afraid you face a choice. In the age to which we are travelling, a female trader would not be credible. We need another cover for you. Which is it to be – a serving woman or my wife?'

'Your wife,' said Edwina May promptly.

'The year will be 1260. Kubilai – for that is the correct Tartar form of Kubla Khan's name – has been on the throne of the Khaghan for almost one year. We do not know how firmly he is established on the throne, for his succession was certainly contested. His campaign to confirm and extend his power over the Mongol empire and beyond has already begun. At his *khuriltai* or coronation he promulgated an edict in which he adopted a name for his reign. The name is *Chung-t'ung* or the point of balance. Already he sees history at a pivotal point.'

'If we are to defeat Khan in his attempt to overthrow world history, we must first understand his plans. We know that the Mongol empire was one of the most powerful and menacing institutions in the history of the world. Just how Khan plans to turn it to his own purposes remains to be seen.'

'Let us suppose,' said Konrad Dubendorf, 'that in some way he changed the course of history. What would happen?'

'I don't know,' said Steerforth candidly. 'Perhaps if we fail we shall simply return to a world that is changed beyond all recognition, a world in which all the history books have ceased to exist.'

Next morning at ten o'clock the Magus crew was once again transported to the timecraft. Mr Steele, who drove the small bus out to the airstrip, was somewhat disappointed by Steerforth's final insistence that he must remain with the servants at Bain Brook. Steerforth had always said as much but Steele was hoping to persuade him at the last moment to relent. At length we said our farewells and watched the bus trundle down the path to Bain Brook. We boarded the Magus III and stowed the few things we had brought with us. We were to assemble on the bridge for our time shift just before eleven o'clock. I sat for a few moments gathering myself for the experience ahead. My thoughts had changed. Ever since Steerforth had begun to tell me about the Magus experiments I had been forced to try to wrap my aged mind round the concept of time travel. Once I accepted the idea of time as a fourth dimension, the idea of *not* being able to travel in time became as absurd as finding oneself utterly immobile in space. Naturally one moved about the three-dimensional world on one's daily business, on journeys of greater or lesser significance. We even make rendezvous in space and time: 'I'll see you in Paris next week,' we say. But though our journey through space is planned and controlled, our journey through time had been (thus far) linear and unchangeable. Now our relation with time could be normalised. Yet all that theoretical knowledge counted for little now. I forced myself to sit in front of the mirror in the washroom and look myself in the eye. I noticed that despite the importance of the occasion I had shaved in a rather haphazard fashion.

'You are a silly old man dying of cancer sitting in a washroom and talking to himself,' I told my friend in the mirror. 'But for all your silliness the fact is that in a few minutes of your subjective time this age will cease to hold you and you will find yourself in thirteenth century China.' The thought seemed too fantastic to contemplate longer alone, so I went to join the rest of the crew, reflecting as I went that we were all at the mercy of our new Chronogator. I hoped she knew which buttons to press to take us in a few microseconds hurtling back in time past two world wars, past the industrial revolution, past the age of reason, past the wars of the roses and into the era of the Tartar emperors. And I hoped too that she knew how to get us back.

When we were all assembled on the bridge, Steerforth asked us to take our seats in front of the big screen. Without hesitation Steerforth handed over control of the launch to our new Chronogator and Executive Officer.

'Magus display current time data and go data. Display,' said Edwina May in a firm, clear voice. At once the screen showed a display of the actual time, ticking onward in tenths of a second. Beside it was our programmed departure time, now less than three minutes away. For some reason the last thought that flashed through my mind as we approached our programmed departure time was that in a few seconds I would again be in the same time and country as Abigail. The next thought that filled my mind was that the Magus had failed. I looked along the row of seats. Edwina May, Steerforth and Konrad were all looking at the screen with unchanged expressions. There had been no sensation of movement or vibration. Then I realised that the actual time and date display had changed. It showed that it was now just after midday on a June day in the year 1260 AD. If our coordinates were correct too, we were within the realm of the man that Marco Polo had described as 'the mightiest man, whether in respect of subjects or of territory or of treasure, who is in the world today or who ever has been, from Adam our first parent down to the present moment'. I could not help but wonder whether Messer Marco's admiration for his employer would have been further enhanced if he had known that Khan had celebrated his eighteenth birthday in 1954 – a year which also marked the seven hundredth anniversary of Marco's birth.

'External display please,' said Edwina May as soon as she had recovered her composure.

'At last,' murmured Steerforth, 'we have arrived.' The huge screen was filled with a picture of a pleasant upland scene, grassy and sunkissed. In every direction that the eye could see were gently undulating hills and valleys. Through some of the valleys the eye could detect the glint of distant streams. Some way off towards the right of the screen ran a double row of tall trees. Edwina May told the Magus computers to rotate the view, and we saw that to the north the gentle slope broke into rockier heights. At Steerforth's command the Magus lowered itself gently to the ground, coming to rest on the grass at a slight tilt. The doors were opened and we stepped out on to the hillside. I stooped and touched the grass. It felt no different from the grass of the modern world. Not far off were some pats of dung, perhaps from cow or deer. No animals were in view, though I suppose the sudden materialisation of a large timecraft might have prompted the instant departure of any that had been about. Apart from the distant trees, which we could now see marched in carefully planted lines towards the northern horizon, there was no sign of human habitation.

'Right,' said Steerforth, 'our first tasks are to find a place to park the Magus that's reasonably inconspicuous and then to assume our disguise as Frankish merchants. We are certainly in the right place. Those trees are planted to mark the main highways, for the benefit of travellers who've lost their way. That should be the main road from Cho-chau to Khan-Balik.' It also transpired that Steerforth had planned the date of our arrival quite carefully. According to Marco Polo it was Kubilai Khan's habit to spend the months of June, July and August at his northern capital of Kai-ping-fu, which he would later rename Shang-tu or Xanadu. Thus we might have several weeks to accustom ourselves to life in Khan-Balik without the immediate danger of being recognised as strangers and taken at once into the court of the Great Khan.

Like so many children allowed a brief excursion into the open air between classes, the Magus crew were soon ushered back to their places in front of the big screen.

'It won't be exactly easy to find a hiding-place for something as big as the Magus III, will it?' I asked innocently.

'What we can't find we may have to make,' said Steerforth, as
he lifted the Magus gently into the air. 'Rotate 180 degrees,' he
told the computers, and the smooth scrolling of the panorama
across the screen told us his command was being obeyed. The
Magus climbed slowly up the green hillside for a few miles until
the grass gave way to patches of scrub amidst scattered rocks.
Magus III rotated once more to give us a complete view of the
surrounding countryside. There seemed to be no evidence of
human habitation, nor did the terrain seem likely to appeal to
nomadic Mongols and their herds. The rocky patch over which we
now hovered seemed the highest land for some distance around. I
was about to suggest that the Magus, perched on top of a rocky
incline, would be about as inconspicuous as the Eiffel Tower, when
Steerforth demonstrated what he meant by making a hiding-place.
He slowly elevated the timecraft until it was several hundred feet
above the ground. Then he gave his instructions to the computers.

'We need a hole large enough to hide the Magus III from sight
and with a reasonable clearance round the circumference – say
two metres. Can you do that?'

'Is the use of lasers acceptable?' asked Magus III.

'We detect no sign of human habitation. Do you agree?'

'Yes,' said the Magus.

'Then the lasers may be used.'

'Ready to execute,' said Magus III.

'Execute,' said Steerforth. A faint pulse ran through the ship as
the laser guns fired. Almost at once great clouds of smoke, dust
and vaporised rock hurtled up past the big screen, obscuring our
view of the outside world. The laser burn lasted for perhaps four
or five minutes. Then Steerforth backed the timecraft far enough
for us to inspect the job Magus had done. It was astonishing. The
Magus had carved out of the solid rock a flat-bottomed indentation
about thirty feet deep. It was easily large enough to accommodate
the timecraft, and the edges of the hole had been very considerably
raked so as to make entry and exit easy for the passengers. The
rock was still hot and we had to hover there for another half-hour
before we could sink into our hiding-place. When we did, the huge
vessel fitted as neatly into its mooring as a plastic cup in a holder.
It was necessary to wait some further time for the rocks to cool
enough for us to leave the craft. We passed the time by taking a
meal and by exchanging our twentieth-century clothes for those of
travelling merchants in the thirteenth. The clothes Steerforth had
prepared for us looked authentic enough to me, though whether

they would convince our new contemporaries was yet unproven. Given that it was summer they seemed a little heavy. We each wore stockings of dull grey wool, an undershirt of cotton with long sleeves and a knee-length skirt, and a short-sleeved overall falling to our ankles. We all wore stout sandals of leather tied up with leather laces and wide-brimmed hats made of felt. We were to carry our possessions – including a change of clothes, though Steerforth warned us that we would risk detection if we changed our clothes more than once a fortnight – in leather bags with a drawstring at the neck. Each of us also strapped on a money-belt carrying small ingots of gold and silver. At Edwina May's insistence Steerforth reluctantly agreed that we might keep our modern underwear, plus one or two items of twentieth century luxury which she regarded as indispensable.

'Without a toothbrush I don't leave this ship,' she stated flatly. Steerforth himself also packed a hand-weapon in his travel bag, preferring I suppose to risk detection rather than to leave us defenceless. Edwina May and Dr Dubendorf, both of whom normally wore spectacles, had been fitted out with contact lenses. The only other concession to modernity was that a pocket computer was hidden in the bottom of Konrad Dubendorf's bag, where we hoped it would never be discovered.

'How are we to travel to Khan-Balik?' asked Edwina May.

'It's less than forty miles from Cho-chau to the capital,' said Steerforth, 'so we could go on foot. But I think there may be a big advantage in having the gembikes close at hand, in case we need to get out of the city in a hurry. Therefore I propose that we should ride down at night, relying on the sonar and radar to keep us on the road. There is a risk, of course, even at night. But if anyone spots us, we'll have to hope he attributes us to an excess of mare's milk wine.'

As darkness fell we rode the gembikes out of the timecraft and up the slope to the lip of Magus's hiding-place. Looking down at the polished metal surface of our vehicle we knew that it was safe from detection unless anyone happened to climb to the very rim of the pit. Steerforth switched on both the panel and lights of his own machine and the radar lock that would keep us all in a tight arrowhead formation. We set off slowly down the hillside, feeling our bikes rise gently over the boulders strewn along the slope and the soft warm air on our faces. In half an hour we passed the spot where the Magus had first come to rest. Away to the north-east we saw again the two lines of tall trees that marked the highway silhouetted now against the darkening sky. In the south-east we saw for the first time some signs of human habitation, a long flat building with dimly lighted windows.

'Cho-chau is a well-known religious centre,' said Steerforth. 'That is probably a Buddhist seminary.' We joined the dark highway just north of the township, some miles beyond the point where the road forks eastward towards the ancient South Chinese province of Manzi and westward to Cathay. Far to the south-east the Sung emperor Tu-tsong still held court in the ancient city of Kinsai, in total defiance of the Khan of Khans. He would continue to do so for another eight years, when Kubilai's cunning general Bayan Ching-siang whose nickname was 'Hundred-eyes' would by a combination of military power and diplomatic cunning drive Tu-tsong into exile and persuade the dowager empress Sie-chi to surrender his kingdom to the Tartars. Marco Polo records that at the time of this, our first visit to the Mongol empire, the gentle Sung emperor in his southern citadel ran a state-aided adoption and marriage agency that dealt with 20,000 cases a year. He says nothing of what happened to these cases when the grimmer suzerainty of the Mongols extended over them.

It was as well for us that we took to the road by gembike rather than on foot. For though the Mongol Khans were justly famous in their own time for the roads with which their empire was traversed, the surface we now rode upon was hardly what the twentieth century calls a highway. It was liberally scattered with quite large rocks and in places so deeply pitted and cracked that a man walking might easily fall and break his leg. To be fair, I do not suppose the roads were designed for use at night: we certainly met no travellers on the road. Once or twice we passed a roadside cottage or an inn with oil lamps burning inside, but no one ventured out. Once we passed a group of horses tethered at the roadside, tall gaunt creatures with gleaming eyes. I expected them to rear and neigh as the gembikes swept round the corner in the road, but they just stared at us with fierce incredulous eyes and we were gone. I wondered for a time that it was considered safe to leave horses unguarded by the roadside. Later Steerforth guessed that this was one of the stations of the famous Mongol postal system where horses were kept in constant readiness for the Khan's messengers. The personal property of the Khan of Khans was not at risk, under whatever circumstances it might be found.

As the gembikes purred onward in their tightly controlled formation I found myself once again seized with momentary terror at the prospect of the adventure ahead of us. Running through my head like a dismal refrain were the sonorous lines from the *Historia Regum Francorum* by Philippe de Mousket:

> Et li Tartare fort et rice
> Gueroiierent viers Osterrice
> Et viers Hungrie derement. . . .
> Et s'ierent encor li Tataire
> Dieu anemi, Dieu aviersaire
> En la grant tiere de Roussie
> Et voloient destruire Austriie.

Such was the contemporary European view of the savage and pitiless people among whom we had cast ourselves. In preparation for my task as the chronicler of the expedition I had looked up in the Magus III's universal database these gloomy lines from the old Flemish versifier. They had led me on, almost against my better judgement, to a contemporary eye-witness account of the Mongolian hordes at work and play. When the Tartars streamed across the frozen Danube into Austria and prepared to lay siege to Wiener Neustadt, the heretic French cleric Yvo de Narbonne had been faced with a singularly unpalatable dilemma. Should he turn westward and face the Papal inquisition or sit tight and risk capture by the Mongols? It is a tribute to the discipline of the Church of Rome that he elected to face the invading armies of Batu Khan rather than the correction of the Vicar of Christ.

This present Summer, wrote Yvo, the foresaid Nation, being called Tartars, departing out of Hungarie, which they had surprised by Treason, layd siege unto the very same Towne, wherein I myself abode, with many thousands of soldiers.

Neither were there in the said Towne on our part above 50 men of warre whom, together with 20 Crosse-bowes, the Captaine had left in Garrison. All these, out of certaine high places, beholding the enemies vast Armie, and abhorring the beastly cruelty of Anti-Christ his accomplices, signified forthwith unto their Governor.

The hideous lamentations of his Christian subjects, who suddenly being surprised in all the Provinces adioyning, without any difference or respect of condition, Fortune, Sexe or Age, were by manifold cruelties, all of them destroyed; with whose carkasses, the Tartarian chieftaines, and their brutish and savage followers, glutting themselves as with delicious cakes, left nothing for vultures but the bare bones. And a strange thing it is to consider that the greedy and ravenous vultures disdained to prey upon any of the reliques which remained.

Old and deformed Women they gave, as it were for daylie sustenance, unto their Dog-headed Cannibals; the beautiful devoured they not, but smothered them, lamenting and scritching, with forced and unnatural ravishments. Like barbarous miscreants, they deflowered Virgins until they died of exhaustion, and cutting off their tender Paps to present for dainties unto their chiefs, they engorged themselves with their Bodies. . . .

I could not forbear a glance at the shadowy figure of Edwina May, whizzing along in her appointed place in our formation, as these hideous words formed in my mind. The fractured and inconsequent grammar of the passage seems only to add to its force, as if the author was partly distracted in the act of composition by the very screams of the dying maidens. And it was against such a people, with Inayat Khan at their head, that we had pitted ourselves! A nuclear physicist, a postgraduate student, a noble publisher and a senile professor. . . . Even Steerforth's cricket caps seemed inadequate in the face of such a foe.

But in a moment my attention was jerked away from these macabre visions. For a mile or so we had been descending gently into a river valley. I wondered for a moment whether we would have to steal a ferry-boat to get ourselves across or whether the gembikes would work equally well on water. I need not have concerned myself. For as the sound of the rippling water grew louder in our ears Steerforth slowed and halted.

'This is the river Pulisanghin,' he said, 'or as it is known in our time the Sang-kan ho. Ahead of us is the famous marble bridge, which Marco Polo described as incomparable in all the world. Let us see whether the old adventurer was right.' As we advanced, I was amused to reflect that while it was undoubtedly understandable that Steerforth should refer to Messer Marco in these terms, the author of *Divisament dou Monde* was at this moment a child of six or seven years in faraway Venice, while his father and uncle were stranded by war in the western court of Barka Khan on the banks of the Volga and would not set foot in China for another six or seven years. But by the light of the stars we could tell that the bridge, when we rode on it, did not fall short of Marco's claim.

The span of the marble bridge was well above a furlong and its width on either bank about twenty-five feet. The gembikes retained their arrowhead formation without difficulty as we crossed. Looking down we could see the water foaming and swirling round the massive marble piers on which it rested, of which there were twenty-four in all. The bridge sloped upward as we moved forward and the roadway narrowed a little. The long central span was horizontal and walled with marble slabs on either hand, presumably for safety's sake. At the top of the rising section rose a column with a marble tortoise at its foot and a marble lion at its head. Five feet further on was another column. It was these columns that made the frame for the engraved panels of marble that walled the bridge. On the central panel of the bridge on either hand were engraved two Chinese symbols which Steerforth identified as those of the Chung-t'ung, the point of balance, the symbol of Kubilai's reign. They looked freshly carved as if the symbols of Kubilai had only recently replaced those of Mongu Khan, his predecessor. As we coasted gently down the slope towards the northern bank of the Pulisanghin river, Steerforth informed us that we were now only ten miles from Khan-Balik.

We rode a few more miles towards the city. Then Steerforth decided that the time had come to cache the gembikes and proceed on foot. Near a bend in the road, where the sound of a small stream tinkled in our ears, a footpath rose sharply from the highway only to peter out in rocky ground.

'Look,' said Dubendorf, 'isn't that the mouth of a cave?' And so it was, heavily shadowed by a rocky overhang and quite invisible from the road.

'Be careful,' said Edwina May. 'Our garage may be home sweet home to a bunch of bears or wolves.'

'Or lions,' added Steerforth.

'Lions?' I asked, a shade more nervously than I meant.

'Yes. Big brutes they are too, with horizontal stripes of black, orange and white. The Tartars use them for hunting wild boar and bulls. Those are just the tame ones, of course.' In spite of these forebodings the cave turned out to contain nothing more menacing than a few bats and rather a lot of cobwebs when we shone the beam of a gembike's headlamp into its interior. It was about as large inside as a reasonable-sized bicycle shed in an Oxford college, and scarcely any damper. There were no signs that it had ever been used for human or animal habitation. With the gembike motors still running they were weightless, so that it was an easy matter to manhandle them into the cave. Once they were inside, we spent another thirty minutes or so gathering branches and fronds of fern from the rocky hillside to camouflage the entrance to the cave. At length we felt that our garage was as well hidden as we could contrive and found our way carefully down the road.

'Wait just a moment,' said Steerforth, reaching into his travel bag. He took out a pocket knife of decidedly archaic design and began to cut a star-shaped incision into the tree nearest the footpath. 'It would be something of a disaster if we couldn't find our way back to the garage.' We stood waiting for him to finish, trying to memorise the place as best we could in the gloom. I felt a sudden cool breeze blowing from the north, perhaps from the region of the legendary Xanadu where (if we had planned right) Kubilai Khan was now passing his days. I was suddenly glad of the warm clothing we had on. But perhaps it was a shiver of apprehension rather than the chill. We walked on slowly down the highway, keeping as near the middle of the road as we could and using the tall trees planted on either side as our guides. There was still need for caution, for even in the proximity of the capital the road was still badly pitted. I was beginning to think that after travelling so far in space and time in the blink of an eye it would take us the rest of the night to travel the few miles into Khan-Balik when we came in sight of a lighted building. As we approached we saw that it was a well-built single-storey house made from wooden beams. The beams were sealed with lime or mud and two unglazed windows faced the road.

'We may be in luck,' said Steerforth. 'I think this is an inn.' The wooden door was slung on leather hinges and was unlatched.

In the centre of the room was a small fireplace where a fire of wood and coal was burning, the smoke rising to a vent-hole in the roof. Near the fire were a table and benches. Dozing at the fireside was our first example of thirteenth century *homo sapiens*. He was small, no more than five feet in height. His skin was pale and slightly creamy in colour. He was dressed in a single and rather tattered garment of dark material. As we entered he awoke suddenly and sat up to face us. His hair was very black and he wore a thin moustache and beard. I guessed that he was in his middle thirties. I suppose the four of us must have made a pretty startling sight, stepping in and out of the darkness. For a moment alarm was written across his features. I wondered how we were to communicate with him, for I was nearly sure that none of us spoke

a word of the Tartar or Chinese tongue. Then I saw Steerforth
had anticipated me. He had taken a gold ingot from his money-
belt and this he placed on the table before our host, then held his
hands open and outstretched in the universal gesture of one who
comes unarmed. The Tartar stood for a second gazing at the gold.
Then he ran with a furtive, shuffling gait to the doorway and
stood looking out into the night. He looked left and right, then
ran back and lowered the felt covers over the two windows. He
even glanced uneasily up at the vent-hole in the ceiling as if he
half-suspected an observer there. Only then did he pick up the
ingot and weigh it in his hand, looking hard at Steerforth all the
while as if the stranger's bearing would indicate the value of the
gold. He seemed satisfied with what he felt and saw. He put the
ingot in some pocket hidden in the interior of his robe, went to a
wooden cupboard in a corner of the room and came back with an
earthenware pitcher and mugs. He was talking all the time in his
own language, a rather high-pitched stream that was quite un-
intelligible to us. Then he seemed to grasp that we were strangers
and filled the mugs in silence. We drank. It was a white wine,
harsh and strong and warm – but white wine none the less.

'T'ai-yuan-fu,' said the Mongol, pointing to the pitcher. He
repeated it two or three times before we realised that he was
naming the origin of the wine, the Chinese city away to the south-
west.

'T'ai-yuan-fu,' we all repeated and he beamed with pleasure,
for all the world like a *sommelier* in a top-class restaurant who
sees his art appreciated by the guests. Thus encouraged he left us
for a moment but soon returned with some rough dark bread, a
few onions and a slab of what we later discovered was mare's milk
cheese. We sat on the benches by the fire and did justice to the
food. Our host hovered over us all the time, bringing out a pitcher
of milk when the wine was gone. The milk tasted creamy and
slightly rancid.

The innkeeper had built up the fire and we all began to feel
sleepy. When he had cleared away the vestiges of the meal, Konrad
Dubendorf indicated to him that we were tired. He understood at
once and, picking up one of the oil lamps, led us into a larger
adjoining room. Here we found two rows of pallets laid out on
the wooden floor and neatly piled blankets. The room was dark
and airless, but reasonably clean. On a table in one corner was a
pitcher of clean water. When our host left us, Edwina May was
able to indulge her only concession to modernity by cleaning her

teeth. Then we all lay down as we were, pulled the rough blankets over our tired bodies and prepared to sleep. Konrad Dubendorf blew out the oil lamp and I closed my eyes.

'You Europeans may find this situation odd,' said Edwina May softly as we drowsed off, 'but at least you can imagine that thousands of miles to the west your countries exist in some recognisable form. But as for me – why Columbus doesn't set sail for another two hundred and thirty years!' In the night I woke suddenly to the noise of horses on the road outside the inn. Had we already been detected? Presently the riders (perhaps two or three in number) rode away into the night towards the south.

Next morning we rose early but found our host already up and about. He served us a breakfast of bread and mare's milk, which we were to find were the staple Mongol foods near towns. It then transpired that he wished by sign language to conduct a financial transaction and to offer us a piece of advice. He took from his pocket the small bar of gold with which Steerforth had paid for our night's food and lodging, and set it on the table.

'*Altan*,' he said, pointing at the gold. We had learnt our first word of mediaeval Mongolian. He picked up the gold, smiled and pocketed it, conveying quite clearly its acceptability to him. Then he pointed down the road towards the city, and creased his face into a hideous grimace.

'*Altan*,' he said again, drawing his finger across his throat.

'To use gold in Khan-Balik is to die,' said Konrad softly. The innkeeper pointed at each of us in turn, drawing his finger across his throat with a blood-chilling leer. If any of us used gold in the city, all would suffer the same fate. In the babble of strange words with which he accompanied this warning, two words struck my ear. '*Altan Khaghan . . .*' he repeated several times. The gold belonged to the Khan of Khans. I explained this to my friends, then held my hands helplessly upward: what then should we use for money? He understood at once and took from his pocket a roll of small paper notes. He gave one to us to examine, obviously amused by our ignorance. It was black in colour and silky in texture. It was covered in closely written Chinese characters. It also carried a vermilion seal deeply embossed into the texture of the paper. Apparently this was the paper money of the Khan's empire. We later found that its use was widespread and indeed obligatory on penalty of death. But for the advice of our host, we might have found ourselves in trouble with the currency police on our first day in Khan-Balik.

'If it's as dangerous as that to accept gold, why did he take ours?' I wondered aloud.

'He checked very carefully that we were alone last night,' said Konrad. 'Perhaps the value of the bar he was offered so far exceeds his normal charge that he is willing to take the risk.' We all laughed at that, for Konrad had spoken like the canny Swiss he was, with an eye for a worthwhile financial proposition. Our host joined in the merriment, despite the fact that he cannot have understood a word we said. With cries of encouragement and many waves he saw us off down the road to Khan-Balik. As he stood in the doorway, another figure joined him, smaller and slimmer even than himself. We presumed it was his wife, kept out of the way until then for some unknown reason. Perhaps foreigners were considered inherently dangerous.

We walked briskly down the highway towards the city. On the road we began to pass more and more travellers, nearly all Mongols. Both men and women wore a long, voluminous garment rather like an academic gown tied tightly round the waist, with cotton trousers underneath. The men wore boots of felt or leather but the women went mostly barefoot.

'Sex discrimination here too,' muttered Edwina May, though the women seemed contented enough to walk barefoot over the warm stones of the highway. We passed an open field where a Mongol encampment had been set up. Some cattle, horses and ponies were tethered to the branches of the trees. For the first time we saw the traditional travelling home of the Mongol tribesmen, the *yurt*, with its circular wooden walls, domed roof and felt covers.

There were half a dozen tents in this group, all pitched to face the south as is the Mongol custom. Nearby were the small, two-wheeled trollies with felt coverings in which they carried their precious or sacred objects. All around the tents were women busying themselves with housework, stitching clothes, tending the cattle and looking after the children. At first I thought the figure standing watch over the women was a warrior in a plumed helmet, but then I saw that it was a woman wearing the feather-crested bonnet, the *boktag* that marked superior from inferior females. She had a stick in her hand and would occasionally lash out at one of the women if she was not satisfied with the work rate, or at one of the children if its play seemed likely to attract the displeasure of the lords and masters. The men all sat in front of the largest *yurt*, relaxing on blankets of felt or fur. Despite the warmth of the day, the leader of this group was wrapped in a huge fur, presumably as a display of wealth and power. He did not trouble to glance aside as the group of strangers, tall and pallid, passed his camp. Some of the children ran over to the edge of the field to watch us pass. On their faces, as on those of the passers-by, were expressions of mild curiosity but none of hostility. Our disguise as Frankish traders appeared to have passed the first test.

Suddenly everyone in sight made swiftly to the verges of the highway, almost as if they expected to be strafed by a low-flying aircraft. Instinctively we did the same, but without the faintest idea why. We soon found out. Down the road came riding a group of thirty or so Mongol warriors in full battle-gear, pushing their tough little horses forward at a brisk canter. They were a fearsome sight. Their heads were covered with conical steel helmets with leather flaps down to their shoulders. Each man had two bows tied at his back, one long and one short. Two quivers of arrows rattled at their hips and two swords were sheathed at their waists. Each carried a stout leather shield or target. Their saddles were simple pads of leather or felt tied to the mounts with leather thongs. Both men and mounts gazed steadfastly ahead and paid no notice to the people on either side of the road. Looking at the fierce features of these nomad warriors as they stormed past, I was struck with the fact that many of them bore a striking resemblance to a historical figure of our own era. For a moment I could not think who, but then I realised that it was the architect of the Russian revolution, Lenin himself. Imagine a cavalry charge of Lenins in barbaric armour and weaponry, if you can. Then you will have a faint appreciation of the impact made upon us by our first glimpse of a Tartar fighting force. And they weren't even fighting! They were perhaps part of the imperial guard just relieved from their period of duty at the palace and riding gently back to barracks. It took no effort of the imagination to understand how Batu Khan nineteen years earlier with a great army of such warriors had ripped open the doors of central Europe and knocked with such ferocity on the door of Christendom. And it took little imagination to understand the terror these nomad warriors had struck into the defending armies and the population at large. The clatter of horses' hooves seemed to keep pace in my mind with the sonorous beat of de Mousket's lines:

> Et li Tartare fort et rice
> Gueroiierent viers Osterrice
> Et viers Hungrie derement. . . .

The city of Khan-Balik was in reality three cities in one, though the third part of it had only just begun to be built. The first city was the old walled town of Chung-tu, which we now saw in the middle distance. Between us and Chung-tu sprawled huge and rambling suburbs where the common traders and passing nomads stayed. Further off was the vast twenty-four-mile-square p. : where Kubilai was already preparing to build the new city of Ta-Tu (or Taidu as Messer Marco called it). The streets of the suburbs were narrow and crowded with Chinese, Mongol and Arab traders and with noisy women and children. Some of the larger buildings were of stone. The smaller ones were just shacks with wooden frames and felt coverings. There were innumerable stalls where cooked meats, milk, cheese and clothing of every kind were on sale. The babble of voices and the ceaseless activity of a market town seemed no different from any commercial centre of our own age, so that I had to keep reminding myself that we were seven centuries away from our own time. It was nearly midday by now and we cast covetous eyes at the food and drink on the stalls: but we took the advice proffered by our host of the previous evening and kept our gold out of sight. At least in such a crowd of different tongues we seemed to attract little attention in our alien garb. So preoccupied did the people seem with their own affairs that we might have ridden through the crowd on our gembikes without being noticed – or perhaps not. We saw a number of other European faces in the crowd, and marked them down as Italian, French or German traders. One of them had a bolt of silk over his arm and was striding purposefully along with a tiny Chinese trader trotting beside him.

'That fellow seems to know where he is going,' said Konrad. 'Why not follow him?' The trader wore a long robe of yellow cotton over his vest and trousers, making it easy for us to trail him through several winding streets deeper into the suburbs. At length he and his Chinese companion halted before a small brick-built edifice set somewhat apart from the rest of the buildings. We saw a Chinese appear at the window of the building and speak for a moment to the trader. He disappeared and returned a moment later with a pair of scales. From a purse hung round his neck the merchant produced a handful of silver coins. The official carefully weighed them, examined them closely for quality, and at last counted out a substantial roll of the same blackish bank notes we had seen at the hostel. The trader paid his Chinese supplier, pocketed his change and set off alone with the silk under his arm.

We had discovered the means of legally changing our gold.

'*Altan,*' said Steerforth boldly, placing three small ingots in front of the official. The gold was carefully weighed and scrutinised. It struck me that he could not possibly detect real precious metal from a good job of plating without further equipment. But then I remembered our host's graphic gesture of throat-slitting, illustrating the penalties for improper financial dealings. The Khan of Khans had his own ways of encouraging probity. The official handed over a bundle of Mongol bank notes which seemed gratifyingly thick, though we had no means of checking the transaction. We retraced our steps and bought bread, cold meat and milk from roadside stalls. We sat on a low wall and ate our simple meal, watching the people mill past.

Our greatest need now was to find a place to stay in the suburbs of Khan-Balik. We had noticed a number of houses with some kind of display outside them, but none of us could tell which might be hostels.

'Look,' said Edwina May at last, 'there's our friend in the yellow robe. He might be staying in a hostel somewhere. Perhaps we should follow him again.' We fell in behind him as unostentatiously as possible and within an hour, having made several minor purchases in the market, he turned as if satisfied with his day's work and set off for home. He led us to a large stone building in a quiet and tree-lined side street. We waited in the road for a while before entering. When we went in, the man in the yellow robe was showing his purchases to another fellow seated on a sort of divan. To our astonishment we realised that we could understand what they were saying to each other. They were speaking an archaic and heavily accented form of French – but French none the less. Steerforth stepped forward as the two men turned to face us.

'Excuse me sirs,' he said in his best Parisian accent. 'You are French?'

'Yes we are,' said the seated man. 'And though you speak our language after a fashion you are clearly not.'

'No sirs,' said Steerforth. 'We are travellers from a distant country to the north of yours. We believe we are the first of our nation to have reached Khan-Balik.'

'You are traders like us?' asked the man in the yellow robe. Steerforth nodded agreement.

'Yes, I thought so,' said the Frenchman. 'I saw you at the money-changer's office.' We sat down and talked for a while to the two Frenchmen. This was indeed a hostel, one which served mainly as a lodging place for French merchants. They explained that the proprietor, a Chinese, was a friendly and honest fellow who would certainly make us welcome. And so it proved. Our new host was a tiny, shrewd-eyed man who accepted two or three notes from Steerforth's bankroll and showed us to our rooms. Compared with our lodgings on the road, they were luxurious indeed. He put three rooms at our disposal, of which Steerforth took one, Konrad and I another, and the third was left for Edwina May alone. He showed us where a well in the garden provided fresh water and, rather too close for our liking, a little privy stood. Each of us had a wooden cot to sleep on and blankets and furs to keep us warm. The two Frenchmen had a smattering of Chinese and passable Mongolian, so they served as interpreters whenever difficulty arose.

We were to stay for eight weeks in the house of the Frankish merchants, as we learned to call it. Our French friends could not have been more helpful. It transpired that they were cousins, and had come to China on a trading mission partly at the prompting of the French court. Later I was to recall this French commercial and diplomatic interest in the Mongol empire. It was only seven years earlier in 1253 that Louis IX had sent the Franciscan friar Guillaume de Roubrouck to Karakorum to sound out Mongu Khan on the prospects for Catholicism in the Mongol world. Our friends were obviously the commercial counterparts of this spiritual mission. We made it our practice to take our evening meal with them. Gradually we acquired a better grasp of their ancient French dialect. They even taught us a reasonable smattering of the Mongol language. One evening over dinner the conversation turned quite naturally to political matters. We learned that Kubilai Khan did not exercise quite the degree of unified control over the Mongol empire that we had expected.

'Kubilai Khan first came to prominence here about ten years ago when Mongu was the Khan of Khans,' said the Frenchman. 'By Mongu he was claimed as a blood-brother, the son of Tolui and the grandson of Chinghiz, the great originator of the Mongol empire. But his enemies say that Tolui had only three sons, Mongu, Hulagu and Arik Boge and that Kubilai was a foreigner who came first as a *darkhan* – a freeman follower – to the *yurt* of Mongu Khan. Later the story is that he showed great military skill and great magical powers and was adopted as Mongu's *anda* or sworn brother. In this case Kubilai could have no claim to the throne of Chinghiz, for only the blood line inherits the throne.' We gazed at each other in silence. We had often wondered how Inayat Khan had managed to insinuate himself into the Mongol royal family.

'Mongu Khan ascended the Tartar throne in the year of Our Lord 1251. Kubilai became the chief of his generals and led a force of seven *tumen* – seventy thousand warriors – against the Chinese kingdom in the south. Kubilai was suspected of secretly favouring the Chinese people above the Mongols. He seldom massacred whole populations, as is the Mongol custom when they conquer a foe. And then two years ago Kubilai persuaded his brother – if that is what he is – to move the imperial city from the old city of Karakorum. It was agreed that the new summer capital would be at Kai-ping-fu in the north and the new winter capital here in Khan-Balik. A new city is being built here for the purpose. But the Mongol people were greatly displeased. They believed that in both places the Khan of Khans would be surrounded by Chinese advisors and corrupted and weakened by them. Chinghiz had been proud that he wore the same tatters as his warriors, drank *kumiss* with them and sucked the blood from his horse's veins on campaign. There was a great uproar against Kubilai led by Arik Boge. He claimed that Kubilai was not his brother, but was a foreigner conspiring to enslave the Mongols to the Chinese. In the summer of last year both Mongu Khan and Kubilai were campaigning against Chinese rebels. Arik Boge remained in Karakorum. In the heat of the summer campaign, Mongu Khan fell ill of a disease and died. In the end Arik Boge was declared Khan of Khans at a *khuriltai* in Karakorum, while Kubilai was elected Khan in Khan-Balik. They remain today struggling for the true throne.'

'What of the barons, whom do they support?' asked Konrad.

'They too are divided,' answered the Frenchman. 'Hulagu the Khan of the Levant supports Kubilai, though it is said that he does not accept him as a blood-brother but only as an *anda*. But Barka Khan, the Khan of the Golden Horde, still supports Arik Boge. No one knows when the battle for the throne of Chinghiz Khan will be settled once and for all.' I could see that Steerforth was most interested to learn that Khan's grip on the Mongol empire was not yet secure. But we were to learn no more on this occasion. For the Frenchmen, feeling no doubt that they had furnished us with useful information, were beginning to grow a little inquisitive of us.

'Tell us about yourselves,' said one of them, 'you traders who neither buy nor sell, you who speak French that is not French and English that is not English. Where is this strange northern land you claim to come from?' We prevaricated as politely as we could. I supposed we could have told him any yarn and it would have been more plausible than the plain truth. But it was worrying that our cover story seemed so implausible.

A few days later Steerforth and Dubendorf were stopped and questioned by the city guards. They were returning from the market with food they had purchased. The guards were under instruction to question every foreigner in Khan-Balik. Steerforth was able to tell them the name of the street where we lived and the hostel proprietor's name. At length they were persuaded that the two Frankish traders might be released. We all agreed that we must be careful in future to be as unobtrusive as possible.

One afternoon while we were resting in our rooms we heard a sound of music approaching. We went into the street and joined a growing crowd of Mongols, Chinese and foreigners. We heard the procession long before we saw it, the high-pitched rattle of the *nakkaras* drums and the wail of the trumpets echoing up the road. At length there came in sight two or three hundred mounted warriors with the drummers and trumpeters in their midst. They rode onward at a trot through the streets of Khan-Balik, looking neither to the right nor left. The trumpets shrieked deafeningly as they passed by, the hooves of the horses throwing up great clouds of dust. After the horses came two huge war-elephants, the first we had seen. Each carried on its back a wooden shelter decorated with gold and fur. The shelter on the first elephant was decked in the striped skins of the Mongolian lion. In it sat a woman and a boy. This, we learned, was the *khatun* or first wife of the Khan of Khans. A great cry of 'Chingkim!' told us that the boy was the son of Kubilai, the heir apparent. We watched them ride by on their mighty elephants. The *khatun* was dressed in a simple silk gown but wore an elaborate *boktag* on her head. The boy was bright-eyed and alert, his skin a darker brown than his mother's. It was difficult to believe as we watched this mediaeval princeling ride by on his war-elephant that his father was a reputed twentieth century physicist. The second elephant evidently carried some of the senior officials of the court sent back from the summer palace to accompany the heir apparent and to conduct essential business in Khan-Balik. Among them we noticed a tall, thin-faced Arab in a brilliant white robe. He glanced suspiciously around the whole time, as if no one and nothing were to his liking. We were later to learn that this was none other than Ahmad, the Khan's Grand Vizier (to use an appropriately Moslem term) and expert tax raiser. Beside the Khan of Khans he wielded greater political power than any other man in the Mongol empire. He was cordially detested by Mongols and Chinese alike, and was reputed to have enriched himself to an unbelievable extent at the expense of his enemies – of whom there were many. All too soon we were to find ourselves in the uncomfortable position of needing some help from Ahmad.

The time was now approaching when we must return to the twentieth century and to the comfort of Bain Brook, there to reflect upon what we had learned of Khan and his plans. I know that Steerforth was looking forward to a pipe of tobacco, I to a glass of sherry and Edwina May to a shower and a Martini cocktail. Konrad seemed to miss the amenities of the modern age less acutely, or at least was less prone to admit his longings.

When disaster struck it came suddenly and without warning. We had made our way once more to one of the six official offices of the currency exchange, to turn some more gold into the black paper money of the Mongols. In a side street we came up to a group of Mongols, soldiers and civilians mixed. We moved to the other side of the street to avoid disturbing them. Pinned to the wall where they stood was a kind of rag doll made of scraps of felt and silk. It looked somewhat like a crudely made Guy for November fifth. Spread on the ground under this image were some items of food and drink. We could not have been expected to realise that this bunch of rags was as holy to these men as a monstrance to a Catholic, for it is a symbol of the Mongol ancestor-worship, an *ongon* of the spirit of the sage-like martial emperor, Chingiz Khan himself. The next moment two of the soldiers had simply grabbed Edwina May and propelled her into the space before the *ongon*. They pointed to the symbol, jabbering unintelligibly but making clear their intention by bobbing down reverentially before it. Edwina May was required to do homage to the symbol. There was a moment of silence. Then one of the soldiers lifted from the ground a jug of *kumiss* and flung the liquid into the air. It spattered over all of us, Mongols and strangers alike. Again the Mongol soldiers pointed to the *ongon* and jabbered their instructions. Edwina May turned on them, wiping the *kumiss* from her cheeks.

'Kiss my ass!' she said. It was perhaps fortunate that the Mongol soldiers did not understand the words she spoke, but her message was unmistakable. Before our horrified eyes and with nothing we could do to prevent it, the soldiers arrested the girl from Oak Bluffs on a charge of sacrilege. It was lucky that she was a foreigner and a woman. Otherwise she would have been beheaded on the spot. We stood in silence and watched as the soldiers marched her away under armed escort. Faced with their glinting swords there was nothing even Steerforth could have done, though his face was tense with frustrated fury as the woman he loved was led away to God knew what fate. In truth it was her American spirit of independence that had led her to violate the *Great Yasa*, the code of conduct on which all behaviour in the Mongol empire was based. It was a dispirited bunch of Frankish traders that made its way, one member missing, back to the hostel. In conversation with our French friends, who had a better knowledge of Mongol affairs than we, the true nature of Edwina May's offence became obvious. The *ongon* she had insulted represented not only the spirit of the sage-like martial emperor Chingiz Khan but also the symbol of the *Yeke Mongol ulus*, the Mongol nation. Failure to do the requisite obeisance to the *ongon* was a capital offence, which only the Khan of Khans might mitigate. As we explained what had happened, the Frenchmen became more and more concerned.

'Your friend has behaved very unwisely,' they said. 'There may be nothing you can do to save her. Perhaps it would be best if you returned at once to your own country.' Steerforth explained that it was contrary to the customs of our country to leave a friend in distress. The Frenchmen shrugged their shoulders, a gesture they appeared to have transmitted to their descendants unchanged by the passage of seven hundred years. We took that evening a sad and unappreciated evening meal, much to the disappointment of our Chinese landlord. The Frenchmen explained to him the disaster that had overtaken us. He nodded gravely. When the meal was over he came solemnly to our table carrying a bundle of wooden rods.

'What's this?' said Konrad. 'Surely he doesn't expect us to join in his heathen games at a time like this?'

'He wishes to do you the honour of consulting the *tolga*, the rods, concerning the destiny of your friend. It is a great honour he extends to a foreigner,' said the Frenchman. Only when the Chinaman began to toss the rods gently into patterns on the floor did I realise that he was consulting the traditional oracle of the Book of Changes, the *I Ching*, which survives until our own day. What the rods showed was clearly something of a surprise to him.

'Your friend is in conflict with the *ch'ien-yuan*, the original creative force in the universe. Hence the ill-spirit that led her to insult the *ongon* of the sage-like martial emperor. Yet the *tolga* also state a curious thing, foreigner. They say that the foreign woman was not destined to die before she was born. This would be contrary to the natural law. I do not know what this signifies. How could she die before she was born?'

'All too easily, I fear,' muttered Steerforth: but we all took it as a good omen. On a more practical note our landlord suggested that, if we had the necessary funds, we should approach the Grand Vizier Ahmad and offer him a bribe to liberate Edwina May. What had begun to worry Steerforth was that Edwina May might be interrogated by the Khan's police and that some hint of her true origin might be dropped. After all, the soldiers had already been cross-examining foreigners in the streets of Khan-Balik. No doubt the Khan himself would be intrigued to discover an American girl in his mediaeval prison.

Next day it was agreed that Steerforth and I should go alone to the office of the Grand Vizier. This necessitated for the first time our venturing into the city itself. We made our way through the noisy streets of the suburbs and presented ourselves at one of the gates in the central city walls. At first the Mongol guards refused us entry, but a handful of black banknotes at length overcame their suspicions. We had not the slightest idea where to go. The buildings of the central city were all stone-built and much grander than those of the suburbs. The streets were also less crowded and many of the buildings were guarded by armed warriors who stared suspiciously at us as we passed. We wandered about for nearly two hours before we met a Mongol in civilian dress who understood our intent, and led us a few blocks down the street to a palace with pleasant gardens. Carved on the wooden door of this palace were the two symbols of the *Chung-t'ung*, the royal symbol of Kubilai Khan. We were met, of course, by a junior official who took a long time and another bundle of banknotes before he would hand us on to his superior. By mid-afternoon we were – albeit tired and a good deal poorer than when we started – waiting in the ante-room of the Grand Vizier. An hour later an aide emerged and beckoned us to follow him.

Ahmad was seated in a chair so solid and ornate that it was almost a throne. A small table stood beside him, at which his emanuensis sat writing with a bone stylus in Arabic script. Ahmad himself was a very sharp-faced man with greying hair and a quiet, rather menacing voice. When he spoke, it was (to our relief) in the mediaeval French to which we had now become accustomed.

'You are friends of the English woman who was arrested yesterday? There is little I can do to help you.' So Edwina May had claimed to be English: however dangerous such an admission, it was undoubtedly sensible. Trying to explain that she was American two centuries before Columbus would have been a thankless task.

'The offence which our friend committed was inadvertent,' said Steerforth. 'We are simple travellers who do not know the ways of your people. No insult was intended to the memory of the sagelike martial emperor.' Ahmad's eyes glinted a little at this precise formulation of Chinghiz Khan's title. Perhaps the travellers were not as simple as they claimed, he seemed to hint.

'Nevertheless the offence is grave,' he pointed out. 'Reverence to the *ongon* is prescribed by the *Great Yasa* and is obligatory on the Mongol *ulus* or state and all the *unagan bogol* – the conquered peoples. This includes not only you and your friends but also servants of the Khaghan like myself.' His eyes flickered momentarily towards the wall where hung a replica of the earth goddess Nachigai. But a slight sardonic smile hung on his lips as he spoke, as if he knew that Moslems and Christians alike might secretly despise the crude superstitions of the shamanist Mongol nomads. For some time the Grand Vizier went on, elaborating upon the heinous nature of Edwina's May's offence and on the unwisdom of travellers who failed to acquaint themselves with the customs of the lands they traversed. We forebore to point out that not only distance but seven centuries of time separated us from this particular country and its ways.

'This much I could do to help you,' said the Grand Vizier at length. 'In two weeks from today the great Khan of Khans will return from his summer palace at Kai-ping-fu. When he returns he will hold a great feast in the palace. At the end of the feast the Khan of Khans will declare an amnesty for all those charged with crimes against him. Such is the merciful spirit of the Great Khan. Perhaps it might be arranged that your friend will not be brought to trial and execution before the feast. In that case she may benefit from the amnesty. If that is the will of Heaven, I cannot say.' He sat brooding for a moment, his hands folded over his knees. His emanuensis laid down his stylus and gazed at us. It seemed that some reciprocal gesture was expected.

'Is it possible, Grand Vizier, to make some gift in order to demonstrate our appreciation in advance of such a gratifying outcome?' I asked. I had no idea of how overtly a bribe might be offered. Ahmad nodded and smiled, as if the very novelty of such a suggestion lent it a certain appeal.

'We have learned that it is contrary to the law to trade in gold,' remarked Steerforth.

'All gold belongs to the Khaghan,' said Ahmad promptly. 'But since I myself am nought but the Khan's possession, you may justly return to me what is in fact the Khan's.' Steerforth produced a dozen of the small gold ingots and set them in a row on the table. The Grand Vizier's eyes gleamed with pleasure: he was beyond question a most avaricious man. This time he deigned to stand when we left the room. We were apparently considered suitable clients for his august patronage.

The two weeks that passed after our visit to the Grand Vizier were wearisome indeed. For safety's sake Steerforth decided that we should stay as much as possible within the hostel. We had none of the amenities with us that modern folk turn to for relief from tedium: though I was the official chronicler of our journey, I had neither writing paper nor pen. I had to content myself with sitting in the downstairs chamber that served as a residents' lounge and – as far as I was able – putting my recollections into better mental order. It is a process I have always found far less rewarding than the making of written notes. Konrad seemed as restless as I, while Steerforth himself was sunk in a most uncharacteristic despondency. I knew that there were two anxieties pressing upon his mind. For all that the Grand Vizier had taken our gold and held out at least the hope that Edwina May's life might be preserved until the return of the Khaghan, we had no means of telling whether that hope would be fulfilled. For all we knew she might already be dead, or subject in concubinage to some *noyan* of the Mongols. On top of this, Steerforth was also aware that the cautious plan he had made for our first visit was now in tatters. We had intended to spend several weeks exploring Khan-Balik and finding out about the Mongol empire at a time chosen expressly to coincide with Kubilai Khan's absence from the capital. Now it seemed that if we were to save Edwina May's life we might have to face the dangers of an interview with Kubilai – who I had to keep reminding myself was also Inayat Khan. I know it crossed my mind, and perhaps Steerforth's too – that in view of the importance of our mission to the whole of mankind past, present and future, we ought, if we were to take the cold detached military view of our duties that Major Tolson might have taken, to consider abandoning Edwina May to her fate and returning to the safety of the twentieth century. If Augustus Steerforth ever envisaged such a dire expedient he never mentioned it to me, nor I to him.

Steerforth went alone to the Grand Vizier's palace once more. I suppose he unburdened himself once more of a tidy sum in gold and banknotes, but he returned with the information that we should present ourselves at Ahmad's offices just before sunset two days hence.

The next day witnessed a number of hurried and somewhat secretive consultations between Steerforth and Konrad Dubendorf, the purpose of which remained a mystery to me. At length, however, Steerforth explained that Dubendorf would not be accompanying us to the Grand Vizier's office as he had other urgent duties to attend to. That afternoon Dubendorf packed his few belongings in his leather travel bag and, after a brief farewell, left us. I watched him walk off down the street in the shade of the overhanging trees. For all the disguise as a Frankish merchant, he had never looked to me like anything but a Swiss scientist and as I watched him now I could swear his precise gait would betray him to the first soldier he met. We were to learn that Dr Dubendorf was made of sterner stuff, in our hour of direst need.

At the appointed hour we too packed our few belongings and took our leave. The two French merchants, who knew that our friend had been arrested, understood at once that we were trying to arrange her release. They wished us good fortune, with a great deal of warmth but little conviction. Our Chinese host also sent us on our way with expressions of goodwill no less fervent if less easily comprehended. The two of us made our way slowly through the streets of Khan-Balik. As we neared the Grand Vizier's offices a kind of gloomy jitteriness spread over me, the like of which I have never known before. We were unprepared for the sight that met our eyes when we finally reached Ahmad's office. Clearly the forgiveness of sins was a serious business in Khan-Balik, for there were close to two hundred assorted people gathered outside the office. Most of them were jostling about in front of the wooden doors with the symbol of the Chung-t'ung carved upon them, presumably in an attempt to demonstrate their loyalty to the Khaghan. We attached ourselves rather cautiously to the exterior of the crowd, trying to appear dignified and aloof while not missing our turn in this ramshackle array of supplicants. We need not have worried. As the day declined the Vizier's officials emerged from his office and began to impose some kind of discipline upon the crowd. We found ourselves separated into groups, presumably on the basis of the size of bribe we had offered. Steerforth and I were in an elite group alone with a short but very fat Chinaman who gazed at us with barely disguised resentment.

'I imagine his gift was so lavish that he expected to be in a category of his own,' I ventured.

'I've always been prone to overtip,' said Steerforth. Most of the crowd of supplicants were ushered into two or three larger groups, though not a few (their attempts at bribery presumably considered *infra dignitatem*) were sent miserably away. Their accused relatives or friends would, we supposed, be left to face unaided the Mongolian interpretation of the will of heaven, invariably unpleasant and generally terminal. When the categories were firmly established the Grand Vizier himself emerged into the courtyard. In his brilliant white robes he made an impressive figure, but the sighs and clucks of admiration that rose from the group of supplicants owed more, I thought, to sycophancy than to true regard. Without a glance at us, the Grand Vizier set off down the street accompanied by a guard of a dozen or so Mongol soldiers. Like so many schoolchildren on their way to church, we followed on behind. Deeper into the old city of Khan-Balik we passed, along streets with well-built stone houses and palaces on either hand. In later years Kubilai Khan was to abandon the old city and set up his administration in the newly built city of Ta-Tu, the foundations of which were already being prepared. But this was for political reasons, not because the old city was in any sense less than magnificent.

At last we came within sight of the old palace, a huge stone-built hall with massive wooden doors. We supplicants were the last to arrive except for the royal party. The Khaghan's guests were already seated, well over a thousand of them, at long dining tables. At the top of the hall was erected a dais on several levels where we presumed the royal party would be seated. High on the walls of the hall flamed great torches, spreading a lurid golden light over the scene. At the entrance of the hall stood an official accompanied by two large slaves with wooden clubs. He pointed downwards and shouted something at us. For a moment I was about to prostrate myself, but the fat Chinaman knew the court protocol and made a great fuss of stepping clear across the threshold. We did the same, while the official watched and the slaves longingly fingered their murderous-looking clubs. Apparently it was a sign of disrespect to step on the threshold. We supplicants were not given seats but ushered to the corner of the hall furtherest from the royal dais.

'Look over there, in the opposite corner,' I whispered. To the right of the royal dais was another group of standing figures. They were the accused. Easily identifiable among them was the slim figure of Edwina May McGrath. Steerforth's eyes burned as he caught sight of the woman he loved. But he said nothing and made no gesture of recognition. I could not tell whether Edwina May had recognised us or not.

Into the great hall marched a group of soldiers carrying musical instruments, bugles and horns and *nakkar* drums. The light from the torches glinted on the bronze of their drums as they marched to their appointed places round the hall. As the first note of their harsh music rang out, everyone in the hall rose to their feet. A few seconds later all were prostrate on the stone floor. The Khaghan was approaching.

It was more than a decade of physiological time since I had set eyes on Inayat Khan. As he strode into the hall, decked in the finery of a Mongol emperor and confronted by his adoring subjects, the first impression I had was that he had not aged much – certainly not as much as Steerforth who had sacrificed three years of his life in the future age. He had grown a moustache and a small pointed beard, very much in the Mongol style. He was decked out in a huge cloth of gold robe, with a silk sash or cummerbund round his waist. He wore a kind of skullcap of decorated material with a flap that covered his neck, but this he swept from his head as he marched into the hall. The royal party consisted of about twenty people, among whom we recognised the *khatun* or first wife, the mother of Chingkim. The biggest shock was to see the tall and stately figure of Abigail in the royal group. She too was little changed, her hair still plaited into dreadlocks, her walk still pliant and majestic. Was it my imagination, or did her personality outshine all but the Khan himself? For a second I believed that her eye would catch mine and that she would instantly detect us. What are these modern strangers doing in this ancient place? But the royal party passed by without a glance at the miserable supplicants: for the moment we were safe.

The Khan and his party now mounted the dais at the end of the hall and took their places on its different levels. The Khan himself was on the highest level, perched some twenty feet above the floor of the hall. The bugles blared again and everyone was seated. But there was still silence through the great hall. A servant emerged from a kitchen area to the left of the great dais, carrying a silver goblet large enough to hold at least a quart of wine. He walked into the middle aisle of the hall and carefully set down the cup on the stone flags. Then he stepped back in reverential pose. We craned our necks to see what was happening. What good was the Khan's wine down there while he was seated in his lofty throne? For a second it seemed that there was a tiny, electronic hum in the air. Then the silver chalice rose slowly in the air. There was a gasp of stifled awe from all the guests. When it was level with the Khaghan's throne the chalice stopped, hovering unsupported above the diners' heads. Then it moved slowly towards the dais until it came to rest in reach of his hand. The trumpets blared again. Khan took the cup out of the air and raised it to his lips. Noisy and nervous chattering broke out all over the hall, and servants began to circulate with huge flagons of milk and wine and platters of food. Great mounds of cooked meat, bread, cheese and fruit were placed before the guests and they fell to with a will.

'How do you suppose the trick with the silver cup was done?' I muttered.

'Some form of traction beam, I imagine,' answered Steerforth. 'It must have been taken from some future century.' The serving of food and drink went on for an hour or more. These Mongol nobles and their ladies were certainly formidable in their appetites. Before the meal was over some of them were already red of face and loud of voice. When at last the food was cleared away, a rough and ready cabaret took place with jugglers and acrobats. The dinner guests appeared to enjoy these entertainments hugely, though I noticed that the Khaghan sat impassively throughout them. Four or five levels below him on the dais, Abigail also watched silently as the wooden balls flashed in the air and the bodies of the acrobats spun and whirled. For a further hour, it seemed, the entertainment continued. Then at last the Grand Vizier Ahmad stepped forward, a roll of paper in his hand, and read out what we took to be the statement of amnesty proclaimed on behalf of the Khan of Khans. When the proclamation had been read, the courtiers all nodded appreciatively and beat the tables with their hands in obsequious recognition of the Khan's clemency. An official stepped forward and shepherded the supplicants up the central aisle. We were now less than thirty feet from the dais. As we glanced up at the face of the Khaghan, a face so well known to us in former years, it seemed unthinkable that he should not look down and recognise us. But as the process of the royal amnesty began, I thought we might have a chance of escape. One of the accused was led out in front of the Khan's throne. Those who had interceded on behalf of the prisoner were also led forward. Prisoner and supplicants alike fell face down before the throne, their arms stretched out in prayers and obeisance. The Khan raised one hand in a dismissive gesture and the prisoner and his friends literally crawled away and slunk out of the hall. Grand Vizier Ahmad watched this process with a smile on his thin lips, though whether he was relishing the mercy of the Khan or counting up the bribes was far from obvious.

'Our best chance is to flatten ourselves as quickly as we can,' muttered Steerforth. 'Khan looks pretty bored with this farce, he may not even see our faces at all.'

At last Edwina May was led forward. She gazed for a moment upwards at the throne. Clearly it was against the grain for this independent-minded young American woman to prostrate herself before anyone. As one man, Steerforth and I flung ourselves flat on the stone floor. The impact winded me for a moment but when I stole a look at Edwina May she had picked up her cue and was also prostrate. We wriggled along the ground like so many worms and came to rest under the dais front. I did not even dare look up to see if the Khaghan had dismissed us. In a moment an official stepped forward and turned us roughly away from the throne. We crawled away until we were level with the first tables. The faces of the courtiers were turned towards us in mocking smiles. I took no notice. We were within sight of freedom. Then, with success within our grasp, disaster struck. As we rose to our feet Steerforth half-turned to grasp Edwina May's arm. In that instant his features were clearly visible in the light of the great flares. Even then the Khan did not recognise his old schoolmate and scientific collaborator. But a more vigilant pair of eyes was also on the dais. As we walked with bowed heads between the tables towards the door of the hall, a single word rang out.

'Steerforth!' We turned in horror. Abigail had risen to her feet, her hand outstretched and finger pointing. At once Khan too leapt to his feet.

'Steerforth?' he cried in English. 'Is it really you?' And then in the language of the Mongols he called to the soldiers to hold us. At once we were surrounded and the doors of the hall were blocked by soldiers. There was an eerie silence as the Khan of Khans gazed down on us in disbelief.

'How in the name of heaven did you get here?' said Khan.

'They have built a time machine,' said Abigail. 'Look, there is the old professor with him.'

'So you have tracked me down. My clues must have been too obvious. But how did you build a machine? That intrigues me. Perhaps you hoped to interfere with my plans. If so you have failed. Do you know what punishment is inflicted on the enemies of Kubilai Khan?' The courtiers looked at each other in puzzlement as the Khan carried on this conversation in a strange tongue. He gestured for the soldiers to bring us nearer the throne.

'Who is this woman who accompanies you, Steerforth? What has she to do with your expedition into the past?'

'She is the one who tracked you down. She is a Coleridge scholar. She recognised all your clues, the light of two candles, your pseudonyms. Even the Abyssinian maid, the damsel with a dulcimer.'

'Indeed?' said Khan, seating himself again. 'What a pity that all that cleverness should be in vain.'

'Do you think so?' said Steerforth.

'Well, you have lost,' said Khan reasonably, with a flash of his old smile. 'You are in my power.' Steerforth nodded, then suddenly said something rather unexpected.

'But can we have our money back?'

'Your money?' said Khan, and Abigail laughed out loud.

'Yes,' insisted Steerforth. 'We paid a great deal of money to get our friend released. In gold too. Your friend Ahmad is taking bribes from everyone, but at least he must deliver against his promises. Is that not fair?' Ahmad, standing with the list of supplicants in his hand, understood not a word of what had been said. But he heard his name spoken, saw the way Steerforth glanced at him and noticed the look of anger that passed across Khan's face. Steerforth turned to face the Grand Vizier.

'*Altan, altan,*' he said, holding out his hand in mimicry of a man asking a bribe. Then he turned his back to Khan and hid his hand under his robe, with a crafty leer. For a moment there was silence. Khan gazed at Ahmad and Ahmad gazed at Steerforth, each with venom in his eyes. Then someone laughed. Then another, and another, until the hall was echoing to the merriment. Most of these people had been blackmailed by Ahmad in the past. This I knew from reading Messer Marco. Ahmad had extorted money from the men and sexual compliance from the women. They were delighted to see him exposed in public by this weird stranger. They must all have realised that Khan knew of Ahmad's crimes: how could he not? But it was another thing to have the matter out in the open. Thus Steerforth's little charade had done much more than cause merriment. It had exposed Ahmad as a villain and (closer to his real intent) made Khan look a fool in front of his own subjects.

Suddenly Ahmad's anger boiled over. He drew a dagger and hurled himself at Steerforth. The sheer force of Ahmad's onslaught knocked Steerforth to the floor, but he managed to grab the hand holding the dagger and keep it from his throat. Khan shouted a command. Soldiers leaped upon Ahmad and dragged him from Steerforth. Pandemonium now broke out in the hall, with courtiers screaming abuse and accusations at Ahmad, the soldiers trying to restore order. Who struck the first blow in anger, I could not say. But I saw one man, almost demented with hatred, try to stick a knife in Ahmad; a soldier clubbed him to the ground. The age-old hatred of the Mongol for the Chinese and of both for Khan's Arab officials now erupted into a full-scale riot. The soldiers had more to worry about than us prisoners. Steerforth grabbed Edwina May in one arm and me in the other. We were carried along by a struggling mass of people trying to get out of the hall, prisoners and courtiers alike. I looked back as we reached the door. Khan was standing with a look of baffled rage on his face. Abigail, to her great credit, was shaking with helpless laughter.

Outside the hall people were milling about in the darkness. We stood to one side and watched as they ran off towards their homes. But suddenly the fleeing courtiers turned back in panic. Moving up the hill towards the palace were four brilliant lights.

'Konrad!' said Steerforth. And Dubendorf it was, riding a gembike up the hill with three more slaved behind him. As we mounted the bikes a group of soldiers burst from the palace and ran towards us. Still under the control of Konrad's machine, we shot forward. I gripped the handlebars as tight as I could. The sonar controls steered us round the soldiers and we hurtled off down the hill. Courtiers flung themselves in all their finery into the ditch as we rushed by, our headlamps on full beam. And so, creating panic wherever we were seen, we left the streets of Khan-Balik and sped down the Cho-chau road.

I had hoped that we might return at once to the twentieth century. But Steerforth had other ideas. He wished to know what action Khan would take against Ahmad. For three weeks more we remained in Khan's kingdom, camping near the Magus and venturing out only to buy food in obscure hostelries.

On a hill outside Ta-Tu the final chapters of Ahmad's career were played out. During his lengthy period of office he had made many enemies by extortion and blackmail. Once he was threatened with the Khaghan's disfavour, there was no shortage of witnesses against him and his family. From the safety of a copse on the other side of the valley, we observed the scene. First seven of Ahmad's sons were stripped naked, tied to posts and flayed to death with whips. They died slowly and in great agony. Edwina May turned pale but she did not flinch from watching the administration of the Khan's justice. Then Khan read out an edict in Mongolian laying the practices of the Moslem faith under the strictest of prohibitions. Finally Ahmad himself was scourged to the point of death, then flung down the hill to a pack of starving dogs.

Even from our distance across the valley, Steerforth and I could guess the revulsion with which Khan watched this spectacle. The Mongol crowd laughed and cheered most keenly. Just for a moment Khan seemed to me to be the lost, tormented little boy who had come to England with nothing but his terrifying memories, the boy who had sought consolation in the study of science and in grandiose dreams of power. Soon we would face the final battle to determine whether those dreams would be fulfilled.

CHAPTER 8

A Light Half Unearthly

Mr Steele went round the breakfast table at Bain Brook, refilling all our cups with fragrant hot coffee. Exactly a week had elapsed since our return from the Yuan empire, a week in which we had relished all the comforts of modern living.

'It seems to me,' said Konrad Dubendorf, gazing down with satisfaction at a plate which a few moments earlier had contained three scrambled eggs, two rashers of bacon, grilled tomatoes and spicy sausages, 'that despite the unhappy chance of Edwina May's capture, our first expedition was a modest success. We have learned a good deal about Kubilai Khan and his empire. We stirred up a first-class row over Ahmad and his family, and forced Kubilai to sacrifice one of his most effective advisors.'

'Yet we have not touched Khan himself,' said Edwina May sharply, glancing at Konrad keenly over her spectacles, now restored to her after the obligatory contact lenses. 'The essence of a monarchy is the monarch. Taking even the major bit players like Ahmad and his sons out of the game is marginally helpful, but the only way to stop the whole thing is to take Inayat Khan out of the action.' I noticed that she used Khan's modern name, as if to emphasise that Steerforth must accept the elimination of one who had once been his closest friend.

On the mantelshelf in the breakfast room Steerforth still kept a photograph of Khan in academic dress. Slowly he rose from the table, coffee cup in hand, and went to study the picture, as if seeing it for the first time. I was inescapably reminded of the preoccupied way he had examined the pictures in my Oxford room on that stormy night when he first told me of the Magus project.

'Preferably we would kidnap him and isolate him in some period of history where he can do no harm,' said Steerforth.

'That might be difficult,' said Konrad, 'his security will be very tight. We have now forfeited the element of surprise, too. His guards will be on the look-out for us, and will probably die in hundreds rather than see any harm come to him.' Steerforth nodded his agreement and set down the picture of Khan.

'Alternatively we might just have to murder the bastard,' he said at last. He smiled as he spoke these words, in mimicry of Edwina May's accent and idiom. Yet his eyes burned fiercely and sadly as he spoke.

'Now you're talking,' said Edwina May softly. And so was sealed our resolve to stop Khan at any cost, even at that of his life. For Steerforth it represented the crossing of a final Rubicon, the acceptance that Khan's plans could be thwarted only by intervention as direct and indefensible as the plans themselves.

'Now we are two of a kind,' Steerforth would later comment in private. 'All that stands between us is that I believe my goals are preferable to Khan's, and that is just a matter of judgement. This is the absolute power that Acton says corrupts absolutely.' From this point onwards I noticed too that Steerforth no longer exercised the sole leadership of our team as he had been wont, but rather worked in a dyarchy with Edwina May and even deferred to her. As a leader in dire straits he lacked something, call it toughness of mind or ruthlessness. The cricket he had played had left him with an ingrained sense of decency, in this case a serious disadvantage. We needed someone who was willing, so to speak, to run Khan out at the bowler's end for backing up too far – and without a warning.

'The historical Kubilai Khan,' said Steerforth, 'ruled the Mongol empire from 1260 until 1294. It seems astonishing to me that Khan should need so long to put his plans in place. What do you think is happening?'

'According to Marco Polo,' I said, 'Kubilai spent his whole reign trying to cope with the internal conflicts of his empire, Chinese against Mongol, both against his Arab officials. There was an endless stream of civil wars against other members of the imperial family trying to oust Kubilai, because they believed (rightly, we now see) that he was an outsider who had usurped the throne of the sage-like martial emperor. There was a foreign war against Japan which cost him most of his fleet. All of these problems have to be dealt with. It may be that he just doesn't get the time he needs to plan for the alternative world.'

'How many soldiers would he need trained in modern weapons?' asked Edwina May. 'Perhaps five or six thousand? We have seen how poorly they take to high technology. It's obvious that selecting and training them would be a huge job. And Messer Marco tells us how reluctant Kubilai was to delegate anything.'

'There is another factor which may also be at work,' said Konrad Dubendorf, his voice deep but quiet. 'We have always wondered what would happen if Khan succeeded in changing history. Would the old world flicker instantaneously out of existence, the new world suddenly be created? Maybe the fabric of history is not so easily torn asunder.... Maybe history has a certain – inertia. Events that have happened may be too many and too weighty suddenly to make unhappen. I don't know....'

We pondered in silence this encouraging thought.

'Why don't we go take a look?' asked Edwina May. Steerforth slowly nodded.

'We must go to 1294 and see how close Khan is to readiness,' said Steerforth. 'But this time we must go not to Khan-Balik, but to the palace of Xanadu. For that, I think, will be the base for his attack.' Happily Steerforth decided to delay our departure for a further week, allowing Edwina May and Konrad some further use of their spectacles, while Steerforth and I might enjoy an occasional glass of whisky or claret.

On the evening before our departure I sat on the bridge of the Magus, scanning the description of the Khaghan's annual progress to Xanadu in the pages of Friar Odoric of Pordenone:

Now this lord passeth the summer at a place which is called Sandu, situated towards the north, and the coolest habitation in the world. But in the winter season he abideth in Cambalech. And when he will ride from one place to the other this is the order thereof. He hath four armies of horsemen, one of which goeth a day's march in front of him, one at each side, and one a day's march in the rear, so that he goeth always, as it were, in the middle of a cross.... The king travelleth in a two-wheeled carriage, in which is formed a very goodly chamber, all of lign-aloes and gold, and covered over with fine and great skins, and set with many precious stones. And the carriage is drawn by four elephants, well broken in and harnessed, and also by four splendid horses, richly caparisoned.

The next day we found ourselves disguised once again as Frankish merchants and travelling along that same road, having hidden the Magus in a copse about halfway between Khan-Balik and Shang-tu. Modern travellers along this road have commented upon its narrowness and dilapidation, and have therefore expressed scepticism that it could have accommodated such a grandiose vehicle as Friar Odoric describes, but it must be badly ruined in modern times for the road we now saw was as wide and flat as many main roads of the twentieth century. At a way station near Sindachu we bought some horses to carry our possessions and ourselves and made good time as far as the Great Wall. There we had to deal with the usual obstacle of Mongol soldiers and officials, who explained that we were not permitted to advance much further up the road to the north-east. Some money changed hands and we were on our way again. But as we set off, one of the Mongol soldiers followed us a few yards down the road.

'Let's see what he wants,' said Edwina May. We turned back and went to meet the soldier.

'Be careful, careful,' he said, with some urgency and an unusual degree of concern for our safety. 'At Shang-tu you will find the Upas. The Upas.'

'The Upas?' said Steerforth. 'What is that?'

'The Upas tree,' answered the soldier. 'No man or animal that passes near it can live. All die.'

We were stunned. The very thing we had suspected in the hotel at Broadway so early in our investigation appeared to be true. Coleridge's Upas tree, or rather his Tartarean forest full of Upas trees, was some kind of defensive array on the road to Xanadu. It seemed worthwhile to try to exploit this fellow's knowledge of the terrain. We sat down by the side of the road with him and offered him a drink from a leather flagon of *koumiss*, which he accepted with pleasure.

'Do you know well the road between here and Shang-tu?' said Steerforth.

'Oh well, well,' he answered, rolling his eyes at the inanity of the question. 'You will not be allowed to go nearer than one day's ride from the Khaghan's palace. The Upas is there. After that...' and he drew his hand across his throat.

'Could you take us as far as that? We will pay you well.'

'For me, yes, I would take you. But the patrol leader....' We looked back at the wall where the other soldiers were watching us

with interest. It seemed that we were not the first travellers to
have sought guidance from the soldiers. Perhaps they had an
arrangement with the bandits who undoubtedly preyed upon
travellers on this lonely road. A sum was expected for the guide
himself (whose name turned out to be Boga), a sum for the patrol
leader for making Boga available, and a sum for each of the
soldiers who would have to work overtime to cover for Boga.

'These guys are the lineal ancestors of New York cabbies!' said
Edwina May when the deal was done. But we had secured the
services of our guide for a trivial sum, by modern standards.
Nevertheless, to judge by the shouts and laughter which accompanied the sharing out of the money, the Mongols were well
pleased with the transaction.

Boga was a sturdy-looking fellow a trifle under five feet in
height. He wore a shirt and voluminous trousers, and carried a
rough blanket on his shoulder, presumably for the nights. He wore
large boots of felt tied up with string, and carried a murderous-
looking dagger at his waist.

'If he's in the game I want him on my team,' said Edwina May
admiringly. He laughed aloud with delight when we invited him to
ride the most lightly loaded packhorse, and sprang to its back like
a jack-in-the-box. His zest raised all our spirits. I tried not to
reflect upon the undoubted fact that he had little idea of the perils
we faced.

That night we camped in a field where several Mongol families
had established their *yurts*. Whatever story Boga told them about
us they seemed readily to accept. But on the following day's march
we noticed most of the Mongol travellers taking side turnings off
the main road for villages to the south-west of Shang-tu. Soon we
had the road to ourselves. We approached a large brick gateway
which bore the imperial crest in bas-relief. Boga stopped and
pointed down the road.

'The Upas begins here,' he said simply. We sat down on the
safe side of the gate and watched in silence. On either side of the
road at intervals of three or four hundred yards stood wooden
posts about ten feet in height. Atop each post was a small black
box, most anachronistic in this mediaeval setting. Each box had a
hood to protect it from the weather and a glass lens inside.

'Look!' said Boga at last. 'Watch that animal.' A large buck
rabbit was working its way up the slope towards the road. While
it was still fifty or sixty yards from the road, one of the Upas trees
glowed red and a beam shot out and hit the rabbit. The creature

screamed briefly before it died. It was a most effective demonstration.

'How does it work?' said Steerforth, for some reason speaking in a low voice.

'A network of passive infra-red beams, probably,' said Dubendorf. 'When a number of the beams identify a three-dimensional moving object, one of them is programmed to eliminate it with the laser beam. It's a very effective defence system.'

There seemed little opportunity to skirt round the Upas defences. Other systems were visible further down the slope and Boga told us that the whole perimeter of Shang-tu was similarly protected.

'Show us what your box of tricks can do, Dubendorf,' said Steerforth. Konrad drew from his knapsack the portable computer terminal hidden there, which was (along with a safety first kit and two electric torches) one of the few items of modern equipment that Steerforth had agreed might accompany us. It was, admittedly, unlikely to attract attention. It was very small, about the size of a book. I had completely forgotten that he had it with him. The terminal was equipped with a small aerial, which Konrad now pointed at the nearest Upas tree.

'Let's see if we can get them to talk to us,' he murmured. He adjusted the controls on the terminal and two curves appeared on the screen. Fine adjustment of the controls caused the two curves to converge.

'The individual Upas trees are controlled on a fibre optic local area network,' he said. 'When the infra-red beam detects movement, it checks with three or four others and fires the laser beam if the intrusion is validated.'

'How does the system distinguish between bad guys and good guys?' asked Edwina May.

'I'm just trying to find out,' said Dubendorf. 'But for that I have to work back through the LAN to the central controller.' Boga was squatting beside Konrad, staring with the utmost interest at the screen. He looked at us, grinned and shook his head, as if to acknowledge that there was no end to the ingenuity of the Frankish. 'The system is deadlocked, of course,' said Konrad. 'Every message that passes along the network has to satisfy a security handshake before it is treated as valid. Fortunately this little friend of mine can try several billion code combinations a second, so randomly we break the code in a few minutes. Ah, now I'm talking to the boss computer. I've come in through a port that's designed for software maintenance engineers. It thinks I'm a systems programmer working for a thirteenth century monarch.' Dubendorf typed in some code and the remote computer, presumably installed in Shang-tu itself, replied. After half an hour's trial and error, Konrad had established how the Upas system recognised authorised travellers to Shang-tu.

'A good security system not only eliminates intruders but also allows the host and his friends to move around the place without being flash-fried,' said Konrad. 'The main Upas computer has a library of holographic records of authorised travellers. It recognises what Edwina May calls the good guys and allows them to pass unhurt.'

'How about deleting Khan's image from the library?' said Edwina at once. 'Next time he leaves the palace he'll be reduced by his own system to a heap of smoking ashes.'

'Not possible,' said Konrad, 'for the same reason as I cannot insert our images in the library. Any insertion or deletion among the holograms triggers an alarm circuit, probably sends a big bell ringing on the master terminal. Khan would know at once that someone was monkeying with his system.'

'Do we suppose that Khan acquired this defence system from some future age in one of his time trips?' said Edwina May.

'Presumably so,' said Konrad.

'Is it then impossible to fool the Upas system?' asked Steerforth.

'Not necessarily,' said Konrad slowly. 'There is one way that I can scramble the input to the sensing system. In our time, the way aircraft try to penetrate radar systems is by projecting false images. I can use this terminal to tell the Upas computer that it sees not just the few of us but literally millions of people passing up the street. I can also randomise the timing circuits so that where we are is where it thinks we were or will be.'

'What will the effect be?' I asked.

'It's hard to be certain,' admitted Konrad. 'The recognition circuits may become overloaded. No two Upas trees may agree on what is a valid target. When they unanimously select a valid target, I hope it will be a phantom target and not one of us.'

'Only hope?' asked Edwina May.

'That's all,' said Konrad Dubendorf. Without more certainty than that we took our first steps along the road to Xanadu. We now abandoned all but our essential possessions, turned the horses loose and pointed them back down the road to Khan-Balik. There was no point in risking their lives. Seeing us step out under the Upas trees, Boga's eyes bulged somewhat, but he did not question our wisdom. He had an exaggerated trust in Frankish technology, which must have seemed to him indistinguishable from magic. We had advanced perhaps thirty yards along the road when the first Upas tree fired. A patch of road twenty yards ahead of us glowed red in the beam, then one a few yards behind us.

'What happens if the computer fails?' whispered Edwina May.

'On that score at least I can comfort you, dear lady. You would die so fast that you would never know it had happened,' said Konrad with a smile. All in all the laser beams must have shot out some fifteen to twenty times during our journey. It was easy to allow one's imagination to run riot, to conceive of the unreal figures scythed down by the Upas beams as the spirits of those doomed not to be born in Khan's new world. When history was changed in a sufficiently fundamental way, their lives would flicker out of existence as the rabbit had died in the laser. The closest call was when a beam hit the road about a yard from where Konrad Dubendorf was walking. Edwina May screamed but if Konrad was jittery, he masked it well.

We came at last, in my case wearily enough, to the end of the road guarded by the Upas trees. At a safe distance, Konrad closed down the link to the control system and put away his computer. The road now became a gravel track which ran for half a mile or so along the base of a scree, high enough to block our view of the country ahead. I was lagging somewhat behind when Edwina May emerged on the crest of the scree with a clear view ahead. She stopped, uttered a nearly silent exclamation and (it seemed) almost sank to her knees.

'"So twice five miles of fertile ground/With walls and towers were girdled round,"' said Edwina May. A mile or so away stood the palace of Xanadu in its walled grounds.

My first impression was that it soared into the sky like the mountain from which it had been carved, as if at any moment it might break free of gravity and vault into the sky. The walls alone, each of them some three miles in extent, rose a hundred feet into the air. At each corner of the walls was built a watchtower reaching a further thirty feet or so towards the sky. We were too far from the palace to see how the towers were manned or equipped. Inside the walls the land rose gently at first but then steeply, so that the palace itself rested on a plateau high above the tops of the walls. To our left a ragged ravine ran from the summit to the base of the enclosed area. As Coleridge had promised, a forest of cedars covered the hillside on either side of the ravine. The slope that faced us had been carefully landscaped into a series of terraced gardens and lakes, the water pouring from a fountain at the upper level and descending from one ornate lake to the next. In the brilliant sunshine, the spume from the fountain floated like mist, rainbows occasionally and briefly flowering in the air. We were too distant to make out the details of the fountain.

As we had expected, the shape of the palace itself was domed, resting upon a torus. But we had been unprepared for the sheer scale and grandeur of Xanadu. The dome stood some five or six hundred feet in height. The radius of the torus was as great. The dome was not solid, but constructed in curved vanes or panels, like the blades of a mighty turbine engine, which rotated slowly so that the whole building seemed to shimmer and spin. The walls and the dome were built of a dark grey, near-black material – perhaps the natural colour of the rock from Mount Cadillac. From the interior of the dome came a pale and flickering light that was alternately masked and revealed by the moving panels, like sunlight flashing on crystals. Between the torus below and the dome above were visible two levels of rooms with wide glass windows. These might be the living quarters amd storerooms of the palace. The main gate of the palace was near the fountain, a wide portico with columns not unlike those that distinguished our old school, though far larger.

How would one gain access? From the main entrance of the palace a huge staircase was built, which seemed to run all the way down the hill. The stairs were steep and apparently innumerable. I could hardly imagine a young, fit man climbing them, let alone a creature like myself.

This then was the building that towered above us. Because of its size and colour, it seemed to brood over the land like a great cloud. What technology from what future age had gone into the creation of it was a mystery to me, though not perhaps to Steerforth, who had lived in the future to build his own Magus machine. Apart from Khan and Abigail, no modern eye had rested upon the palace since the old vagabond witnessed its departure on Mount Desert Island. We were dumbfounded, we who knew what to expect: imagine then the feelings of those who saw the palace in its own time, like Messer Marco and the unnamed witnesses whose testimony came down through Purchas to Samuel Taylor Coleridge.

The steeply sloped grounds of the palace also contained a number of copses and gardens less formal than those surrounding the lakes. At one point we saw a herd of deer cropping the grass. An aviary for doves had been built. High in the sky two eagles soared over Xanadu. We saw a small building, perhaps a hunting lodge, on a terraced ledge below the palace.

At first we were too overwhelmed by the building and its surroundings to notice any signs of human life. Then a person – male or female we could not tell – emerged on the portico, stepped on to the staircase and began to be carried downwards. The motion of the staircase was not that of a modern escalator. There were no mechanical links between the steps. Rather the fabric of the stone seemed to melt, flow and ripple to form new steps under the passenger's feet. As we watched, another person appeared above the top of the wall, travelling upwards on the same staircase. As the two passengers met, the rippling motion ceased and they stood and talked for a while. Then their journeys began again.

Away to our left we suddenly glimpsed a vehicle moving between the trees. It emerged into open territory. It was an armoured personnel carrier about the size of a modern car, carrying four Mongol soldiers in modern uniforms. It passed within a quarter of a mile of us, heading for the palace.

'Where is the gate?' muttered Steerforth. But when the vehicle reached the walls, the near-black fabric suddenly began to dilate like an opening flower. A semicircular porthole appeared, the vehicle passed through and the hole closed behind it.

Under cover of the trees we advanced to within a quarter of a mile of the palace walls. From this range we could see that the fabric of the walls glistened in the ebbing sunlight, like polished marble.

'That is the same sheen that I saw on the surface of the mountain where Khan made his machine,' said Steerforth. 'Whatever power Khan uses to shape his artifacts leaves that glazed effect, as if the rock is melted and fused to his design.'

We stared up at the watchtower high above us. It was equipped with radiation antennae and a long, black tube that looked like a laser cannon. As we watched, a Mongol soldier raised a pair of binoculars to his eyes and scanned the horizon.

We retreated into the forest and found a place in the shelter of two fallen trees to make a camp for the night. Before we slept, Steerforth summarised our position. 'It's hard to see how we can even get into the palace grounds, let alone the building itself. The portholes for Khan and his men are obviously created in response to an electronic signal. Heaven knows what it is.'

'Could Konrad try to fox the system, the way he did the Upas trees?' asked Edwina May.

'The towers are equipped with electronic monitoring devices,' muttered Steerforth. 'If they detected us, we'd be finished. Maybe we'll have to go back and fetch the gembikes, or even the Magus III itself.'

'We've gotten so far on our own, it would seem so disappointing to have to turn back.' We wrapped ourselves in our blankets and tried to sleep. Later that night I awoke when the wind got up. I saw a flicker of red light away to the south-west; some luckless and now lifeless creature had wandered under the eye of the Upas trees.

We awoke the next morning. To my surprise I felt refreshed and lively, though my joints creaked a little from the damp earth. Again we approached the palace under the cover of the trees.

'Look at the ravine that runs down from the palace,' said Konrad Dubendorf. 'Is there something within it? A pipe?'

'The sacred river,' said Boga. 'It runs under the walls of the palace and into a deep cave.'

'Sacred? Why sacred?' said Edwina May.

'It is the river of the Khaghan,' said Boga, as if any fool would know that.

'Where is the cave?' asked Steerforth. Boga looked uncomfortable, then gestured vaguely towards the west.

'No man has ever entered the cave and returned alive,' he said quietly, as if to forestall any suggestion Steerforth might make.

'Let's take a look,' said Edwina May.

Within half a mile we could hear the distant rumbling of a waterfall. Boga walked uneasily at the head of our party. Steerforth supported my creaking bones over the rougher sections of the path. The noise of the water became louder and deeper.

We came to the entrance of the cave at the foot of a hill. The ground sloped steeply above us towards the distant walls of Xanadu. The cave entrance was not large, only eight feet high and five feet wide. But by now the noise of the water was deafening. As we entered the cave, some bats shrieked and gibbered and flew off into the darkness. We found ourselves standing on a rocky ledge. It was impossible to make oneself heard. As our eyes grew accustomed to the dim light, we saw an underground waterfall. The sacred river traversed a concrete lip, then fell headlong into the bowels of the earth. How far below us was the underground reservoir into which the torrent fell, we could not guess. It was like standing on the edge of a subterranean Niagara. Konrad gestured us to remain for a moment where we were. He took out his pocket computer and switched on its Geiger counter. Then he picked up a stone and scratched a message on the tunnel wall.

'Mildly radioactive. Coolant from Khan's powerhouse,' he wrote. Steerforth and Dubendorf produced electric torches and we advanced into the tunnel through which the sacred river flowed. Without warning we were in the mouth of a huge cave, its walls having the same dark lustre as the walls of Xanadu. Steerforth shone his torch up the wall of the cave. The roof of the cave was still in darkness, high above us. Khan had sculpted the cave out of the sheer rock inside the massive hill leading up to the walls of Xanadu. It was indeed a cavern measureless to man. Boga looked uneasy but did not demur when Steerforth moved forward into the cavern. I believe that having contracted himself to us and taken the money, he felt obligated to perform whatever task was demanded of him. He had become our bondsman. So at least I theorise about the Mongol mentality.

Beside the sacred river was a walkway some four feet across. In single file we walked upstream. As we advanced, the noise of the waterfall faded and conversation became possible. The course of the river turned a hairpin bend.

'Why does the course of the river follow this complex path?' I asked.

'The water from the nuclear plant must be very radioactive,' said Dubendorf. 'It is processed and diluted on the way down. The channel meanders in order to slow the progress of the water and allow the dilution to take place.'

'"Five miles meandering with a mazy motion . . ."' said Edwina May. 'It is like this because Coleridge said it would be.' The course of the river continued to loop this way and that, climbing up the floor of the cavern as a switchback road climbs a mountain face. I tried in vain to calculate where we might be. Had we yet passed under the walls of Xanadu?

We came to a point in the river where a stream of unpolluted water joined the main current, the walkway crossing both streams. At the conduit of this confluence Boga stopped and raised a warning hand. Something moved in the shadows. Boga took a step back, then two forward. In the light of the torches I saw him take out his long-bladed knife. From the shadows of the conduit something was slowly advancing towards him, slowly and sideways. As it emerged into the light we saw that it was a crab about the size of a small donkey.

'The thing has mutated in the radiation,' muttered Konrad. The eyes of the giant crab glittered in the torchlight. Behind it we glimpsed piles of bones, some human, some animal, a skull of a human being. In the last few metres it moved with staggering swiftness. Its claws were raised and opened, each the size of a pair of garden shears. Boga had thrust himself forward between the claws. He grasped the monster's shell with one hand and stabbed repeatedly with the other, trying to find a gap in the carapace where its brain might be penetrated. He seemed to succeed, the crab jerking and writhing away from him as if in agony. Then, slowly and with meticulous care, the crab lowered its claws to the soft areas on either side of Boga's body between his ribs and his hips and ripped two huge, ragged wounds in the flesh. Boga screamed once. With the frenzied strength of the dying, he turned the crab round in a clumsy dance and pushed it from him and over the tunnel lip. In a moment the river had swept it away. Boga stood facing us, his hands pressing in on his torn sides. His head turned slowly towards the distant tunnel end.

'Be careful, careful,' he said, 'the Khaghan is dangerous.' He turned again to face us, then looked slowly round the walls of the tunnel as if seeking his last resting place. His face was deathly pallid. The water gurgled below, silence else. Boga took his hands from his sides and looked at them, red with his lifeblood. He stepped towards the brink and looked down into the water. He lay down on the edge for a moment, then slowly rolled his body over it and fell to the waters below. In a moment he too had disappeared from sight, his lifeless remains soon to be buried in the lifeless ocean.

'Come along,' said Edwina May softly. 'He took his chances with the rest of us. He probably knew the risks better than we. Besides, there may be more of those monsters around.' And thus we continued our journey without our guide, Konrad Dubendorf regularly taking measurements of the radiation. At length we emerged from the cavern measureless to man into a smaller chamber carved from the rock.

'As best I can, allowing for the meanders, I estimate that we have walked about five miles from the tunnel entrance,' said Steerforth. 'If I am right we can't be far from the palace.' But here we met a further obstacle. Set in the tunnel wall was a steel door with neither a handle nor a lock. The walkway came to an end. There seemed no way to penetrate further until we spotted a set of iron rungs set in the rockface. Steerforth set off to climb up and see where the rungs led. In a few minutes he was back.

'About thirty feet above us there is an installation,' he reported. 'It looks like a decontamination centre for the heavily radioactive water that comes down from Khan's nuclear pile. The water is processed there, then mixed with the uncontaminated river water for disposal. The plant is automated. I guess that the radiation level in the chamber is sky-high. No one could go in there without a protective suit.'

'Is there a way up to the palace from the chamber?' asked Konrad.

'I couldn't see for sure,' said Steerforth. 'But there was a staircase at the back. It looks as if it comes down to this steel door and up to the palace.'

'And can one gain access to the decontamination plant from this side?' I asked.

'The whole place is enclosed in glass an inch thick, but there is a lead-sealed door with a handle on this side. If we had a suit, one of us could go through and open the steel door.' I realised at once what I must do.

'I will go through and open the doors,' I said.

'But we have no suit,' said Edwina May and Steerforth at once.

'My friends, we have come so far that we cannot turn back. We have faced the Upas trees and the sacred river and the caverns measureless to man, and that grim guardian that took Boga's life. Just think. Even if we fetched the gembikes from the Magus, we would encounter other obstacles. As you well know, my life will end soon whatever happens. My doctor has told me as much. When I consented to be part of this mad expedition, I half-thought a time might come when a man whose life is expendable would be useful. That time has come.'

'Out of the question,' said Edwina May and Steerforth nodded emphatically.

'Not at all,' I answered, 'but the obvious thing to do. After all, our friend Boga, who was in good health and knew nothing of our necessities, has given his life for our cause. How can I, a man condemned to death and quite familiar with the dangers of Khan's empire, choose to offer less?' Still Steerforth and Edwina May tried to brush aside my proposal.

'Think carefully before you reject Hawkesworth's suggestion,' said Dubendorf, weighing his words with care. 'It has the merit of logic. His life, as we know, is threatened by a terminal disease. The whole success of our venture, and therefore the future of the world as we know it, may depend on our passing this obstacle. If Hawkesworth is already doomed, he sacrifices little. He would not make such an offer frivolously.'

In the end I resolved the question by handing my knapsack to Konrad Dubendorf and beginning to mount the iron rungs up the rockface. Edwina May moved as if to restrain me, but Steerforth took her arm and she turned her face to his shoulder. If the truth be known, I felt exhilarated and grateful for the chance to serve the expedition in a way for which I was uniquely fitted. I climbed slowly and finally reached the upper level. The processing room was large and brightly lighted. Its central area contained a deep pool full of water and criss-crossed by metal tubes. At one side was a control panel with lights and buttons galore. I stood on the paved area outside the processing room and took a deep breath. The door of the room was heavy and edged with lead strips, but it opened easily when I turned the steel handle. I stepped inside. I imagined the lethal radiation flooding my body, but I felt nothing. I skirted the pool and found the door to the staircase, which opened as easily as the first. Beside the stairs ran the big metal pipe that brought the radioactive water down from the palace through the ravine. Down below, I found a green button which electrically opened the steel door and a red button that closed it when my friends had passed. They looked at me in silence, as if searching for traces of the deadly waves.

'Let us proceed,' I said sharply, and we all moved up the stairs. Another hundred feet up a sloping walkway brought us into the open air. We were indeed well inside the walls, less than a mile from the palace itself. We hid in the bushes near the tunnel exit. The palace seemed to float in the sky above us, threatening to crush us at every instant.

'We cannot assume that our arrival has gone unnoticed,' said Konrad Dubendorf. 'Although we have seen nothing as lethal as the Upas trees, there may be other detection systems.'

'I agree,' said Steerforth. 'All we can do is lie low for the night and hope to find a way into the palace tomorrow.'

Using the trees and bushes as cover, we began to search for a temporary camp. That night a wild wind sprang up and we heard the trees and bushes thrashing about in the darkness. I began to feel a sense of impending disaster. My head ached and my throat was dry and sore. My eyes itched intolerably. I had not discussed with Konrad Dubendorf how long it would take for the symptoms of the lethal radiation to take effect, but suddenly it seemed to me that in this time and place so remote from my own I should die of a modern sickness. Would a twentieth century archaeologist ever dig up the bones of a contemporary man who died of radiation poisoning in the thirteenth century? If so, what would he make of it? In the night I awoke groaning or screaming, I knew not which and Edwina May came to me with a handkerchief soaked in cool water. She wiped my face and neck. I slept again.

When I awoke, I was looking down the barrel of a weapon held by a Mongol soldier. A personnel carrier was parked nearby. The soldiers stood all about us.

'Good God,' muttered Edwina May. Instead of their traditional garb the Mongol soldiers wore modern army uniforms. Their faces were quite expressionless. In their hands were squat, metal weapons that looked futuristic even by our standards.

'Probably laser rifles,' muttered Steerforth.

'Where is the fifth who was with you?' said the patrol leader.

'He is dead,' said Steerforth. 'The guardian of the cavern measureless to man took him.' The patrol leader nodded without surprise. He gestured towards the personnel carrier. In a few moments our possessions were gathered up and we were ushered into the vehicle. It moved off silently up the hill, obviously powered by some mechanism more advanced than the internal combustion engine.

'The Khaghan's eyes have been upon you ever since you entered the sacred river,' said the patrol leader, gesturing towards the surveillance equipment on his vehicle. 'The Khaghan has given instructions that you be brought alive to the palace, but if you try to escape, we are to kill you. With these weapons we will give you no chance. You understand?'

This time we approached the palace openly. The patrol leader took from his pocket a small transceiver and spoke into it. Doubtless he was in contact with his headquarters in the palace. It seemed that at last Khan's Mongol troops had come to terms with modern technology. As we approached the palace gates our worst fears were confirmed. A convoy of modern rocket launchers was driving down the hill towards the distant walls of Xanadu. It was difficult to imagine the impact of such weapons on the mediaeval world.

The carrier took us to the foot of the huge staircase. The patrol leader and six other soldiers jumped out of the vehicle and shepherded us on to the stairs. The leader shouted a command to the staircase. We began to ascend. The stone stairs rippled and flowed under our feet. We passed the formal gardens and the lakes. The water murmured softly as it fell from level to level. Now we could see that the fountain at the top of the waterway took the form of a monumental replica of the *Chung-t'ung*, the imperial emblem, from the centre of which the water poured.

At the summit we stepped off the moving staircase and on to the portico. Its blackish pillars were huge and stately. Now at last we entered the palace of Xanadu, albeit as prisoners. I glanced at Steerforth: his face was grim. I glanced at Edwina May: even in this predicament, her eyes blazed with excitement as she entered the palace of Coleridge's vision. We passed under the portico and emerged inside the dome. High above our heads the inner surfaces of the panels corruscated and rotated in the dazzling light. In the dead centre of the palace was built a large control room, through the plate glass windows of which we could see complex computer and communications equipment. Only one technician was on duty, a Mongol in a uniform of dark green. He glanced up as we passed. Here was a man born in the thirteenth century supervising a computer with operating systems and applications perhaps more advanced than those we had left behind in the 1980s. We were led off to the left along a corridor of the same blackish stone, but brightly lighted from concealed lamps.

'In here,' said the patrol leader, punching an access code at a heavy wooden door. He guided us inside, then left us alone, closing the door after him. We found ourselves in a large common room, airy and well-lighted, more like a villa than a prison. On one side of the room were large windows that looked out over the grassy slopes, the fountains and the staircase. On the other were modern bedrooms and bathrooms. We found the bathrooms equipped with soap, shampoo, towels and shaving equipment. On all our beds were simple but functional clothes, tunics and trousers, underwear and socks all apparently brand new. It was very clear that Khan had been expecting us.

'What do we do?' asked Edwina May.

'About what?' said Steerforth.

'About all this babying. Do we use the bathrooms and the clothes or do we not?'

'I think we should use them,' said Steerforth. 'There is scarcely any point in maintaining the pretence that we are humble Frankish merchants, is there?'

'OK, I was dying for a shower anyway,' said Edwina May. I forced myself to bath and put on the clean clothes that had been provided for me, though I felt more like lying down on the bed and trying to sleep. When we were clean and dressed in the somewhat pyjama-like attire, a Mongol soldier opened the doors of our new home and two women brought bread, meat, cheese and milk. I was not hungry, but simply lay on my bed with my pounding head and burning throat. Edwina May coaxed me into trying to drink some milk, but without success. I rested as best I could while my companions ate a little, and talked quietly among themselves in tones that were far from joyful. It seemed that our expedition, undertaken in such a mood of confidence and determination, had ended in a failure that was both immediate and complete. How foolish now seemed our talk about whether it was necessary or justifiable to murder the Khan of Khans. Our fates lay now in his hands.

As evening fell the soldiers returned to collect us. We were taken past the control room to the apartments on the other side of the palace. These were somewhat grander than ours. On the door of the main chamber was the imperial emblem. We were led inside and left to wait. The room was sparely but exquisitely furnished with a mixture of traditional Mongol furniture and some ultra-modern lights and fittings. We discovered that it was a conference room attached to Khan's personal quarters. It was also a secure area. For as we waited, a gallery that ran all the way round the room near the ceiling suddenly became visible. Gazing up, we saw half a dozen Mongol soldiers with laser guns looking down at us. Suddenly the wall became opaque again.

'Very clever,' said Steerforth. 'They can see us all the time, we see them only when they want us to. Hence we never know for sure whether they are there.'

'Augustus,' said Edwina May, 'I am most concerned about poor Hawkesworth.' And it was true that I was feeling far from well. My hair was falling out, my fingernails were loosened, my bowels were in turmoil and a hot, coppery taste in my mouth told me that my gums were bleeding.

'What can we do for you?' said Edwina May.

'Little enough, I fear,' said I. 'But please do not concern yourself for me. My end was near, it comes only a little faster. Think of how you can escape and defeat Khan.'

'There is little enough chance of that,' said a familiar voice from the door, and Khan entered the room. In this his citadel, Khan had no need of the trappings of a mediaeval monarch. He wore a simple tunic and trousers. He had shaved off the beard he wore in Khan-Balik, and now looked unchanged from the man we had known in the twentieth century. I wondered if Khan was using drugs or surgery to restrict the process of growing old.

'Sit down, sit down. You may as well be comfortable in your captivity. Welcome to Shang-tu. I am sorry to greet you as enemies, I would have wished it otherwise.' A servant came in and poured wine for us. Steerforth saw no reason to refuse; the rest of us followed suit.

'Is this the same lady who was with you in Khan-Balik, the Coleridge scholar who cleverly unravelled all my clues?' asked Khan. Steerforth introduced Edwina May simply as Dr McGrath. Khan smiled graciously, but Edwina May coldly glared, her eyes glittering with resentment.

'Well, Konrad Dubendorf, this is the first opportunity I have had to congratulate you on your spectacular rescue at Khan-Balik.' Dubendorf smiled rather frostily, and said nothing.

'Hawkesworth, my friend,' said Khan, 'you do not look well. Was it you who entered the high radiation area to unlock the doors?'

'It was.'

'That was a lethal task for you to undertake. Steerforth, do you not know that you have killed our old friend?'

'It was I who chose the task,' I said swiftly. 'I had little enough time remaining anyway.'

'You have been sick? Mortally sick?' asked Khan. I nodded.

'Then it was a defensible self-sacrifice, though, as we see, a vain one.'

'Khan,' said I, 'will you excuse me? I am very sorry that I am not up to socialising this evening. If I may, I would dearly like to turn in.'

'Of course, of course,' said Khan. 'I fully understand. Steerforth and I will be together, as in the old days. Our ladies will have a chance to become acquainted. What could be more agreeable?' That then was the end of the evening for me. The guards escorted me back to our quarters and I took to my bed, tolerably certain that I would never rise from it again. For the rest of my account of that first evening in Xanadu, I am of course indebted to the recollections of the others.

'Do you mind telling us what you plan for the future?' asked Steerforth.

'Not in the slightest,' said Khan. 'It has taken me far longer than I expected to reach this stage of preparedness. Events conspired to create confusion and delay. But now I am ready. I have a force of ten thousand soldiers trained in the use of modern weapons. I have a cadre of some forty men who are reliable satraps. My plan is first to conquer Europe, as my predecessors so nearly did half a century ago. Europe will be divided into a northern and southern kingdom. Both kings will be personally bound to me, and will rule their kingdoms with unremitting zeal. Then I will turn to Africa and southern Asia. The Empires of Persia, Egypt and India will be taken over, reorganised and revitalised under my nominees. Before the end of this century, I shall build a fleet of nuclear-powered ships to conquer America, Australia and Japan. I shall have communication satellites in orbit before 1300 and a factory for space vehicles in production soon afterwards.'

At that moment a soldier opened the door of the room and admitted Abigail. She too wore modern and simple clothes, a shirt and trousers. Her hair was still dressed in dreadlocks. She seemed ageless.

'So these Romans are back again,' she said, running her eyes over us. 'Why do you keep them here? Why not take them out in the yard and kill them now? They wish us nothing but ill. Is this your woman, Steerforth? Did she unravel all the clues that Khan left behind? What a clever woman! She need not have bothered. Men can find their own end without clever women to lead them astray.'

'Listen and learn, Mr Khan,' said Edwina May, and Abigail's eyes glittered with cold fury. Not long after this exchange, Khan arranged for his prisoners to be escorted back to their quarters. Unexpectedly he decided to accompany them.

'I want to have a look at Hawkesworth,' he said. He came into my bedroom, with two armed guards on hand, and spent some time with me. I was asleep, or in a trance.

I awoke the next morning feeble and bedridden, but awake I did. During the days that followed I began to feel slightly stronger. I could eat and drink, and my hair loss and bleeding gums ceased. I began to wonder whether, against all expectation, I should live long enough to die of my disease – unless of course Abigail prevailed upon Khan to take us out into the yard and kill us all.

During those days of captivity, my three companions went about the palace under armed guard and were even taken out into the grounds for exercise. They were never more than a few yards from their captors. But it was infinitely preferable to passing the whole day in our quarters.

The lower levels of the palace were devoted entirely to living space and storerooms. On one side were Khan and Abigail's rooms, on the other ours. The technicians for the control centre and the resident guards numbered some twenty people, most of the soldiers being garrisoned somewhere outside Xanadu. High up in the dome of the palace there was a gallery, similar to the whispering gallery at St Paul's, except that within the dome were moored great silver vehicles, flying machines we conjectured. When we first had leisure to inspect the gallery from below, there was a guard walking round the gallery and looking down at us.

'How do the soldiers get up there?' whispered Edwina May. 'I don't see a staircase or an elevator.' Just then an officer emerged from the control centre and called to the man in the gallery to descend. We watched in silent horror as the soldier walked to a gateway in the gallery and stepped out into space. Edwina May gasped and looked away, but instead of falling four hundred feet to his death, the soldier drifted slowly to the ground in a sparkling beam of light.

'Do you recall the tractor beam that moved the silver cup at Khan-Balik?' said Steerforth. 'This is the same force at work.' There were tractor beams at several different points in Xanadu, used by Khan and his followers to move around the palace. In operation, the beams gave off a crystalline sparkle. This, together with the rotation of the panels in the dome, created the impression in the eyes of an outside observer that one was looking into a deep crystal structure – a cave of ice. The panels of the dome were closed at night, or in the daytime when the weather was poor. On the first day that I rose from my bed and began to totter about my room, Edwina May told me that she had seen the panels of the dome open completely, like the petals of a flower. One of the flying machines, without propellers or jets, had risen and left the palace. Dubendorf surmised that it too was powered by the same electro-magnetic traction beam.

Soon I too was permitted to join the others in a brief and heavily guarded excursion into the palace grounds.

    ' "But O, that deep romantic chasm which slanted
      Down the green hill athwart a cedarn cover!" '

quoted Edwina May, as we sat upon the grass on the brink of the ravine. Buried deep in the ravine was the mighty pipe that took the nuclear waste from the palace to the sacred river. Above our heads the cedars were as large and numinous as those at the old school, and far more plentiful. Far below us, one of Khan's servants walked a hunting lion on a lead; another rode up the moving staircase, a hooded falcon on his arm. A fragrant, almost narcotic, perfume from the trees and flower beds of the formal gardens drifted across the hill. The fountain murmured, the birds sang. From the palace behind us we heard the sound of music. Abigail was playing her *kissar*. She played for an hour or more, playing in deep, ruminative chords. She played a slow, melodic version of the song of Mount Abuya Myeda, but did not sing. It was hard to believe the force of evil that this sumptuous place commanded.

With the unfailing politeness they always showed, the guards now indicated that it was time to return to our chambers. Our way along the portico led past Khan's quarters. We looked through the open window as we passed, to see Abigail at her instrument. She looked up at us, without expression, hands moving gently over the strings. In the next room Khan was standing facing the window, which was closed. His hands were spread wide, as if to give emphasis to something he was saying. A man was sitting facing him, listening to his words.

Framed thus in the window, Khan looked for all the world as he had done when I saw him explaining to Steerforth about the flames of two candles so many years before – six and a half centuries later. Our impression of Khan's companion was fleeting but precise.

'I could have sworn that he was a European,' said Steerforth.

'He wore clothes like these,' agreed Dubendorf. 'But who could he be?'

'Good God,' said Edwina May. 'It could have been Messer Marco!' And so we decided it probably was – for we knew that Marco Polo had visited both the palaces, Khan-Balik and Shangtu. Modern scholars have entertained justifiable doubts about the role of the author of the *Divisament dou Monde* in the events he describes. His claim that he served as governor of Yang-Chau province is unsubstantiated in the records. His position as personal confidant of the Khaghan is also open to doubt. But that he visited the palaces and met Kubilai is certain. It was indeed exciting to think that he was at this moment in the same complex of buildings as ourselves. Would he later find himself writing about some Europeans executed by the Khaghan with mysterious weapons?

One morning Khan sent for us to come to his conference room. He greeted us cordially. There was no sign of Abigail. 'How are you, Hawkesworth?' he asked, with every sign of concern.

'Astonishingly enough, a good deal better,' I replied. The guards looked down at us from the gallery, then at a sign from Khan they opaqued the wall. A servant brought in fruit juice and iced water. Khan sat down among us with every sign of friendliness.

'Steerforth,' he said at last, 'I want to ask a favour of you. For old time's sake, may I?'

'Of course,' replied Steerforth. 'Anything within reason.'

'When we were boys and young men, did we not try to train ourselves in the real virtue of a scientist, namely to look at every question not as it might be, nor as we might wish it to be, but exactly as it is? Wouldn't you agree?'

'Of course,' said Steerforth. 'How could I not?'

'All scientists must follow that discipline,' added Konrad.

'Well then,' said Khan, leaning forward and spreading his hands wide, 'will you look for a moment at what I am doing and why you and your friends feel obliged to oppose me? I don't mean just go over the same old arguments again, but fight for a clear vision of the truth, wherever the argument leads us. Just as we used to do in the old days, remember?'

'And then what?' said Edwina May.

'Why then,' said Khan, 'we shall see if we can agree. And if Steerforth persuades me that I am wrong, I shall send this palace and everything in it crashing into infinity. But if Steerforth agrees that I am right, if you will agree, we shall shake hands and become friends again and you will be my loyal and dedicated helpers.'

'It's wrong, Khan, that you and I should be opposed to each other,' said Steerforth at length. 'It's wrong because we were friends for so long, and it's wrong because we have great power through the Magus machines, and should not use that power simply to damage each other. I am willing to listen to your arguments, if you have new ones.'

Khan glanced at Konrad and me. We nodded our assent to Steerforth's proposition.

'And you, Dr McGrath,' said Khan. 'Do you assent?'

'Let me first ask you a question,' said Edwina May. 'Suppose for a moment that we persuade you to abandon your mission. How would Abigail respond?'

'She would think me a fool, a madman. But I think she would place her trust in me. We love each other, you see.' Edwina May smiled. Whether through simple truthfulness or cunning, Khan had given the one answer she could not challenge or fail to respect.

'Then like the wedding guest, I cannot choose but hear,' she said.

'Oddly enough,' said Khan, 'it is the example of your own country that most persuades me that I'm right.' He smiled broadly as he made this remark, knowing that Edwina May would react.

'The USA? How do you figure that?'

'Think of it. America had both the atom bomb and the hydrogen bomb long before the communists. It should have been possible to shape a new world, based on firm diplomacy and the threat of unprecedented destruction. Perhaps a test explosion off the Soviet coast. Some American officials favoured this approach. But the liberals won the day.'

'Nuclear blackmail would have been repugnant to the American people,' said Edwina May.

'Only to those too short-sighted to see,' said Khan. 'Look at the alternative. For forty years until your time the world has been hagridden by the fear of nuclear war. Huge expense that could have gone to feed the hungry, cure the sick, educate the ignorant, has gone to build weapons of war. It's simple madness! And let me ask you a question, Dr McGrath. In your worldline as it now stands, do you really believe the peacemakers can succeed indefinitely? Do you?'

At this, Khan stretched out his hand and touched Edwina May on the cheek, lightly and lovingly as a brother might touch a sister. She looked aghast, not at his gesture but at his question.

'The question is unfair,' said Khan at length. 'I have looked into the future and know the answer. The peacemakers fail.' In the silence that followed, Steerforth poured a cup of water for Edwina May. As a boy, Khan had watched his family slaughtered. As a man he had looked at a world where civilisation had been mutually annihilated. For a moment it was easy, almost inescapable, to think of him as the man of vision and sanity, the architect of a sane new world for the mad old one.

'Somehow in our dealings, Augustus,' said Khan at length, 'I have been cast in the role of the reckless overthrower of the established order, the revolutionary, the wrecker. Consider carefully whether this is fair. Stop any sensible person in the street in the twentieth century, and offer him or her the chance to abolish the threat of nuclear war. What do you think they would say? Answer that, then tell me who is the eccentric between us!'

'But when you say that,' said Konrad Dubendorf at length, 'reasonable as it sounds on the surface, I hear a disturbing echo of another voice. Pointing up the ills of a chaotic, liberal world and the benefits of an ordered, disciplined and controlled world ... such arguments were abundant in the German-speaking world when I was a child.'

'But the Third Reich is one of the very things I want to save the world from,' explained Khan quietly and patiently. 'In your passive, non-interventionist frame you can only lament the victims of the holocaust and their pain. I can actually prevent it. Augustus, you know that my family died at the time of the partition of India. And died most horribly. Your mother's brother died in the Great War, I believe. What was his name?'

'Augustus,' answered Steerforth.

'She was a child when he died. Twenty years later she named her only child for him. What a cry of grief! Multiply that grief a billion, billion times, and you have the history of the human race as we now know it. The waste, the waste ... all now remediable.'

'Yet this is the oldest sin of all,' said Edwina May, 'the sin of *hubris*, of overweening pride, the sin of men who play gods.'

'Is it?' said Khan, suddenly waspish. 'If it is, then who is Steerforth to rebuke me for it? The beam in his eye is greater than the mote in mine.'

'You are right in that,' said Steerforth quickly. 'I have had serious doubts about coming back in time to try to frustrate your plans. We are two of a kind.'

'You misunderstand me,' countered Khan, speaking suddenly with conviction, even passion. 'I don't rebuke you for trying to defeat me. Given your beliefs, that is a practical and honourable thing to do. If you have a chance to kill me, you should take it. I propose to give you no such chance.' Khan smiled as he spoke these words, as if they were debating the next move in a game of chess.

'My criticism lies elsewhere. You are enslaved to a false objection, as weak-kneed as it is illogical. Your objection to my plan, as I understand it, is that it is beyond Man's realm to rewrite history, to tamper with what the moving finger has written. But that is now nonsense. We are today in the thirteenth century. What you call history lies in the future, and as such is as yet unmade. It is now seven centuries before our original time.'

At this point Khan rose to his feet and stepped across to the plate glass window. He gazed out towards the cedar trees and the distant walls of Xanadu.

'Think of the hundreds of millions of people destined to die in misery and agony if your leave-well-alone philosophy were somehow to prevail. Think of the millions who will die in the Great Plague, from which your ancestors will flee in terror to Bain Brook. Think of the women and babies who will be burned alive in the Great Fire. Think of the Thirty Years War, the American War of Independence and their Civil War, think of Mons and Ypres, think of Belsen and Auschwitz, Hiroshima and Nagasaki. Think of the holocaust that all sane men fear – and are right to fear – is inevitable in your world. Hundreds, perhaps thousands of millions of people *as yet unborn* stretch out their hands to you in supplication, asking you to save them from brutal lives and agonising death.' He stood in front of Steerforth with his hand extended. 'I hold out my hand on their behalf. All you have to do is take it, and their futile suffering is averted. In your world the very future of mankind is at risk. In mine it is assured. Which of us is the true humanitarian?'

Steerforth's eyes rose slowly to meet Khan's. For a moment he looked defeated, overwhelmed not only by the force of Khan's arguments but also by the miracles Khan had wrought to give effect to his ideas and the apparently ineluctable way they were being accomplished. To me, perhaps also to the others, Khan seemed in that moment truly to embody the man of sanity and vision described in the *Republic*.

Steerforth in contrast looked hagridden and possessed, as if the burden of his argument had become insupportable to him. It was clear that Khan had won a decisive victory in the dialogue. I wondered if he had usually done so, when he and Steerforth were boys. Perhaps Steerforth was crushed by the experience of being exposed again to the sheer force with which Khan deployed his argument. As Steerforth almost cringed before Khan, I glanced at Edwina May; she stared in horror as at the corpse of the man she had loved.

'But this is nonsense!' she cried. 'Remember the description of the Mongols hacking their way through Europe in 1242? It will be the same again, only with lasers and nuclear bombs. It's unthinkable, Augustus! Unthinkable.'

'You are right,' said Dubendorf, as if emerging from a trance. 'Freedom is never an easy cause to espouse, peaceful slavery always a seductive proposition.'

'Dubendorf, do you say this?' said Khan gently, as if more in puzzlement than anger. 'You, who claim to be a scientist? Are you so proud of what Steerforth's world has done for you? Thousands of your colleagues who could be working for the good of mankind are forced to work in weaponry. Space travel has been invented, then starved of funds. Time travel was invented, then suppressed, until I liberated it. This woman is the Coleridge expert. Can she tell us what future the great poet foresaw for his fellow men in the universe? You know the passage to which I refer?'

' "In his loneliness and fixedness he yearneth towards the journeying moon," ' said Edwina May, speaking slowly and with seeming reluctance, yet even she bent to comply with Khan's will, ' "and the stars that still sojourn, yet still move onwards; and every where the blue sky belongs to them, and is their appointed rest, and their native country and their own natural homes, which they enter unannounced, as lords that are certainly expected and yet there is a silent joy at their arrival." '

'A silent joy,' repeated Khan. 'Do you know, Dubendorf, what other lords await us in the stars, wait to greet us as equals with a silent joy? I don't yet know. But in my world we shall begin to find out by the fourteenth or fifteenth century.'

'Yet,' said Dubendorf, 'what is that to us? If we were to join you and live with you in the thirteenth century, what is the importance to us of all that might happen in the fourteenth or fifteenth?'

'On that score, set your mind at rest,' said Khan swiftly, with his dazzling smile. 'You will live to see far later centuries than those, if you will only join me.'

Konrad Dubendorf rose to his feet and walked across the room to face the Khaghan. The Mongol soldiers in the gallery above us made the wall transparent and trained their weapons on the Swiss scientist. But instead of hitting Khan, Dubendorf reached out and grasped Khan's hand.

'That is enough for me,' he said. 'Conquest of the universe is enough of a prize for me. Just as my conscience drove me to help Steerforth in the cause of science, so it drives me now to organise the first expedition to make contact with an alien intelligence. And this before the age of Shakespeare! How can I refuse? I am first and foremost a scientist, after all.'

I will draw a veil over the bitter words that were said by Steerforth and particularly by Edwina May as our chief scientist defected to Khan's side. Dubendorf made no attempt to defend or explain his decision, but simply waited with a stony face for us to be led away.

'If you say, Hawkesworth, that it is a mistake fully to trust any man who has never played cricket, I think I shall brain you,' said Steerforth, as we took our gloomy meal that evening. Events now began to follow on with unexampled swiftness. Within a week we saw, on one of our morning escorted walks, our own Magus machine stationed on a rocky terrace a few hundred yards from the dome of Xanadu. Dubendorf had obviously been to fetch it from its hiding-place.

'The gembikes and our weaponry will be of great value to Khan in the assault on western Europe,' said Steerforth glumly. I could imagine the gembikes bearing armed warriors through central Europe to France and the Lowlands, into Spain and Italy and Greece, even across the English channel, warriors with laser cannon and rocket launchers, perhaps with nuclear grenades or chemical weapons, who would cast terror into the hearts of the English yeomen. Half a dozen such troops could conquer any mediaeval country. Seven centuries of recorded history would flicker out of existence.

One afternoon Khan and Dubendorf came to see us.

'Konrad wishes me to offer you one last chance to join me,' said Khan. 'There is now no possibility of your overturning my plans. Konrad thinks you might be impressed by the opportunity at least to influence the direction of future events. Besides, think what I can offer you. Do you, young and beautiful woman as you are, not fear the onset of age? Most of us do, men and women alike. I have drugs and surgical techniques that are undreamed of in the twentieth century. So far only Abigail, Chingkim and I have profited from them. You too could do so, if you would only join us.'

'You will live for ever?' asked Steerforth.

'No one can live for ever,' answered Khan softly. 'But we will live long. We will live for centuries, perhaps for millennia. We will live for so long that when we die, it will seem that we have lived for ever.'

'You go to hell,' said Edwina May. After a few more minutes of futile exchanges, Khan and his new ally left us. When they had done so, I thought Edwina May was close to tears at the spectacle of Dubendorf's duplicity. As unostentatiously as possible, in case we were observed by secret watchers, I handed her and Steerforth the note that Konrad Dubendorf had slipped me. 'Be ready for escape tonight.'

None of us could sleep. It was, by accident or by Konrad's design, the night of the full moon. The moonlight glittered on the fountain and the lakes, and streamed in through the window of our common room.

From the corridor outside our door came a muffled shout. A flash of red light flickered under the door. Then silence. A few minutes later the door opened. Konrad Dubendorf stood there, a laser gun in one hand and his pocket computer in the other. Two Mongol guards lay at his feet, whether stunned or killed I could not tell.

'Sorry for the delay,' he murmured, 'I had to work out the access code for this door.' Edwina May warmly embraced Konrad, Steerforth and I shook his hand.

'I never really believed you were a traitor,' said Edwina May.

'Thank you, Edwina May. I hoped your faith would survive my little deception. Abigail did not believe me either. She kept telling Khan I was plotting something. But he was so keen to get his hands on our machine, he wanted to believe me. It may be the first time he has ever disregarded her advice. So much the worse for him, I'm sure she will regularly remind him of his error! But there is no time to spare. We have work to do!'

'How did you manage to escape?' I asked Konrad.

'Khan sent me under guard to collect the Magus III. I was planning to travel forward in time to rescue you – and myself, so to speak. But the guards never took their eyes off me. I managed to get my pocket computer back by pretending that the access codes to some of the Magus functions were programmed into it. Then I detected enough of the access codes of the Xanadu machine to get out of my quarters and move around the palace. In the end, however, I resorted to simple means. I hit my guard on the head with the leg of a table and stole his weapon. And here I am.'

'Let's go!' said Edwina May.

'Not yet,' said Konrad. 'We have one task to perform. I want to destroy this palace before we leave!'

'Destroy it?' said Steerforth. 'How?'

'First we have to connect this computer to the Xanadu machine. But it must be in a place where we can establish line of sight microwave communication from our own Magus.'

'Where is that?' I asked.

'The control room is no good,' said Dubendorf. 'It is too near the centre of the building. The palace is wired up with a fibre optic local area net. There is an access point at the level of the gallery. We can ride up there on the traction beam.'

Silently we made our way along the corridor. We saw no guards. We emerged under the central dome of the palace. The panels of the dome were closed, but moonlight streamed in through the windows. The traction beam spots were marked with white circles on the gleaming, blackish floor.

'I hope the beams are left on at night,' whispered Edwina May.

'We'll soon find out,' said Steerforth, stepping forward. But as he spoke, Konrad seized his arm and pulled him back into the shadows. Brilliant moonlight began to flood the chamber. The dome of Xanadu was opening.

From the direction of Khan's quarters came voices. A Mongol guard came and turned on the lights in the control room. The dome was flooded with light. We drew back further into the shadows of the corridor. Now Abigail and Khan entered the chamber, she glancing upwards at the unfolding petals of the dome. She was dressed in a flowing robe of silk. A servant followed her with a leather carrying bag.

'Safe journey,' said Khan, and took her in his arms.

'I will return tomorrow or the next day,' said Abigail. 'Unless that fool Chingkim can work more reliably, we will have to drop him from the plan. He is too much influenced by the Chinese. This is the last time I will sort out his problems. Make sure you don't take any risks with Dubendorf. I don't trust him. Once you've got what you want from him, kill him. Kill the rest tomorrow.'

Even at this late stage in his plans, it seemed that Khan could not wholly depend upon his family: now his son seemed to be a weak link in the chain of command. Abigail gestured to the servant. He immediately stepped into the traction beam, which burst into light and carried him up to the gallery. He began to stow Abigail's bag in one of Khan's flying machines. He started the engine, which generated only a mild humming noise. Slowly the machine sank down to the floor of the palace. Abigail kissed Khan for the last time, and stepped aboard the flier. It was silvery in colour and slightly wedge-shaped. Silently it rose until it cleared the petals of the dome, then moved off southward out of sight. Khan left the chamber. The petals began to close. The guard switched off the lights. We were alone.

Dubendorf and Steerforth stepped into the beam. I watched my friends rising slowly through the air, carried only by a brilliant beam of light. They carried the pocket computer to the access point and plugged it into the Xanadu network, using a connector that Dubendorf had taken from the Magus III. Dubendorf fully extended the aerial of the computer and placed it in a window from which the Magus III was directly visible. Then they came down the traction beam. We watched them descend, knowing that it would take only the turn of a switch to send them to their deaths.

Silently we crossed the central chamber of the palace and made for the main entrance. Dubendorf already knew the code required to open this door. In seconds we were stepping across the smooth stone of the portico, then half-walking, half-sliding down the steep lawns towards the ledge where the Magus III was stationed. I breathed a deep sigh of relief as Steerforth punched the access code of our time machine and we entered it safely.

'Do you mind if I take over for this operation?' asked Konrad, when we were all seated at the Magus control panel. Steerforth and Edwina May instantly agreed.

'Power up all circuits, visual display of exterior,' said Dubendorf. The palace of Xanadu instantly appeared on the screen.

'Align microwave link with visual display,' said Konrad. At once a pair of crosshairs appeared on the screen, such as are used in rifle sights. Konrad used a joystick to elevate the camera angle.

'Zoom in,' he said. A picture of the window near the gallery filled the screen. Konrad's pocket computer was clearly visible. He positioned the crosshairs precisely on the tip of the aerial.

'Are you now connected to the Xanadu computer?' asked Dubendorf.

'I am. The Xanadu machine is demanding my access password,' said the Magus computer.

'Try random permutations of words from the works of Samuel Taylor Coleridge,' said Edwina May.

'Good idea,' said Steerforth.

'Access code accepted,' said Magus. 'I am terminal user "Holy Dread".'

'Very good, Holy Dread. Access the power output display and show the display on screen.' For a few seconds the screen of the Magus III was covered with flying symbols and equations. Then a graph appeared. It showed a red line and a green.

'The green line is the actual power being generated by the Xanadu reactor,' said Dubendorf. 'The red line is the nominal level; the level at which the reactor was designed to operate.' The green line squirmed across the screen, dipping and peaking occasionally but never more than a fraction off the red.

'Limit of safety in output?' asked Konrad.

'Minus 15 per cent, plus 10,' said Magus III.

'Power consumption monitor, please.' A new display flashed on to the screen. It showed the power being consumed in the palace. The squirming line in this case was very close to the lower axis of the graph.

'Power consumption is very low,' said I. Konrad Dubendorf smiled at me, as if this somewhat obvious remark were the key to a riddle.

'Not for long,' he remarked. 'Magus, please listen carefully. There are three switching systems that measure the power consumption of the palace and the power yield of the generator. Correct?'

'Yes.'

'Excellent. Can you try to access them? The transaction code is AQ 7564.'

'Access established,' said Magus after a fractional pause.

'Report to the systems that power utilisation is increasing at zero point eight per cent per minute, via terminal Holy Dread,' said Dubendorf.

'Transaction complete,' said Magus.

'The Xanadu computer now thinks that this terminal, Holy Dread, is a massive user of energy – perhaps a powerful turbine or a transportation system like the staircase. We now have to tell it that its power output is declining.' Dubendorf smiled thinly as he resumed his dialogue with the Magus computer.

'Report power generated declining at zero point six per cent per minute,' said Dubendorf.

'The fail-safe system wants to know why the power output is declining,' said Magus. Steerforth, Dubendorf, Edwina May and I stared at each other in bafflement. What could we say?

'Tell it we'd like to know too,' said Konrad.

'Command provisionally accepted. Full circuit check in progress,' said Magus.

'Quickly, then, change the transaction code from AQ 7564 to something else.'

'What?'

'EM 1234,' said Steerforth.

'Transaction complete,' said Magus III. Dubendorf sat back and wiped his brow.

'Display power output,' he ordered. Once again the red and green lines appeared, but now the power generated was beginning to climb on the graph.

'The palace is doomed,' said Dubendorf gravely. 'I have persuaded the Xanadu computer that it requires more and more power and is generating less and less. I have changed the transaction code so that the error cannot be corrected. In a few minutes from now, the power will exceed the safety limit. A few minutes after that, the palace will be destroyed in the world's first nuclear accident.'

'Will it be a nuclear explosion?' asked Edwina May.

'No. There will be some leakage of nuclear material, but fission or fusion will not take place.'

Even as he spoke we could see on the screen the first sign of the destruction of Xanadu. The panels of the dome seemed to be rotating faster, the traction beam lights flashed wildly, bright lights lit up the interior of the portico. Lights began to come on also in the living quarters, as people awoke in chaos. We felt the Magus III vibrate slightly as the ground under the palace began to buck and heave. Suddenly and simultaneously the huge pipe that took away the radioactive water down the ravine exploded, and another explosion lit up the interior of the dome. The ravine burst open with a roar. The lovely cedar trees were ravished. The force of the explosion hurled huge rocks into the air. Mongol soldiers ran this way and that in panic as the boulders fell to earth.

' "Huge fragments vaulted like rebounding hail . . ." ' I half-heard Edwina May mutter. Now the panels of the dome were detaching themselves, falling to the ground and smashing.

'I think it's time to leave, you guys,' said Edwina May.

'Konrad, I'll take over,' said Steerforth. He keyed into the Magus III the coordinates of Bain Brook in the twentieth century. 'Chronogator, ready to go?'

'You bet,' said Edwina May. 'I mean – ready.' Her finger was poised on the GO button.

'Wait!' said Steerforth. Across the green hill two figures were moving towards us, stumbling and sliding down the slope, hands outstretched in supplication. One was Khan, the other a stranger to my eyes, a heavily built man in a dark robe, who was staggering and reeling as if on the point of collapse.

'Who is that with Khan?' asked Konrad Dubendorf.

'It's the European, the one we saw through Khan's window,' said Steerforth. 'The one Edwina May thought might be Messer Marco. Khan is trying to help him to escape.'

'Leave them!' cried Edwina May. 'This is just Khan's latest stratagem. To hell with him. Let him die in the time and place of his own creation.' Still Steerforth hesitated.

'Edwina May is right,' said Dubendorf softly. 'If we leave Khan stranded in the thirteenth century, with Xanadu destroyed, why then we know the world is safe. If we take him back to the twentieth century, who knows what he may achieve? We may face the same threats all over again. Let us shipwreck him here.' Steerforth hesitated for a moment longer.

'Hawkesworth, what do you say?' he cried.

'We have no choice. Khan has brought this fate upon himself,' I answered. Steerforth shook his head in sorrow, then turned to Edwina May and was on the point of giving the command to go.

'Wait!' said Edwina May, for some unaccountable reason changing her mind. She stared with mounting incredulity at the scene depicted on the Magus screen. A massive ball of orange fire seemed to be lifting the dome of the palace into the night sky. Khan was now half-carrying his companion to the doors of the Magus machine.

'Open the doors. Let them in,' said Edwina May in a tone that seemed to brook no debate and no delay. Steerforth hit the controls. In seconds the doors were opened and the fugitives admitted. Steerforth gave the go command and instantaneously we were back in Bain Brook in the twentieth century. The external display showed only the walls of Steerforth's hangar. Khan's companion was slumped unconscious in his arms.

'You must get this man back to his own time and place,' said Khan urgently. 'He has already seen more than enough that he will not understand.' The man's face was fat and pallid, his breathing laboured and ragged. He looked distinctly unhealthy and when we came to move him seemed to weigh a ton. Steerforth quietly keyed in the codes that secured the doors to the rooms; he did not want Khan getting into the weapons room.

'Where do we take him? Is Venice or Khan-Balik the appropriate place for Messer Marco?' asked Steerforth.

'Neither,' said Edwina May. 'We take him to a farmhouse between Porlock and Linton in 1797. This is not Messer Marco. I thought it might be he, but later when I had time to think I remembered that in 1294 Messer Marco was on the long sea voyage back to Europe. So this could not be Messer Marco. Haven't any of you guys ever seen the Vandyke portrait in the National Gallery? This man is Samuel Taylor Coleridge.'

Through Paradise in a Dream

Why am I not dead? Of all the mysteries in this affair, I find this the most puzzling. The maximum expectation given to me by my doctor is now close to expiration. If I add to the elapsed time in the twentieth century those weeks also passed in the thirteenth, then I am far beyond the time when I should be dead. On top of that, I have no doubt that Konrad Dubendorf was right when he said that I had been exposed in the chamber below Xanadu to a lethal dose of radiation. To my surprise, the symptoms of the radiation sickness actually began to regress as soon as I returned to modern times. My hair and fingernails began to grow back, at an almost alarming rate. I feel stronger now than I have for several years; the other day I accidentally missed my nap after lunch, and felt no ill-effects. For a time I flirted with the most unlikely notion. A lethal dose of radiation would quickly kill a healthy person. Was it possible that the same radiation would cure someone who was mortally sick? Could the radiation have killed the tumour and left me well? Stupid as it seems, I have been reluctant to visit my doctor. Even to me, my motives in this matter are far from clear. I tell myself that I do not want him to tackle me on the matter of the radiation poisoning. How would I explain it? But in my heart I suspect that I will not go to the doctor because he might tell me my respite is normal and will be brief. Sooner or later I know I will have to face him. Let it be later.

Not long after our return, Steerforth paid a business visit to his bank in the Strand. Even at a bank as prestigious as this, Steerforth is regarded as a VIP. He was quickly ushered into the manager's office.

'I have a rather unusual request to make,' he began, laying on the table a box no bigger than the kind used to hold a pair of cufflinks. 'This box is small, but it contains something of vital concern to me and my family. I want you to place it in the family strongbox and to be absolutely certain that you do not release it to anyone but me. Is that understood?'

'Completely, my lord,' said the manager.

'Be clear, even if someone comes here with a power of attorney signed by me, this box must not be handed over. I am to remarry in the near future. If the new Lady Steerforth were to ask for the box, you must send her away empty-handed. After I am dead, the right of withdrawal may pass to my heir. That will be dealt with in my will. Otherwise that box will stay in the vault till kingdom come.' The bank manager gulped and sent for the custodian of the vault. He would never know what the little box contained. In fact it contained the results of several weeks of work by Konrad Dubendorf. It was essential, with Khan back in the twentieth century, that the time travel module at the Torus Centre and Steerforth's Magus machine should both be immobilised. But at the same time it seemed reckless simply to destroy them. Dubendorf came up with the ideal solution. He fitted a scrambler circuit to the logic channels on both machines. Commands received by either machine, whether keyed in or spoken, looked like gibberish. The code to unscramble these circuits was recorded on two microchips. These chips were now to be immured behind several feet of concrete and steel beneath the pavement of the Strand. No one but Steerforth would ever authorise further use of the time machines.

'Could not the code be found by trial and error, Konrad,' said Edwina May, 'just as you unravelled the code of the Upas trees?'

'In theory, yes,' admitted Konrad. 'But the randomising algorithm is so complex and dynamic that even with a picosecond speed computer, it would take several million years to hit on the right solution.'

'Several million years?' said Edwina May thoughtfully.

'At least,' said Konrad, rather smugly.

'So that if someone began the task today, and handed it on as a sacred trust to generation after generation of his descendants, one of them would eventually crack the code?'

Konrad nodded reluctantly.

'Why then, that descendant would use the Magus to travel back in time and solve the problem today!' We were lunching at Bain

Brook when this conversation took place. Steerforth picked up a bread roll and, with the throwing skill that had once made him an outstanding cover-point, dotted his wife-to-be on the nose.

Because Steerforth's first wife was still alive, though by now remarried in California, the marriage of Steerforth and Edwina May McGrath took place in a registry office. The college chaplain, however, offered to conduct a service of blessing in the chapel. His offer was happily accepted. On the day before the wedding I had at last visited my doctor.

'Hawkesworth,' he said, 'I hardly know just how to tell you this. Every once in a while the world of medicine hears of a case of spontaneous remission of a tumour. No one knows why, but the thing just goes away. Such cases are very rare, one chance in millions. I don't know what you have done to deserve it, but you are cured. The new X-rays show conclusively that your tumour has disappeared.' I suppose that if I had been to Lourdes instead of Xanadu, I should now be claimed as a miracle. The doctor said nothing of the radiation sickness. I saw no reason to raise the subject myself. I walked out of his surgery and accepted my good fortune at face value. Just as she had wept when she learned by chance of my death sentence, Edwina May wept at my reprieve. This time her tears were more joyful.

The college choir began to sing the anthem. Steerforth had selected the Hymnus Eucharisticus, *Te Deum Patrem colimus.* . . . The newly married couple entered the chapel and took their seats. The college chaplain prepared to read the first lesson of the service of blessing. Dubendorf and Mr Steele were there, together with a number of the staff from Bain Brook. There were assorted members of the Steerforth clan and Edwina May's widowed father from Oak Bluffs, a quiet and friendly man old by most standards but mine. Just as the service was about to begin, the chapel door was quietly opened and a latecomer took his place in a pew nearby – a dark figure in a blue suit wearing tinted spectacles and carrying a hat. Inayat Khan had come to celebrate the marriage of his old friend. After the service, I caught him up in the college quadrangle. He did not make much effort to elude me. His face was fleshier than before, his eye duller and his hair at last beginning to grey. He looked like a slightly seedy Asian businessman, on his way to a negotiation.

'It was kind of you to come,' I said. 'I know Steerforth will have appreciated it.'

'I doubt if the same is true of the new Lady Steerforth,' said

Khan with a smile. 'You look well, Hawkesworth, better than when I last saw you.'

'I feel well, Inayat, better than I have any right to feel. As you know I was gravely ill, mortally ill, I was told. For some reason I have made a miraculous recovery. No one can understand why.'

'Because you led a blameless life and did not waste your substance on women,' he said, with the old swift smile. I smiled too, but I was momentarily sad for him, cut off by nearly seven centuries from the woman he loved. It was strange to reflect too that his son Chingkim must have been dead for many centuries.

'I understand that Lady Steerforth's book is a great success,' said Khan suddenly. It was true: Edwina May's thesis had been published by the house of Steerforth and was that literary rarity, a *succès d'estime* and a best-seller. Such was the success of the book that I had even heard Edwina May's name put forward as a candidate to be the new professor of poetry at Oxford.

I shook Khan's hand as we parted. Whatever his faults, he was still the same man who had told me the horrific story of his parents' death that night on the Oxford train, still the same Inayat whom Steerforth had seen returning to Bain Brook in the middle of the night, his cheeks bejewelled with tears. Abigail and he had been very close. He lived alone now, I gathered, in a house in Woodstock. His needs were amply covered by the money in his family trust, though Steerforth had checked carefully that he had nothing like the money needed to build a new Magus machine. Now, if ever, I could imagine Abigail on the desolate hill beside the ruined palace, now truly 'woman wailing for her demon lover'. I watched him cross the road in the direction of the college car park. He was a lonely, detached figure, no longer the man of vision and sanity that Sokrates saw as the natural ruler of mankind; it was almost as if the thirteenth century was his true home, as if this middle-aged man in a blue suit really was the Khaghan or no one at all.

A month later I came across Edwina May, sitting alone in the library at Bain Brook. She looked sad and withdrawn, a book held slackly in her lap. I wondered if she had been crying.

'What is it?' I asked.

'Oh nothing, nothing,' she answered. 'What can I do for you?'

'I have just had a telephone call from the Warden of the college. The election for the chair of poetry – the result is in. You have been elected.' Now the chair of poetry at Oxford is one of the oddest chairs at any university. Both the stipend and the duties are negligible. But the honour of holding the chair is great. I took Edwina May in my arms and hugged her tightly. When her husband came home, having heard the news on the radio in the Rolls, I thought he would crack her ribs with his embrace.

By tradition, the new professor dresses up in academic garb and gives an inaugural lecture at the Sheldonian theatre. So it came about that, a few months later, Steerforth and I went to hear Edwina May's lecture. Her title was simply 'Imagery'. She was dwarfed in size by the tall figure of the vice-chancellor, but if she suffered a trace of nerves she utterly concealed the fact.

'At the heart of every great work of art,' said Edwina May, 'there is a mystery. But at the heart of 'Kubla Khan' there lies a mystery within a mystery. First there is the mystery of the poem's origins and significance. Seldom has a poem exercised such a powerful grip on the imagination of generations of scholars and ordinary readers, without anyone being able to say with any precision what the poem is about. The famous description at the end of the poem, for example, refers to – whom? Does the poet envisage himself with "flashing eyes" and "floating hair"? Truly? Is this the same STC who elsewhere writes of his own appearance: "As to me, my face, unless when animated by immediate eloquence, expresses great Sloth, & great, indeed almost ideotic, good nature. 'Tis a mere carcase of a face, fat, flabby & expressive chiefly of inexpression . . ."? But if not the poet, then who? Kubla Khan himself? The contemporary portraits of Kubilai do him less than justice, one suspects, and are for propaganda reasons deliberately sinified. But why should the reader see Kubilai at this point, when it is apparently the poet himself who resurrects the image of the pleasure-dome, stimulated by the recollection of the Abyssinian maid's music? And the chaotic scene with the rocks bounding in the fountain – is this supposed to be an abiding feature of the palace scenery? If so, it is far from easy to understand how the "mingled measure/From the fountain and the caves" could be heard at all. Perhaps the "ceaseless turmoil" and the "dancing rocks" are images from a different scene, arguably that of the destruction of the palace.' I glanced at Steerforth and he frowned back; Edwina May was venturing on to perilous ground.

'Secondly,' went on Edwina May, 'there is the mystery of the date of composition and publication of the poem. Let us consider these questions in reverse order. "Kubla Khan" was published in

1816, together with that other weird masterpiece "Christabel" and "The Pains of Sleep". As usual, STC was stony broke' – this unscholarly interpolation occasioned some mirth – 'but as usual some well-wisher came to the rescue. The poet's account of these transactions is shot through with his characteristic blend of evasiveness and self-mockery. "Mr Murray called on me," writes STC, "in consequence of some flashes of praise, which Lord Byron had coruscated. . . . Murray urged me to publish it, and offered me 80 pounds. . . . The publication was utterly against my feelings and my Judgement – but poor Morgan's Necessities, including his Wife & Sister, were urgent & clamorous. . . . With many a pang & many a groan . . . I concluded the bargain – and gave the 80 pounds to Morgan." Naturally the money was not for STC himself. Naturally the advocate of publication is as irresistible as only Byron could be. And naturally, too, STC's harridan of a wife makes things even tougher for him than they need be. "He has been so unwise," she writes, "as to publish his fragments of *Christabel* and *Koula-Khan* (sic). We were all sadly vexed when we read the advertisement." ' Edwina May turned over a page of her notes and took a sip of water before continuing.

'This is, to begin with, hardly the fanfare one might expect to herald the publication of one of the greatest English poems ever written. Let us now turn to the compositional questions. The depiction of "Kubla Khan" as a visionary poem written "without any sensation or consciousness of effort" after taking an "anodyne" and the description of the horrors of addiction in "The Pains of Sleep" together established Coleridge in the public eye as a self-confessed and notorious opium-eater. Then as now, famous junkies were big news. Whatever debts, monetary or moral, Coleridge owed to the Morgans were fully expunged by the willing and foolish sacrifice of his reputation. Yet behind all this, doubts still lurk. The story of the stay at the country cottage, the anodyne, the vision, the interruption by the person from Porlock – all of this is as well known as any yarn ever devised to hype a literary opus. The story crumbles under the most superficial analysis. The poet gives 1797 as the date of these far-fetched events. Ernest Hartley Coleridge suggested that the visit to the cottage took place in 1798. "Kubla Khan" followed rather than preceded "The Ancient Mariner". Yet even so, this wonderful poem was concealed from the world for eighteen years. It was never considered for inclusion in *Lyrical Ballads*, nor for the planned edition of Coleridge poems for 1798. When Coleridge was desperate for poems to send to *The Morning Post*, "Kubla Khan" was neglected. Neither in his notebooks, where he frequently lists work in hand, nor in his letters, where he runs frequent previews of forthcoming attractions, does the Khan of Khans rate a mention. The argument is *e silentio* and therefore inconclusive, but nevertheless cogent. Is it after all possible that the poem was written much later than 1798? Perhaps not long before its publication? Coleridge might have fabricated the story of the earlier publication, merely in order to suggest that he was a reformed rather than a current dope fiend. Yet this interpretation, plausible enough on some grounds, itself falls to the ground. By 1816 – indeed by 1800, the poetic *annus mirabilis* of which I have written, Coleridge's poetic talent was in ruins. His prose still soars, but his verse creeps. By then the Muse had visited him, found his sad, self-deceptive, self-destructive world uncongenial, and deserted him. Is it really possible that this wonderful poem is just a single flower in what is otherwise a poetic desert? For my part, I have a simple rule. Coleridge is such an indefatigable liar, that when he tells me things that are highly plausible, I mistrust them. By the same token, when he tells me things that are preposterous, I am inclined to believe them. I think that "Kubla Khan" was written in 1797, as Coleridge tells us. I think Ernest Hartley Coleridge became a trifle confused over the dates. The poet enjoyed, or perhaps more correctly endured, some experience, some vision, some hallucinatory contact with the world of the Mongol emperor. More than that. . . .' She paused. The audience waited. Slowly her eyes rose to meet her husband's. 'More than that is not given us to know.' The rest of her speech, referring to Keats, Shelley, Byron and Wordsworth, was stimulating and perceptive. Naturally it is the Esteesian moments that live most clearly in my mind.

   She had, I think, most certainly been crying when I met her in the library to tell her of her election. I think I know what had caused her tears. No Coleridge scholar has ever failed to be moved, perhaps even torn, by the way STC's life fell apart after 1797. Look at the portrait by Vandyke in the National Portrait Gallery, painted in 1795. The face is juvenile, almost babyish, the lips open as if to speak, the eyes soft but keen, the hair fluffy and dark. Compare this with the portrait by Washington Allston in the same gallery. The face is bloated and slack, the eyes dull, the hair white. In nineteen years, STC has become an old, old man. There is no doubt in my mind that drink, drugs and family problems contributed to this rapid decline. A scurrilous novel partly based upon

Coleridge's public character was published in 1798. His son Berkeley died in 1799 at the age of two. But Edwina May divined its true cause.

Khan took the poet out of his own age and into the thirteenth century, for how long we do not know, perhaps at most a week or two. What he saw there we alone knew. We returned him to the eighteenth century only a few chronological hours after he had left it. Perhaps he was drugged when Khan took him. He was certainly unconscious when we returned him. No wonder he struggled for nineteen years to understand and absorb such an experience. No wonder he wrote of the poem that "all the images rose up before him as *things* . . .". After I had spoken to Edwina May about her election to the chair of poetry, she left the room to greet Steerforth on his return. I took up the book she had been holding in her lap. It was Coleridge's *Anima Poetae*. It was bookmarked at a certain page, and a certain passage was marked for emphasis in the margin. As I read it, all the poet's confusion and despair spoke aloud to me, and I too was close to tears. "If a man could pass," wrote Coleridge, "through Paradise in a dream, and have a flower presented to him as a pledge that his soul had really been there, and if he found that flower in his hand when he awoke – Ay! and what then?"

Who was the person from Porlock who interrupted Coleridge's account of his time voyage? Was it necessary for Steerforth to return to the eighteenth century, lest the poet write more than we have received, and the world of poetry as we know it would be different? I have never asked and do not wish to know. On the whole I prefer to believe that the person from Porlock was a plumber or a carpenter, come to quote for some job that needed doing in the cottage. On the subject of Samuel Taylor Coleridge and 'Kubla Khan' I have nothing more to say. One other mystery was unravelled one evening when Steerforth was away and Edwina May and I were alone at Bain Brook. When we first arrived at Xanadu I appeared to be mortally sick of the radiation poisoning. On our first night in the palace while I slept, Khan came and administered an injection. He said only that it would lower my temperature. Whatever drugs Khan and Abigail had, taken from the medical skills of some future century, it was clear that I too had profited from them. The radiation sickness and the tumour had been cleared.

Next morning I looked at my face with renewed interest in the shaving mirror. I looked and felt a decade younger than when I had set out for Xanadu. Under these new circumstances, how long could I expect to survive? Like Khan and Abigail, I too had drunk the milk of Paradise. "Close your eyes in holy dread," the poet had commanded. I obeyed.